SOLSTICE
THE GODDESS AWAKENS

BY

J.S. COMISKEY

A CIP record for this book is available in from the British Library

Paperback ISBN: 9780993092305

This book is dedicated to my family,
especially my parents, Gemma and Gerard Savage.
You are the best parents a child could have
and I'm truly glad I chose you to be my Ma and Da.

ACKNOWLEDGEMENTS

Writing can be a very lonely process and from time to time when the words slide off the page, seemingly lifeless, you find yourself wondering if you should continue at all. With that in mind I would like to give a special mention of thanks to Mark, Angela and my mother for their encouragement, they might not realise just how much they helped to keep me going in those very early days.

I would also like to thank Janet, Kelly and Joan, three people who took time out of their lives to read Solstice. Their feedback and very gracious encouragement will never be forgotten and their kindness and honesty will always be appreciated.

I also owe a great debt of gratitude to the lovely Emma Warnock, from Editing Works, for proofing my work, it was no easy task and this book would not be in your hands without her. That is also the same for Barry Rooney, from BO!D Design, who is the brainchild behind this eye-catching cover sleeve and the book production. Barry's creative acumen has enabled me to transform my dream into a physical reality.

I want to thank Stephen and Tony at Gemini International Limited for their guidance, patience, expertise and help throughout the entire printing process. I couldn't have done this without them.

I would like to thank my husband Neil for his continuous support, advice and help along the way, as well as the constant reminders that I should be writing.
Finally, I would sincerely like to thank you the reader. I hope you enjoy this story. If you do, make sure to pass it on.

Eternally thankful,
J.S. COMISKEY

When you walk through the storm
Hold your head up high
And don't be afraid of the dark
At the end of the storm
There's a golden sky
And the sweet silver song of the lark

Walk on, through the wind
Walk on, through the rain
Though your dreams be tossed and blown
Walk on, walk on, with hope in your heart
And you'll never walk alone
You'll never walk alone

PROLOGUE
(IRELAND 3,500 BC)

Brigid glided silently through the familiar forest, which was now wrapped in a silver blanket of snow. Her footprints were the only evidence that she had passed through. Of course, they could lead her pursuers straight to her, but she couldn't worry about that now. It was almost dawn and time was running out. A thin wind whispered through the densely-packed pines and conifers, muffling the gentle crunch of Brigid's feet and the sound of her accelerated breath as she sped towards hallowed ground. Her guardians would be waiting for her there.

She could see it now as the thick copse of trees began to thin out. The granite temple stood aloft a small hillock like a sentinel, its quartz face illuminated in the metallic moonlight. Thick flakes of snow continued to fall in torrents, settling like petals on Brigid's flame-red hair before melting. It was risky, careless to carry everything with her tonight. Yet, it was her duty, and hers alone, to ensure that the secrets of the House of Dé Danann were preserved. She understood this made it worth the risk.

Reading her thoughts, the precious cargo that she carried over her shoulders in a goatskin bag began to awaken, recognising that it was almost home. The stone amulet that rested around her pale neck

1

pre-empted the danger. The delicate object began to gently pulse, emitting a piercing orb of blue light. The colour of lapis lazuli, the bright beam swelled until it encapsulated Brigid's entire body in its warm womb. Instinctively, Brigid reached for the hilt of her sword. Pulling it out of its sheath, she ran her steely gaze over the cold blade which had been hers since birth. An Claidheamh Soluis – the Sword of Light. Her steady hand moulded perfectly around the ornate hilt which bore the symbol of her tribe. The triple spiral. The symbol of life eternal. Brigid extended the Sword of Light in front of her, catching a glimpse of her own pallid face and eyes of emerald green in its cold gleam. She looked older than her eight and ten years. Her duty, however wilfully she'd accepted it, had clearly taken its toll. Brigid inhaled slowly. Dropping her eyelids, she channelled the scalding adrenaline that coursed through her veins. She'd performed this magick countless times before, but never with so much at stake. A circuit of sacred energy poured from Brigid's body into the receptive sword. Her shut lids detected the light as a pure white flame travelled up the length of the glimmering blade.

A loud snarl tore through the darkness, momentarily shattering the silence. Crouching at the forest's edge now, Brigid adjusted her position slowly. The dim flame of a torch punctured the black depths of the forest, casting shadows on the glistening snow as it made a steady pace towards her. With just enough time to get the Cube and Oracle to safety, she broke cover, bolting through the knee-deep snow towards the circular stone temple two hundred yards ahead.

The cold air cut the back of her throat as she came to an abrupt stop at the mouth of the temple. Fixing her amulet against the triple spiral on the large granite capstone, Brigid waited as her anxious eyes followed the thin amber flame coiling around the deep grooves in the stone. Brigid glanced over her shoulder, her eyes searching through the darkness for those who pursued her. Finally, the large edifice groaned open, permitting the young goddess to enter.
Safe now that she was inside, Brigid allowed her sword to illuminate the way to the inner chamber, where she found the four guardians waiting. She could taste the fear. Perhaps it was hers. Perhaps it did not belong to her faithful servants.

Three recesses lay before her in the large cavernous vault. Her footsteps rang off the narrow walls as she came to a standstill at the north inlet. There was no time for pageantry, tonight she would have to be swift. Bobbing her head forward, she beckoned the guardians towards her with a wave. Dipping her hand into the leather bag, Brigid plucked a large crystal cube from its depths. Releasing her hold, it defied gravity as it rotated on its side, suspended in mid-air as if by some magical force. There was a soft whisper of metal on metal as Brigid once again removed Soluis from its scabbard, the tip still hot with light. As the translucent crystal cube continued to slowly rotate, Brigid reached out and touched it with the point of her sword.

'What lies within, reflects without.'

Her majestic voice reverberated off ancient stone and crystal quartz. As she spoke the hallowed words, warm amber light spilled from the vessel as it obediently shifted and broke apart, until all that remained were five unique crystalline forms.

'Luna, come forward,' invited Brigid, her voice revealing no trace of her trepidation. 'I give to you the dodecahedron. Protect it.' The young girl with flaxen hair and pale blue eyes bowed as she gracefully stepped back into line while the older of the two women took her place in front of Brigid.

'Rocha. You are a wise sage and your many years have taught you much. To you, I entrust the icosahedron.' Removing the intricately cut crystal, Brigid guided it into the old woman's weathered hands before addressing the young man who stood trembling in front of her. He was the youngest of the group and as she looked into his dark eyes, Brigid could see the fear that coursed through them.

'Manus,' said Brigid gently. 'Take this octahedron. You understand that you must protect this with your life?' The young man nodded gravely, taking his place alongside his fraternity. Finally, the eldest of the guardians was summoned forward. He was Brigid's most loved and trusted counsellor. He had been like a father to her throughout her short life. It would be hard for her to leave him, but destiny offered her no choice. 'Delphius.' The name caught in her throat like a barb. 'To you I entrust the House of Danu's most sacred items. You must have the tetrahedron and Cube. Also, please take these.' Brigid slid a long silver chain over her head and placed the amulet into the worn and callused hands of Delphius.

Her vibrant eyes scanned his face, a face where each wrinkle and each crease housed millennia of wisdom. 'The spirit of my people will protect you wherever you go. Keep this amulet with you. Always.' After placing the chain over his head, Delphius then slid both crystals inside his elk-pelt cloak. 'Fear not, my druid,' soothed Brigid, in response to the anguish in his eyes. 'We will meet again. You will know me and I will know you.'

For the first time there was an edge to Brigid's voice. 'I trust you still have the Oracle, teacher?'

Nodding his head, Delphius tapped the side of his saddle bag, all modes of speech having abandoned him.

Gathering them into a close embrace, Brigid once more stirred Soluis. 'It is almost dawn and soon the first rays of our sacred sun will saturate this dark chamber. I will leave a sign to all those who come seeking knowledge and hope in the dark age that is to come. It will be an eternal sign. As eternal as the rocks in which we now take shelter. It will be a sign that my people will return. As the House of Dé Danann retreats to our Far World, we must give way to the dark aspects of this vast universe. But know this, our light will once again radiate.'

Brigid effortlessly slid her sword through the air in a circular motion, carving a triple spiral on the back wall of the stone chamber. 'This,' she announced proudly, 'will be evidence that we lived and that we will return to our sacred Brú. Each solstice the universal light of the divine will expel the darkness, illuminating this sacred and magickal symbol. But you must go now, my faithful followers, for our enemy is close at hand. A time will come when this Cube can be made whole again. Until then each of you is bound by our sacred treaty to keep its pieces safe from those who wish to destroy it.'

Bowing, one by one the guardians exited along a warren of tunnels. Delphius was last to leave.

'Goodbye, Delphius. For now,' hushed Brigid, as she pushed her sword into his reluctant hands. Closing her eyes, Brigid stood in the enveloping darkness. Alone and unarmed, she waited for her nemesis to enter.

CHAPTER 1

'Okay. Okay. I'm awake. I'm awake,' groaned Lola defiantly to no one in particular. Her dad had been calling her for the past ten minutes. Warm sunlight assaulted her weary eyes as she forced herself out of bed. It only seemed like minutes had passed since she had gone back to sleep. She had woken in a panic in the middle of the night again. At exactly the same time as every other night – 1.05am – with the residue of the familiar nightmare clinging to her like sweat. Beyond her bedroom window she could hear the thrum of traffic as Ballyvalley began its working day. At least it's Friday, Lola told herself, the start of the weekend. Avoiding the mirror, Lola washed and dressed quickly, before making her way downstairs where she was greeted by her dad busying about in the kitchen.

'You finally decided to get out of bed, love,' grinned her dad. 'Here, drink that, your toast's on the way.' Lola took the cup of hot tea from him gratefully and sat at the worn kitchen table.

'Thanks, Da.'

'Are you feeling okay, love? You look awful. Did you not sleep last night?' quizzed her father suspiciously.

Lola didn't feel the need to lie to him. She rarely lied to her parents, or had to, but she didn't want to get into the details of her recurring dreams. She was too tired for that this morning. Besides, she hadn't told anyone about it – not even Arthur. Not even her girls.

'You're not worrying about that place. Are you, pet? If you don't like it just leave! Arthur will understand.'

Her father obviously thought that her lack of sleep was due to her internship at the local paper, but that was another nightmare entirely.

'No, Da, it's nothing like that,' protested Lola, trying to sound as convincing as possible. 'It was really warm last night and I just couldn't get over to sleep.'

Her dad narrowed his eyes, staring at her waiting for the truth he knew she was hiding, but, much to Lola's relief, he didn't push the matter, continuing to make her breakfast as he'd done since she was a child. When she was very young, Lola remembered coming into the same kitchen on winter mornings, along with her brothers. She would always find her school uniform lying over the chair in front of the open gas oven, warming her clothes before she put them on.

Being an only girl in a house with four boys meant that she had a special bond with her dad – most of the time anyway. They were very much alike in temperament –fiery. Both had the innate ability of pointing out each other's flaws. Joseph Paige was a joiner by trade. Working all his life in the construction business had taken its toll on him. He was almost fifty, and both his age and his affection for a pint of Guinness had resulted in him developing a little pot belly. In his youth he'd been a very slim and attractive man standing at five foot ten. He still had the same kind, sparkling blue eyes, fair hair with hardly a trace of grey and the same moustache for over thirty years.

'There you are, love, eat that up before it gets cold,' advised her dad as he set the steaming toast with strawberry jam on top of the gingham table cloth.

'Thanks, Da, that's lovely. Hopefully we'll not be too busy today, and I might get away early to enjoy the sunshine – while it lasts. It'll give me the chance to get ready for the weekend. It'll be the last time we will be together for the whole summer.'

For weeks Lola had been dreading the mass exodus and now the time was nearly upon them. In just under a week, Ruby, Clara and Orla would be abandoning her for America, while she was trapped working in the seventh circle of hell. Perhaps that's what the nightmares were all about. Maybe she was worried about the girls heading away. Lola's mind drifted back to the cold and lifeless chamber as she gazed absently into the wisps of steam rising from her black tea.

Once again the darkness enveloped her as it had done every night for the past six months. The chamber was lifeless, like the limp body she held in her aching arms. She couldn't see who it was, but somehow she knew the person she clung to so helplessly was dead and, with them, all hope. Lola couldn't get her bearings, all she could feel was the frigid dusty earth beneath her paralysed body. In desperation her fingertips reached out into the blackness, only to find more stone. As her hands moved across the enormous stone edifice they detected grooves embedded deep into the columns. She could recall, so vividly, the excruciating pain emanating from her ankle that prevented her from concentrating on any of these observations. Lola's skin prickled as she relived the fear that exploded through every particle of her body, knowing that someone was just inches away in the darkness, waiting to finish her off.

'Lola! Lola! Earth to Lola. It's time you got a move on, love, it's almost nine!' urged her dad, waving his hands in front of her blind eyes. 'Are you still sleeping, Lola? God knows you haven't changed much, pet, you'd sleep on a clothes line.'

Coming to, she glanced at her watch. She was late. Gulping down the last of her tea and toast, Lola planted a kiss on her dad's stubbly cheek before bolting through the front door of thirty-three Cottage Park. This was Lola's favourite stretch of road in town, not just as it was the road her house was on, but because she loved the sights and smells of the Scarvagh Road. However, her mind was otherwise engaged this morning, so she had no time to indulge in the picturesque cherry blossoms that lined the left-hand side of the road as she crossed over to where the sun chose to shine. The morning sun hung low in the sky, the beautiful hazy blue hue indicating that it was going to be another hot one. But the warmth never seemed to touch Lola. Her dream flickered through her mind's eye like a roll of film. Something was different about last night's episode, she mused. Something that she couldn't quite pinpoint. Some detail she was missing.

She buttoned up her powder-blue mac, regretting her choice of wardrobe – a light lemon skater dress with a pair of white pumps. The weather had been fantastic over the last couple of weeks, at least by

Irish standards, but as much as she loved the sun, Lola's fair complexion never changed. Her girlfriends often jibed that it was easier to stare directly at the sun than to look at the glare off her white legs. Glancing down at her slim, toned legs, she couldn't disagree. Lola had learned the hard way that subjecting her body to the gruelling job of tanning was futile. No matter how much she forced her inherently Irish melanin to turn her skin golden brown, it refused to give in. The best she could hope for was a healthy glow and a smattering of freckles across her cheeks and nose.

It was only a five-minute walk into town, but as Lola got closer to the Ballyvalley News, which would be her place of work for the next three months, she began to slow down. She had just completed her first year as a journalism student at Queen's University, Belfast. It was mandatory that she take up an internship each summer in her field. One week in, she was cursing herself for turning down the top provincial paper in Northern Ireland for her local weekly. It had been on Arthur's advice. After his counsel, they'd both agreed that she might learn more there. Get more hands-on experience. But for the first time in her life she felt he may have been wrong. It had been a tough week for her. Instinctively, Lola paused at the entrance to the Ballyvalley News. As she pushed the creaking door open, she retreated from the sunny street into the district's oldest news hub.

CHAPTER 2

As the worn sign on the front of the aged building indicated, the Ballyvalley News had been in circulation since 1835, making it the oldest paper in the county. Hasn't changed much in over one hundred years, scoffed Lola to herself as she made her way around the walnut-panelled counter at reception. Jane wasn't at her usual station this morning. She must have gone to make some tea, thought Lola as she approached the back office gingerly, hoping that she was the first to arrive. Delighted that she was alone, Lola hung her coat up on the mahogany stand and took a seat at her desk. The new Apple Mac desktop computers offered a stark contrast to their surroundings. The epitome of a modern technological age trapped in another era. Stepping into the Ballyvalley News was like stepping back in time. Lola's eyes travelled around the bland room, taking in the worn brown carpet tiles and old office desks that no doubt had been purchased back in the 1970s. The walls were a sickly white and the light that flooded the reception area was prevented from entering the back office by a large wooden partition. The doorway between the rooms had panes of glass high up on the panelling, but visibility was so poor that the halogen lights were always on.

Hitting the 'On' button, Lola organised some press releases as her computer whirred to life. Her desk faced a peeling wall, forcing her to sit with her back towards her colleagues, which only compounded her unease. She couldn't quite explain it, but the place seemed to be devoid of any positive energy. Forcing those observations to the back of her mind, Lola tried to focus on the banal workload.

'Morning, Lola,' greeted Abbey Williams in her sugary, high-pitched voice. This was as much conversation as Lola would get from her all day if the last week was anything to go by. Abbey hadn't exactly been welcoming and Lola wasn't exactly sure how to feel about her. Abbey was the type of girl that viewed other women as competition. Determined to make an effort, Lola turned to greet her new colleague.

'Morning, Abbey. It's a great day, isn't it?' she offered genially. Both women exchanged pleasantries, but it was strained. Abbey's attention quickly moved to Drew, her sidekick, as he, Sebastian and Bryce all arrived into work. As Drew and Abbey gradually excluded her from their conversation, Lola turned her attention back to the pile of dreaded press releases on her desk. She hated the damn things but she was the 'newbie' and this was how she was supposed to learn her trade, despite the fact that she had worked all year for the university paper. It was something to do, and certainly better than sitting idle.

It was after lunch when the desk phone rang. Lola had been having difficulty working out the ring patterns: two rings in close succession indicated an internal call, and one long ring an external call. Preoccupied as the dream invaded her mind again, she didn't recognise the ring pattern and lifted the phone in automatic pilot.

'Hello. Ballyvalley News. News Desk, can I help you?'
'You still haven't figured out the ring patterns, Lola!' said a brisk, well-spoken voice on the other end of the line. A light pink blush covered Lola's face; it was Bryce Neal, editor-in-chief of the Ballyvalley News.

'Oh. Hi, Mr Neal. Sorry about that,' laughed Lola tentatively. 'How can I help?'

'Could you come up to my office, please? I'd like to have a word with you.'

Heat started to rush in waves through Lola's body as she tried to think why he might want to see her. She could tell that Abbey, who hadn't spoken to her since this morning, was straining hard to listen. Lola rose from her desk, nervously smoothing down the light creases in her cotton dress, and climbed the moaning stairs to the editor's office. She tried to compose herself as she knocked on the door, and was relieved when a pleasant voice beckoned her in.

'Please, take a seat,' said Bryce, motioning to the plush green leather chair in front of his desk. Lola sat down as instructed, trying to disguise her apprehension. The last time she had been sitting in that chair was during her interview, and it wasn't as comfortable as it looked. Bryce Neal was quite handsome and this only served to compound Lola's embarrassment. He was the youngest editor the Bally-valley News had ever had, and he was keen, by his own admission, to bring it kicking and screaming into the twenty-first century. His dark hair was neatly styled and Lola couldn't help but notice a well-toned torso under his pale blue shirt and navy suit. His cufflinks had little owls with red eyes. They looked expensive. She guessed that he was in his early thirties, he couldn't be much older.

'So, Lola, how did your first week go?' he asked, his youthful face breaking into a warm smile. 'I'm sorry I haven't had much time to get down and see you, but you know how it is. I've been very busy. Sebastian tells me you're doing very well though.' Sebastian was the paper's deputy editor and proofreader. He was the only one who had been welcoming to Lola, but she suspected he'd told Bryce that she might've been feeling a bit uncomfortable in the office.

'It's been good. It's always hard being the new person, but I've enjoyed my first week.' Lola was the worst liar. She forced a smile, working hard to sell the lie she had just told her editor.

'Well, Lola, we're very glad to have you! Not only are you local, but you have an excellent academic record, and I think you will do very well here.' Bryce smiled reassuringly. 'Arthur tells me that you had a lot of other offers. But, you chose us, and that says a great deal to me. We are only a weekly newspaper, but you'll get to work across the entire paper, in terms of news, features and sport. You'll also get a chance to learn how to edit pages and lay them out. I see you've already some experience of page make-up at the university paper. I must say, Lola, I was very impressed by some of your copy, especially your piece on the recent hike in student tuition fees. I dare say you'll make quite the investigative journalist.'

It had been a very hard week for Lola and she was grateful that her editor had sensed this, or indeed acted on Sebastian's information. Not sure what to say, she smiled and nodded, thankful for the effort made to give her a few words of encouragement.

'Thank you, Mr Neal, I want to learn as much as I can while I'm here,' offered Lola, realising how tense she sounded.

'Well, it's a lovely day out there and everything is about done here. So, why don't you take the rest of the day off? Go and enjoy the sunshine.'

'I won't need to be told that twice! Thank you, sir, and have a great weekend.'

Leaving the office, Lola felt as though a weight had been lifted off her weary shoulders. She was surprised at the impact a little bit of reassurance could have on her. In truth, since coming to the paper, her confidence had plummeted, but then self-belief was something she constantly battled with. As Lola emerged from the dark office into the bright street, her phone rang. 'You'll Never Walk Alone' rose into the summer air as Lola fumbled about in her bag. She managed to get to it before the caller hung up.

'Well, Rubes! Sorry about that, my phone was at the bottom of my bag. What's the craic?'

'Hi, honey,' responded the chirpy voice at the end of the line. 'At least you have it with you today!'

'Very funny! I've just got out of work, the boss let me go early.'

'Great, that's why I was calling. I'm just coming out of work too! Do ya fancy meeting me in the park?'

'Sounds like a plan. I'll see you there in five.'

'Ok, hun, loves ya.'

'Yeah, me too!'

With that the phone went dead, and Lola made her way to the park to meet Ruby Carter.

CHAPTER 3

Lola felt instantly lighter as she soaked up every last ray of sunshine walking through the town towards Solitude Park, which was nestled in the middle of Ballyvalley on the banks of the River Bann. Lola couldn't believe how the place had been transformed. The once drab play park now had a Japanese garden with small oriental winding pathways lined with lavender. There were mini-satellite mounds dressed in wooden benches and willow trees and, in the centre, a new outdoor amphitheatre, harking back to ancient Greece. Steps had been introduced down by the river's edge and that was where Ruby sat waving at her.

Ruby Carter always seemed to bring a smile to Lola's face – no matter how bad she was feeling. That's why she was one of her oldest and dearest friends. She was different to Lola in many ways, but their friendship worked.

'Well, how was work today?' asked Ruby, her facial expression indicating she already knew the answer.

'It was alright. The gruesome twosome were pretty much the same, but the editor called me up for a bit of a pep talk before I left, and that made me feel a bit better,' replied Lola, with all the optimism she could muster. There must have been a slight break in her tone that alerted her friend that she was bluffing.

'Just spit it out, Lola,' demanded Ruby. 'Stop trying to be so decent! They're prats! Just go ahead and let it all out. I mean look at you! You look like you've been dragged through a ditch backwards.'

'Oh thanks, Ruby! We can't all be as fabulous looking as you, you know!' retorted Lola, a bit stung by her friend's comments. If Lola looked as drained as she had felt over the past week, then she was sure Ruby was right! But it wasn't work that was troubling her and she didn't want to get into it with Ruby.

'Don't be such an idiot, Lo! You know what I meant.' Ruby's tone immediately softened, the genuine concern written on her face.

'You are so much better than them. You shouldn't let them get to you like this – that's all I meant. Some day you'll work for The Guardian and they'll still be stuck where they belong in the Ballyvalley News.'

Lola knew she was right, well about the 'not letting them get to her' part anyway. After the week she'd had, she wasn't sure about The Guardian.

'I know, Rubes. I know. It's just… Listen, I refuse to waste any more energy talking about it. I'm off! It's the weekend, we're heading away and I can't wait! So, are you organised?'

Lola listened intently as her friend rambled on about make-up and whatever outfit she was going to wear. Ruby was the epitome of female, not just her curves and the way she looked, everything about her; she was a real girl. She loved make-up, her glossy celebrity magazines and high fashion.

'So, Lo, what are you planning on wearing?'

'I've finished my dress, after what seems a lifetime, so I think I'll wear it with my red shoes. You know, the patent ones with the peep-toe and little bow?'

Ruby's face looked blank.

'The ones I got for two quid in the charity shop?' reminded Lola.

'Oh yes,' sighed Ruby. 'They're lovely,' she offered, but Lola wasn't fooled.

'Yeah right,' Lola laughed, 'like you would buy anything in a charity shop, Ruby Carter! You wouldn't be caught dead!'

Feigning offence and indignation, Ruby tried to muster a response. 'What? What do you mean? I go into charity shops.' Lola raised her eyebrow, unconvinced. 'I do!' continued Ruby, in vain. 'I do ... to give clothes and stuff.'

With perfect timing, Ruby's phone started to ring and buzz, Madonna's 'Material Girl' cutting through the tranquillity of the park.

'I rest my case,' laughed Lola. Indignant, Ruby answered the phone. Her tone changed immediately. Lola could tell it was a member of the opposite sex that was calling. Who it might be – well that was another thing entirely. She found it very difficult to keep up with all her friend's admirers. Lying with her back on the smooth, hot stone, Lola closed her eyes and listened to the birds going about their work. The gentle gushing of the nearby river encouraged her to relax. She blocked out Ruby's chat, forcing herself to remember what had been different in her dream the previous night. The warm sunlight filtered soft yellow through her fine eyelids. Too embarrassed to talk to anyone about the dreams, Lola had finally turned to the great oracle – the internet – for solace.

After sieving through various articles, from the sublime to the ridiculous, one particular item stood out. It detailed how Native Americans believed recurring dreams were messages from the other world, such as warnings or omens. Lola thought that this notion was a bit far-fetched, like one of Arthur's stories, but she was aware of an unease deep within her. A feeling she couldn't suppress no matter how much she tried. The light behind her eyes momentarily faded as the sun slipped behind a thin veil of cloud, only to re-emerge. There it was, in an instant she had it. The thing that had eluded her memory. Until last night there had only ever been darkness in the chamber, but now, now there was light. From where or what, she couldn't tell.

'Well, slackers!' The familiar voice made Lola jump, and she turned with a start to see Clara and Orla approaching.

'Well, ladies.' Lola struggled to re-adjust her eyes to the light. 'So are we all ready for our road trip?'

'Yep, I'm packed and all,' said Clara brightly.

The fact that Clara Stewart was packed didn't surprise Lola or any of the girls. It was a well-known fact that she had a serious case of OCD. She'd probably had her bag packed for a full week. This was good in some respects, but living with someone who was obsessed with tidiness caused tension in their university house from time to time, especially between her and Lola.

'I'm almost sorted,' offered Orla. 'I'm really looking forward to getting away.'

'Has this got anything to do with a certain boy called Peter, by any chance?' jibed Lola.

Orla's robust denial did nothing to convince her friends. The traitorous blush rising to her cheeks told them all she needed to know.

'No it has not,' snapped Orla defensively.

Seeing the resolve on Orla's face, Lola, Clara and Ruby – who had just ended her call – looked down at the ground and towards each other, seeming fully scolded. Unable to keep up the pretence any longer, they all broke into fits of laughter, even Orla couldn't resist.

'Right, my lovely ladies, as I am sure you can guess, I'm not ready. So I'll have to make tracks.' Gathering her jacket and bag, Lola arranged to meet the girls in an hour. Leaving the park, she made her way through the busy town and headed towards home to pack her bag for what would be their last weekend together for three whole months. She would be without her girls but at least she still had Arthur. For the first time that week, Lola felt a glimmer of hope.

CHAPTER 4

The moist sand felt cool between Lola's toes as she strode across the golden beach, passing the few stragglers that were still enjoying what was left of the evening sun. Cranking up the volume on her new iPhone, she slowly gravitated towards the shore where the white foamy waves lapped at her feet, before ebbing back to the sea. Since she could remember, she'd always been drawn to water. Just being beside a river or a fountain helped her to think, helped to clear her troubled head. Even having a bath made her feel instantly better. It was as though the water spoke to her soul, soothing and purging her worries, giving her clarity of mind. But, being by the seaside, especially on a warm day like today, was as good as it could get. Feeling the nip of the icy Atlantic Ocean, Lola retreated to a sunny spot at the bottom of one of the nearby sand dunes.

Towards the horizon, where the sea had turned a deep azure, a few drifting clouds appeared in the sky. Lola could see four solitary surfers bobbing up and down on the water, patiently waiting for the next wave to come along and carry them back to shore. It looked so peaceful out there. Closing her eyes, Lola removed her earphones to hear the song of the waves as they peaked and troughed before crashing on the sand.

Dreams, work, the girls leaving – Lola wished she could just expunge it all from her mind. Her green eyes drank in the different hues of blue on blue, the glistening sand and contrasting rocks. Absentmindedly she lifted a handful of sand, letting it slowly fall between her fingers. Glancing down at the miniscule grains glistening like tiny diamonds on her fingertips, she suddenly remembered the lines of a William Blake poem she had read countless times before.

'To see a world in a grain of sand, And a heaven in a wild flower, Hold Infinity in the Palm of your hand, and Eternity in an hour,' recited Lola silently as she admired the natural beauty of the scene before her. This was written in gold leaf along the top of Arthur's observatory, back at Brook Mill Manor.

It had been a few days since she had actually seen Arthur, which was most unlike her, but she had been busy with work and football training. Her brother Michael had them training three nights a week in preparation for the Summer League Cup final. It wouldn't be so bad this summer, Lola told herself. After all, she had Arthur. At seventy-five years of age, there was very little chance that he would come clubbing with her, but he was one of her closest friends. Arthur Delphian never ceased to amaze Lola. Of course, he was uber-intelligent, a true polymath. By profession he was a retired astronomer, but his vast knowledge spread well beyond the stars. She was only eight years old when she first met him. Like all the kids on her council estate, she had heard the stories. Each day after school, Lola played with her friends in the fields that surrounded the mysterious Brook Mill Manor. Only the bravest of the group would breach the large perimeter wall of the estate or venture up the overgrown driveway that snaked up to the mansion. Lola, who was usually with her brothers and some of the other boys from her estate, was the only one who had not completed the covert mission into enemy territory, much to her annoyance. Back then the place held such reverence and mystery for her – in many ways it still did. But when she was a child, Brook Mill Manor was the unknown. It was intriguing and a little bit scary. So, when her dad came home one night and announced that he would be working at the manor for a couple of weeks, Lola tortured him to take her with him. She'd thought how impressive it would be – she would be the envy of all her friends. Not only could she say she'd been in the large garden, but also that she had been inside the Delphian mansion.

Growing up in Ballyvalley, the Delphian family had always been very prominent. They owned most of the real estate in town and even owned the local football team, Ballyvalley United. Arthur's great-great-grandfather had made his fortune in the linen and textile trade back in the nineteenth century and had employed hundreds of people in the factory beside the family estate. The looms of Brook Mill Factory had long since fallen silent, the factory itself was only a crumbling relic of the past.

In all the time Lola had spent playing in the adjoining fields and around the old factory, she had never met Arthur Delphian in person. People said he was a recluse, she had even heard people say that he was into dark magic. There was no way she was going to miss the opportunity to see for herself, so eventually she wore her father down.

'What's the fascination you have, Lola, with Arthur Delphian and Brook Mill Manor?' spluttered Joseph Paige. Although he never admitted it to his daughter, he knew exactly what it was that captivated her. It was the same things that had captivated him as a young boy. 'You shouldn't believe the tittle-tattle you hear about the estate, Lo,' he had admonished her.

'I heard that he does black magic, Da, so I want to see for myself. Do a bit of investigating. You know?' She had been so sure she was going to expose Arthur Delphian's dark secrets.

'Dark magic, you say?' answered her dad, managing to keep his face straight. 'Well, our Lo, if he has anything to hide, pet, I've no doubt a super sleuth like you will uncover it! You can come with me tomorrow, but you'd better be on your best behaviour, young lady.'

Of course she'd promised him she would. The night before the big meeting she could hardly sleep with the excitement. Lola could still recall the plethora of emotions that she went through that morning, as they approached the gate lodges at the top of the avenue. Her stomach churned as the butterflies danced around it. Clutching onto her beloved notebook, she took her dad's hand, gripping it tightly, not sure what she was about to discover. As they approached the house the sun shone on the perfectly manicured lawns of Brook Mill Manor. A plush viridian, they were unlike anything Lola had ever seen before. The flower beds, which lined the stone driveway, were brimming with yellow and pink roses, and in the far corner of the front garden, along the perimeter wall, was a mass of sweet pea, its perfume drifting across the garden.

Then there was the house. It was the biggest house she had ever seen. Lola counted at least twenty windows at the front. Her house had only seven, and that was the entire building. She was instantly smitten by the beautiful neo-classical house; with its perfect symmetry and white exterior, it was breathtaking. Passing the large black front door, Lola noticed it had the face of an old man with a long beard made of holly attached to it. Looking more closely, she realised it was a door knocker.

Following her father around to the side of the house, she stopped dead in her tracks, straining to take in the large circular building attached to the side of the house. It didn't seem to be part of the original building, but it looked spectacular.

'That's Arthur's observatory. He's an astronomer.' The word was new to Lola. 'That means he works in the observatory in Armagh. His job is to look at the stars,' her dad had explained, answering all her questions before she'd asked, like he always did.

Lola's eyes were transfixed on the mini-observatory. This was way better than anything she could have imagined. Gazing at the large circular structure, she heard the crunch of footsteps behind her. Her father greeted Arthur casually as she swung round to get a look at the man of legend. The deflation must have been evident on Lola's face, she saw nothing of the man she expected to find. Intuitively, Arthur read her disappointment.

'Not what you were expecting, Miss Paige?' asked Arthur bemused.

Lola, never one for lying, remembered blurting out the first thing that came into her head, much to her dad's mortification. 'Well no, Mr Delphian,' she answered crisply. 'Not really. I mean you don't look like someone that's into dark magic to me! In fact you look more like Santa Claus, with your grey beard and big belly.'

At that, Arthur Delphian let out a blistering roar of laughter, a sound that Lola would come to love. It was so infectious. At the time though, she didn't join in because she felt like she'd been cheated. She had been after her first exclusive story. Embarrassed by his daughter's candidness, Joseph began to apologise to Arthur, but he wouldn't hear of it.

'Joseph, you have a gem there. What lies within, reflects without.' Still chuckling, Arthur gestured to the observatory. 'Lola, my dear, how would you like me to introduce you to the cosmos, and the transcendental order of this great universe?'

Laughing, Lola followed eagerly. She liked Arthur instantly. 'Come let's away. I think you and I are going to become the best of friends,' chuckled Arthur, as he led the way into the observatory. That was her hooked. From then on, she would visit Arthur every day at the manor or at least talk to him on the phone.

The slow rumbling in Lola's stomach indicated that it was time to return to the cottage. She wanted to give Arthur a call, she felt bad that she hadn't told him about her dreams. He would know what to say. What it all meant. He always had the answers. Looking up the sandy pathway, Lola could see Pebble Cottage perched at the top of the road, guarding the entrance to the beach. Ruby's father had purchased the house the previous year as a 'precaution', in case his daughter went to university in Coleraine rather than Belfast. Ruby called it a 'little cottage', which always made Lola laugh because it was about five times bigger than her parents' house. It had five bedrooms, each with its own en-suite, and a massive kitchen and living room. All the rooms were completed to the finest spec, but what the house chiefly offered was the most wonderful view of the beach and the sea. The white timber-framed house, equipped with an all-American white picket fence, would not have been out of place in Cape Cod. The interior was decorated from a pallet of greys, blues and whites, complementing the deep blue sea beyond the cottage's large bay windows.

Lola glanced at the cliffs that jutted out into the sea as she strode down the beach. A flicker of white caught the side of her eye. On first inspection, all she could see were the large rugged cliffs that, in the evening sun, blended almost perfectly with the yellow sand. Straining to see clearly in the light, Lola put on her sunglasses, her shielded eyes tracing out a balcony where a young man stood. His white shirt was unbuttoned and flapped in the breeze. Looking more closely, Lola realised that the balcony was made out of glass as a house seemed to materialise out of the cliff face behind him.

Lola had been to the Strand Beach on countless occasions, but she had never noticed this cavernous structure before. It was like a massive sandcastle, with two large round towers at each side, and three enormous arched windows in the centre of the building that dropped to the ground. The entire house appeared to be carved out of the cliff itself. The young man, barely visible but for his tousled blonde hair and open shirt, seemed to be staring back at her. Turning away in embarrassment, Lola fumbled with her music. When she lifted her head again, he was no longer there.

CHAPTER 5

Alex Stein savoured the rays of warm sun on his exposed flesh.
Despite the fact that he was fair-haired he always tanned.
Admiring his well-toned torso, he leaned over the balcony, soaking up
the scenery. He had a lot on his mind today. There was much to do and
he was in charge. The thought made his empty stomach churn. His
father had travelled back home to America to visit his brethren at
Bohemian Grove. Alex had been there numerous times before, but
wasn't that impressed by its pageantry.

Each year the 'Club' hosted a two-week camp, attracting global
heads of state, prominent businessmen, former presidents and other
such esteemed guests. Alex understood that the majority of those
people had no real understanding of the true purpose of such
gatherings. All the ceremonies were merely an elaborate display. The
Cremation of Care Ceremony, which mimicked human sacrifice, was
understood to be symbolic by the majority of participants. But there
were those amongst them that practised and preferred the real thing.
His father was one of those people – as was he.

While Alex scoffed at their ignorance, Carl Stein often told his son it provided the perfect cover to meet the other members of the Club in order to discuss their global agenda. Scanning the distant shoreline, Alex located the solitary outline of Mussenden Temple, perched on the cliff's edge one hundred and twenty feet above the sea. The temple had been built in the eighteenth century as a personal library for the Bishop of Derry. Architecturally, it was modelled on the Temple of Vesta in Tivoli, Italy. That's what had drawn him and his father to it. Even from this distance Alex could see the tiny dots that were tourists milling around the exterior, observing the breathtaking views of the rugged Irish coast.

It amused him that they were so oblivious to what really took place at Mussenden. How blind they were to the dark energy that radiated from the place. He had been there many times with his father and other members of their exclusive coven and soon the burden of responsibility would lie on his shoulders. This was his first real test and already he was beginning to feel weary of the Club's – and his father's – expectations. This was his destiny. There was no alternative for him. Alex understood that his only option was to step up to the plate, as his father and countless generations of his family had done before him.

The beach was almost empty now, except for one lone figure that seemed to be looking up towards him. The house had been specifically designed to blend perfectly with its surroundings, depending on the movement of light. Its design was quite an achievement and had taken Alex months to perfect. Judging by the look on the girl's face, she hadn't noticed the house before that moment. Alex returned the slim brunette's stare but his sport was soon interrupted by the telephone ringing inside – it wasn't safe to use his mobile. Returning to the house, he was relieved when he lifted the receiver and heard the familiar voice at the other end.

'Alex?' the smooth, deep voice enquired.

'Yes, it's me. Is everything in place for tonight?' Despite his best efforts at restraint, the urgency and angst in his voice was clearly evident to the caller.

'Yes, everything is in place. You have nothing to worry about. Once the job is completed I will contact you on this line. If all goes to plan – which it will,' added the man assuredly, 'you can expect my call around 1.30am.'

'It had better go to plan,' warned Alex, a hint of menace in his voice. This was met by a peal of laughter.

'I see your father has taught you well, young man. You can be assured this will go to plan. I have waited a long time for this opportunity and will enjoy every second of it.'

Alex hung up the phone, a sudden wave of nausea sweeping over him. Tonight was his biggest test. He did not want to disappoint his father. He couldn't bear to think of the consequences if he did. One last time he put himself over the plan. The party was organised and the appropriate candidate selected. There was no doubt that she would be there, willing to please him in whatever way she could, like all of the women he met. Although his father had not said it, Alex understood that this was his real initiation into the Club.

CHAPTER 6

'Hurry up, Ruby, it's nearly 10 o'clock and we won't get in anywhere!'

Normally Orla was very laid back, but tonight she was clearly on edge. Finally Ruby emerged from the bedroom looking as glamorous as ever in a sparkly silver designer dress with matching shoes.

'Okay, can we go now?' snapped Orla, already halfway up the garden path. Rolling her eyes, Ruby locked the door behind her and followed behind Lola and Clara.

'I think Peter is going to be at the club tonight,' said Clara, raising her voice just loud enough so Orla could hear.

'Oh is that right? Is that why I nearly got my head bitten off then?' added Ruby mischievously. Orla continued to lead the pack at a steady pace, pretending not to hear her friends ribbing her. Lola increased her stride, eventually catching her up.

'Do you hear them? You'd think they'd give it a rest,' she hissed at Lola.

'Ach Orla, they're only messing with you. Come on, lighten up,' chided Lola lightly.

'You're one to talk! You haven't exactly been a barrel of laughs this weekend!'

Lola was momentarily taken aback, but she didn't want to darken the mood, so she tried to lighten the conversation.

'It's still lovely out, isn't it?' Hearing the humour in her friend's tone, Orla felt guilty for being so brash.

'Sorry, Lola, that was out of order.'

'Don't be silly, pet,' said Lola magnanimously, wrapping her arm around her friend's shoulder. 'I know it gets to you, us always winding you up about Peter. You know we just think you'd be a great couple, that's all.'

'I know, Lo, I know,' said Orla with a deep sigh, resting her head on Lola's shoulder.

'It will happen between you two. It's written in the stars. I can feel it!'

'Do you really think it's written in the stars?' giggled Orla.

'Of course! You know I know about these things, plus I'll ask Arthur to check, just in case,' laughed Lola. 'Anyway, enough about boys, it's all about the ladies tonight. So, let's just have a great time before you all head off and leave me.'

The night seemed to fly by as they danced and laughed the hours away. Lola couldn't remember the last time she had felt so carefree. Leaving the club, Lola's feet began to throb in pain. She realised that she hadn't actually sat down all night as she retreated to the nearest seat, waiting for the others to emerge from the stuffy club.

'There you are,' said Orla. Lola fought hard to contain her delight at seeing Orla and Peter coming towards her holding hands.

'Well, Lola, long time no see. Did you have a good night?' asked Peter, who now resembled a Cheshire cat, his smile stretching from ear to ear.

'Hi, Peter. I'm doing great! I've had a brilliant night, and by the looks of it so have you,' replied Lola, cheerily gesturing towards Orla with a slight nod of the head.

Instinctively, Peter pulled Orla closer to his side. His dark eyes glistened as he looked at her in admiration.

'The best night I've had in a long time, Lola,' he winked.

Lola liked Peter, they all did. He was easy-going and very funny. Lola and the girls knew that he totally adored their best friend. She was so happy to see them together after all this time she thought she might burst with excitement, but she knew better than to say anything for fear of Orla's wrath.

'Where are the rest of them?' asked Orla, trying to remain non-chalant, just as Clara and Ruby emerged from the crowd.

Catching sight of Orla and Peter together, they pretended not to notice, perching themselves on the bench alongside Lola.

'So what's the plan of attack now?' chirped Ruby.

'Bed!' offered Lola wearily rubbing her feet. The last of her energy had evaporated in minutes. 'Dancing all night in heels doesn't seem such a good idea now!'

'Bed!' protested Ruby. 'The night is young, and since this is our last night together for three months, I intend to make the most of it, Miss Paige.'

'There's a party at my friend's house, if you fancy coming?' Peter said, looking at the girls hopefully.

The pleading look on Orla's face made it impossible for Lola to say no. 'Sure why not.'

'A house party – great!' exclaimed Ruby. 'Let's go!'

Ruby leapt off the seat, pulling a reluctant Clara and Lola with her.

'So is it anyone we know, Peter?' enquired Ruby as they made the short journey to the exclusive Strand Road. Knowing her, it was more than likely someone she knew, thought Lola.

'It's Alex Stein's place. Do you know him?'

'Yes, doesn't everyone? You would have to be on another planet not to know Alex!'

'Yeah, he seems to have that effect on most people he meets,' chuckled Peter.

'Alex Stein, Alex Stein…,' mouthed Lola to herself. The name sounded vaguely familiar, but she couldn't think where she had heard it before.

'The name sounds familiar, Peter, is he in your law class?' Lola asked.

'No, he studies architecture at Yale. He's home for the summer. Actually, I think he's home for his year out. His father owns Stein Corporations, so he'll be working for him. You obviously haven't met him, Lola. You would definitely remember Alex! He leaves quite an impression on the ladies. But I don't think he would be your cup of tea,' added Peter, with a wry smile.

'I would buy front-row tickets for that encounter,' sniggered Ruby in agreement, clearly enjoying the private joke. Lola pretended not to hear them. Turning onto the Strand Road, it was clear that the Stein party was the hottest in town. Droves of revellers swarmed towards the cliff-side mansion.

'Which house is it, Ruby?' enquired Lola. They were almost at the end of the street and as far as she could see there was only one other house and it seemed too modest to fit the description of the Stein residence.

'It's actually built into the side of the cliff; they've been working on it for years. Word is that Alex was the main architect on the project. You want to see it, Lo! It's like some gothic castle. I'm dying to get a look inside!'

'Oh! I saw that place today. From the beach. When I was out walking. One minute it was there and the next it was gone.' Lola had forgotten to ask Ruby about the house and the young man on the balcony when she had returned from her walk earlier. Falling into step with Peter and Orla, they turned into a brightly lit asphalt lane. A sandstone wall flanked the driveway on either side with two large stone owls perched on pillars at the end. Below the owl on the left-hand side was a small plaque inscribed with the words Chateau Bacchus. The cacophony of laughter and sound spilled out of the open door into the cool night air.

'Chateau Bacchus – how apt,' mused Lola as she walked into the throng, hit by a wall of music.

CHAPTER 7

Lola strained to hear Orla's voice over the music; all she could do was nod her head as Orla gestured towards the far corner of the house where Peter had disappeared.

'OKAY, I'LL SEE YOU LATER,' shouted Lola over the din. Turning to speak to Clara and Ruby, Lola was annoyed to find her friends were nowhere to be found. It was impossible to see where she was going as she pushed her way through the sea of bouncing bodies. Searching for her phone in her bag, Lola suddenly remembered she'd left it on the bed back at the cottage. Cursing herself for leaving it behind, she scrambled through the mass in a vain attempt to find her friends. Suddenly she was brought to an abrupt and very painful halt. Slightly dazed, she thought she had been struck by something or by someone. Rubbing her head she looked around for a culprit, but the crowd seemed to be oblivious to her pain. It wasn't until she extended her hand out in front of her that she found it. As if out of thin air, a spiral staircase materialised before her watering eyes. Fearing she was hallucinating, Lola took a closer look, and was relieved when she realised it was made from glass.

'Stupid bloody staircase! Who the hell would have a staircase that you can't even see?' seethed Lola. Had there been a hammer at hand she would gladly have gone to work on the offending feature.

'Tha happind da me a minute ago.' Lola turned to see a boy about her own age pressing down on her. He held a glass containing a bluish liquid, which was now sloshing out. 'Are ye alrigh?' Judging by the accent, Lola could tell he was a local boy, and a quite intoxicated local at that.

'Yeah, I'm fine. Thanks. It'll maybe knock some sense into me,' replied Lola, trying to laugh off her embarrassment. Not wanting to be rude, she continued to talk to the boy, but she could see where this was going. Then two things happened at once, which Lola had seen coming, but still couldn't move quickly enough to avoid. Misunderstanding her congeniality to be an invitation to get intimate, the boy bent down in a futile attempt to kiss her. At the same time someone was trying to pass by him, and in the process practically knocked the young Lothario on top of her as the entire contents of his glass spilled all over her hair, dress and legs. Self-restraint had never been one of Lola's strong points. Assessing her options, she considered the first, which involved punching the culprit right in the face. She decided, however, to settle for the second, and capitalised on the distraction. Making a quick exit, Lola dashed up the glass stairs, muttering the worst insults under her breath.

'That's it! I have had about enough for one night,' she fumed, talking to no one in particular.

She was now standing at the top of a dimly-lit hallway with large black wooden doors leading off into numerous rooms. The walls were a crisp white, decorated with various works, all seemingly by the same artist. To Lola it just looked like a child had splashed paint along the surface of the canvas. It wasn't exactly Caravaggio.

Kicking off her sodden shoes, the thick red carpet felt fantastic beneath her tired and cramped feet. At the end of the corridor she could see a door slightly ajar, the light spilling out into the hall. Assuming it was the bathroom, Lola slowly padded down towards the open door. As she approached the room she thought she heard someone talking. Stopping short, she strained to hear over the music filtering up from below. At first it was very faint and she couldn't make it out, then suddenly the voice became louder.

'Have you completed the job?' quizzed the young man. There was an edge of authority to the polished American accent but there was no reply. Lola realised that whoever it was must be speaking on the phone. There was a sudden change of tone as the largely calm voice became more aggressive, with an edge of panic.

'What do you mean, you didn't get it? Very well, I will let my father know.' It sounded more like a threat than a statement. Lola felt ill at ease wandering around a stranger's house listening, albeit accidentally, to their conversation. Deciding to leave, Lola turned back towards the stairs. She didn't hear anyone approaching on the cushioned carpet, so she let out a gasp when an iron grip clasped her arm.

'What do you think you are doing up here?' said a furious voice as Lola was twisted around to face her accuser. His beauty momentarily stunned her. Even though his face was contorted in anger, it was still perfectly breathtaking. His eyebrows furrowed over deep blue eyes as he spat the accusation at her.

'Were you eavesdropping?' Lola was shocked and mortified. Just when she thought her night couldn't get any worse. She laboured to find her voice, distracted by this siren that held on to her.

'I... I...,' attempted Lola, shaking her head in a futile attempt to order her thoughts. She finally spat out her answer in a splurge. 'I was looking for a bathroom. Someone spilled the contents of their glass down my dress, in case you haven't noticed!' Lola's heart sank as she looked down at her handcrafted dress. The white cotton fabric with little red anchors had turned a bubblegum blue. Raising an eyebrow, Alex pushed Lola out disdainfully as if she were contagious. Lola watched as his arrogant eyes surveyed her dress, her wet legs and the absence of shoes. No longer detracted by his beauty, Lola allowed her embarrassment to be replaced by anger. 'And by the way, I was not listening to your conversation,' she shouted back at him. Her captor seemed momentarily taken aback by her delayed reaction. 'Don't be so arrogant as to assume that anything you might have to say would be worth listening to!' Her angst was spilling out now. 'And could you please, let go of my arm!' she shouted pulling herself free.

Lola could feel the burn of his grip as he let go, leaving a crimson ring on her pale skin. For a moment Alex had forgotten he was even holding on to her. 'The party is downstairs, you shouldn't be up here!' he said in a calm, now softened tone, as he stared down into the most wonderful pair of emerald green eyes he had ever seen, full of energy and defiance. It had been a stressful day for him and he felt abashed that he had lost his cool so easily. He rarely lost control of his emotions, but he had a lot on his mind, and there was still much to do tonight.

'You look like you need to get cleaned up! The bathroom is at the end of the hall.'

'You have the audacity to offer me the use of your bathroom after the way you've just spoken to me,' snorted Lola disdainfully. 'I'm not sure what sort of people you are used to dealing with, mister,' she continued, poking him in the chest with her index finger, 'but there is no substitute for good manners! Oh, and one more thing, you are right, I shouldn't be here! So, shove your party and shove your bathroom, and you can take that stupid grin off your face and all!' A broad smile spread across the boy's gorgeous face, momentarily disorientating Lola. Forcing herself to turn, she strode up the hallway with her shoes in her hands.

CHAPTER 8

Pausing at the top of the stairs, Lola could see that Clara was heading towards the door, the expression on her face indicating that the party had ended for her too.

'Is it home time, Clara?'

'It is for me, Lo. You coming too?'

'Yes, I've had enough,' said Lola, forcing a smile, while holding up her dress. 'Look at the state of me! First of all I walk into an invisible staircase, and then some idiot tries to put the lips on me, ruining my dress in the process. It took me almost a month to make this, and then I try to find a bathroom and get accosted by some first-class aaaa...'

'Alex! Alex!' Lola turned towards the high-pitched voice. A leggy blonde in a blood-red dress that caressed her slim figure embraced Alex at the foot of the staircase. Lola wasn't one bit repentant as she realised he'd been behind her the entire time.

'There you are! I've been looking for you all night, where've you been?' said Alex smoothly. Lola watched as the blonde girl coiled herself around the American like a purring cat. She was certainly stunning, just the type he would go for, thought Lola. A hint of something unfamiliar stirred deep inside her. Unmoved by the blonde girl's attention, Alex's eyes were still firmly on Lola. His female companion flicked her head towards Lola as her thick ringlets cascaded around her perfect face. Lola registered the distain in her pale blue eyes. She was clearly confused as to why she wasn't commanding Alex's undivided attention.

'Bye, Lola. It was a pleasure meeting you and I'm sorry about your dress. You can bill me for it!' laughed Alex, but Lola didn't turn around. No longer governed by her hot temper, she gritted her teeth refusing to let the mocking voice of Alex Stein ignite a reaction. Lola stepped outside with Clara, closing the door behind her. She sucked in the fresh sea air as she stood on the warm asphalt, barefoot.

'What was all that about?' quizzed Clara. Rolling her eyes, Lola didn't have the energy to get into it.

'You don't want to know! Come on, let's go!' Linking onto Clara's arm, Lola began to walk up the drive towards home.

Lola's feet throbbed as she stood in the shower, washing the blue syrup out of her hair and off her legs. Drying off her hair, she checked her phone, before climbing into the large double bed where Clara already lay, fast asleep. She had one missed call from Arthur. According to the phone display he'd called at 12.30am. Lola glanced at the bedside clock. The neon display read 2.30am. Worried, she considered calling him back, but decided it was too late. Resting her head on the soft pillow, Lola fell into a deep sleep.

Suddenly she was back at Brook Mill Manor. She was walking with Arthur towards their regular seat in his herb garden. The entire garden was covered in a light frost that glistened in the winter sun. Even though she and Arthur were deep in conversation, Lola couldn't exactly make out what he was saying. The sky started to darken, turning a dull grey and it looked as though it might snow. Arthur began to stir, rising from his seat. He turned to Lola and spoke.

'You are so intuitive, Lola; you have the innate ability to see all aspects of the soul, both the light and the dark.' Reaching down he embraced her, kissing her on the cheek. 'You must trust your instincts and follow the signs.'

Lola couldn't understand what was happening. Although Arthur was smiling at her, she saw sadness in his earthen eyes. Suddenly a bright silvery light radiated from Arthur's solar plexus.

'I have always seen the greatness and the goddess in you. You shine like a beacon and, in these dark times that are to come, there are many who will need your light. I have imparted many secrets over the years, and now you must journey on your own. Trust your insights, for they will keep you from harm, my dear.'

With that, Arthur got up off the seat and walked towards the bottom of the garden. Lola rose and tried to follow him but she was rooted to the spot. Panicking, she called after him. 'What do you mean, Arthur? Where are you going?'

'You cannot come with me! It is time for me to leave you now, but know this: I love you dearly and I have faith in you. You have the answers. You alone hold the key.' Walking to the back of the garden, the bright light emanating from Arthur's core grew larger and brighter. It was so blinding that Lola could no longer look at him directly. Then, in an instant, he was gone, disappearing into a million particles of light.

CHAPTER 9

Alex Stein slid out from under the black satin sheets, catching the sweet scent of perfume from the side of the bed that Victoria Jones had vacated. It was still warm. The dark bedroom was illuminated by the cold moonbeams as they bounced off the calm sea below, allowing him to locate his robe with ease. Pulling on his red silk cloak, Alex lifted the golden Scaramouch off its stand in the closet and headed towards the library.

Tracing his finger down the spine of a worn book, he waited impatiently as the bookshelf glided open revealing a dank stairwell. Stepping over the threshold, the door closed with a gentle click behind him. The familiar briny smell of the sea caught his nostrils as he descended the rugged stone steps to the bowels of the cliff. Detecting his approach the light sensors guided his path, expelling a dim orange light which extinguished again as he passed. In truth, he would have been quite capable of making the journey unaided, but it would not be long until dawn, so the light helped to speed proceedings.

Tonight Alex would be Grotto Master, a role that his father had been preparing him for all his life. A rush of electricity weaved its way through his body and he began to mentally ready himself for the task ahead. Almost everything had gone to plan, which pleased him, but they had failed to secure the ring and the Cube. Nonetheless the Club had plenty to celebrate tonight, he mused, as he boarded the small hydro-electric rail carriage that waited at the bottom of the stairs. Alex welcomed the fact that the next part of his journey would be taken in complete darkness. It gave him time to focus his thoughts. His blood-red cloak flailed out behind him as the small craft gathered speed, racing now through the blackened subterranean passageway. This was Alex's pièce de résistance. After all, it had been his idea to incorporate a means of access to the temple from their mansion. It had taken almost two years to complete, but it proved to be invaluable. The hidden transport system allowed members of the Club to move to and from the temple without detection.

Suddenly his carriage began to slow down; he was almost there. As he opened his eyes again he could see a faint red light up ahead, and the entrance to the lift shaft. Alex pulled on his mask as the craft came to a halt. It was a vital prop in tonight's little get-together.

He entered the lift, pulling the iron cage closed and ascended towards the temple. As the lift climbed up the cliff, he could hear the baritone chants of his fellow Club members growing louder and louder against the hysterical soprano screams of a woman. There was no better sound in the world. It was quite a symphony, smiled Alex to himself. Flicking up his hood, Alex emerged dramatically from behind a large granite wall at the top of the make-shift altar. The chanting immediately stopped. The only sounds now were the helpless sobs of the pretty blonde who lay sprawled out on the large stone altar. Her pale limbs were stretched out like a star with a black candle burning at each point of her extended body. Victoria Jones's eyes danced frantically around the sea of black robes and the ghostly white masks, whose long menacing beaks were blind to her terror. Alex cocked his head, studying the fear and confusion in her eyes as she writhed against an unseen restraint. No ties or chains secured Victoria Jones to the table yet she could not move.

Calling order, Alex Stein addressed the Hell Fire Club. 'Brothers,' he announced in a deep guttural voice, unfamiliar even to him. 'We are gathered here tonight in the presence of our Great God – the one true bringer of light – to celebrate the extermination of our deadly foe. We of the left-hand path know the true nature of this universe and the human condition, and so we renounce the fallacy of a divine architect, this creator and saviour of humanity. We, the brethren of the Hell Fire Club, are gods of our own fate and thus together we will profess our faith.' A cacophony of sound saturated the small chamber as each faceless man added his voice to the prayer.

'I proclaim the Great God as my one and only God. I promise to recognise and honour him in all things, desiring in return his manifold assistance in the true success of my dark endeavours.'

Alex held up his right hand, revealing a slender silver knife. Each man followed his lead as he cut a small incision across the palm of his left hand, allowing the warm droplets of blood to fall into a small glass made out of finely cut crystal. Silently the men took their positions around their sacrifice, making room for Alex at the head of the stone table. Alex's cold eyes considered Victoria Jones. Her red dress was torn at the sides and a steady stream of black tears traced down her once perfect face. The passion and pleasure that they had shared just hours ago had evaporated. He had feasted on the carnal pleasures that Victoria Jones's beautiful body offered but now he meant to feast on her soul. She meant nothing to him. She was only ever a pawn in his game, but, as Alex traced his eyes along her slender body, he understood that she would make a worthy sacrifice.

Alex raised his hand again, giving the command for silence and obedience. Victoria Jones's breathless sobs were the only sound that punctured the eerie quiet. Closing his eyes, Alex focused on his offering, he could hear it, he could taste the fear that was coursing through every particle of Victoria Jones's perfect body. Meditating, he began to feed off this raw life force. He could feel the pure adrenaline coursing through his veins as he spoke. 'Great Lord, you have bestowed wondrous fortune on us tonight and thus we offer you this sacrifice in return.' A deafening shriek pierced the room. Crying desperately, Victoria Jones begged the faceless strangers for her life.

'No, no please let me go! Let me go! Oh God, please, please!'

With a mocking sneer, Alex Stein bent in close and whispered into her ear. 'Your God can't save you now, Victoria!' Her name rolled off his tongue like silk. For the first time Victoria Jones fell still, sheer horror rendering her mute. Alex could see confusion mingle with disbelief, as she struggled to find her voice. He slipped off his mask to confirm her worst fears, smiling as her hysteria reached fever pitch.

Alex lifted his knife again and carved a single line down the inside of the girl's outstretched arm, watching hungrily as her blood flowed into the thirteen deep crevices etched into the table. Each of the men collected Victoria's Jones's warm blood into their chalices that sat along the edges of the table. Raising their offering, Alex cast the spell, 'Power without be whole and true, as we drink this cup let her soul ensue.' The familiar words sounded wrong as they rolled off his novice tongue. For a second Alex wondered if they would be as powerful pouring from his mouth as they had been the countless times his father had spoken them. In seconds Alex got his answer. Each cup began to glow a pale blue as the life-rich blood and magick pirouetted and fused in a deathly dance. The dying girl's life force coursed through Alex's body like wild-fire as he downed the contents of his chalice.

This was the ultimate high for him. He had never taken drugs and didn't drink alcohol. To him his body was the ultimate temple and he refused to pollute it with mere chemicals. But this, the fear-rich blood, fused with his dark magick, was the true organic high. He could feel his own strength and magick growing. He was becoming stronger.

Alex glanced down at the limp lifeless body of Victoria Jones, her glazed eyes confirming that the last vestiges of life were now fully extinguished. With dawn fast approaching he ordered his men to start the cleansing ritual before leaving for the mansion. His father was due back later today and would be expecting a full debriefing.

CHAPTER 10

'Pick up, pick up, come on, Arthur, pick up the phone!' pleaded Lola for the umpteenth time.

'Relax, Lola. He's alright, it was just a dream,' calmed Clara. 'He's probably out in the garden with Cuchulain that's why no one's answering the phone.'

Lola nodded absentmindedly. No matter how the girls tried to reason with her, and no matter how much she wanted to believe they were right, she couldn't control the waves of sheer panic that had taken hold of her. Last night's dream had felt so real. She just needed to talk to Arthur, to hear his voice, and then she would be content.

'We're nearly home, Lo, I'll drop you off at Arthur's if you want,' offered Ruby.

'I'll just try calling once more,' said Lola. Lifting her mobile, she pressed redial, but again there was no answer.

They arrived in Ballyvalley in record time. Ruby's father's Range Rover Sport had made the journey seem short.

'Arthur's. Is it?' asked Ruby.

'No,' Lola hesitated. 'No, I think I should go home first.' Ruby looked confused but brought the jeep to a standstill at the side of the busy road. Lola lifted her overnight bag and hopped out. Shouting her goodbyes over her shoulder, she climbed the steps to her house two at a time. Bombing through the front door, she went straight for the telephone. Just as she was about to dial Arthur's number her mother came through the living room door into the hall. Eileen Paige's face was ashen and her green eyes were swollen and red.

Without a word Lola replaced the handset and followed her mum into the living room, where her brothers Michael, Brendan, Christopher and Liam sat, along with her dad, all wearing the same glum expression. None of them had to say a word. Their faces confirmed exactly what Lola had known. What she had sensed all weekend. Her legs registered the panic first as wave after scalding cold wave washed over her body.

Collapsing onto the floor, Lola broke down, her aching sobs almost inaudible. Her mother was the first to her side holding her tight, rocking back and forth in perfect motion with Lola. No one seemed to question how she knew, but each took their turn to console her.

Lola felt completely numb. She had never experienced pain like it. Broken, she couldn't even bare to think Arthur's name. She couldn't bear to think of a world, or a universe, that didn't hold Arthur Delphian. She could hear her own sobbing. Her head felt as if it were about to explode. Yet, it felt like it was someone other than her that was crumpled on the floor, crying frantically.

After some time, someone guided her upstairs to her room, laying by her side in an attempt to control her body as it convulsed on the bed.

CHAPTER 11

Disorientated and dehydrated, Lola woke to find her bedroom flooded in soft amber light. Her thoughts were fuzzy as she tried to calculate what time of day it was and how long she had actually slept for. Labouring out of bed, Lola felt lethargic, almost as if she had been drugged. Her legs and arms were like lead weights, as though they hadn't been used in a long time. Fumbling into her nightgown, she went downstairs to find her mum in the kitchen, gazing blankly out of the kitchen window. She looked as bad as Lola felt. The scrape of the kitchen chair broke her reverie.

'Lola. You're up, pet! Do you feel like having a wee bit of breakfast?' At first the thought of food was repulsive to Lola but as she was about to decline her stomach protested, giving a loud rumble of discontent as she took a seat at the kitchen table.

'Yes, Mum, I'm starving,' croaked Lola, her voice faint and husky.

Lola found it difficult to focus on one thing for any length of time but she was perceptive enough to notice her mother's furtive glances. Lola knew that look on her mum's face. Her mother had worn the same anxious expression many times. It was usually when she was debating how to break some bad news, like the time Lola had wanted to go on a school trip to Paris. She had been alight when she'd brought the letter home from school. Arthur had told her all about the sights and smells of Paris. Her mother had smiled and told her she would see. To a fourteen-year-old Lola that was as good as a yes. She and the girls had talked about nothing else. A few days later Lola came home from school to find her mum at the kitchen window, the same look of turmoil on her face. Lola didn't need her to explain, she understood how tight money was for them. Arthur had offered to pay but she couldn't have embarrassed her parents like that. Her mum cried for hours afterwards. Looking at her now, Lola understood that her mum felt every bit of her pain, such was their bond. She wasn't the only one that had lost him. In the time since Lola had befriended Arthur Delphian, he had become an important part of the entire family's life.

By the time her mum sat the large plate of food down in front of her, Lola was ready for it. 'There you are, pet, a big Ulster fry, it'll sort you out.' Eileen Paige planted a soft kiss on Lola's head, taking a seat at the table beside her. Lola was ravenous and gulped down the greasy fare in large mouthfuls, hardly taking the time to chew her food.

'What time is it, Mum? I must have slept all day,' spat Lola, her mouth still full of soda bread and bacon. Lola noticed her mum shift uncomfortably in her seat.

'It's just gone 2pm, love,' she smiled. 'Today is Wednesday. Wednesday the 16th June.'

'Wednesday?' spluttered Lola. 'I've been out of it for four days! Oh my God!'

Lola started to feel a bit hysterical. 'The girls are heading away today! I... I'll have to go and see them. What about work? What about... What about Arthur?'

' Settle down, Lo.' Lola's mum reached across the table to calm her. 'Orla called last night, she said that they would be calling today to see you before they head off to the airport. I called your boss at the paper and explained the situation. He couldn't have been more understanding. He said that you weren't to come back until you felt ready. He understands how much...,' her mother broke off. Lola prayed she wouldn't say his name. She couldn't bear to hear it. 'He knew how much Arthur meant to all of us, Lola.' The name hit Lola like a kick to the stomach. Looking at her mother's face, Lola could see the dark circles under her eyes. She looked like she hadn't slept in days.

'What about the funeral? Have I missed it?' whispered Lola. The thought was unbearable. She could sense her mother's trepidation.

'Mmmm, no, pet,' she hesitated. 'Of course you haven't missed the funeral. We'd have wheeled you there if we'd had too! But, there have been some, some... complications.'

Leaving the table, Eileen got up to fill the kettle. 'What is it, Mum? What's wrong?' asked Lola fearfully. Lola had known it since she had come into the kitchen. Her mother was holding something back. After the last few days, she could understand why. Her mum was clearly worried that Lola couldn't take much more and Lola conceded that she may be right. She looked at the dilemma playing out on her mother's face. Lola could tell that she was debating whether or not to tell her the truth.

'Listen, pet, why don't you go and get a bath? Straighten yourself up a bit and we'll talk then,' smiled Eileen, hopeful that Lola would accept the decoy. But, before the words had even left her mouth, Lola mounted her protest.

'Mum, I'm fine! Tell me. Tell me now! What's going on?'

Sighing, her mum caved in.' Well, the post-mortem was carried out as usual, but they found traces of some sort of toxin in Arthur's system.' Eileen stood for a moment wringing the dish towel in her hands while gingerly surveying Lola's reaction. 'They think Arthur may have been poisoned.'

Lola couldn't believe what she was hearing. Her brain felt fuzzy again. She sank her head into her hands, trying to comprehend what her mum was actually saying.

'Poison?' questioned Lola. 'That means that someone must have... What're you saying, Ma? That Arthur was murdered? That's ridiculous. Who'd want to bloody murder Arthur?' Angry tears dripped from Lola's chin onto the table. It was all too much. It had to be one big nightmare. She couldn't bear to think of Arthur laying there on his own or how he may have suffered.

'I'm so sorry, Lo. I shouldn't have told you this! Not now!' her mum pulled her close, smothering her sobs.

'Don't be silly, Mum,' said Lola, lifting her head to look at her. 'I was going to find out sooner or later. 'Was there anything missing from his house? How did they manage to get in past Cuchulain?' Lola's head was reeling.

'We don't know much at this stage, honey. At first they thought it was... you know... suicide, but the young detective in charge ruled that out. The police aren't telling us anything. Strictly speaking we aren't Arthur's family.'

'Yes we are!' blurted Lola indignantly. 'We are the closest thing he's got to a family. Who's leading the investigation? What about the paper? Have they been covering it?'

'I think the head detective is a DCI Campbell. Your dad is dealing with him.'

Eileen handed Lola the latest copy of the Ballyvalley News. Lola glared at the headline smeared across the front page.

Ballyvalley News
LOCAL COMMUNITY IN SHOCK AT SUDDEN DEATH OF ARTHUR DELPHIAN
STORY, BY ABBEY WILLIAMS.

Lola felt sick. There it was in black and white. The confirmation that Arthur was really gone. And, to add insult to injury, Abbey was covering the story, someone that knew nothing of the man. Unable to bring herself to read any more, she flung the paper across the table. Getting up, Lola turned to find her mum staring out the window again, clearly regretting her decision. Beckoning her mother towards her, Lola embraced her with the sturdiest hug her weakened body could muster.

'I don't know what I'd do without you, Mum, I love you so much. I'll be alright. So don't be worrying. Okay? I just need a bit of time to get my head around all this.'

Looking at her mother, Lola admired those same vivid green eyes.

'I'll be fine, Mum, honestly!' she reassured her, planting a kiss on her cheek. 'Sure don't I have the best family in the world? I'm just going to miss him so much.'

'I know you'll miss him, honey, we all will. But in time the pain will dull and all you'll be left with are the happy memories.'

'I hope so, Mum, I really do,' said Lola sadly, her mind drifting again, as she suddenly thought about the funeral arrangements, and Arthur's poor lonely dog. 'Who's sorting out the funeral arrangements, Mum, and who's looking after the dog?'

Cuchulain was Arthur's best friend and his loyal steed – a giant Irish wolfhound. Lola had been terrified the first time that she'd seen him. Up on his hind legs he stood at over six feet tall and looked more like a small pony than a dog. He'd never been parted from Arthur. Arthur had named him after the great hero of Irish mythology, Cuchulain. When Lola was young, that was one of her favourite stories. She used to make Arthur tell it to her all the time.

There was no doubt that the coarse, wiry grey coat and vast stature of Cuchulain was a formidable sight, but that's where the menace ended. He was the most lovable dog Lola had ever known. Sweet-tempered and intelligent, he was fiercely loyal to Arthur and those he loved. He patrolled the grounds of Brook Mill Manor with much gusto, immediately at Arthur's side if any stranger approached. It made Lola wonder how Arthur's killer had got past him. The dog never left his master's side.

'The dog's fine, Lola. Your dad and Liam have been looking after him. They've been helping with the funeral arrangements as well. In fact, honey,' continued her mum, a look of confusion on her face, 'Arthur seems to have been very well prepared, he's done most of the organising himself.'

Lola left her mum in the kitchen and went upstairs to take a much needed bath.

CHAPTER 12

As always, she did all her best thinking in the bath. When she finally emerged from the steamy room, she was delighted to find her three best friends sitting in her bedroom waiting for her.

Talking to the girls instantly made her feel better. They chatted about Arthur – each giving Lola their condolences – and the impending trip to America. Lola knew they were really excited, but understood they were playing it down because of the present circumstances, and the fact that Lola would be left behind. None of the girls mentioned the dream, or how Lola had been acting the weekend Arthur died.

Although it had only happened a few days ago, to Lola it felt like months instead of days. Finally, it was time for Ruby, Clara and Orla to go, their flight was leaving in a few hours. They all said their goodbyes as Lola walked them to the front door.

'Oh, here, I nearly forgot,' said Ruby, taking Lola's hand before dropping a metal object into it. 'I thought you might make use of her over the summer.'

Ruby smiled as she turned to leave. Looking down, Lola realised that Ruby had given her the keys to her car.

'No! Ruby, not your car!' exclaimed Lola in disbelief.

'She loves the summer, Lo! I can't have her locked away in a garage for three months. She'd never forgive me!'

Embracing Ruby, Lola thought she was going to cry again.

'Thanks, Rubes, thank you so much!'

With that the girls were gone. Lola was about to head back to her room when she heard her dad calling. He put his head around the living room door and handed her a rectangular package wrapped in brown paper.

'This came for you the other day, love.'

Taking the package, Lola wracked her brains to think what it could be. As far as she could remember she hadn't ordered anything online.

'When did you say this arrived, Da?' asked Lola. She could tell that her dad was curious. In fact, she was surprised that he hadn't opened it already.

'I think it arrived on Monday, but the stamp date says it was posted last Saturday.'

Looking at the stamp Lola could see that her dad was right. It had been posted on Saturday and, according to the postage mark, it had been sent from Belfast.

'Thanks, Dad, it's maybe just something I ordered online.'

Lola returned to her room to open the package in private, intrigued as to what it might be. Lola quickly ripped off the brown paper to find a white box beneath. Opening the cardboard box, Lola lifted out a thick square envelope with a golden wax seal. She recognised the crest immediately. It was an oak tree with the sun radiating from its centre and just beneath the sun lay a crescent moon. Lola recognised it because this symbol appeared on a pane of glass above the door that led to Arthur's observatory and study.

Breaking the seal, she unfolded the stiff piece of parchment to find a note on the inside in writing she had seen countless times before.

DEAREST LOLA,

YOU ARE CORDIALLY INVITED TO ATTEND MY CREMATION, WHICH WILL TAKE PLACE AT MY BELOVED LISNAGADE FORT. PROCEEDINGS WILL BEGIN AT 6PM SHARP AND MAKE SURE TO DRESS FOR THE CELEBRATION, AS I KNOW YOU WILL! I HAVE ENCLOSED TWO PARTING GIFTS.

WEAR ONE AT ALL TIMES. IT WILL BRING YOU MUCH PROTECTION IN THE CHALLENGING TIMES AHEAD. THE OTHER, GAZE UPON IT WITH INFINITE WONDER AND DISCOVER ALL THE POWER IT POSSESSES, CONTEMPLATE ITS MYSTIC CRYSTAL REVELATIONS IN YOUR VOYAGE TO THE MIND'S TRUE LIBERATION. REMEMBER, WHAT LIES WITHIN, REFLECTS WITHOUT. AND I PROMISE 'YOU'LL NEVER WALK ALONE'.

LOVE ALWAYS,

Arthur

Tears streaming from Lola's eyes dropped onto the letter, as she read and re-read the note. Looking into the box, Lola could see a large object wrapped in white tissue paper. Unwrapping it, she let out a gasp as she examined the criss-crossed pink crystal, each end pointed. Lifting it up, it reminded her of a marionette handle, only instead of a puppet attached to its strings this strange object held five perfect three-dimensional prisms.

Examining it closer, Lola could see that each shape was different. There was a triangle-shaped prism that resembled a pyramid, a cube and another had twelve sides. Taking a closer look at it, Lola could make out lots of miniature pentagons. There was a shape with twenty faces, all making tiny little equilateral triangles. There was an octagon and a hexagon.

Getting up off her bed, Lola pulled back the curtains, permitting the last of the evening sun to enter her room.

Lifting the prism holder up towards the light, each translucent crystal caught the sun, splashing tiny rainbows across the walls of Lola's bedroom. It was the most intricate and beautiful thing she had ever seen. Although each prism was only about three inches in diameter and height, along with the handle it was quite heavy. Noticing a little silver hook on the top of the handle, Lola stood on her bed and attached it to her curtain pole. Perfect, she thought, as she admired the spectrum of light flashing across her room.

Turning her attention to the box again, Lola rummaged about finally pulling out a small box made of oak. The modest case bore the same symbol as the wax seal on the envelope. Opening it, Lola saw Arthur's ring. Arthur had always worn this small ring on his little finger. It was a thick gold band, with a square granite stone embedded into it. On the stone there was an intricate Celtic triple spiral. The ring had a long golden chain attached. Lola removed it from the worn box and placed the chain around her neck, stuffing it down her top to conceal it. She sat quietly in her room for over an hour reading and re-reading the note that Arthur had left, trying to figure out what it meant and what had happened. It was all so confusing. Did Arthur know he was going to die? Lola tried to repel the thought. How could he have known? Why would he let someone poison him? He wouldn't do that. He wouldn't leave her without saying goodbye. Lola remembered the missed phone call. No. No. There had to be another explanation. Without thinking Lola lifted her mobile phone and called Ballyvalley police station. She was re-reading the note Arthur had left her when a voice broke on the line.

'Hello, this is DCI Campbell, how can I help you?' The young man's voice momentarily threw Lola. He didn't sound much older than her.

'Oh! Hi. Detective, my name is Lola Paige and I am calling to get an update on the Arthur Delphian case.' Lola tried to sound as stern and confident as she could. But as she had anticipated, the young detective was reluctant to give her any information.

'I understand that, Detective, but you need to understand where I'm coming from! Someone very close to me has been murdered, and I think I have a right to some information.' Lola's patience was wearing thin.

'I'm aware of that, strictly speaking,' hissed Lola. 'I know I'm not a blood relative, but I am family, let me make that very clear!'

'Listen, Miss Paige, I understand you're upset, but my hands are tied here. I'm trying to run a murder investigation.'

'I'm well aware of that, but I only want to know what the coroner's findings were.'

'Okay, okay,' sighed DCI Campbell as he reluctantly explained. 'The post-mortem noted that the cause of death was due to a very high volume of coniine in the system, causing a blockage in the neuromuscular junction, which resulted in muscular paralysis of the respiratory muscles. This meant death due to lack of oxygen to the heart and brain.'

Lola fell silent as she tried to unravel what the detective had just said, searching for words that she understood. Giving up, she targeted the one that stood out the most. 'Coniine, is that some sort of a poison?'

'No. Not as such, Lola. The coroner said that coniine is a neurotoxin that can be procured from some plants. It can be found in hemlock.'

'Hemlock, as in Socrates hemlock?' spluttered Lola, her mind racing ahead. 'He was put to death after being charged with corrupting the youth of Athens by failing to recognise certain gods and introducing some new ones.' Lola immediately regretted her outburst as there was a sharp change in the detective's tone.

'What did you say about Socrates, Miss Paige?'

'Nothing,' bluffed Lola. 'It was just the hemlock thing. You know, he was put to death, forced to drink hemlock, or as we call it here in Ireland "the Devil's Porridge". Why do you ask, Detective?'

There was a short pause on the line, as if he was deciding whether or not to respond to her question. Finally, DCI Campbell answered. *The end of life is to be like God, and the soul following God will be like her.* Does this mean anything to you, Miss Paige?'

Lola didn't like where this was going. As a true journalist she decided to throw his question back at him.

'What do you mean, Detective?'

'I mean do those words mean anything to you?' he repeated dryly.

'Well, if by that question, you mean do I recognise them, then, the answer is yes, I do. They belong to Socrates, well most of them anyway.'

'What do you mean most of them?' asked the detective, growing more impatient.

'All of them apart from the word "Her", that wasn't Socrates's word. He preferred to think of God as a He. But, I'm guessing you already know that, being a detective and all.' Lola couldn't resist the jibe, but taking her sarcasm in good humour, DCI Campbell wasn't one to be outdone.

'Indeed, Lola. Indeed! I think this is a chat we had best have in person. I have to go out this afternoon, but I will be in touch.'

Unmoved by the subtle threat, Lola thanked him before hanging up the phone. Her stomach churned. There was so much that she wasn't seeing. Not only was Arthur dead, but he had been killed. Then there was the added confusion of the ring and the note. There was a deep unease within her. In some part of her subconscious – or as Arthur called it, her soul – had she known that this moment had been coming? One thing was for sure, someone had murdered her dearest friend, and she would not rest until she found out who had killed him and why.

CHAPTER 13

Aibgrene Moone struggled with the key in the door. Finally, after a little forced coercion she heard a faint clunk and the door opened. The morning sun had finally hit the side of the street where her family's shop sat, catching the many crystals and prisms that were hanging in the window display and around the shop. The familiar and comforting smell of white sage welcomed her as she entered the building. Flicking on the lights, she propped the door ajar and flipped the sign from closed to open.

It had been an unusually busy week at Mystic Moone. Not only was there a great deal of walk-in trade, but orders from her online store were mounting up as well. Usually her mother was there to help, but she had other important business to attend to today. The shop, which sold everything from crystals to cauldrons, had been in the Moone family for decades. Many people had come through its doors, from the curious to the experienced. A full-time maths and philosophy student, Aibgrene loved to take time out from her studies and work at the shop. As it was the start of the summer break, she was delighted to be able to do this every day now. Belfast's Cathedral Quarter, as it was now called, had become increasingly popular since the end of the conflict. Her mother and grandmother had been in business for many years, and they could see the difference the regeneration had made to the area. In her mind though, it would never compare to their old shop, which had been in North Street Arcade. Mystic Moone had survived even the darkest days of the conflict in Northern Ireland, but it was a random arson attack on the complex that had forced her mother to move around the corner to Waring Street. The street name still didn't sit well with her. Aibgrene's mother had always had her suspicions about the fire; she suspected foul play. For years developers had been trying to push her and other shop owners into selling up, but they resisted. North Street was a central location for the multinational development company, Stein Corporations, in their expansion of the Cathedral Quarter.

Aibgrene was feeling quite sentimental today. Raised in the ways of the old religion her world was very different to that of her peers. It never prevented her from socialising or integrating; in fact it was quite the opposite. She had none of the tribal baggage that religion and politics had entrenched into most of the people in Northern Ireland. When she was young she used to worry about bringing her friends home, as her mother never made any attempt to hide her lifestyle and spiritual leanings. Of course there were those parents that wouldn't allow their children to play with her, and those kids that called her a witch. Even then, it didn't bother Aibgrene. The way she looked at it, she was a witch and a proud one at that. Just like her mother and her grandmother before her. In fact she came from a long line of Bhean Draoi. Bhean Draoi was an Irish word and it was the word used to describe who and what the Moone women were. They were women with magick, druidesses, and wise women. Each had their own personal strength and since she was very young, Aibgrene Moone had decided she would follow in the footsteps of her grandmother and become a healer. She had a talent for it. The Craft was as natural to her as it was for some people to go to church or go shopping. Her church was an open field or a sacred tree. She engaged with the Goddess and God through a reverence with nature and the many herbs she cultivated and healed with. But there was still much she had to learn about her path, the art of healing and the world in which she lived.

Aibgrene felt on edge today. The next couple of weeks were very important as her Seanóir was coming up. This was the third and final part of her initiation and not one that she would enter into lightly. It was on her eighteenth birthday, almost three years ago, that the first of the ancient secrets were passed down. Further knowledge was divulged on her nineteenth and twentieth birthdays, and now in a matter of days, the final and most challenging initiation would take place. The ritual was always the same – fire, drums and meditation. These secrets were never spoken, not in the literal sense. They were communicated telepathically into her consciousness. Not so much words, but a mixture of flashing images, aided by magick and an innate understanding of what they meant. Even now Aibgrene couldn't fully comprehend how this worked, or where this understanding emanated from. Yet it was deep within. It felt as though it had always been there, hidden in her DNA, just waiting to be activated. Her spiritual awakening was still something of an enigma to her. Her mother had explained that she had been preparing her for this moment all her life, and when it was her turn to have a child, she would do the same.

The walk from the café to the shop had completely rejuvenated Aibgrene; she had thoroughly needed her lunch break. Over the past number of weeks the night visions she had been experiencing had intensified. She had discussed this with her mother, and they both agreed that something very significant was about to be put into motion which only time would reveal. The heavy feeling inside her indicated that the events ahead were not going to be altogether positive, but significant nonetheless. She recalled her dream of the cold megalithic chamber, with the symbols of spirit, body and soul etched into the ancient stone. She remembered how it was briefly illuminated and that a person was there. The girl was about her own age, maybe a bit younger. Aibgrene remembered the girl's vivid warm green eyes.

The sensor above the door bleeped, indicating a customer. Aibgrene Moone smiled as she greeted the young lady by name. She was a regular customer and no doubt she had come into purchase her herbs for the upcoming Solstice celebrations.

CHAPTER 14

Alex Stein strode confidently into the packed church, the service had just begun. The soft melodic tap of his designer shoes on the old tile floor aroused the curiosity of the silent gathering. Shuffling in their seats, they turned to see who was approaching. A thin sliver of the summer sun illuminated the centre aisle of St Patrick's Church, shrouding the approaching silhouette in golden light. Alex met the curious stares as he always did, with a gentle nod. He had become well accustomed to people staring at him; he had his fair share of admirers both male and female. His father was one of the wealthiest and most influential businessmen in Northern Ireland, so he was often pictured in the 'Who's who' section of the Tatler and other society magazines.

Quickly locating a small gap in the seat, he effortlessly settled into the narrow pew in one swift motion. Alex felt slightly uncomfortable inside the church – even though this was nothing new to him. Looking at the altar, his eyes were drawn to the single most iconic image of Christianity. The ideology at the very heart of their faith, embodied in that ragged man nailed to the cross.
Self-sacrifice was not something Alex Stein believed in. It was all a fallacy. The Abrahamic faiths – Christianity, Judaism, Islam – all were

just glorified sun worshippers. They were no different than the countless other tribes. Each story was malleable, easily twisted to suit the teller. Arthur Delphian's hypocrisy amused him. This church service was a charade, so far removed from the old man's true faith. Arthur's place of worship was not so different to his, he thought, though their ideologies were poles apart. Self-sacrifice was certainly not part of Alex's mantra. Sacrifice though, that was a different matter altogether. The thought brought a wry smile to his perfect face.

Indifferent to the service, Alex turned his attention to the people around him. There were a few faces in the church that he recognised, which was exactly why his father had sent him. Alex didn't notice her at first, but a flash of red caught the corner of his eye. Shifting his head slightly to his left, he examined the brunette who sat with her head bowed, gently sobbing into her tissue. Intrigued that she was wearing the brightest red dress at a funeral, Alex continued to stare. From what he could see she looked to be around his age, but it wasn't until she lifted her head that he realised who she was. How was she connected to Delphian? Her long dark hair and pale oval face gave her a certain appeal, he thought, but it was her eyes – a vivid and most unusual shade of green with flecks of gold around the pupils – that placed her. Lola Paige was her name. He had got her first name that night, but it took a bit of research to get her second name. He'd been told that she was studying journalism. She certainly had fire. Momentarily interrupted as the mourners rose from their seats, Alex continued his appraisal. His eyes traced the contours of her slim, yet well-proportioned frame. The vintage, fitted dress that flared at the waist accentuated her figure. She must have sensed that he was looking at her, for she quickly glanced to her right. Alex made no attempt to look away and gave her a knowing nod. But, unlike every other female he had ever met, she didn't respond with the customary smile, instead she held his stare for a second, her face like stone, flicking her eyes before abruptly looking away.

Momentarily distracted by the god at the end of the booth, Lola wondered what on earth Alex Stein was doing at Arthur's funeral. The sound of a bell tinkling from the altar focused Lola's thoughts once again. The service was nearing its end. It was almost time for her to speak. Lola's stomach tightened in response to the thought.

'And we ask you oh Lord, God of all creation, to take your

beloved son Arthur into your perpetual light. May he rest in peace and may his soul and the souls of all the faithful departed, through the mercy of God rest in peace. Amen.' The priest finished off the service before addressing Lola. 'I would now like to invite Lola Paige up to the altar to say a few words about Arthur. Lola.' With a warm comforting smile, Father McGinn beckoned her towards him.

Suddenly nervous, Lola struggled to compose herself. Rising from her seat, she excused herself passing those who sat beside her, until she came to the edge of the pew where Alex sat. Much to Lola's frustration, he made very little attempt to move out of her way. Anger rose in Lola, sparked in part by her embarrassment at their previous meeting, and the fact that curiously he seemed to be enjoying himself at her expense for the second time. In an attempt to pass, her leg caught the inside of his and he seemed to hold it there for just a second, long enough to stop Lola's movement. Glancing down at him, Peter's words came back to her: 'Once you meet Alex, you will never forget him,' he had said with a knowing laugh. Looking at him now she acknowledged that it was certainly not a face that anyone would forget in a hurry. Alex Stein was a beautiful man. He was even more god-like in the daylight. His blonde bed-head hair, sculpted bone structure and perfect facial proportion matched the rest of his sophisticated, toned appearance. He was tall, over six feet, guessed Lola, very athletic looking, and wore an immaculate fitted light grey Armani suit. As he lifted his eyes to meet hers, Lola tried to muster the coldest look she could manage. This wasn't the first time their eyes had met but in the light she could get a better look. Lola couldn't explain what she found there. Despite his irises being the most vibrant shade of blue, she had never before seen eyes so devoid of warmth. If the eyes were the windows to the soul, thought Lola, then Alex Stein's soul was a cold and frigid one. Lola almost stumbled out into the central aisle, but she felt a firm stone grip around her waist which kept her upright.

'You should watch where you're going, Lola,' said Alex, a hint of mocking in his well-polished American voice. It was a voice that was so far removed from Lola's reality, it almost made her laugh. She wondered if his supermodel girlfriend was with him. She probably was, waiting to coil herself around his Davidesque physique. Lola subtly shrugged Alex Stein off and made her way to the altar, taking deep breaths as she went.

Standing behind the pulpit Lola stared out into the large crowd, her eyes were swollen and her head throbbing from all the crying. She knew exactly what she was going to say, but still she chose to look at the sheet in front of her. This was preferable to gazing down at the faces now staring at her intently. Alex Stein's being one of them. She could see her brothers and her parents. They sat close to the front. Her mouth was dry and she took a few seconds to compose herself before she began.

'Arthur Delphian,' Lola swallowed as the name stuck in her throat like a razor blade. Just saying his name made her feel as though her heart had been stabbed, such was the pain. Using every bit of will she had, Lola began again. 'Arthur Delphian was one of the most amazing people I have ever had the good fortune of meeting. Although in his long life I only knew him for a relatively short time, during which he watched me grow from a precocious little girl to a precocious young woman.' There was faint rumbling of laughter, which helped Lola shrug off the tears for a bit longer. 'He was like the grandfather I never had. And I often told him that I was like the granddaughter he never wanted. To which his characteristically kind rebuttal was always the same. "Lola, my dear," he would say, "you are like the granddaughter I hoped and prayed for."' Lola paused for a moment before continuing. 'Some of you here today will have known Arthur for many years. In fact, in some ways, you will have known him a great deal better than I did. But he was my oracle, my sage. He taught me the value of true friendship and of the light that exists in us all if we would just believe it. His passion for astronomy, Irish my-thology and cosmology was infectious. Most of it was over my head, but I loved to hear him talk about his passions. Arthur Delphian not only had an amazing mind, but also an inspirational lust for life. He loved all things, not just his fellow human beings, but the beauty and abundance in nature. It was easy to love Arthur, those playful earthen eyes and warm laugh made anything else impossible. His humanity, social consciousness and genuine decency made him stand out in a crowd. I find it.....' Lola finally broke down, the tears teaming down her face. Father McGinn stepped forward offering her a handkerchief, encouraging her to continue. Finally, finding her voice once again, Lola continued. 'I find it inconceivable that anyone would want to harm someone as gentle and wonderful as Arthur Delphian. A light in this world has gone out; we have lost a truly enlightened soul. The world is a colder place today. Well I know mine certainly is.'

Lola spoke her last line so low that she was unsure if anyone even heard her. There was a moment of silence and then a deafening round of applause erupted around the church as the gathering rose to their feet. Lola felt like she was floating down from the altar. The applause still rang around the building, but to her it sounded like a faint hum in her head. She couldn't bear to stay in the church for a moment longer. She had to get out into the air. She wasn't sure she was even breathing anymore. The sun was still illuminating the central aisle, as Lola walked past her seat and instead followed the golden light to the back of the church. She pushed out through one of the huge old oak doors to the outside. Lola had struggled to hold herself together, but now the grief poured out in her. Waves of unbidden sorrow crashed over her as she realised once more what she had lost. She was grief stricken and as well as that there was something else troubling her deeply: guilt. She felt guilty. Guilty that she had missed his call the night he died. What if he was calling her for help? The thought was torturous. Lola felt that perhaps she could have done something.

The mourners were now making their way out of the church. They emerged into the sun which offered a comforting contrast to the cold church. Lola was relieved to be outside. She was grateful for the soft breeze now drying her tear-stained face. Finding refuge under one of the cherry blossom trees dotted around the church grounds, she located a small pocket mirror and checked to make sure that her mascara had not run too badly. Lola didn't hear anyone approach on the mossy grass, so she was slightly startled by the gentle tap on her shoulder.

'Excuse me, Miss Paige. Sorry to startle you, but would it be at all possible to speak with you for a moment?' enquired a well-groomed gentleman, who Lola failed to recognise. He spoke with a heavy Oxford accent, which made her Northern Irish brogue sound very harsh in comparison. He was not much taller than her, dressed in a pale cream linen suit, with a red silk handkerchief hanging from his lapel pocket and a matching bow tie. On his head he wore a panama hat. He looked to be in his early seventies and carried a beautifully engraved walking stick that seemed to be more for dramatic effect than for use. His overall appearance gave an aura of eccentricity. Lola noticed the small signet ring on his little finger. It caught her eye since Arthur had worn exactly the same ring. Similarly, this ring was granite and had a golden Celtic triple spiral engraved deep into it.

'Surely you can,' said Lola. 'How can I help you, sir?' Her confusion must have been apparent because the gentleman began to speak almost to himself at first.

'Oh ya! Of course. Of course! How rude of me! My name is Markus Holmes, Arthur and I....' His face meant nothing to Lola, but the name meant everything, she interjected before he could finish his introduction.

'Arthur and you were best friends at university. I'm so sorry, Markus, we've never met but I've heard about all your exploits. Arthur talked about you all the time. He has a picture of the two of you in his observatory, when you were at Oxford, but you were both a lot younger then. So I'm so sorry I didn't recognise you.'

'No no, not at all my dear. That seems like a lifetime ago.' His eyes began to well up. 'I've certainly changed a bit from then,' he chuckled. 'Arthur spoke very highly of you, my dear, and you did him very proud in there today.'

'I don't know about that, Markus,' cringed Lola. Lola never quite learned how to take a compliment. Glancing over towards the thinning crowd she caught Alex Stein looking over. He turned away immediately when he realised Lola and Markus were looking in his direction. Lola turned her attention back to the charming old man. 'It's lovely to meet you. I just wish it had been under different circumstances.'

'I know. I will miss him ever so much, and the circumstances surrounding his death are very perturbing, my dear, very perturbing indeed!' Gently taking Lola by the elbow, Markus guided her away from the few stragglers that were within earshot. He looked over his shoulder like he was about to divulge a major secret.

'Lola, I know this is neither the time nor the place to discuss such matters, but there is much you do not know about Arthur Delphian. His murder is of major significance, and a horrific chain of events has been set in motion.' Lola's face was blank, as was her mind; she wasn't at all sure what she was hearing. She tried to gather her thoughts and turned to face the old man.

'Sorry, Markus, I know that Arthur was a bit eccentric, and of course there's the cremation, later on this evening, but what exactly are you saying?' There was a hint of accusation in Lola's tone. Markus sensed that it was perhaps best to leave, but he held his hand on her shoulder clearly concerned. She looked exhausted, and he was unsure how much more he could tell her. For the first time in his life Markus questioned his friend Arthur's judgement. Lola was only a girl, perhaps his old friend had got it wrong.

'Lola, I just wanted to prepare you for what you will see and hear at the cremation. You know Tom is a friend of Arthur's?' Lola glanced over towards the robust undertaker as he stood solemnly awaiting Arthur's coffin. 'He will take care of all the legalities, the general public believe that the burial is a private affair and you understand that it must remain that way? I trust you have not told anyone about the arrangements later? You've clearly been through quite a lot, my dear.' Lola could see how worried Markus was. She could sense his anxiety, and she immediately felt guilty for being so abrasive. Arthur had been his friend too. She wasn't the only one to have lost him; the crowd in the packed church today was evidence of that.

'I will speak to you later this evening, dear girl, and this will all make more sense.' Markus tipped his hat and walked away. Lola noticed a very attractive woman was waiting for him. She looked as though she was in her early forties, too young to be his wife, thought Lola. They both smiled and nodded at Lola as they turned to leave. Lola couldn't take her eyes from her long golden hair and the way her crushed velvet dress swayed as she walked, the light catching the various shades of lilac and gold.

A guard of honour had formed along the sweeping driveway of the church as her brothers and her father gently slid Arthur's coffin into the back of the waiting hearse. Lola forced herself to look as Tom secured the back door; he gave Markus and his lady friend a curt nod before slipping into the driver's seat.

CHAPTER 15

The large circular copse of trees that was Lisnagade Fort could be seen from all over Ballyvalley, lying high on a hilltop three miles out of town. Lola turned off the narrow country road onto a thin dirt track that was obscured by the heavy shrubbery on either side. She had made this journey countless times before otherwise it would have been quite easy to miss the turn-off that led to the ancient site. Slipping the car into second gear, Lola slowly made her ascent up the winding road, the overgrown hawthorn hedges gently tapping the side of the car. Finally she came to a halt on the side of the skirting track.

A fresh wave of panic began to erupt in Lola's stomach as she wrestled with the thought of turning back and going home, but she was distracted by the news report booming from the car radio. Lola listened absently to the voice.

Another teenage girl has gone missing from the seaside town of Portstewart, the second in as many weeks. Former Miss Northern Ireland, Victoria Jones was last seen at a house party on Saturday 12th June. The 19-year-old media student is described as being 5 foot 10, slim build with long blonde hair. On the night she disappeared she was wearing a red dress with red shoes. Police are currently appealing for anyone that may have seen or spoken to Victoria before or after the party to please come forward with any information they may have. The Causeway Police have not said if they believe this recent disappearance is connected with that of Karen Watson who disappeared a week previously. An information hotline has been set up to help with inquiries.

Lola had had enough bad news for one day. Shutting off the engine she calmed herself and stepped out of the car wondering what was ahead of her. The large iron gate that usually sealed the entrance to the site was open and as she rounded the trees Lola could see why. Five cars were neatly parked into the small inlet. Lola realised that she was the last to arrive. The sun was still very strong even though it was almost 6.30pm.

Following the overgrown path, Lola finally reached the large granite steps that led to the outer ring of the fort. She stepped softly to the central pathway between all three tiers. She briefly admired the wild primroses that decorated the steep banks of the fort. As she came closer to the inner ring her senses were immediately ignited by a profusion of scents. A warm summer breeze rustled around the surrounding ancient oaks carrying the aroma with it.

As Lola inhaled the soothing smells, her tense body seemed to relax. In the unfamiliar fusion she could detect lemon, mint, and a hint of something earthy, which was totally intoxicating. Each intake of breath seemed to lighten Lola's mood. Finally, approaching the inner ring she could hear the soft murmur of voices. No one seemed aware of her arrival; the small group were deeply engrossed in conversation. She lingered at the edge of the inner circle soaking in the enchanting sight that lay before her eyes.

The rath, which had been there for over a thousand years, had been completely transformed beyond recognition. There were two seats positioned at the top of a loose circle, with five seats positioned at each side, and one directly opposite the two at the top. Each seat was draped with white linen.

Each piece of cloth had an intricate symbol embroidered on it in vivid gold thread. The symbol was of an oak tree and in the centre of the tree was a large sun disc, its beams of light radiating in every direction. At the foot of the oak, just beneath the sun, lay a crescent moon. The linen covers with the golden thread were complemented by the emerald green grass underfoot, which provided a natural carpet. Turning her attention to the twelve people now gathered at the centre of the makeshift circle, Lola noticed that they were wearing cloaks. The long-hooded garments mirrored the seat coverings, and were identical, apart from two of them. Markus and the lady that Lola had seen him leave the church with were the exceptions. Their garments were of a deep rich purple, and they both wore ornate garlands on their heads. It was clear even to Lola's uneducated eye that they were in charge. Standing wide-eyed, Lola drank in every last detail. It was still warm as the leafy trees around them formed the most perfect canopy, which allowed shafts of sunlight to spill through and illuminate the floor of the fort.

Suddenly Lola could hear Arthur's voice, it was so clear that she turned around, believing he was right behind her.

The pair had come here many times. She loved to hear about this ancient fairy ring that he said dated right back to the Neolithic period. At school she had been taught that it was just a dwelling place for farmers and the people that worked the land. But Arthur's tales of fairy battles, royal feasts, mating ceremonies and burials from the mists of time were always much more entertaining.

'This place holds such powerful energy, Lola, that only a few can feel and see,' he used to say. 'It's a triple-ringed fort and that is very special indeed, three is a very powerful number.' For some reason Lola had never asked any questions – she had hated to interrupt his reverie. Instead, she loved to listen to him, and so desperately wanted to believe him, but to her it was just superstitious nonsense, mythology and nothing more.

However, standing now observing the spectacle in front of her, the energy was tangible; the air was thick with it.

Finally her presence was detected. Markus beckoned her to join the group. As she approached the gathering she was greeted by faces she had never seen before. Each person wore a kind smile. Lola concentrated hard to see if she recognised any of them from the church. The large wooden pyre that sat in the centre of the fort escaped her attention until she finally reached Markus.

'I'm sure this is very strange for you, Lola,' he apologised. 'But Arthur specifically said he wanted you to be here.'

Her eyes darted back and forth to the massive rectangular basket behind him. Examining it, Lola could see large pieces of reed and wattle intricately interwoven. She admired the beautiful roses, angelica and yarrow which were delicately threaded through for decoration. Finally, she allowed her eyes to reach the top of the pyre where she could clearly trace the contours of a body under the fine linen shroud – it was Arthur.

Abruptly, Lola turned her head as if that would somehow erase the sight from her memory. Markus had stopped talking now and was looking worriedly from Lola to the lady beside him.

'It certainly is strange, Markus. But I'm fine really, there's no need to worry,' Lola answered eventually. She lifted her head to look directly at him, though he didn't appear convinced. 'Honestly, I'm fine; it's confusing more than anything. I'm glad I'm here,' assured Lola, forcing a smile. 'It's what Arthur wanted.'

Lola looked down at her feet feeling a little awkward. She prayed that she had said enough to convince Markus that she could handle the situation and whatever it was that she was about to learn.

'Welcome, Lola. I'm Celeste Moone,' said the woman dressed similarly to Markus who had remained silent until now. Her voice was like liquid velvet and almost rendered Lola into a trance. The lady extended a graceful hand towards Lola, and spoke in a hypnotic tone. The name made Lola want to laugh a little. It sounded as though it had been made up. 'Arthur had a lot of faith in you, and trusted you very much. It has taken a lot of courage for you to come here today, not knowing what you'd find. I'm sure you are scared and confused, but hopefully everything will become a bit clearer after the ceremony.'

Celeste guided Lola to her seat at the bottom of the circle while the others took their positions along the flanks, with Markus and

Celeste standing at the top. Now holding everyone's attention, Markus began the ancient burial ceremony.

'Brothers and sisters of the Ancient Order of the Golden Dawn, for centuries we have gathered on this most sacred day, the Summer Solstice, to celebrate the ancient secrets we have been bound together to protect for millennia. We also gather to celebrate and give thanks for all that is good in our lives and the bounties our earth has provided. On this most sacred of festivals, when the veils between this world and the far world is at its thinnest, the symbolism could not be more poignant.'

'Our most high priest and druid Arthur, who throughout his rich lives often shared in this celebration, has now made the ultimate sacrifice in laying down his life for those most sacred secrets. Today, not only do we celebrate the end of the summer, the light half of our year, the unity of the God and Goddess, we also celebrate the life and regal soul that was Arthur Delphian.'

Lola sat transfixed, listening to every word spoken by Markus.

'On this great festival of fire and here on this hallowed site where we are flanked by our sacred oaks and protected by the smouldering vervain, mugwort and lemon balm, we cast the infinite soul of Arthur Delphian out into the great cosmos, back from whence it came and wish him well on his transcendental journey back to the divine, the source of all life.'

Plumes of white smoke began to emerge from the pyre as it ignited, but Lola didn't see anyone move from their stations to light the kindling. Markus continued to speak as the fire crackled. Lola's attention was drawn in by the flames, finding something comforting in their warmth and gentleness, as they licked and caressed the reeds and flowers. Gathering pace the orange, blue and yellow flames intensified, as did the citrus aroma, rising higher and higher until they finally enveloped and consumed the earthly remains of Arthur Delphian.

A well of emotion erupted inside Lola, in tandem with the accelerating flames, she began to weep again. This time, though, she didn't feel sad and pained; instead she felt joy and peace. Joy that Arthur was now spirited away to a better place than this one, yet she could feel that in some way he was still with her. Her attention fell back to Markus.

'We ask for help in the dark days that are to come, the battles that

must be fought and won. The flames guide away Arthur's spirit but
they also signify the waning of our glorious and life-sustaining sun
and the coming of the dark. This year, my friends, our resolve will be
tested in this time of darkness. So we must endeavour to stand together and keep our resolve.'

Markus's face was sombre yet his voice was full of authority.
The intimate gathering began to murmur, the gravity of the ceremony
clear on their faces. A robust man then rose to his feet. Lola guessed
he was in his fifties, portly, with auburn hair and a weathered complexion. He spoke with a soft voice in a distinct southern-Irish accent,
which suggested he was from the west of Ireland. Like Markus he
spoke with confidence.

'So what are ye sayin, Markus?' asked the gentleman. 'I mean, is
this da beginnin? They've killed Arthur, our leader, so does this mean
we should all fear for our lives? What about the objects that Arthur
had in his possession? Does the Hell Fire Club have dem now?'

Lola played over those words again – 'beginning', 'killed', 'Arthur', 'Hell Fire Club'. Celeste elegantly rose to her feet in one fluid
motion and placed a hand on Markus's shoulder. He sat down, giving
her the floor as she turned to answer the questions. She looked at the
man as a mother would her disobedient child.

'Eoin,' said Celeste calmly. 'You are one of the oldest and most
loyal members of our Order. You more than anyone should know what
this turn of events means! Arthur had fore-warned us for the past year
that an attempt on his life would be made, which they unsuccessfully
have tried to disguise as a suicide. Time is beginning to run out for the
Hell Fire Club so, as Arthur predicted, they are becoming desperate!'
Warning them for the past year? Lola soaked up those words, wondering who they were talking about. It couldn't possibly have been her
Arthur! He would have said! He would have told her if someone was
trying to kill him.

'They have little time to achieve their aims as soon the new epoch will be upon us.' Celeste's voice remained temperate and reassuring as she turned to address the rest of the group. 'Sisters and brothers, Arthur's death is a great blow to us all, but we must implement
the plan that he has laid out for us. The Hell Fire Club's global agenda
is almost complete, yet we must prevail. Arthur has revealed to us the
ancient key. It has been returned to this realm and he has sought out

and nurtured it. It is our duty, as it has been our duty for millennia to protect it at all costs. If our foes should discover it, all hope for the new epoch would be lost.'

Lola watched on in bewilderment as the man they called Eoin contemplated what Celeste had said. Lola was waiting for Arthur to burst from behind a tree and tell her it was some joke. She even wondered if she was still sleeping. All this was so far removed from her reality it was almost funny. These people were weird. Arthur was nothing like them.

'That's all well and good, Celeste,' continued Eoin. 'We will not desert our duty, but are you sure this key,' Lola noticed how he emphasised the word key, 'is what we seek? Can we trust that this is the true key of prophecy?'

For a moment everyone seemed to be looking at Lola, some nodding in agreement with Eoin. All she could do was smile at them. Some faces smiled back, others seemed to be studying her as if she were some curiosity. Lola supposed to them she probably was!

'I understand your concerns,' reasoned Celeste in her soft tones. 'All of your concerns, some of which I share. But, I pose this question to you, Eoin. To you all! Do you trust Arthur?'

Eoin wore a sudden look of indignation. 'Our trust in Arthur is not in question!' he hissed, clearly annoyed at any accusation. 'We trusted him beyond any doubt!'

'Well then,' continued Celeste. 'Arthur trusted in the ancient key beyond and above any doubt. He did so for a reason, reasons that he was not prepared to divulge to all of us. But I believe these reasons will be justified in due course. This is a very challenging and uncertain time for us, but only together can we hope to achieve our sole purpose.'

The crowd began to settle, somewhat appeased by Celeste's words. A toast was raised to Arthur and prayer offered to the God and Goddess. It was almost twilight when the ceremony ended. Lola watched the last of the embers burn as Celeste dismissed the gathering.

'Before we part let us raise our vibrations in loving memory of Arthur Delphian, druid, healer and sage. Let us pray for the strength and courage to ensure his death has not been in vain. We must now go our separate ways. Each of us has our own part to play. The road ahead is an uncertain and perilous one but we will prevail.'

Lola had never seen anything like this in her life and was completely lost for words. It was certainly dazzling, but what did this all mean? It was so hard to digest, though only the beginning for her. Could this really be the same Arthur Delphian she loved? Her mind slipped back to the package she had received and to the dreams she had been having. Any fool could see that it was linked. But still Lola's mind screamed in defiance, even though she understood that her life had changed forever. He had wanted to tell her something the night he died. But what could she offer, what did Arthur want from her? Why had he brought her to these people and why could he not have told her all this before he died? Lola began to feel the anger burning inside her stomach. After all, what could she do? She was only a young girl. How could she fight this Hell Fire Club?

CHAPTER 16

The group began to disperse, but Lola was reluctant to leave the fort, she felt relaxed now and in some way closer to Arthur. The pyre that once held his earthly vessel was reduced to nothing more than a pile of smouldering embers. Walking over to it, Lola watched a few feathery flakes of ash as they floated towards the leafy canopy above.

A gentle hand touched her shoulder, and she turned to find Celeste standing by her side. Lola felt drawn to Celeste, she felt safe and calm beside her. Both women stood in silence, their thoughts with Arthur.

'Celeste, Lola.' Both women turned in unison towards the voice. 'I'm awfully sorry, but I must dash, my flight leaves in an hour,' offered Markus apologetically. 'I hope you'll forgive me, Lola, but there is much I need to do. I will try to get in touch with you. But, as you can imagine these are very troubling times and the Hell Fire Club's reach goes far and wide. I will need to go away for a while. But I will contact you when the time is right.'

'I understand, Markus, thank you for everything,' said Lola, knowing that she would understand these events soon. Markus embraced her tightly as if it was the last time he might see her. He promised that he would be in touch soon, and then he left to catch his flight back to Glastonbury.

'We have much to discuss, Lola,' said Celeste, as she guided Lola out of the fort. 'If you are half as inquisitive as Arthur said you were, then I'm sure you have a lot of questions,' laughed Celeste. 'You seem to be taking this all very well. It is a lot to accept,' she added a look of disquiet on her face.

'I can't really explain it, Celeste,' replied Lola. 'It sounds crazy, but I'm not shocked or surprised. I mean, I know I should be. Any sane person would be running a mile from this. When I first spoke to Markus at the church today, I couldn't bear the thought that Arthur had this secret life, that he was someone other than my Arthur. But I suppose, deep down, I always knew he was special. Not just to me, but....' Lola trailed off, trying to find the right words. 'I can't really explain it.'

Lola felt quite ashamed at opening up to Celeste, but she couldn't help it, she was so easy to talk to. Celeste was about to speak, but paused when she realised they had company. Lola instantly recognised the man that stood at the entrance waiting for them, a wide smile on his face. He had made Lola feel very uncomfortable throughout the entire ceremony. She wondered who he was and what he was doing here. A faint shiver touched her, but Celeste appeared oblivious to her discomfort, as she genially greeted the man at the end of the path.

'Cyril, how are you? I'm sorry I didn't get chance to speak to you earlier.'

'Not at all, Celeste! Not at all. You have much on your mind in these very troubling times,' replied Cyril, a sympathetic smile spreading across his face, though it never seemed to reach his eyes.

His voice was languid and a bit too high pitched for a man. And, even though he was speaking to Celeste, he never once took his black beady eyes off Lola. Celeste followed his gaze.

'Oh how rude of me, Cyril, let me introduce you to Miss Lola Paige. Lola was a very close friend of Arthur's.'

The man extended a slender hand towards Lola, and she reluctantly reciprocated. His hand shake was limp and his palms were cold and clammy, which only compounded her uneasiness.

'Very nice to meet you, Lola! You are a most unusual girl,' he was surveying her now, as if she was a prize cow. 'You must have been very special to Arthur, very special indeed.'

Lola didn't like the tone in his sickly voice, there was something quite menacing in it, as if he was contemplating something. Instinctively, she pulled her hand from his.

'I'm not special at all, no more than anyone else,' said Lola, unable to hide the fact that she didn't like, nor trust this man.

'You're a feisty young lady, aren't you?' he replied, his cackling snigger irritating her even more than his voice. But before Lola could answer him, he had turned to speak to Celeste.

'I just wanted to know if you needed a lift back to Belfast, Celeste?' the same false smile returning to his face. 'I have business in the city this evening.'

'That's very kind of you, Cyril, but I've got to stop at Arthur's place and wouldn't want to keep you back. I can make my own way home, but thanks for the offer.'

'I've plenty of time, I can wait for you. Or go to Arthur's with you, I really don't mind,' he pressed.

'Okay, if you're sure. How about I meet you in town? By the Town Hall, would that suit?' Celeste didn't seem unsettled by Cyril's eagerness to give her a lift home, which frustrated Lola. She would say something, once they were on their own again. 'I'll travel into to town with Lola, and I'll see you in about thirty minutes.'

'Well if you're sure,' he spat, thinly disguising his disappointment at not being invited to join her at Arthur's.

'I'll see you in town then,' replied Celeste, as Cyril turned and left the clearing, before climbing into his car. Lola and Celeste followed, making the short journey back into town.

'That man gives me the creeps, Celeste! I can give you a lift back to Belfast if you want,' offered Lola. That same maternal smile returned to Celeste's face as she reassured Lola that she would be fine.

'Oh Cyril is harmless enough, a bit peculiar, but he's okay, Lola.'

'What about the fort, all the chairs and stuff, aren't you worried that someone might see it?' asked Lola.

'Oh, no one will see it, Lola,' assured Celeste. 'We have made sure of that, the fort will be as it was in just a few minutes, like we were never there.'

'But how?' asked Lola.

'Well that's easily answered, Lola, magick, of course,' said Celeste, emphasising the 'K' sound at the end of the word.

Lola scoffed. 'So where's your magic wand then, Celeste?' Lola burst out laughing, expecting her passenger to join in the joke, but much to Lola's embarrassment she didn't. Smiling at Lola in her usual temperate manner, Celeste answered, her tone very matter of fact.

'Magick wands are things of fairy tale and fantasy, Lola, surely you know that. But magick isn't. To answer your question, I use a crystal, rose quartz to be exact. In fact, I don't really need an object to perform magick, but sometimes it helps me to direct and channel my energy.'

Lola's mouth dropped open, all traces of jest gone. After what she had seen and heard today, was it so inconceivable that there was such a thing as real magick? In truth she wasn't so sure that it was all stuff of legend and fantasy! Lola was lost for words.

Turning into the avenue that led to Brook Mill Manor, Celeste motioned for Lola to stop. Pulling up at the side of the road, she cut the ignition. Looking at the strange and beautiful woman beside her, Lola could find no traces of irritation. Instead, Celeste patiently continued. 'Magick is certainly real, Lola, and it's not something to be underestimated. In the wrong hands, or the wrong soul, it can be a very potent and destructive force. Arthur's death is evidence of that.' Celeste looked beseechingly at her, and for the first time Lola could see how anxious she was. 'I was born into the craft; it has always been part of my life and part of who I am. At the age of twenty-one my sister and I were both inducted into the Ancient Order of the Golden Dawn, as our mother had been before us.' Celeste thought of how happy she was then, how exciting it had all been for her and her sister Aurora.

Lifting her head she looked at Lola and felt pity for her. For the first time her faith in Arthur was wavering. Here was this young girl, alien to their world, their way of life and their rules, and yet their future depended on her. An eighteen-year-old girl with no concept of what was at stake. 'Being initiated into the Order is the single greatest honour that could be bestowed on followers of the right-hand path, Lola,' Celeste continued.

'At that ceremony, in the fort, almost twenty-three years ago, I met Arthur Delphian for the first time. I had heard about him, but to meet him in person was something else. Aurora, my sister, hardly slept for a week, she was so excited.' Celeste laughed to herself as she thought of her sister. 'He was a very powerful druid and high priest, and the Order was extremely powerful, a shining beacon. We stood strong in the fight against the darkness, awaiting the return of the cosmic Age of Aquarius and the return of the mystical Tuatha Dé Danann, to their ancestral homeland.' Lola listened, but struggled to recognise the Arthur that Celeste described; to her he was pipe and slippers, grey hair and grey beard, gentle and loving. It was still hard for her to think of him as something other than what he was to her. In some ways she felt hurt and cheated that he hadn't confided in her. He could have at least given her some insight to this alternative lifestyle. Lola couldn't bear to talk any more about Arthur, and so she changed the subject.

'You have a sister? Aurora? What a beautiful name, was she at the ceremony today?'

Celeste's face dropped at her sister's name, the pain clearly visible. Lola cursed herself for being so tactless. How many times was she going to insult or upset Celeste today?

'Don't be silly, Lola dear, it's fine,' assured Celeste. 'No she wasn't at the ceremony today, but she would have loved to have been there. She would have been at Markus's side instead of me. Aurora, lived up to her name, she really was like the Goddess of the Dawn, bringing light and love everywhere she went. She was much more talented than I was, but she saw the goodness in everyone, even in those souls where none existed.' Lola just listened not wanting to break Celeste's flowing words, clearly she was still in grief at the loss of her sister.

'We were twins,' Celeste continued, 'and like twins, we had a unique and unbreakable bond. We shared everything and had no secrets from each other, that's until she met the love of her life. He swept her off her feet and like her she practised magick. So she never had to hide who or what she was. But her love made her blind to him, to his true and vile nature.' Lola was startled by the sudden anger and revulsion in Celeste's voice, dropping to a faint whisper, tears welling up in her beautiful hazel eyes.

Reaching over Lola took her hand, squeezing it tightly. 'I'm so sorry, Celeste, I didn't mean to pry.'

'Lola, you have nothing to apologise for, you are handling all this so well. I can't imagine how hard this must be for you,' replied Celeste, squeezing Lola's hand in return. 'You need to know all of this. About the Hell Fire Club, the Age of Aquarius and the legend of the Tuatha Dé Danann, but what we have taken a lifetime to learn, you are having to digest in days.'

Celeste took a deep breath, controlling her emotions, instantly returning back to her normal serene self. Lola had heard of the Tuatha Dé Danann, Arthur had told her all about their sagas in Irish mythology. They were said to be the most iconic and enlightened peoples ever to settle in Ireland, possessing great spiritual knowledge and powerful magick.

'The Age of Aquarius, is that not some cheesy song from a 1960s musical or something?' asked Lola bewildered, her apathy instantly bringing a smile to Celeste's face.

'There's much you still have to learn, Lola, and I'll be happy to teach you all I can. It's vital that we figure out what part you play in all of this. There is still much to talk about, but unfortunately now is not the time. It's my daughter's birthday, she turns twenty-one today, and of course it's the Summer Solstice, which is a very important festival in our tradition, so I need to get back home.'

'What exactly is so important about the summer solstice? I heard what Markus said earlier but I didn't really understand,' enquired Lola, as she started up the car again. She was genuinely interested, she had a million questions running through her head, and was a bit surprised that Celeste was just going to go, as if it was all perfectly normal.

'Well, in our tradition and other earth religions, this midsummer festival celebrates the apex of light which is symbolised in the crowning of the Oak King, God of the waxing year. At his crowning, the Oak King falls to his darker aspect, the Holly King, God of the waning year. You see Arthur was like our Oak King, he was the apex of light to our organisation. The Hell Fire Club knew this, and they knew that by murdering him close to the Solstice the symbolism would not be lost on us.'

'You must understand,' continued Celeste sombrely. 'Like everything in our wonderful universe, all material has an opposing side. This does not always mean that it is a negative aspect, but in this case I'm afraid it does. If there is light, Lola, there must also be darkness.' Lola silently nodded her head in acknowledgement. She was beginning to comprehend the symbolism and the full impact of Arthur's death. Until now she had only ever thought of her grief, her pain and her sense of loss, but looking at the angst on Celeste's face, she recognised that there were more important issues at hand.

Driving back out onto the main road, heading for town, Lola was relieved that they didn't go up to the manor; she wasn't ready for that yet. Celeste gazed out of the window, silent as they made the journey. She was only too aware of the evil that dark magick could spread. She had seen from first-hand experience what it could do, having lost her sister at the hands of the Hell Fire Club, and now they'd taken Arthur, their leader. They were almost at the Town Hall when she finally broke the silence.

Shifting in her seat to look at Lola, Celeste began to speak, the melodic rhythm of her soothing voice captivating Lola once again. 'You've an innate ability to see people as they truly are, Lola, to see deep into their souls. That's a very powerful gift to have and I must warn you, that while you may be unaware of it, there are those that can and will detect it.' Celeste reached out, gently tucking a few strands of loose hair behind Lola's ear. 'The warmth and light that radiates from you is very potent and those that may wish to harm you can see that. What you dismiss as mere hunches, or as gut feeling, is something much more. You must learn to trust your divine intuition and use it to find your way.'

There was urgency in her voice now, which worried Lola. 'Arthur didn't say too much about your role in all of this, because he wanted to protect you from the forces of darkness. They're everywhere. I fear the Hell Fire Club have even infiltrated our most sacred Order.' Celeste's head dropped, the burden of the revelation seeming too much for her to bear. Pulling the car into an empty parking space, Lola could see a black Mercedes parked outside the town hall. The windows were blackened out, so she couldn't see the driver, but she guessed it was Cyril inside. Celeste reached over and embraced Lola before getting out of the car. 'Remember, what lies within, reflects without. There are those who will try and hide what they truly are, Lola, but if you have faith in yourself you will be able to see through them.'

With that Celeste was gone. Lola watched as she stepped into the waiting car, and then watched the car speed off. Lola drove out and turned towards home. The sun was still bright as she drove through the deserted town centre. Approaching a junction, Lola checked her rear view mirror, before breaking hard and bringing the car to a standstill. For a split second, she'd thought she'd seen a pair of steely blue eyes reflecting back at her, but when she looked again they were gone.

It was almost eight-thirty when she arrived home to find the house empty. The note on the kitchen table, in her mother's handwriting, explained that they had gone to Arthur's to feed the dog. Lola didn't know if she would ever be able to set foot back in Brook Mill Manor again. Totally drained after what had been a long and emotional day, Lola climbed into bed and for the first time in weeks fell into a deep and dreamless sleep.

CHAPTER 17

Lola berated herself for sleeping in again as she bounded through the doors of the Ballyvalley News, colliding with Jane, and almost knocking the middle-aged woman over, sending the paper in her hands flying all over the reception area. Jane was head of advertising at the paper and had been an employee there for over thirty years. She was conservative in her dress sense, but Lola found her to be warm and approachable.

'Goodness me, Lola, where's the fire?' gasped Jane, pressing her hand over her heart. 'You scared me half to death!'

'I'm so sorry, Jane,' cringed Lola sheepishly. 'I didn't see you there. Let me pick those up for you.'

Lola scooped up the pages from the floor. Turning over one of the posters, she saw the striking face of Victoria Jones smiling back at her. Her dazzling white teeth, and perfectly styled long blonde hair, gave her the look of perfection.

'The girl's family asked us to put one of these up in the window and leave a few on the counter,' explained Jane, as she returned behind her reception desk with Lola in tow. 'Do you recognise her?'

Lola hadn't really been concentrating on what Jane was saying, her eyes transfixed on the picture of the girl she had seen fleetingly at Alex Stein's party.

'The girl in the picture, Lola, do you recognise her?' repeated

Jane.

'Sorry, Jane, I didn't hear you there. No, No, I don't,' lied Lola.

'My heart goes out to her family,' continued Jane sympathetically. 'I'm sure it's every parent's worst nightmare, wondering where she is, and if she's okay. I've none of my own but I know I'd be distracted.'

'Yeah I know, it's awful,' replied Lola, as she made her way into the back office still looking at the picture. Abbey and Sebastian were hard at work, both lifting their heads to greet Lola as she came in.

'Afternoon, Lola,' jibed Sebastian looking at his watch. 'We weren't expecting you back so soon, how have you been?'

'I'm good thanks. I just need to get back to normal, you know, take my mind off things,' replied Lola.

'Well I've plenty of stuff here for you to work on,' smiled Sebastian, as he gestured to the pile of paper on his desk.

'Yeah, Lola, I'm glad you're feeling better,' added Abbey. 'I'm working on a few things and could do with a bit of help, only if you don't mind?'

Despite her instincts, Lola forced herself to be nice. She and Abbey hadn't exactly got off on the right foot, but if she was going to be working with her all summer Lola was keen to put the past behind her and move on.

'Sure, what are you working on?' chirped Lola trying her best to be genial. She turned and switched on her computer.

'Well I've got the police report on Arthur's death, so I'm looking into that, and the disappearance of Victoria Jones. I don't know if you've heard about it?'

Lola couldn't believe how tactless Abbey was. Lola had no intention of working on anything to do with Arthur, she couldn't face it. Lola had quite enough to digest for the moment. Being so close to him, she didn't think it as a good idea anyway. She was grateful that Abbey wanted to involve her, so she didn't want her to think she wasn't interested in helping.

'To be honest, Abbey, I don't think it would be such a good idea for me to work on Arthur's story, just because I'm so close to it. But I'll certainly help with the other piece.'

'Of course, Lola! I understand. Sorry, I wasn't thinking,' replied Abbey. Lola doubted that it was a mistake but smiled anyway. 'Help with the Victoria Jones story would be great,' continued Abbey. 'I've a lot on this week.'

Abbey filled Lola in on the background detail to the story. Lola already knew a bit of the background, having actually seen her at the party, but she felt it would be best to keep that information to herself for the time being.

'Where's she from, Abbey?' Lola wondered why the paper would be covering it, as she was sure that Victoria was not from Ballyvalley.

'She's actually from Blackskull, which is in our catchment area. Her family have been on the phone, and would like to do an interview for the paper.'

Lola had only ever been in Blackskull a few times – it was about seven miles outside of Ballyvalley. It was a tiny place, not even as big as a village, more of a townland. It was the last place on earth that she would expect someone as glamorous as Victoria Jones to call home. That explains the posters and the coverage, thought Lola.

First things first, Lola would make a few calls, starting with the police press office. It was doubtful whether they would give her any more information than what was already out there. Another girl had gone missing, and Lola was interested to know whether they considered the disappearances to be connected. It seemed more than a coincidence to her.

Lola was just about to dial the number for the press office, when Jane came into the back office, handing her a piece of paper with two numbers and a name neatly written on it.

'I almost forgot about these, Lola. A man called in yesterday asking to speak to you. He said he was from Tennyson and Tennyson's Solicitors. He left a number and asked that you call him back. The other call,' said Jane, motioning to a note in Lola's hand, 'was from a girl. She called first thing this morning. She didn't leave her name, but said it was urgent.'

Looking at the numbers, Lola could see that both had Belfast area codes. Thanking Jane, she lifted the receiver and dialled the first number. The call was answered after a few rings.

'Hello, Tennyson and Tennyson, Daphne speaking. How can I help you?'

'Hi, my name is Lola Paige. I received a call from your office yesterday?'

'Do you know who called you, dear?' enquired the chirpy voice.

'I'm sorry I don't,' replied Lola.

'One moment please. I'll just put you on hold while I make some enquiries.'

Lola was enjoying the soft music filtering through the telephone until it was interrupted by a man's voice. The well-spoken voice was deep and gravely, Lola guessed the gentleman to be elderly.

'Miss Paige?'

'Yes hello, how are you? What can I do for you?'

'I'm very well. Thank you for getting back to me. My name is Felix Tennyson and I am Arthur Delphian's solicitor. I am also the executor of his will.'

'Oh right, how can I help you, Mr Tennyson?' asked Lola struggling to understand why he was interested in speaking to her.

'Well, Arthur has left an envelope here for you, and he specifically wanted you to pick it up at our office. There are a few other matters I would like to discuss with you as well, but I would prefer to do that in person, if you don't mind?'

'No. Not at all! You're in Belfast I take it? When would be a good time?'

'Yes, we are in Belfast. Our offices are situated just off Waring Street. Are you familiar with the city?'

'Yes, I know Waring Street,' repeated Lola. 'When would suit you, Mr Tennyson?'

'Would you be able to make it tonight, say around six-thirty? It's quite urgent, Lola,' he added. Lola repeated the time to make sure she had heard him correctly.

'Okay, I'll see you at six-thirty then,' confirmed Lola.

For a moment she had thought he had hung up, as there was a soft click at the other end, but Felix Tennyson said goodbye and put down the receiver. She wondered how much more intrigue she would have to handle. She set about calling the second number, which was answered after only three short rings.

The shaky voice of a young girl answered, 'Hello, Mystic Moone.' There was urgency in the answer. Lola could tell that the girl was clearly upset about something.

'Hi, my name is Lola Paige, I.....', but before Lola could finish the girl on the other end of the line interrupted.

'Oh, Lola,' said the voice with a deep sigh. 'Thank God. Thank you for calling me back. My name is Aibgrene Moone, you don't know me, but you may have met my mother.'

Lola didn't quite catch her first name, all she could make out was that it began with A, but she could tell it was a Gaelic name. However, she immediately recognised her surname, Moone. It was the same as Celeste's, and Lola remembered her saying that she had a daughter. 'Is your mum called Celeste?' asked Lola, making sure she hadn't made a mistake.

'Yes. Yes!'

'I met your mother yesterday. Is she okay? Is everything alright?' questioned Lola, she had a feeling that it wasn't, but waited for Aibgrene to explain.

'I'm so sorry for calling you, but you're the only person I can trust,' said Aibgrene, knowing how crazy she sounded calling a girl that she had only ever met in a dream. But she was desperate and Lola was the only lead she had. Lola's name was the only name her mother had spoken when she appeared at the foot of her bed in a haze the night before.

'Find Lola Paige,' Celeste had said. Then in her mind's eye Aibgrene remembered seeing a copy of the Ballyvalley News.
Lola still hadn't replied, Aibgrene thought for a moment that Lola might have hung up. 'Hello, Hello?'

'I'm still here,' answered Lola. 'How did you find me?'

'It's a long story and I'm not sure how secure this line is, Lola. When did you last see my mother?'

Aibgrene listened intently as Lola told her about the events of the day before, skirting around the confidential parts. She guessed that Aibgrene probably knew more about the Order than she did.

'Cyril?' repeated Aibgrene. 'I've never heard my mum talking about anyone called Cyril before. You say she knew him?'

'Well she seemed to,' replied Lola, knowing that he was not to be trusted. She wanted to say this to Aibgrene, but the time didn't feel right. The poor girl sounded sick with worry, and Lola didn't want to further compound her anguish.

'I have to go to Belfast tonight, why don't we meet up so we can talk properly?' suggested Lola. 'In the meantime keep trying your mum's mobile phone and call everyone she knows.'

Aibgrene knew there was no point in calling her mother's phone again – she would not be answering anytime soon. All she knew was that her mother was alive. Last night's vision was proof of that. Aibgrene knew that her mother could travel on the astral plain, but she could only do this if she was alive. Her captors must not have realised this yet, and she prayed that they would never discover it. But now was not the time to explain this to Lola.

'Okay, I'll do that,' she said flatly. 'Where would you like to meet, Lola?'

'Well, I'll be on Waring Street, are you anywhere near there?'

'Our shop, Mystic Moone is just around the corner, we live just above it. I'm in the shop now, so I'll meet you here at about 7.30pm, is that okay?' asked Aibgrene.

Lola agreed to the time and gave her mobile number to Aibgrene in case she needed to contact her. Hanging up the phone, Lola dedicated herself to her work again. The rest of the day flew by as she researched the Victoria Jones story, placing calls to the police press office and the former Miss Northern Ireland's friends and family.

As always, she was waiting on the press office getting back to her, and she knew that this would probably take a while. Scanning the social networking sites, Lola started to build a profile on the missing girl. Not only was she beautiful, she was also very popular and according to her academic record, very smart as well. Coming from a wealthy background, she seemed to have everything going for her.

There was something in Lola's gut that told her that it was unlikely that Victoria had run away, or thrown herself off the nearest cliff. All evidence seemed to point towards foul play. Glancing at the clock, Lola was pleasantly surprised to see that it was home time. Closing down her computer, she lifted her bag and headed for the door and the short walk home.

CHAPTER 18

Lola told her mum and dad about the call from the solicitors and explained that she had arranged to go to Belfast that night. Her parents offered to accompany her, but Lola told them that she would be meeting a friend afterwards and that she would be fine. Changing into her favourite pair of skinny jeans, flat pumps and a white cotton t-shirt, she set off for Belfast. She'd never driven in the city before and was relieved to find that she had missed the rush hour traffic.

It was exactly six-thirty when she pulled up outside Tennyson and Tennyson's Solicitors. The building, like the creaking sign above the door, was aged, and the external cream paint was flaking off the front of the building. Pushing on the glass door, Lola realised it was locked. Suddenly the buzzer sounded and the door clicked open.

Climbing the stairs to the first floor, Lola found the reception area deserted, as was the rest of the office.

'Hello, Hello! Is anyone there?' shouted Lola, beginning to feel a bit edgy and wishing she had brought company.

'In here, dear!' Lola recognised the voice; it was the same man she had spoken to on the phone earlier that day.

She entered a large spacious office to find a frail little man hunched over a mahogany desk, dressed in a dark grey suit, which seemed to be as old as he was. Sweeping his snow-white hair back across his face, Felix Tennyson extended his hand to greet Lola.

'Thank you for coming, dear, at such short notice. I'm sorry I didn't go down to meet you at the door. The old bones aren't what they used to be. Please, take a seat, Miss Paige,' said Felix, as he motioned to the plush mahogany chair in front of his desk.

Comfortably seated, Lola eagerly waited for him to explain why she was there.

'You must be wondering why I have asked you to come here tonight, Lola? Well it was at Arthur's request.'

Lola nodded her head in reply and waited for the old man to continue. Slowly getting up from his seat, Felix moved towards a picture hanging on the wall at the back of the room. Pushing the old dusty picture aside, he entered an unlock code for the iron safe embedded into the wall. He gradually made his way back to his desk with a small file and some keys, then fell back into his seat again. He opened the file, glancing at Lola over the top of his smeared spectacles.

'Lola, this is the last will and testament of Arthur Delphian, and I need you to listen carefully.'

Lola nodded, giving Felix Tennyson her undivided attention as he began to read Arthur's will.

THIS IS THE LAST WILL AND TESTAMENT OF ME, ARTHUR DELPHIAN, BORN ON 23RD JULY 1940, OF BROOK MILL MANOR ESTATE, SCARVAGH ROAD, BALLYVALLEY MADE THIS DAY OF WEDNESDAY 7TH JUNE. I HEREBY REVOKE ALL FORMER WILLS AND CODICILS MADE BY ME, AND DECLARE THIS TO BE MY LAST WILL. I APPOINT MY DEAR FRIEND AND SOLICITOR, FELIX TENNYSON, TO BE EXECUTOR OF THIS WILL.

I DEVISE AND BEQUEATH THE RESIDUE OF MY REAL AND PERSONAL ESTATE AND WEALTH TO MY GRANDDAUGHTER THROUGH FATE, MISS LOLA PAIGE.

IN RELATION TO MY BODY, I WISH IT TO BE CREMATED AS DETAILED IN THE LETTER TO MY FELLOW MEMBERS OF THE ANCIENT ORDER OF THE GOLDEN DAWN.

AS WITNESS, MY HAND THE DAY AND YEAR ABOVE WRITTEN, SIGNED:

Arthur Delphian

Handing Lola the piece of thick paper, Felix pointed to the two signatures at the bottom.

'As you can see this has been witnessed by both Markus and I,' confirmed Felix.

Lola was silent; she hadn't noticed that her hands were trembling until she lifted the page. She scanned it again to make sense of what she had just been told. Her face had turned an ashen white and tears began to trickle down her cheeks. Felix looked at her, worried that he had said something wrong.

'Are you okay, dear?' he asked, clearly confused as to why she was upset. 'Usually when people are given such a generous inheritance they jump for joy!'

'I don't deserve this,' was the only reply Lola could muster.

She felt once again humbled by Arthur's virtue. She felt guilty that she had always taken from him and never really given anything in return, at least not in the material sense. He was always there for her, always at hand to listen to whatever problems she was having, always there to give advice. He had taught her so much, given her so much knowledge and so much of his time, but what had she given him? As far as she could see not very much! The thought was unbearable, she didn't deserve this. Lifting her head, her eyes met Felix's.

'I don't want it! Arthur has given me enough. I can't accept this, Mr Tennyson!'

This was clearly not a reaction that the seasoned solicitor was used to.

'You really are something else, Miss Paige,' he chuckled. 'You certainly are one of a kind, Arthur was right there! This is what Arthur wanted, dear. It's irrelevant whether or not you think you deserve it. Arthur thought you worthy. He believed you to be worthy of more than just bricks and mortar and a sizable bank account.'

Lola knew what he was alluding to.

'Speaking of which,' asked Felix, 'did you get the other package I sent you?'

It took Lola a fraction of a second before she realised what he was talking about. 'Oh, you mean the ring and the crystal sun catcher thing?'

'Tut tut tut,' chided the old man. 'The crystal sun catcher thing? Indeed, Lola! Well there is one last part to add to the ring and the other object.' Leaning closer to Lola, Felix's expression was grave.

'Here is the third and final part, it will complete the trilogy and it is of the utmost importance that you never let any of these items out of your sight at any time. Nor should you tell anyone you have them. Do you understand?'

The old man handed Lola a piece of paper wrapped in a plastic gel protective sheath. Taking a closer look, Lola realised that it was actually a page from a very old book. The page was yellowed and frayed around the edges with water marks and creases all over it. Despite this, it had the appearance of a magnificent piece of art. The lettering seemed to have been drawn with a quill and ink in a Celtic script. The page heading was highlighted by the most vivid red and yellow illustrations. Tuatha Dé Danann were the only words that Lola could make out, as the entire text was written in Gaelic.

What am I expected to do with this, she thought to herself. Felix answered her question, as though he had read her mind.

'As you can see the entire text is written in Irish, Lola. Well to be exact it's written in Old Irish. There are only a handful of people on this island who can read that, one of those people was Arthur Delphian.'

'So, for what reason have I been given this? Am I expected to interpret it?' she muttered growing impatient.

'I wish I could tell you, Lola, but I have told you everything that Arthur told me. He just said that it was a very old and sacred text and urged that you keep it safe. As you can see it is written on calf skin and it must not be taken out of its protective casing. That gel sheath is state-of-the-art. It provides the perfect conditions for that text to remain as it is, so do not remove it. As to the other matters, it will take a while for Arthur's assets to be transferred to you, but Brook Mill Manor, well that's yours now!'

Lola caught the set of keys to Brook Mill Manor, as Felix glided them over the desk to her.

'One more thing,' he chuckled. 'Cuchulain is also your dog now! I wish you luck with that. It's getting late now, Lola, and I don't want to keep you any longer. I'll be in touch. Would you mind seeing yourself out?' Getting up Lola thanked Felix. As she was about to leave, he called her back. 'Just one more thing, Lola, please be careful,' he warned in his chalky voice.

'Okay, Mr Tennyson,' said Lola, not really understanding his meaning. 'I will and thank you.'

Tucking the keys and the parchment into her bag, she left the office and headed up the street to Mystic Moone, unaware that she was being followed.

CHAPTER 19

Lola was completely preoccupied as she walked up the deserted street. Her head was swimming as she replayed all that Felix Tennyson had just relayed to her. Tightening her grip on the bag that hung over her shoulder, she instinctively brought it closer to her body, only too aware of its precious contents. She'd had a lot to take in, but the fact that Arthur had left her everything, that for the first time in her life she would not have to worry about money, well, that was inconceivable.

Money had never really mattered to Lola, mostly because her parents never really had any. They had always managed somehow and had always tried to provide what they could. She and her brothers took part-time jobs, which helped with university costs, but like most people they relied on student loans to go there. Lola preferred it that way, always making do with whatever she had. Her mum and dad had taught them to respect people for who they were, not what they had. Perhaps if her parents had been better off financially her outlook may have been different, but as it was, she was content.

The sun had dropped behind the shops on the opposite side of the street suddenly making the area feel very desolate and run-down.

Feeling a sudden chill in the air Lola rubbed her bare arms as goose bumps materialised. So preoccupied by her own thoughts, she hadn't noticed anyone on the street when she emerged from the solicitor's office, but as she became aware of her surroundings and more concerned about the contents of her bag, she began to feel quite on edge. Instinctively, she looked behind her before rounding the corner onto Waring Street and was surprised to find that she was no longer alone.

A few paces behind was a young boy, his face obscured by a baseball cap. He wore dark tracksuit bottoms and a grubby hooded top. Although this was nothing out of the ordinary, Lola quickened her pace as she neared the shop a few yards ahead. She suddenly became aware of the cold stone of the signet ring close to her chest, and for a moment it appeared to be vibrating. It felt as if it was emanating a soft gentle pulse. Lola reasoned that it was simply her accelerated heartbeat. There was no sign of life as she approached Mystic Moone. The shop seemed to be empty as Lola couldn't see anyone through the shop front window. She admired the display, decorated with lots of dream catchers, crystals and prisms of every colour imaginable.

Deciding to try the door, she found it locked. Taking a step back from the entrance, she was about to open her bag for her phone when a sudden movement caught the side of her eye. Lola could see a hand reach out to snatch her bag and she instinctively recoiled and closed her eyes. There was blinding flash of white light, as Lola's attacker was instantly propelled away from the shop. Lola slowly opened her eyes to find that her attacker lay on the street some distance away. Her first instinct was to go and see if he was okay, but she held back knowing that he had tried to snatch her bag. It was the same teenager that had been behind her in the street since she left the solicitor's office. His cap had now come off and his t-shirt seemed to be smouldering. There was a murky grey mist around him, and he was obviously shaken, but he quickly rose to his feet, his face ashen white, and ran down the street.

Suddenly the door of the shop opened, and a pair of gentle hands encouraged her inside.

'That was amazing. I've never seen anything like that! What was it, a repellent spell? You'll have to teach me that one, Lola,' said Aibgrene Moone excitedly.

Lola was in shock, her head throbbing, and her ears ringing from the blast. She struggled to make out Aibgrene's excited words.

'Here, take a sniff of this, it'll bring you around, help clear the head,' soothed Aibgrene.

Lola winced as a small bottle emanating a sharp pungent aroma was forced under her nose. Inhaling, it burnt her throat and nostrils, but appeared to do the trick because her head began to clear.

'What the hell just happened to me? What did that boy do to me?' she asked in disbelief.

'What did he do to you? More like what did you do to him!' laughed Aibgrene.

Aibgrene Moone was very like her mother, only slightly taller, with a familiar set of playful hazel eyes and long golden hair that flowed down her back. She was lean, with angular features, but very pretty. Dressed in cream corduroys, pumps and a brown t-shirt, she reminded Lola of an Amazonian. Lola could see a beautiful apple green haze around her entire body. Clearly her head hadn't cleared that much, she thought.

'What did you give me? I think it's made me worse,' exclaimed Lola as she tried to get up, but her legs refused to respond. 'I'm seeing things. I think I might need to go to the hospital!'

Rolling her eyes, Aibgrene knelt down beside her, and held her hand in front of Lola. 'How many fingers am I holding up?'

'Two,' answered Lola, with a sigh.

'What's your name and where do you live?'

'Lola Paige and I live in Ballyvalley.'

'Where are you now?'

'I'm lying on the floor of what I presume is Mystic Moone.'

'I think you're fine, Lola!'

Lola was becoming more irate. This girl wasn't taking her seriously at all. 'Well then why is everything around you all green?' snapped Lola.

'That's interesting. You can see auras as well as perform powerful magick.'

'Auras? Magick?' quizzed Lola, growing more impatient by the second. 'What are you on about? Have you been sniffing that stuff too? I can't do magick and I can't see auras, whatever they are. I don't even believe in magick, never mind powerful magick.'

Lola didn't care that she was being quite rude. Anyway, Aibgrene didn't seem to be offended in the slightest. Bending down she helped Lola up off the floor and onto a chair. Much to Lola's irritation nothing seemed to break Aibgrene's mood, she was positively beaming.

'Hi, I'm Aibgrene Moone, lovely to meet you.'

Lola stared blankly at her. She already knew it was Aibgrene; she had after all planned to meet her here at the shop. Aibgrene, assuming the perplexed look on Lola's face was because of her unusual name proceeded to break it down phonetically for a dazed Lola.

'Oh, a lot of people have never heard of my name before,' she explained. 'So they're a bit wary of pronouncing it. It's pronounced A-grain-ya. It means radiant sunshine in Irish,' she added cheerily. 'And you must be Lola Paige. It's very nice to meet you. Well to meet you again!' added Aibgrene with a mischievous grin.

Lola shook her hand, slightly bemused. 'Again?' I don't think we've actually met before.'

'Yes we have. Well technically it was in a dream,' explained Aibgrene in a matter-of-fact tone.

Lola rolled her eyes, the girl was clearly delusional at best, but for some reason she felt drawn to her, as she had been to her mother. She immediately felt that she could trust her, and the truth was that she needed to, because Lola knew she was on her own and Aibgrene – as naïve as she appeared – was her best chance of making sense of this mess.

'Listen, Lola, I'm sorry if I'm freaking you out a bit at the moment, but you'll get used to it.'

'No, I'm the one who should be apologising, Aibgrene. Sorry. I haven't been very pleasant. What happened out there really scared me. All this is new to me. There's been so much to digest and take in, most of which I can't understand. I just don't know why Arthur would do this to me. He's made a mistake. And now your mum has gone missing, it's just too much.'

Aibgrene sat beside Lola. She knew that Lola Paige would in time become her closest friend, and she gave Lola the reassurance she so desperately needed.'Listen Lola, you don't need to apologise,' said Aibgrene looking right into Lola's eyes. 'This is scary stuff, there is no denying that, but we have to stick together, and if Arthur trusted you, you must trust him. You have to accept the possibility that there were things that he knew about you, things that you're yet to discover or acknowledge.'

Lola felt Aibgrene was placing too much faith in her. What happened outside had not been her doing. What she was saying was so absurd to her. Magick. If it wasn't so serious Lola would have laughed in her face.

'Look, Aibgrene, you must believe me, that wasn't me out there, I didn't do that, but that's something we can figure out later. What upsets me more is the fact that that boy was after my bag. Well not my bag, but what's in it.'

Aibgrene was unaware that Lola had just left Tennyson and Tennyson solicitors. In fact, the only people that knew this were the old solicitor himself and her parents, both unlikely to hire the assailant. Despite Felix's words of caution about telling anyone what she had in her possession, Lola felt it was only right to inform Aibgrene. After all, she had been advised by Arthur and Celeste to trust her inner voice. She couldn't explain why, but she knew she could trust this girl. Aibgrene could help Lola understand the world she was being forced to enter, because she was part of it. Besides, she felt that Aibgrene had a right to know, it might help them find her mother before it was too late.

'Listen, Aibgrene, the things that I have been told and experienced in the last few days have completely turned my world upside down and challenged my sanity to say the least. I want to tell you everything I know so far, but I don't think this is the place. That was no random attack out there, that boy was sent by someone, and I'm certain he was after what I have in my bag. In fact, he could have already told our enemies where we are and more importantly that we are together.'

Aibgrene nodded in agreement. 'I have a few enchantments on the place, but I think you're right, Lola, it's no longer safe here.' There was sadness in Aibgrene's voice as she looked around her family shop. Lola focused her mind, she knew her life was not the only one that was affected by Arthur's death, there was no doubt that both women had been brought together for a reason, and that they must rely on each other from now on.

'You can't stay on your own here, why don't you come back to Ballyvalley with me and we'll take it from there?' asked Lola.

'A road trip! Excellent! Let me get a few of my things together, we'll need all the help we can get!'

Lola watched intently as Aibgrene busied about the shop, lifting tiny bottles with various herbs and oils, adding a few multi-coloured crystals and some other items. She placed them into a small leather case that already housed a tiny mortar and pestle, a set of brass scales and long silver knife with an ornate crystal handle. Disappearing upstairs, she returned with a hold-all with some clothes and toiletries packed inside.

'That's me. I think I have everything I need,' confirmed Aibgrene.

'Are you sure?' laughed Lola. 'I think the kitchen sink is still there.'

'Good woman, Lola, I almost forgot.'

Lola looked on in amazement as Aibgrene disappeared into the small kitchen at the back of the shop, emerging, not with the sink, but a small broom.

'Oh, don't tell me we're going to fly to Ballyvalley,' scoffed Lola as she surveyed the miniature broom.

'Of course not,' said Aibgrene indignantly. 'This isn't some movie, Lola. We traditionally use the broom for dispersing negative energy, among other things, and I can see I'm going to need it!'

'Oh, negative energy, how did I not know that?' added Lola sarcastically.

It was twilight when the girls emerged from the shop. Taking one last look around, Aibgrene locked the door, pulling the shutters down on Mystic Moone. The street was deserted once more as they approached Ruby's buttercup yellow Figaro. Once inside, the doors were locked and they set off for Ballyvalley.

Lola was reluctant to speak about what she had in her bag, and the numerous other things that she had been privy to over the last couple of weeks, until she was back home. Aibgrene must have read her mind, or perhaps her thoughts were with her mother, as both remained in silence.

CHAPTER 20

Celeste Moone could feel her strength waning, it was taking every ounce of her power to fight back the heavy force field of dark energy that constantly tried to constrict her. Normally it was effortless for her to expand her vibrant violet auric shell. But she was fighting strong magick, stronger than she had ever faced before. She could tell the person emitting it was quite some distance away from her, but still their power was potent. It was like a massive black hole consuming her soul's life force. The fact that she hadn't had anything to eat for two days didn't help matters, but she knew this was all part of her captor's plans.

Her head was still a bit groggy even though the effects of the chloroform had worn off. She hadn't noticed the person sitting in the back of the blacked out car until she felt a rag being clamped over her mouth and nose, forcing her to inhale the sickly sweet odour. When she came around she had been completely disorientated by the sensory deprivation of her dank cell. It had taken Celeste a while to figure out where she was.

Sensing the full moon, she had used the little strength she had to vacate her body. Rising out of the cell, she travelled up through the cliff like a ghost. Hovering above the rugged edifice, she could see a large mansion embedded into its side illuminated by the moon, a shining beacon in the clear night sky. Tonight it was her accomplice, its mystical powers the only reason she could perform her magick in such a weakened state.

Drifting towards home, her astral spectre found her daughter asleep in the room above their shop. She could feel the protective spells that Aibgrene had put in place as she sat watching her daughter sleep. The potency of her astral body was draining by the second and all she could give her daughter was a name before she succumbed to the sinister power that was forcing her back into her body. Lying now in the darkness, Celeste could taste the saline air and hear the sea crashing against the rocks below. Suddenly there was a twist of a key in the thick iron door of her room. She strained her eyes to see who was entering. Celeste was momentarily blinded by the light that spilled in from the passageway. Her eyes were covered and she felt a firm grip on her arm, as she was hauled out of her cell and up spiralling stone steps.

Shrugging off the firm grip of her guard, she was permitted to remove the blindfold, which allowed her eyes to adjust slowly to the room around her. As her vision returned Celeste found herself standing in a large library.

The interior design of the room was baroque in style. The floors were covered with thick red carpet and the walls were dressed with black panelling trimmed with gold leaf. Each wall was covered in shelving stretching from the floor to the ceiling and crammed with hundreds of books. At the centre of the room sat a large black table with a matching chair. Taking a closer look at the empty seat, she read the initials CS imprinted on the backrest in gold letters. The S initial ran through the bottom of the C. She knew who owned this chair, and this caused anger and rage to rise through her body.

This cannot be happening, she reasoned with herself. But in an instant it all made perfect sense. The man who killed her sister had taken her captive. Clearly he had the same plan in mind for her. This could only mean one thing. Carl Stein was now the Grand Master of the Hell Fire Club, and his brand of magick had become very powerful and extremely dark. She needed to remain calm.

'Sit down,' ordered a gruff voice from behind her. She slowly sat on the chair opposite the desk.

'Well since you asked so nicely, I think I will,' replied Celeste.

The bald, bulky, man who stood behind her now, dressed in a fitted black suit, was the same man that had forced the rag over her mouth in the car. She had caught a fleeting glimpse of him in the rear view mirror. Celeste tried hard to keep her voice even and her anger in check. Closing her eyes she took a deep breath. Steadying her emotions, she determined that a monster like Carl Stein would not break her as easily as he had her sister. Celeste didn't turn around when she heard the familiar southern drawl of the American as he entered the room.

'Well hello, Celeste, it's been quite a long time,' said Carl Stein.

Celeste's stomach churned, and she refused to take his outstretched hand. She looked at him with contempt as he sat down in the chair in front of her.

'Not long enough, Carl,' smiled Celeste serenely. 'But I see you've been quite busy.'

'Only getting what was due to me through my own diligence and hard work, Celeste,' replied Carl with all his usual swagger and charm. Celeste wasn't in the mood to exchange pleasantries, he had taken her for a reason and she wanted to get straight to the point.

'You're as charismatic as ever, Carl! But since we're old friends, feel free to drop the façade. What do you want with me?'

Steadying her resolve, Celeste glared into Carl Stein's cold blue eyes, right into the depths of his frigid soul. Time had been good to him. He had aged well in the twenty years since she had last seen him. She had glimpsed him on television, publicising his many charity events, but not in the flesh. No one delivered pretence like Carl Stein. His adoring public was oblivious to his true, grotesque nature. He was still very handsome; his clean-shaven face, perfect white teeth, and well-groomed grey hair added to his refined appearance. His wealth and intelligence made him the epitome of sophistication, but Celeste knew how hard he worked to make sure that this image never wavered in public.

'You're looking well, Carl. It must be all that "charity work" you are doing that keeps you looking so young and fresh,' jeered Celeste in mock admiration. Ignoring her obvious sarcasm, Carl Stein continued to be congenial.

'You must be famished, dear, would you like something to eat?'

'Don't patronise me, Carl,' snapped Celeste. 'What do you want?'

'I think you know what I want from you, Celeste!' said Carl, the wide smile never leaving his face, but there was no mistaking the malice in his voice.

'I'm not sure I do,' replied Celeste indifferently. 'You've killed Arthur and infiltrated the Order, what more could you possibly want?'

Suddenly his expression darkened. Celeste tried not to react to the agonising burning sensation that flamed across the surface of her skin. She held eye contact with Carl, as the intense coldness of his eyes burned into hers.

'Don't play games with me, Celeste. Your family doesn't have such a good track record against me!' sneered Carl.

Celeste responded in anger, reaching over and striking him across the face. The effect was minimal, as he appeared not to react at all.

'Such anger! Such anger,' laughed Carl darkly. 'I'm impressed, Celeste. Perhaps if Aurora had shown such fire she'd be with you today.' Carl chose his words carefully, fully aware of their evocative effect. He could sense Celeste paining at the mention of her sister's name. 'But she did love me, and as the saying goes too much love can kill you.'

Celeste sat seething as Carl Stein chuckled at his own sick joke. His loaded words were like a cold dagger through her heart. Sadly, she remembered that her sister had truly loved him. Aurora had believed his soul was worth saving. She hadn't known that Carl Stein had sold his soul for wealth and power, long before he had met her.

From the day he had first laid eyes on Aurora he had coveted her power and she was blinded by his charm and beauty. Like a parasite, he had sucked what he needed from her and then disposed of her as if she were nothing. He had consumed her magick, ultimately using it against her.

Celeste had never sought revenge, but sitting in front of the Carl Stein made her want just that. She knew her powers were no good here. He was too strong in this environment, and she was in a weakened state. Without any real options, she calmed her mind once again, awaiting further revelation.

'So where were we? Oh yes, what I need,' continued Carl. 'Well the thing is, we did indeed manage to dispose of your leader. Another trusting fool! But, we didn't get the ring, or the Cube.'

Making his way around the table, Carl stood with his hands on the back of Celeste's chair. He leant down and whispered softly into her ear, his voice smooth and menacing.

'You know I always get what I want, Celeste. One way or another, I always get what I want.'

'I don't know what Arthur did with his ring, or the Cube. He didn't have either in his possession when we were called to the house. We assumed that you had taken them,' said Celeste.

It was clear that the she was telling the truth. Carl sensed a relief in her voice, as she suddenly realised that the Hell Fire Club didn't have any of the objects in their possession. This gave her a renewed hope. Celeste immediately wondered who might have them now.

'In that case, Celeste, who has them? Who would Arthur have entrusted them to, if not you? Who would have fully understood their importance and significance? Who would possess the magick to unlock them?' asked Carl. 'I can only think of one person, my dear, and that is you.'

Celeste could only think of one person too, and that person had no idea of their importance, nor did she possess the ancient magick that would enable her to unlock their power. Celeste wondered how long it would take the Hell Fire Club to figure it out. Cyril had not only betrayed her, Arthur and the Order, but he'd been at the ceremony too. Celeste feared that he too understood how important Lola was to Arthur. And so, with renewed vigour, Celeste directly answered her subjugator. She didn't fear for her own life, and was not intimidated by Carl Stein, but she did care for the life of her daughter Aibgrene and Lola.

'I don't have them, Carl, and even if I did I would die before I told you,' spat Celeste. 'Better people than me have sacrificed their lives to protect our secrets. I have nothing to fear from death.'

This seemed to amuse Carl, as he let out a bitter laugh.

'Who mentioned killing you, Celeste? I plan to inflict worse things on you than death! Believe me, when I've finished with you, you'll be begging me for death,' he hissed into her ear.

Reaching out he placed his long index finger on Celeste's pale collar bone. He watched her contort as black poisonous ink spread along her veins and into the arteries in her chest. Falling off the chair in agony, Celeste tried in vain to repel the toxins that where constricting her airway and lungs. Finally the pain stopped as he took his hand away. Gasping for air, Celeste defiantly clambered to her feet.

Circling now, Carl Stein continued to question her, punishing her in the same way if the answer was not to his liking, all the time goading and provoking her.

'You are much stronger than your sister was, Celeste, she couldn't withstand this much pressure,' he taunted.

Standing upright Celeste spat in his face. Lifting a handkerchief Carl Stein slowly wiped the moisture off, he was tiring. Even in a weakened state Celeste was withstanding his assault, and it was taking a lot out of him. As he readied himself for another attack, a gentle knock came to the library door.

Momentarily distracted, Carl Stein looked up to see his son come into the room. The reprieve gave Celeste time to try to gather herself again, she didn't know how much more her body could take. She sat down on the chair again; all she could think about was her sole purpose for living, her daughter
Aibgrene.

She knew Aibgrene was a shrewd and able witch, but she was young and there was still so much she had to learn. Carl Stein could do what he wanted to her, but the thought that he would harm her daughter, or Lola, was too much to bear. Regaining her vision, she looked at the young man who had entered the room. Wiping her bleary eyes, Celeste struggled to make sense of what or who she was looking at. At first she thought it was more of Carl's dark magic making her hallucinate. The young man – who she guessed was about twenty-one – must be Carl's son for sure yet he looked nothing like his father, apart from his similar piercing blue eyes.

He was taller than his father and his hair was blonde, Carl's hair had always been black in his younger days. Celeste realised that it wasn't Carl Stein that she saw in the boy. He had the same face, lips and nose as her sister. He was so like Aurora in fact that the sight of him brought tears to Celeste's weary eyes, though she struggled to believe that this boy could actually be Aurora's. It didn't add up, her sister had never been pregnant, Celeste would have known, she would have sensed it. As she stared at Alex she remembered how Carl had prevented Aurora from seeing her family for a while before her death – was this why?

Carl Stein watched as the expression on Celeste's face changed from confusion to realisation, and it made him uneasy. Alex relayed the latest news to his father while looking at the strange woman, sitting across the room staring back at him. He recognised her as someone who had been at Arthur's funeral, but she now appeared more familiar to him, though he was sure he had never actually met her before. Celeste struggled in her dazed state to listen to the exchange between them, managing to hear the end of their conversation.

'What do you mean electric shock?' asked Carl impatiently.

'I'm not sure, Father. He said that whatever the solicitor gave her was in her bag, but when he went to snatch the bag he was thrown back about one hundred yards and that he felt like he had been electrocuted. She went into Mystic Moone. The Moone girl was waiting there for her.'

'Thanks for the update, Alex. That is a very interesting development indeed. You'll have to get close to this girl.'

'That shouldn't be too hard,' laughed Alex. 'We are already acquainted.'

'I've taught you well, Son. Now, I have some business to finish here.'

As Alex left the room, Carl Stein turned his attention back to Celeste.

'I've just had some very interesting news, Celeste. It seems you have been holding out on me, how very foolish of you!'

'I'm not the only one that has been holding out, Carl,' spluttered Celeste.

'Like I said, my dear, we can play this game all night and all day. So tell me, who is this Lola Paige?' asked Carl, as Celeste sat rigid refusing to answer. 'Well I have all the time in the world, Celeste, so I suppose that's enough for tonight. I think we will give you a change of accommodation, and a chance to eat and clean up. You might as well make yourself at home – you're going to be here for a while!'

With a nod at the guard, Carl Stein left the room.

CHAPTER 21

Lola began to feel anxious as she turned off the main road towards Brook Mill Manor. A light wind had picked up, rustling through the large oak trees that flanked the narrow avenue. The only light visible now was coming from the car's headlights.

'This is Arthur's house,' whispered Lola as if someone might overhear them. She wasn't sure why she had decided to come here tonight, but something had guided her to Brook Mill Manor and she had decided to go with it.

'I know. I can sense the energy and light. It's amazing, Lola! I've never known magick this powerful, and we haven't even passed through the threshold yet,' exclaimed Aibgrene in wonderment.

For the first time in days Aibgrene felt truly safe. She had known protection spells, she'd even cast many of her own, but this magick was something she had never encountered before. The entire area from the gate, right around the perimeter wall was encapsulated in a mushroom-shaped sphere, which glistened blue under the clear night sky. It wasn't solid or liquid but made of pure ethereal energy, shielding them from those that wished to do harm. Normally any kind of talk regarding magick frightened Lola, but she was becoming accustomed to it now.

'Well they said at the ceremony that Arthur was their high priest, head of this Ancient Order, so he must have been into that stuff,' said Lola. Aibgrene couldn't help herself and burst out laughing at Lola's flippancy.

'Yes he was into that stuff, Lola, and according to my mum, he was the best there was!'

'Well he mustn't have been that good!'

'What do you mean?' asked Aibgrene, slightly offended.

'We'll if this magick, or protection spell, was so amazing, how come he's dead?' Lola didn't want to disguise the hurt and anger in her voice. She was tired of hearing how great a druid Arthur was, but none of it kept him alive. So to her it was all pointless. She quickly jumped out of the car before Aibgrene could answer her. Fumbling with the bunch of keys in her hand, she finally located the right one, and opened the large wrought-iron gate, which was supported by two granite posts. Each pillar was decorated with the moulded head of a golden lion. When she was younger the sight of the two large lions baring their teeth was enough to put her off venturing up the wooded driveway, but she soon got used to them over the years, and even came to love them.

Lola hopped back into the driver's seat and began edging the car forward. Aibgrene got out this time, secured the gates behind them and jumped back into the car, before Lola began the drive up the winding stone drive to the manor. Lola shuddered slightly as a gentle warm vibration rippled through her body; she instinctively turned on the heater, even though the sensation was one of warmth.

'Did you feel that?' asked Aibgrene.

'Feel what? I'm just cold,' said Lola flatly, her indifference clearly beginning to irritate Aibgrene.

The tension between them was quickly building; Lola could feel it and knew she herself was probably the cause.

'I see! It's going to be hard to convince you that any of this is real! That wasn't the cold! We just passed through a very powerful protection enchantment. It'll be safe here,' said Aibgrene, with obvious relief in her voice.

As comforting as that was, Lola didn't share her enthusiasm. After all, someone had managed to breach this invisible force-field before. But, she knew Aibgrene didn't need to hear that right now, she had already been through enough. It was important that Aibgrene felt safe, and Lola felt it was her duty to make sure of that.

'I take it Arthur was a Leo?' remarked Aibgrene. 'He had all the characteristics of a Leo.'

'What do you mean, a Leo? As in his star sign?'

'Yes,' nodded Aibgrene. 'I noticed the golden lions on the gate-posts. That's where the spell starts. I could sense it was very intricate, there's more to it than just protection I think!'

'His birthday's on the 23rd July, it would have been his birthday soon,' said Lola, feeling as though she was going to cry again. She wondered if she was ever going to get used to the fact that Arthur was gone.

'He was a Leo then,' continued Aibgrene, in an attempt to keep up the conversation. 'I suppose it makes sense, with Leo being a sun sign.'

Aibgrene began to explain, sensing that Lola wasn't sharing her logic. 'Sorry, Lola, I'm way ahead of myself. I keep forgetting all this is new to you. Well you know about astrology, you've heard that much?'

'What? It's written in the stars? Is that not just a load of nonsense?' asked Lola, being deliberately petulant.

'Well, we believe that it is very important, and it can tell us a lot about a person and their path in life,' explained Aibgrene, getting frustrated with Lola's indifferent tone.

Finally she lost her cool and confronted Lola. 'What exactly has Arthur been teaching you all these years? I mean, I don't expect you to be aware of all the particulars, Lola, but I assumed that Arthur would have at least explained the basics to you!' said Aibgrene, becoming more animated.

In truth, she had been expecting more from Lola. She was sure that Lola had some answers. But, from what she had observed so far, it looked as if her hopes had been pinned on someone who was in denial of the obvious, a girl completely alien to her world and to the dangers they faced.

'What do you mean by that?' snapped Lola defensively. 'For

your information, I didn't ask for any of this crap to happen to me!'

Lola tried to keep her temper, slowly bringing the car to a halt outside the house. Getting out, she slammed the door, with Aibgrene in hot pursuit.

'We'll I'm sorry if I seem a bit annoyed, Lola. Excuse me! I've bloody lost my mother. I've no idea where the hell she is, or even if she's still alive, and the only clue I have is you. Lola bloody Paige!' Aibgrene's voice became increasingly high pitched as all the stress and worry finally found an outlet. 'A girl that knows nothing of our world, and has no respect for the little she has learnt. A girl that has spent ten years under the tutelage of one of the greatest druids and men our path has ever known and managed to learn nothing!'

Tears began to streak down Aibgrene's face. Stunned by her outburst, Lola stood in silence, cursing herself for being so selfish and tactless. She made no attempt to defend herself again, because every word Aibgrene spoke was true.

Lola was in denial; she couldn't bear the thought that Arthur was something other than the idol that she had constructed in her head. She couldn't bring herself to accept that he was part of some magickal Order, or that magick even existed. To her it was insane, even after everything that had happened, her brain still refused to accept the truth. Lola stared at the ground, unable to look at Aibgrene.

This girl had come to her for help, desperate to find her mother, truly on her own, and she had let her down. Lola suddenly felt ashamed. Celeste had sent her own daughter to find Lola. Now Lola had to honour that faith; it was time for her to re-examine the world around her and everything in it – both visible and invisible.

Reaching out she put a comforting arm around Aibgrene, ushering her towards the house. The stones under their feet crunched as they made their way.

'I'm so sorry. We'll figure this out, I promise. Come on, let's get inside,' said Lola.

Slotting the ornate brass key into the heavy oak door both of them stepped inside the large entrance hall of the two-hundred-year-old Brook Mill Manor.

CHAPTER 22

Lola felt a sudden heaviness of heart as the familiar smell of polish and lillies enveloped her, reminding her why she had put off coming to the Manor for so long – it was simply too painful. Aibgrene closed the door behind them creating a gust of wind that disturbed the large crystal chandelier suspended in middle of the room. The cold moon-beams that spilled through the fanlight above the door illuminated the monochrome tiles that spread out like a large marble chess board beneath their feet, directing them towards the stairs.

'Come on, we'll go to Arthur's study, it's nice and cosy in there,' suggested Lola, as they ascended the large winding staircase towards the east wing of the house where Arthur's library and observatory sat. Making her way down the hallway, Lola glanced back to make sure Aibgrene was following, but she was rooted to the spot, and motioned for her to stop.

'Psst. Psst, Lola! Lola! Stop!'

'What is it now?'

'Shussssh! I think there's someone here! I can feel it!'

Lola's blood ran cold as her mind began to race. Was it Arthur's killer, coming back to finish what they'd started? Trying not to breath, she listened for any sound that might give the intruder's location

away. Then she heard it, a soft padding coming towards them from the
opposite direction. Beckoning Aibgrene towards her, they both stood
behind a small alcove in the long dark hallway, frozen against the
wall. To Lola's left sat an ornate French table with a large vase, one
of Arthur's many accoutrements. The footsteps started to advance and
were soon accompanied by heavy breathing. Lifting the vase, which
was probably a priceless antique, Lola realised that her hands and
knees were trembling. She held the vase as tightly as she could, lifting
it above her head, primed and ready to strike their assailant.

A large shadow appeared up the hallway, stopping abruptly as if
it too sensed there was company. Holding her breath Lola waited for
it to advance. Suddenly, a deep guttural bark ripped through the air,
causing Aibgrene to emit a shrill scream and Lola to drop the delicate
porcelain ornament onto the wooden floor, smashing it into a thousand pieces. Immediately recognising the presence before them, Lola
stepped out into the hallway.

'Cuchulain! You scared me half to death, you silly mutt!'

Hearing Lola's voice, the enormous Irish wolfhound barked with
delight and jumped up knocking her to the ground, licking her face
and wagging his massive tail in amusement.

'Get off! Get off me, you big softy!'

Writhing on the ground, Lola eventually managed to get to her feet,
and headed for the library with the dog by her side. Aibgrene was in
fits of giggles and followed her accordingly.

'I don't know what you're laughing about, missy, so much for
your great sixth sense! It was only Cuchulain, wasn't it, boy? Yes it
was only you, you big wolf,' said Lola, as she ruffled his long grey
wiry coat, stroking him behind the ears. 'I've been awful, haven't I,
pup? Leaving you on your own.' But she knew it would take more
than that to upset him, he was so loyal. Besides, he had been well
looked after by her parents, and her youngest brother Liam had been
up a few times a day with him.

Reaching the library, Lola was surprised to see that the door was
closed. Initially she thought that the police must have been in there at
some point in the investigation, but then she remembered that Arthur's
body had been found in the drawing room downstairs. Twisting the
knob, she found that the door wouldn't budge. It seemed to be locked,
yet there was no visible keyhole. The library had always been open, to

the extent that Lola had never even really noticed the door.

'It's magick,' chirped Aibgrene, seeming fully recovered from her earlier outburst.

'Of course it is,' sighed Lola. 'Now why didn't I think of that?'

'Move and let me have a look at the door please,' requested Aibgrene, moving Lola to one side. Aibgrene bent down closer to examine the brass door knob and panel.

'A bit of light please?' she asked, as Lola turned on the hall light, while Aibgrene further scrutinised the door.

'Ah, there it is! It looks like we need a special key, like a square one with a triple spiral inside it,' confirmed Aibgrene.

'Like this one?' asked Lola, fishing the ring and chain out from under her clothing. She pressed Arthur's signet ring against the small metal panel. It was a perfect fit. There was a soft whoosh and the door clicked open.

'Very impressive, Lola, so that's how you managed to propel that boy about one hundred yards, Arthur's ring!'

'I told you it wasn't me!' confirmed Lola.

'We'll make a witch out of you yet,' smiled Aibgrene.

They entered the library and Aibgrene sat down on the plush sofa, while Lola busied about the room, closing the heavy golden curtains, turning on lamps and lighting the gas fire, bringing the library back to life.

'First things first,' said Lola, as she lifted her phone out of her bag. She called her parents and proceeded to give them a condensed version of that night's events.

Her mum almost fainted when Lola told her Arthur had left them everything, including the house. She explained that she had been given the house keys and would be spending the night at Arthur's. Satisfied that all was safe and well with her parents, Lola said her goodbyes and turned her attention back to Aibgrene, who sat mesmerised at the wonderful bright circular room that sprawled out before her.

'This is amazing. It's full of warmth and light!' Even though she had sat in this book room countless times, Lola could share in her new friend's wonderment. Despite knowing every nook and crevice it always seemed new to her. Surrounded by all those old books – some that she had never even opened or touched – Lola always felt that just by being here she was absorbing the wisdom contained within them, and Arthur had always made sure that there was something new to learn or discover.

'Where does the staircase lead to?' asked Aibgrene. The quirky spiral staircase disappearing through the roof, with its oak steps and iron frame that snaked between two large book shelves, was the first thing that had caught Lola's eye when she entered the room ten years ago as an eight year old.

'Arthur's observatory is up there. It just has his telescope, log books and computer.'

'Log book? What was he logging?'

'Well he was an astronomer, so lots of things, I suppose. But he had been working on a particular project over the past fifty years or so. I don't know much more, but I would sometimes help him. He seemed to be looking at the astrological constellations and the position of the sun at the Spring Equinox each year.'

'That's very interesting,' nodded Aibgrene. She was certain that she knew why he had been interested in documenting that, but decided to look into it a bit more before saying anything to Lola.

'He has it all logged, it's up there if you want to have a look some time. You'd probably make more sense of it than me.'

Lola settled into Arthur's old rocking chair. He always said he did his best thinking there. His woollen cardigan still hung around the back of the seat. It had been a birthday present she had bought him a few years ago. He loved it so much that he wore it all the time. Some buttons were missing and the cuffs were threadbare. Lifting it off the back of the seat she slipped it on, pulling it around herself, inhaling the smell of tobacco and old spice. Rocking back and forward, Lola sat patiently letting Aibgrene absorb the charm of this special room; a room that, for her, resonated with the ghosts of so many fond memories.

'Oh my word! How on earth did it take me so long to notice that?' said Aibgrene leaning back now with her head over the back of the sofa, staring at the domed ceiling.

The room offered much to look at: the mass of books, which reached from the ceiling to the floor, the large bay windows that faced out into Arthur's herb garden, and the unique staircase that seemed to vanish through the roof, but as Lola followed Aibgrene's eyes to the ceiling, she found the room's pièce de résistance.

'It took me a lot longer to discover it than you. It's amazing, isn't it?' agreed Lola.

'That's an understatement, Lola; look at all those tiny quotes around the room.'

The girls drank in the golden domed roof, and the replica of Raphael's masterpiece painted on it.

'The School of Athens – amazing!' exclaimed Aibgrene. 'They're all there, all the great thinkers. Let it be said, some better than others, but they all contributed in their own way, I suppose.'

'I know, that's why Arthur had it painted, only he has made some very notable additions,' replied Lola. 'Can you spot them? You can see all his favourite philosophers are there – Socrates, Plato, and Aristotle, who was a misogynist by the way.'

Aibgrene continued to scrutinise the characters, which were laid out like the original painting. The first thing that struck her was that there seemed to be more women depicted in Arthur's version.

'Raphael even managed to include some women, but there seems to be more here,' said Aibgrene pointing up towards a long red-headed girl with blazing emerald eyes. 'She's new!'

It had taken Lola ages to pick out the changes. They were so subtle, but Aibgrene had no such problems. 'That's Brigid,' Lola explained. 'He has also included his favourite astronomers – Copernicus, Galileo and Kepler – all fathers of the heliocentric movement. Can you see them?'

Aibgrene looked to where Lola was pointing.

'And there's my girl, Lola!' sang Aibgrene enthusiastically. 'Do you see her? The girl looking out of the picture at us. There, in between Pythagoras and Michelangelo?'

Looking to the left-hand side of the picture it took Lola a while to find both men. Stood between them on the step was a fair-haired woman, as Aibgrene said, looking straight at them.

'That's Hypatia,' Aibgrene explained, 'one of the leading minds in mathematics, philosophy and astronomy. She was from Alexandria. Not many people have heard of her, probably because history has been written by men, and we women have been relegated to a mere rib.'

Lola laughed, she liked Aibgrene, it was as if she had known her all her life, it was so easy to be around her, just like it was with her best friends. 'Poor Hypatia was killed by a Christian mob at the behest of the church and cut to pieces. She was as famous a philosopher as her male counterparts, yet history has ignored her,' continued Aibgrene, gravely. 'They accused her of causing religious turmoil with her philosophy on life and death, so of course she had to go. I could sit all day and look at that.'

'So how do you know so much about the School at Athens then?' asked Lola, genuinely impressed.

'I've just finished my degree in maths and philosophy, so I know a bit, but not too much.'

'All I know is that I know nothing. Very Socratic, Aibgrene,' laughed Lola. 'Maths though? I couldn't think of anything worse!'

Maths was Lola's weak subject and it always had been. She hated the ritual humiliation that she'd had to endure at school. The cold sweats and clammy palms at the thought of being asked to answer maths questions. For two years she'd had the worst teacher ever, Ms O'Cole, a complete bully! That, coupled with Lola's inability to hold her tongue, and her obvious weakness in the subject, made her a prime target. Arthur had tried to help her out, but he may as well have been speaking in a foreign language.

'Maths and philosophy, you did it old school, Aibgrene! Like the characters up there!' complimented Lola.

'Yeah, I suppose I did. I mean, back then there was no separation between the sciences and cosmology, not the way there is now. They didn't always get it right, so perhaps it's not a bad thing that they are two different disciplines now.'

The heat from the gas fire was finally starting to warm Lola. With Cuchulain sitting contently at her feet she began to tell Aibgrene what she had learned so far. Sitting in silence, Aibgrene listened intently, as Lola explained the dreams she'd been having, especially the dream she'd on the night Arthur had died. She spoke about the package she had received containing the letter, and the ring and prisms. She told Aibgrene about the ceremony at the church, and what she had learnt at the cremation about the Hell Fire Club, the Order and the Age of Aquarius, before finally arriving at the events of that night.

'You see, I'd got the call at work, just before I called you back. So that's why I was in Belfast. Mr Tennyson also gave me this,' said Lola, reaching into her bag. She pulled out the plastic gel sheath that protected the antiquated parchment, and handed it over to Aibgrene.

'It's written on calf skin. I'm not really sure how old it is. All Felix said was that it was the final part of the trilogy and it was to be protected at all times, and that no one was to know that I had it. Well, there goes one rule!' cringed Lola. 'But clearly someone already knew that I had it, since they tried to steal it from me!'

Aibgrene studied the parchment for a while before speaking.

'I would say that they maybe didn't know what you were there to collect, but, since it was related to Arthur, they might have wanted to take it anyway.'

'Maybe, but what worries me is how did they know I was going to be there? The only people that knew were my parents, and the old man, and I'm sure my parents didn't inform anyone!' said Lola.

'What about this Mr Tennyson?'

'I don't think so. If he was in league with the Hell Fire Club he'd have simply handed it over to them.'

'Aye, I suppose so! So what do you think?' asked Aibgrene glancing at the fragment of parchment in her hands. 'It's certainly old, and it has a great deal of energy around it. It's very potent. Normally I can feel it, but with this I can actually see it. It has a slight phosphorus glow.' Aibgrene looked up at Lola with a serious expression. 'I think this is the key, Lola. This will help us understand what we must do and how we must do it.'

'Well that's just typical, isn't it!' groaned Lola. 'In case you haven't noticed, it's written in Old Irish! And, to add to our problems, there are only a handful of people who can actually translate the text. Arthur being one of them.'

Not for the first time Lola felt a little lost. It was alien to be sitting in the library without Arthur. She had so much that she wanted to ask him, so many questions, and now she feared that she would never get the answers.

'We'll find a way, Lola! I'm positive that Arthur would not have thrown all this at you without giving you the tools to decipher it. Plus, he gave you keys to this place, I think there are answers here too.'

'I don't know where to begin,' said Lola. 'Everything has happened so fast; I've had no time to adjust. What if I can't do it, Aibgrene? What if I can't figure it all out? So many people are relying on me! What if I fail?'

CHAPTER 23

This is what had really been bothering Lola. Her fear of failure. She wasn't sure if she was smart enough or strong enough to succeed, it all seemed a little hopeless. Lola felt everything was way over her head, but also knew that she couldn't quit – she had to at least try.

'Give me a look at that again, Aibgrene,' said Lola.

She began to scan the text and picked out the few words that she miraculously recognised. Lifting a pen and a piece of paper, she wrote them down in capitals

TUATHA DE DANANN, BRUGH NA BOINNE, DAGDA, BEL.

'What've you got?' asked Aibgrene, as Lola turned the page towards her.

'Well, even though it's written in Old Irish, there are a few words that I understand. I'm not sure how, but I do. That's been happening a lot lately. Anyway, it'll get us started. The first is very important I think. It's Tuatha Dé Danann. This is one I do know. Have you ever heard of them?'

For once Aibgrene was at a loss and shook her head. Lola continued.

'Basically translated, Tuatha Dé Danann, means Peoples of the Goddess Dana. They weren't the first, or the last, race of people to settle in Ireland, but, according to Irish mythology, they were the greatest. They were a super intelligent civilisation, who were highly skilled at magick and possessed secret knowledge about the universe and cosmos. No one knows how they came to Ireland, but some believe they descended from the air. With them they brought the stone of destiny, known as the Lia Fail, the Spear of Victory and a magical cauldron.'

Lola was finding the detail from deep within her, as all the stories that Arthur had told her came flooding back, though she hadn't recalled them for years. 'Then there's the Brú na Bóinne, again roughly translated, it means the Palace or Mansion of the Boyne.' Checking that Aibgrene was still following, Lola continued. 'Now, do you know about the Boyne Valley, and its importance in our mythology?'

'We'll I think it's more than lore, its mystical significance is real. Even you must accept that now?' suggested Aibgrene.

'I'm beginning to,' smiled Lola. 'Anyway, it's one of the world's most important archaeological sites. Actually, Arthur would kill me for saying that – he didn't have much time for the archaeologists that discovered and worked on the site over the years, he said they'd done more damage than good, but that's for another time. It's one of the world's oldest spiritual sites.'

'So how does the Brú relate to this mystical race?' asked Aibgrene.

'Well according to the legend this is where they settled and built a temple in honour of their Sun God, the Dagda. This temple, I think, could be Newgrange.'

Aibgrene was following Lola's thread of thought now. 'Yes of course. Newgrange is orientated to catch the first rays of sun on the morning of the Winter Solstice. That's great, Lola, well done! You must have learnt something from Arthur after all!'

But Lola hadn't finished yet.

'That's not all! The last word is Bel.' Lola hesitated for a second. 'Listen, Aibgrene – I don't know where this knowledge is coming from, but I'm pretty sure the word "Bel" means sun in Old Irish. Clearly the sun seems to be an important factor tying in with the Ancient Order of the Golden Dawn. In the Ulster Cycles of Irish mythology, Newgrange was mentioned, but it was referred to as the Temple of the Dawn. The modern Irish term for dawn is "Fainne an Lae" which literally means "the ring of light on the skyline at daybreak".

It's quite a mouthful, I know, but there has to be something in that.'

'Well it's a start,' smiled Aibgrene without further comment.

Lola sat back in the chair, looking around the brightly lit library. She loved it here, she had always felt safe and secure in this room, and now it belonged to her. Turning to Aibgrene, Lola hoped that she might now have some answers too.

'So, we know that the Golden Dawn may be connected to the Brú, but where do the Hell Fire Club come in to it all? And who are they?' asked Lola. That one question had not left her mind since she first learned of their existence during the ceremony at the fort. If they had killed Arthur, and he was aware of them, then what chance did she have? She needed to know what, or who, she was up against.

'We'll that's where I can help you, Lola,' said Aibgrene. 'Many things were to be revealed to me on the night of my birthday, but as you know my mum never showed up!'

Her words quickly reminded them that Celeste was missing, that their situation wasn't a game, that it was real, that Arthur had been murdered, and that Celeste had been taken. The stakes couldn't get any higher. Lola reflected on how she might feel if it had been her mum or dad. She marvelled at how calmly Aibgrene was dealing with it.

'I can't imagine how hard this is for you, Aibgrene. Your mum is an amazing woman and you're so like her,' said Lola.

'I'm okay, Lola. I know I will find her. I have to keep believing that. That's the only thing that keeps me going, knowing that I have to find her. I just can't understand that she didn't know she might be in trouble. I mean you even sensed that Cyril was no good, so how on earth did my mum not see it?' asked Aibgrene.

'Maybe she did know!' replied Lola. She had been thinking about Celeste's behaviour that evening, and how she had dismissed Lola's feelings about Cyril. But there was one thing that troubled her, the look on Celeste's face when she got into the car. It wasn't fear or shock, more resignation.

'We'll find her!' said Lola trying to sound hopeful. Aibgrene nodded her head in acknowledgement, and then expanded upon Lola's initial query.

'Yes, the Hell Fire Club. Well, Lola, you're training to be a journalist, so you might like a good conspiracy theory. Only this one is not so much a conspiracy, it's fact, a fact that many refuse to believe. The Hell Fire Club is made up of a group of extremely wealthy men who are an influential global elite who have studied the mysteries, just like Arthur and my mother. However, they use their knowledge to enslave and control. They alone dictate what happens in the world. They control the banks, the food, governments, law; they have their fingers in many pies. They fund wars, saturate society with materialism, and force us to believe that the latest car or gadget is more important than our fellow man.

'They convince the masses that unless we wear certain shoes, or clothes, or fit in a certain way, then we are somehow lacking. They are businessmen, heads of state, politicians, doctors, priests, judges, teachers. The Hell Fire Club has many members from all walks of life. Now, how long they have been in existence? That I don't know. All I know is that their sole aim is to enslave us, using their tools of religion, race, war, sex, commercialism and consumerism and at the moment they seem to be winning.'

'So what are you saying, Aibgrene, if I go out and buy a new pair of shoes, I'm being corrupted?' asked Lola dismissively.

Aibgrene shook her head, waving off the suggestion. 'No, Lola, you're missing the point. I'm talking about the concept that you are more if you drive a certain car, or wear a certain label on your clothes. When that is engrained into a society, certain members of society cease to fit in when they don't have those things. It creates jealousy, which leads to greed, which leads to violence, which pushes us further and further from each other. That's what I mean!'

Engrossed, Lola nodded for her to continue. 'Anyway, by doing this, ever so subtly, they are ensuring that they keep mankind at war both globally, and on a spiritual level. By doing this they remain in control, keeping the secrets of this great universe for themselves.'

'I'm trying to be open minded, Aibgrene,' said Lola. 'I really am, but this all sounds a bit Orwellian. A shadowy underworld as puppet masters of the masses. And if this is the case, what does it have to do with Arthur and your mum?'

'It's simple, Lola. The Order knows the truth and there will come a day when all of mankind will know and believe this truth. And from what you have told me, I don't think that time is far away.'

'But what truth?' asked Lola. 'I mean that's politics and greed you're talking about, what has that got to do with secret Orders and magick?'

'Let me explain, Lola. The Hell Fire Club is a massive global organisation, a vast network of different groups and subgroups that operate all over the world. They fulfil the aims of their masters, but, while the minions are at their work, there's a small group of about one hundred that are part of the inner circle, each with their own coven. Like the Order they have a high priest, or as they call him, their Grotto Master. They are not only wealthy and powerful, but they also practice magick.'

'What? Like black magick?' asked Lola.

'I suppose, but to be honest we witches don't really think of it in terms of white or black magick. You see magick is magick. It isn't good or bad, Lola. It is what it is. However, whether it's used for good and the good of all is solely down to its exponent. In the case of the Hell Fire Club, it's not used for the good of all. You see, they believe themselves to be gods in their own right. Now, while the Order also believes we are all part of the Source or Creator and therefore are divine, the Hell Fire Club believes that only they are gods because they understand the mysteries of the universe. They wish to maintain their monopoly and will stop at nothing to achieve their aims.'

'And you think they operate here?' said Lola, eyes wide at the truth unfolding in Aibgrene's account.

'Yes, Lola, not only do I believe they operate here, I think the head of the entire organisation lives here! And, for some reason I think that he has my mum! Only very strong magick could hold her and keep her in a weakened state.'

Suddenly the full weight of the day's tribulations washed over Lola. She felt exhausted.

'So what do we do now, Aibgrene?' For the first time that night, Lola could see the toll that Celeste's disappearance was having on Aibgrene. Her face was drained of all colour except the dark circles under her eyes. Smiling, Aibgrene sat up on the chair and stretched.

'It's almost three in the morning, Lola. We won't be able to save my mum or the world tonight, but maybe tomorrow. We'd better get some sleep.'

CHAPTER 24

They awoke early the next morning. Lola had a busy day planned fulfilling her commitments to the Ballyvalley News. She left Aibgrene at Arthur's house with Cuchulain for protection and set off. A million thoughts were running through her mind after last night's discussion. She intended to do a bit of research on the Hell Fire Club to see what she could come up with. However, she spent most of the morning interviewing Vikki Jones's father. It was one of the toughest interviews she'd ever had to do and, as with all sad stories, it really touched her.

She felt emotionally and physically drained when she reached the Ballyvalley News office. Lola often found it difficult to be impartial as a journalist and to suppress emotional responses to such articles, but she knew that if she ever wanted to make it in this field she'd have to be more detached. It was almost one thirty when she lifted her head to check the old clock on the wall.

She was transcribing the interview with Mr Jones, the pain and aching in his voice on the recording sounded even more tangible than when she'd been sitting next to him. Removing her earphones she paused the Dictaphone and re-read her notes.

It struck Lola how Vikki's family refused to accept that she may have run away or taken her own life. This was something that the police had been trying to prepare them for, but Vikki's father remained adamant that his daughter had been happy, and would never have put her family through such an ordeal. The more Lola learned about Vikki Jones, the more she felt that her parents were right. But, she also knew that no matter how close this girl was to her family, like all families, they wouldn't have known everything about their daughter. For that she would have to speak to a close friend, so she was delighted when Mr Jones handed her a number for his daughter's best friend. Searching through the shards of note paper strewn across her desk, Lola found the number. She was hopeful as she rang, but there was no answer, so when the answering machine beeped she left a message.

'Hello, this is a message for Sarah Byrne. My name is Lola Paige and I work for the Ballyvalley News. I spoke to Vikki's parents this morning and they passed on your number. I would appreciate it if you could give me a call when you get this. Thanks.'

Tidying her messy desk, Lola searched for the picture of the missing girl, given to her by Vikki's parents earlier that morning. It was important because it was taken on the night she had disappeared. Finally, she located it under a pile of redundant press releases. Lifting it up she examined the pretty face that smiled out at her. She studied the red dress and shoes. Vikki wore no jewellery, save for an intricate silver charm bracelet, with a heart, a bow, a, shoe and little owl hanging from it. The owl caught Lola's eyes because it was not made of silver but of fine crystal. Staring at the picture, Lola wasn't sure what she was looking for, it was almost as if she was expecting this beautiful stranger to speak to her.

Lola finally lifted her head when she heard her editor come into the office. Bryce greeted Abbey, who had worked in silence all afternoon, and then Lola, as he came by. Lola was convinced that he could sense the tension between her and Abbey, as the room always seemed to have an atmosphere anytime they were there together.

'Are you girls still hard at it?' laughed Bryce. 'That's what I like to see.'

Turning around Lola was momentarily taken back when she realised that her boss was not alone. Standing beside him was a familiar face wearing a now familiar smug expression.

'Ladies this is Alex Stein. He's going to be the architect in charge of the much needed renovations here at the Ballyvalley News. He'll be here for the next few days taking measurements for his drawings. So make sure you help him if he gets lost.'

Alex stared at Lola.

'Hello, Lola, nice to see you again,' he said eloquently.

He was completely different to the first night she had met him, and he continued to smile at her, waiting on some sort of response, until Bryce spoke.

'You two know each other? Good! You'll be able to keep Alex right, Lola, if he needs any help finding his way around the place.'

Lola didn't care that she might seem rude in front of her new boss, there was no way she would be speaking to, or having anything to do with, Alex Stein.

'I wouldn't really be the best person for that, sir, I'm still getting lost myself,' smiled Lola innocently. 'Abbey would be your best bet. Wouldn't you, Abbey?' Abbey, was practically drooling as she gazed at Alex in awe, twisting her hair around her fingers playfully. 'Isn't that right, Abbey?' repeated Lola.

'Oh, yes. Of course, if you need any help, with anything, just ask me,' said Abbey after a momentary silence.

'Thank you, Abbey, I'll make sure I do,' agreed Alex, flashing a flirtatious smile back at her.

'Well, Alex, you have a few measurements to get around the office and reception area, so I'll leave you to it.'

With that Bryce left the room, leaving Alex behind with Lola, who was growing more uncomfortable by the minute. Trying to ignore him, she immediately turned back to her work, but couldn't concentrate. It seemed as if the room was closing in on her as her stomach erupted with butterflies. No matter how much she tried to focus on the screen in front of her all she could sense was Alex's every move as he went about his business.

'He's divine,' proclaimed Abbey, as Alex disappeared into the reception area. 'I've never seen anyone so gorgeous in my life. He's like some Greek god!'

Lola was growing more and more irritated by Abbey, who now appeared doe-eyed, like most women seemed to be around Alex Stein.

'He may look gorgeous, but he's not a nice person, Abbey, you'd be well advised to stay clear,' warned Lola, as Abbey rolled her eyes, quickly turning back to her desk as Alex came back into the room.

'Well, Lola, how are things? Fancy seeing you here!' chirped Alex, as if he'd known her all his life.

This only compounded Lola's bad mood. Who did he think he was? After the way he had spoken to her at the party, and now acting as if they were best friends. Up until a couple of weeks ago she'd had no idea that Alex Stein even existed, and now all of a sudden he was everywhere. First he turned up at Arthur's funeral, which she found extremely odd, and now here at the paper.

His voice spoke volumes about how different their backgrounds were. Lola was proud of her working-class background, and confident that she could engage and talk to anyone. But there was something about Alex Stein that made her feel uncomfortable, that made her feel inferior and she despised it. Yet, she couldn't deny that she was drawn to him, not just because of his astounding beauty, but because he challenged her in ways she'd never been challenged before.

For some reason she felt like she had to prove herself to him. Though he'd had a privileged life, and had grown up with the arrogance that accompanied it, deep down she knew that he was attracted to her. They were from distinctly different backgrounds, with contrasting personalities, all of which seemed to pull them towards each other. The reality was that, like Abbey, Lola also found Alex hugely attractive, and that upset her more than anything. Even standing in the dark hallway the first night they met, she knew there was a spark between them.

'I'm fine, Alex,' replied Lola congenially. 'Fancy seeing you here too! It's beginning to become a bit of a habit. If I didn't know better I'd say you were following me.'

He was right beside her desk now, and she could smell his aftershave – a fresh sharp scent – as he bent down and whispered into her ear.

'Maybe I am.'

Lola's heartbeat began to accelerate slightly, as she tried to force herself to concentrate.

'I have to say though, you look a lot better than the first time I saw you,' jibed Alex smoothly.

'And you're a lot more composed than when I first met you,' retorted Lola with a smile. 'Actually, I think I still have the bruise you gave me as a memento.'

There was a sudden change in Alex's demeanour as he stiffened at the thought of their first encounter. He had been under a lot of stress, but it had been so unlike him to lose his temper. It embarrassed him, made him feel weak for not having been in full control. But when it came to Lola, he sensed that he would never be in control, and the attraction he felt towards her didn't make sense to him. Lola was different from all the other girls, appearing impervious to his charm and wealth. She also had that unexpected connection with Arthur Delphian, what a bonus that could prove, and it made him all the more determined to unravel her.

'You got me on a bad day, Lola,' replied Alex, trying to disguise his obvious discomfort.

The way he said her name knocked Lola off-guard. She was sure he could tell that she was attracted to him, so she worked harder on being petulant towards him.

'Did you have a difficult decision on what pair of designer shoes to wear or something?' she countered. Abbey almost stopped breathing she was listening so intently to their exchange. Alex didn't seem to mind the low blows, instead he played along.

'Don't be ludicrous; I've someone to make those decisions for me,' he replied.

Despite herself, Lola smiled; she needed to get out of there, and quick. Ignoring Alex, she told Abbey that she was taking her lunch break, and grabbing her bag she left the office.

Relieved that she was no longer under his scrutiny, she sat down to her soup, just as her phone beeped with a message. It was Ruby. Lola spent the remainder of her lunch break exchanging messages with her best friend, filling her in on Alex-gate. When she returned to the office Abbey and Alex were both gone, replaced by Sebastian and Drew.

Lola began to follow up some leads on the Jones story. Vikki's father had told her that according to the police report his daughter was seen leaving Chateau Bacchus at around four in the morning by the Stein's cleaners. Lola was just about to make a phone call when he and Abbey returned. Abbey was beaming from head to toe, motioning towards Alex with her eyes. 'Thanks Alex that was a lovely lunch. It was so nice of you,' said Abbey in a raised voice, as Lola pretended not to hear.

'You're welcome, Abbey,' replied Alex, clearly playing along.

Lola caught Sebastian's eye as he mouthed 'Who's he?' nodding towards Alex. Much to Lola's relief, Alex finally left the room, as he continued taking measurements on his way around the building.

'Well, Abbey, dish the dirt, who's your new boyfriend?' teased Sebastian, much to Abbey's delight.

'We were only out to lunch, Sebastian. His name is Alex Stein and he's an architect, or training to be an architect and his dad's company is handling the renovations here. He's so hot, isn't he?' gushed Abbey. 'So how do you know him, Lola?' asked Abbey in a rather pointed manner.

There was a bit too much emphasis on the words 'you' and 'him' for Lola. Clearly Abbey was intrigued as to how someone as ordinary as her would know Alex, but she suspected that her colleague already knew the answer to that question.

'I wouldn't say I know him,' replied Lola. 'We had a brief altercation at a party a couple of weeks ago.' Lola thought about adding that she didn't want to know him either, but not wanting it to sound like sour grapes, she left it at that.

'I think he said something about that. He said it was quite funny that someone had spilt a drink all over your dress and hair,' laughed Abbey, as Lola's temper began to bubble.

Abbey was enjoying every minute of this. But there was no way Lola was going to give her the satisfaction of seeing that it annoyed her. The fact that Abbey knew about their altercation didn't bother Lola, what annoyed her was the fact that Alex had been making fun of her. Lola didn't offer a reply, instead she refocused her attention on her work. Eventually Alex came back into the room. Lola did her best to ignore him but much to her annoyance, he directed most of his conversation to Abbey.

'Aren't you a dark horse, Lola?' said Sebastian, looking at an email that he had been sent from the Ballyvalley Six-a-Side Summer Football League.

Lola had played football since she was a child. Being an only girl in a house full of boys meant she had little choice. But the truth was she loved the game. Ballyvalley didn't have a ladies' team, so she always played football with the boys, and even now at eighteen she was still playing. Lola and her three older brothers Brendan, Michael and Christopher, along with two of their friends, had been playing in the six-a-side league for a couple of years. It was a very competitive league, and Lola was their top goal scorer with fourteen goals so far this season.

'Top goal scorer in the summer league! I didn't know you played,' continued Sebastian, seeming to be really impressed. Lola's face turned a light pink.

'I've always played. It's one of the joys of having four brothers. I suppose someone needs to show you boys how it's done!' said Lola casually, in an attempt to play down Sebastian's praise. She wasn't used to him being serious with her, as he was usually ribbing her about something.

'Your team is in the cup final this Friday night! We'll have to get a photographer down, and of course, we want a back-page lead!'

'You've no chance,' laughed Lola. 'I almost forgot the final was this Friday. We're up against a good side. They've won the cup the last four years in a row, so it's going to be a tight game.'

Looking up Lola could see a grin spreading across Alex's face. He had obviously been listening to their conversation, which only exacerbated her embarrassment.

'And what do you find so amusing?' hissed Lola in his direction.

'Nothing,' smiled Alex, holding his hands up in mock surrender. 'I find it very interesting that you play soccer, but somehow, I can't say it's a surprise.'

'What do you mean by that? I suppose it's too working class for you, Alex, you'd probably prefer a good game of polo or something? And it's football, by the way. Not soccer. You Yanks haven't a clue!' Perhaps she had been a bit over zealous in her rebuke especially with the others watching. But he needed to be brought down a peg or two, reasoned Lola, feeling slightly self-conscious.

'Actually, that's not what I meant,' replied Alex. 'You seem to have a chip on your shoulder, Lola. It's not my fault that you're intimidated by me.'

He was fully aware of the reaction his comment might provoke, and was enjoying the exchange, though Lola quickly realised this. Composing herself she turned back to her computer, grateful when her phone rang.

CHAPTER 25

'Hello, Ballyvalley News,' greeted Lola as she lifted the telephone.

'Hello, Lola, its Sarah Byrne here, you called earlier?'

Lola felt awkward speaking to the girl when Alex was so close by.

'Oh, hi, Sarah, thanks for getting back to me. I was with Vikki's parents this morning and they passed on your number. I was wondering if you would mind helping me out with a few enquiries.'

Aware that Alex was listening, Lola decided that it would be best to have this conversation in private.

'Listen, Sarah, how about we meet up and have a chat, would that suit you?' suggested Lola.

'Yes, that would be great. I have something that I would like you to hear. I don't know if it will help much, but it might.'

'Okay. Would this afternoon suit?'

'Yes, say about three o'clock?'

'Just let Jane at reception know you're here to see me. I'll speak to you then.'

As Lola hung up the phone, a computer email alert flashed on her computer screen. An urgent press release had been sent from the police press office. She clicked the message with the cursor, and as the e-mail opened Lola's heart sank.

TO: lola.paige@ballyvalleynews.com
REPLY-TO: pressoffice@causewaypolice.org
SUBJECT: URGENT PRESS RELEASE

Causeway Police have confirmed that the body of a young woman found on the beach in Castlerock at approximately 8.30am this morning is that of missing teenager Vikki Jones.

Miss Jones (19) was reported missing over a week ago after attending a party in
Portstewart.

The police have now confirmed that they do not suspect foul play. All members of Miss Jones's family have been notified.

Re-reading the message again and again, Lola could only think of Alan Jones and his family. It struck her how profoundly life changing those few lines on the page in front of her would be for them. Clearly Sarah had not got the news yet, so picking up the phone Lola decided to give her a call to tell her not to bother coming in to the office. But she put the phone down immediately, as she became aware of Alex standing behind her, gazing at the screen.

'They found her body?' he asked, all colour drained from his face, before taking the seat next to Lola. 'Can we talk somewhere?'

Lola motioned towards the door, and walked out of the dingy back room to the spacious reception area. Alex followed her and they both sat down on the black leather sofa.

'I know you knew her, Alex. I'm really sorry you had to find out like that,' said Lola apologetically. 'You two were together? I remember seeing you with her at the party.'

Lola didn't want to hear the answer to that, as she sat looking at Alex's perfect face furrowed deep in thought.

'It was nothing serious. You know how it is; we just met up every now and then!'

'I was out with her father this morning. To be honest I think they knew all along she was gone.'

'Why do you think that?'

'I don't know, they had that parent's intuition I suppose. Her dad just kept saying that the police were wrong about her running away or taking her own life. He was adamant that she would never do that, so he must have known she was dead. To be honest, based on what I have learnt about the girl so far, I'm inclined to agree with him.'

Alex sat motionless, the innocent face of Vikki Jones swimming through his head, as it had been for the last week. Every night she invaded his dreams, lying next to him in his bed, her toned, tanned bare body, beckoning him towards her seductively. But as he pulls her closer to him he sees that her wrists have deep gashes cut into them, and her thick warm blood oozes out onto the crisp white silk sheets like black ink on paper.

He was seeing her everywhere he went – there was no escape. He had taken the life of another human being, and he was feeling something he had never felt before: remorse. It was not a word that was in his father's vocabulary, a weakness that his father didn't have, nor would he tolerate it in others, especially the heir to his empire.

Lola could see the torment on Alex's face and her heart sank, thinking that Alex must have felt more for Vikki than he'd been admitting. In the same way she realised that she was more attracted to him than she was admitting. They sat side by side in silence, this was the most civilised they'd been with each other since they first met. A momentary hiatus, thought Lola, no pretence, no mind games, no smug remarks. There was no awkwardness, just a comfortable silence.

'So the police think she took her own life?' asked Alex.

'It looks like it, but I haven't seen the coroner's report yet,' replied Lola. 'I don't believe that Vikki would have taken her own life. I think someone has killed her. She's not the first girl to go missing up there you know. I heard on the news that another girl, around the same age, had gone missing a couple of weeks before. What was her name?'

Lola tried to remember the radio report she'd heard on the day of Arthur's cremation. Searching the far recesses of her brain for a name, she finally got it.

'Yes. Karen. Karen Watson, that's it!'

Alex's stomach leapt, he had known her too. She had been another one of his conquests, and although he was not present at that ritual killing, he had led his father straight to her. He was in trouble and seriously needed to compose himself. There was no way that Lola would put the two together, or would she?

She was full of compassion, underneath that sassy appearance he could feel the light emanate from her, and he was beginning to see that she was very special indeed. He felt different around her, like he was more tuned into his own emotions. She was like his kryptonite, making him feel weak, yet as much as he hated feeling vulnerable, he couldn't resist her.

The door buzzer sounded, interrupting their conversation, as a small red-headed girl came through to reception, heading towards the desk.

'Hi. I'm here to see Lola Paige?' said Vikki's friend.

Hearing her voice, Lola jumped up from the seat, and went to greet Sarah Byrne.

'Hi. You must be Sarah,' said Lola extending her hand. 'I'm Lola. Thank you so much for coming in to see me.'

Sarah's pale blue eyes were bloodshot and puffy, she had clearly been crying.

'I take it you've heard the news? I'm so sorry,' offered Lola, knowing exactly what Sarah Byrne was going through. 'Are you sure you want to do this now?'

'Yes, I want to feel like I'm doing something,' replied Sarah emotionally. 'Vikki didn't kill herself like they're saying, Lola. There's no way. No way!'

Alex remained sitting on the sofa as Lola guided Sarah towards it.

'Sarah, how are you? I'm so sorry,' said Alex, getting up off the seat to embrace her.

Lola noticed that Sarah didn't seem to reciprocate. She wasn't exactly rude, but there was something in her demeanour alerted Lola to the possibility that she didn't seem to like Alex much. That was certainly a first, where females were concerned, apart from her of course.

'I'd better get on with my work,' continued Alex. 'I'll see you later, Lola, and once again, Sarah, I'm really sorry to hear about Vikki.'

'Thanks, Alex, I'll see you around,' replied Sarah.

The atmosphere was suddenly tense. Alex left the reception to find the bathroom, feeling as though he may be sick.

'Why don't we go for a cup of tea? You look like you could do with one and I'd like to get out of the office for a while,' suggested Lola, reassuringly.

'That sounds good.'

'I'm going to get my things, I'll be back in a second.'

Lola gathered her coat, Dictaphone, notepad and the picture of Vikki that sat on her desk, before heading to her favourite cafe with Sarah.

CHAPTER 26

'There's a lovely little place up the street here, it's very private,' Lola suggested warmly.

'That's okay,' replied Sarah.

She seemed drained of all energy and Lola recognised the vacant look of grief in her eyes. The poor girl was trying to understand what was happening, and the events clearly hadn't fully registered with her yet. The warm weather was long gone now and a heavy grey cloud that hung overhead threatened more rain.

'Looks like it's going to rain again,' said Lola, in an attempt to make conversation.

It wasn't long before they reached The Pastry Boutique, a beautiful building hidden in one of the alleyways off the main road. Lola had been coming here for years with her mum and her friends. As they approached the cafe, Sarah stopped to admire the shop front, which was decorated with ornate green and pink flower mosaic tiles that curled around the shop's sign like a beautiful garland. A large wooden-arched window was host to a multitude of colourful pastries and cakes, enticing in all who passed by. Lola loved it there, especially on a dull day like today. The warm yellow glow radiating from inside the cafe spilled out onto the cobbled alleyway.

'I've never noticed this place before, it's so quirky,' croaked Sarah, her voice clearly hoarse from all the crying.

'It's opened a few years now! Wait until you see inside,' said Lola, pushing the door open.

Immediately their senses were ignited by the smell of freshly brewed coffee, cake and chocolate that hung in the air. Lola directed Sarah towards the back room while she gave her order to the warm familiar face behind the counter.

'Well, Lola, where have you been hiding, young lady?' asked Madge, the proprietor of The Pastry Boutique and a very congenial woman.

Lola loved Madge from the first time they met. She was a fantastic character, very attractive for her age, and tall and curvy, reminding Lola of Sophia Lauren. Well into her sixties now her hair had turned silver, but she had a lust for life and people. She loved to hear all about their troubles, which usually revolved around relationships, imparting her words of wisdom where and when she could.

'Hi, Madge, how are you?' smiled Lola, genuinely happy to see her. 'I'm lost without my partners in crime; they're off enjoying themselves in America this summer.'

'And they left you here all on your own? That's terrible, pet,' laughed Madge.

'I know, some friends they are!'

Suddenly Madge's face became sullen, with all traces of humour extinguished, and Lola knew what was coming. In truth that is why she had been avoiding coming to the cafe.

'I'm really sorry to hear about Arthur, pet, I'm sure you were totally devastated. You did him so proud at the funeral, love.'

Emerging from behind the counter in her pale blue frilly apron and matching mules, Madge pulled Lola into a warm embrace.

'I didn't get a chance to speak to you at the service. I miss him terribly you know,' said Madge wiping the sides of her eyes with a tissue, as Lola tried to fight back her own tears.

'Thanks, Madge, I'm still trying to get to grips with it too. We all miss him,' replied Lola.

Trying to compose herself, Madge walked back behind the counter. 'Now what can I get you, love? The usual?'

'Yes please, and a white coffee and a piece of that chocolate cake as well,' smiled Lola, before lifting her tray with black tea and a slice of pavlova on it. In all the time she had been coming to The Pastry Boutique her order had never changed, but today Madge added a little extra serving of two large strawberries smothered in chocolate, onto a small flowery saucer.

Lola found Sarah sitting on the large pale-pink velvet sofa in the back room. It was late in the afternoon, so they had the place to themselves. Setting the tray down tentatively, Lola took a seat opposite her. Sarah was still very emotional. Lola engaged her in light conversation as they drank their tea and coffee, waiting for Sarah to finish, before she started the interview.

'I'm just going to set this on the table, Sarah – it's my Dictaphone. If it's okay with you, I want to record our conversation. No one will hear it only me, it's just for my notes,' explained Lola, trying her best to put Sarah at ease.

'No problem, Lola, I don't mind at all.'

'My shorthand isn't up to speed just yet,' smiled Lola. 'So I cheat a bit using this.'

Sarah smiled, her pale-blue eyes lighting up briefly. She was a bit smaller than Lola, quite petite, with soft auburn hair, which came to her chin in a neat bob. She was very pretty in a natural sort of way, thought Lola, as she examined her features.

'I'm sure you've spoken to the police about this, Sarah, so it won't be that formal. I just want to know about the events of that night, and anything significant you can tell me about Vikki.'

Sarah sat staring at her feet for a moment before she began to speak. 'She didn't kill herself. There is no way, Lola! The police have it wrong. I tried to tell them that but they wouldn't listen!'

'Are you saying you think she was murdered?'

'I don't know, all I know is that she wouldn't have taken her own life,' insisted Sarah.

'Why are you so sure about that?' asked Lola, feeling a little uneasy about interviewing Sarah when she was clearly so upset. She didn't want to push her too far in asking her to talk about her friend's death when it was still so raw. But, she contented herself that Sarah had been keen to help – after all she was Vikki's best friend.

'You didn't know Vikki. She loved life. She was a bit shallow sometimes, but she was a kind person, and she loved her mum and dad. I know she wouldn't have committed suicide. I know because she knew what it was like to almost lose someone that way.'

Sarah fell silent, pulling her sleeves over her hands. Lola's eyes automatically followed the movement and caught a glimpse of the white scars that appeared on Sarah's pale wrists. It was clear why she believed that Vikki had not taken her own life.

'She had helped someone close to her through that,' whispered Sarah faintly.

'Can you tell me about that night, Sarah?' asked Lola after a moment's silence.

'Vikki had been really looking forward to the party for weeks. She'd met Alex around May, after he came back from university in America. It was at one of those functions, you know the sort you would see in The Tatler, with all the beautiful people,' smiled Sarah. 'Vikki was there as part of the whole Miss Northern Ireland thing. She had won it the previous year.

'Anyway, they had a sort of thing going on. Vikki was really taken by him. He was handsome, smart and extremely rich, so he was her ideal man. He seemed quite generous as well. He gave her a charm for her bracelet as a birthday gift. It was a little owl, I think, and it was a two-carat diamond, she was ecstatic. She'd thought she'd met her prince charming. But they only met up every now and then.

'Alex didn't take it as seriously as Vikki did, but she was always on call. So, when he invited her up to his house for the weekend, she was there in a heartbeat. I could tell that Alex Stein wasn't serious about her. I tried to tell her, but she wouldn't listen. He was only using her, and because of that, I didn't really like him much. There was just something about him I didn't trust, Lola.'

Lola wasn't surprised by Sarah's opinion of Alex; she had sensed the tension between them back at the office. She would have been the same if someone had mistreated Clara, Ruby or Orla. Lola felt a little embarrassed, because she had found Alex attractive just as Vikki had. She wasn't really sure what to say or how to respond, so instead she waited until Sarah continued.

'Anyway, Vikki went to this party. I didn't go, it wasn't really my scene to be honest, but I went up with her for the weekend, we stayed at our student house. She left for the party at about 11pm, and that was the last time I saw her.

'I was woken at around 3.30 am by a call to my phone, but I didn't reach it in time. I checked my voicemail and it was Vikki, but she mustn't have hung up straight away as I could hear her talking to someone.'

Sarah was staring into the distance now, deep in thought. Tears began to run down her cheeks, falling in droplets onto her light denim jeans. Lola handed her a tissue not sure whether to continue the interview or not.

'If I'd only answered that call,' wept Sarah, the hurt and anger tangible in her voice. 'Or even if I'd gone with her, Lola, none of this would have happened!'

Lola knew exactly how she was feeling – the what-ifs – but the truth was there was nothing Sarah could have done.

'Listen to this and tell me what you think,' said Sarah handing Lola her mobile phone to hear Vikki's last message.

'Hi, Sarah, it's me,' chirped Vikki's light and airy voice. 'I thought you might still be awake and I was absolutely bursting to get telling you all the gossip! I've had an amazing night. Let's just say that there's more to Alex Stein than meets the eye, he certainly lived up to his reputation,' giggled Vikki excitedly.

The message had been cut off abruptly, while Vikki was in mid-sentence. All Lola could hear now was static, and the click of Vikki's heels on the pavement. Then she heard what Sarah wanted her opinion on, the light purr of a car engine, which sounded like it was slowing down. For some reason Lola got the impression that Vikki recognised the person in the car, as he called out to her. It was a deep male voice with a very distinct Belfast accent. He was offering her a lift. The sound was badly muffled, but Lola could tell that Vikki got into the car and closed the door, and then the call ended.

Lola's mind was racing, how could the police have overlooked this? She knew she was no detective, but this was a vital piece of information. Whoever was in that car could have been the last person to see Vikki Jones alive.

'So what do you think, Lola?' asked Sarah nervously.

She told Lola that she had listened to the message countless times, and believed that she could make out a car and a voice, but when she gave it to the police they seemed less impressed. She had protested, but they said that it was incoherent. Since then she had worried that she'd made it all up in her desperation to find her friend. She was hoping that Lola would agree with her that the message was indeed significant.

'I'm trying to get my head around this, Sarah. I mean how on earth could the police have overlooked this? It's a disgrace!' ranted Lola in disgust. 'Who did you speak to? There is really something wrong here.'

'I had been told that the detective leading the investigation was a DCI Campbell, but when I called he was out. So I spoke to one of his team, I can't remember his name, but he just dismissed it. He made me feel as though I was grasping at straws.'

Lola got a sick churning feeling in the pit of stomach, indicating to her that somewhere in this case there was foul play at work. Hearing what Sarah had to say only strengthened her conviction that Vikki had indeed been murdered. She could feel that this story was more complex than it first appeared. One of the Stein's maids had seen Vikki get into a black car, and here was the proof that she did. Now Lola wondered who, or what, the authorities were protecting. The answer to this question flashed like a neon sign in Lola's mind, but the very thought horrified her.

'Would it be okay for me to take a copy of that voicemail, Sarah?' asked Lola.

'You can do that?' questioned Sarah.

Lola nodded her head, and then lifted out a small memory card from the back of her purse. Inserting the card into Sarah's phone, she saved the voicemail as a media file, and transferred it onto her memory card. Removing it from the phone, she placed it back into her purse again for safe keeping.

'Thanks, Sarah, you've been a great help. I understand how difficult this is for you. Believe me, I do! Losing your best friend like this takes a lot of getting used to, but the pain will get easier to manage in time.'

Lola reached out and squeezed Sarah's hand. She looked so alone.

'My life won't be the same without her,' replied Sarah. 'I suppose you need to be getting back to the office, Lola.'

Sarah sat up to put on her coat.

'You've given me a lot to look into, and I'll try my best to get to the bottom of this, for you and Vikki's family,' promised Lola.

Lola shouted her goodbyes to Madge, as she and Sarah made their way back out onto the main street. It had been raining, but the sun was trying it's best to break through the thick grey clouds. Far off in the distance a rainbow was visible, reminding Lola of the beautiful prisms that hung in her bedroom, a gift from Arthur.

'Once again, Sarah, I can't thank you enough. Take care of yourself and we'll speak soon.'

'No, Lola, thank you for your time, for listening to me, you've been great.'

As Lola turned to leave, Sarah called after her. 'Be careful, Lola!' A quizzical look spread across Lola's face, the last time someone had said that to her she'd been attacked. 'He seems to have a thing for you too,' shouted Sarah, as she walked off in the opposite direction.

Lola immediately knew who the 'He' was in Sarah's warning, and it was not lost on Lola as she returned to the Ballyvalley News, where she tried in vain to get in touch with the young detective. It had been an intense day and Lola was relieved when the clock struck 5pm. It took a while for her computer to close down, so she was the last to leave the office. Stepping outside she was surprised to see Alex leaning up against the wall. The evening sun bounced off Alex Stein's light blonde hair and bronzed skin. His shirt sleeves were rolled up, revealing his taught forearms and his designer watch. He was like a vision, his dazzling smile momentarily disorientating Lola.

'Can I give you a lift home, Lola?' asked Alex confidently.

Lola tried not to look at him, as if by avoiding his gaze would somehow make her immune to his advances. 'No thanks Alex, I'm fine,' she declined, continuing to walk on by in case she changed her mind.

A sharp wave of electricity ran through her body as Alex pulled her by the hand. She turned to face him.

'Look we didn't get off to such a good start. I feel really bad about what happened. How about we start again?' he said, all traces of arrogance now faded from his face, as he looked beseechingly at Lola.

She couldn't resist, she was never one to hold grudges, and despite her better judgement, she wanted to believe him. She also knew that she was falling into the same trap as every other girl Alex Stein had snared. But he'd met her on a bad night in Portstewart and perhaps the same was true of him. However, Lola wasn't willing to give in that easily.

'What is the old saying, Alex? You don't get a second chance to make a first impression. You should think about that,' said Lola cheekily goading his next move.

Lola turned on her heels and strode off towards the town, leaving Alex to watch her walk away from him yet again. Leaning up against the wall, he watched Lola admiringly until she was out of sight. This was going to be a bit harder than he thought, but deep down he knew that his interest in Lola Paige reached beyond that of the Hell Fire Club and her connection to Arthur Delphian.

Lola was buzzing as she walked home, the electricity and butterflies throughout her body still playing havoc. She was in complete denial, putting her present state down to hunger and stress. Suddenly Arthur's words of caution came back to her, he had told her to be wary of new people that came into her life.

Lola had meant what she had said to Alex about first impressions. Her gut feeling about someone was usually correct. She knew Alex had a dark side, of that she was sure, she had first-hand experience of it that night at the party, and she didn't trust him. There was also the small fact that Vikki Jones was with him on the night she disappeared. Yet here she was drawn to him all the same. No matter how she reasoned with herself, for the first time in her life her head and her heart were pulling her in opposite directions. She and Alex had nothing in common at all, they were polar opposites, but like the opposing sides of a magnet, they were attracted to each other, the force field too strong for either of them to withstand.

Never one to give in easily, Lola knew there would have to be a truce between the two, as there had been today. Through Vikki Jones's death they had been able to create a temporary hiatus in their little game of cat and mouse.

CHAPTER 27

The rest of the week passed without incident, and Lola found herself totally preoccupied with the more normal aspects of her life – which were becoming all too rare a thing – as she prepared for the impending cup final. Her brother Michael had them training every night, and although it was tough, it offered Lola a much welcomed break from her efforts to research the dangers of the Hell Fire Club. Friday night came all too soon.

The large crowd had gathered to watch a competitive cup final at Ballyvalley playing fields. But nerves had seemed to play a large part, affecting Lola and the rest of the team, which comprised of her brothers, Michael, Christopher and Brendan, and their friends Aaron and Stephen. They were trailing 2-1 at half time. Lola knew that she could shoulder most of the responsibility for being behind having had several chances to put the game beyond the reach of their opponents. She knew that she was a much better player than the defender she was up against, but her confidence and self-belief was a fragile thing. It always had been.

It frustrated Lola that no matter how good she was at something, she could never really accept or believe it. It only took one person to plant the seed of doubt in her mind and her confidence evaporated. The defender who'd been sent to mark her throughout the game must have had a sixth sense about this and he exploited it to the full, insulting her throughout the game. It was nothing that she hadn't dealt with before on the pitch, the usual insults about women playing football, as well as the tacky sexual innuendo. He had pulled her top, and groped her bottom, all to put her off her game.

Normally Lola shook this off, but tonight it was clearly having an effect on her. So when they gathered for the half-time team talk she had anticipated Michael's verbal onslaught.

'What the hell is going on with you, Lola? You're sleeping up there tonight!' spat Michael. 'I'm gonna have to make a change, drop you into midfield and put our Christopher up front.'

Lola took the criticism, she knew he was right, but she was surprised that there was no mention of the blunder made by Aaron, their goalkeeper, beaten from the halfway line when he clearly should have saved the shot. She was capable of much better, but tonight her marker had rattled her. So she was surprised when Christopher objected to the change.

'Look, Michael, this is the worst twenty minutes our Lola has played in her life, but she's the reason we're in this final. I think she deserves another five minutes up front before you drop her back.'

Before Michael could reply Christopher turned to Lola giving her a much needed pep talk. 'Come on, Lo, you could run rings around that beef cake with your eyes closed. Don't let him get to ya. Use your skill and speed; he's no match for you! Okay, sis?'

Lola felt like crying, but since Michael was already under attack for having a girl in his team, she wasn't about to compound the situation by acting like one. So she just nodded in agreement as the referee blew his whistle calling both teams back onto the pitch. Taking a quick glance at the sidelines she could see her parents and younger brother Liam amongst the large crowd waving vigorously in support. All the spectators were clapping and shouting now, with one major exception. At the back, stood Sebastian and Lola's biggest critic, Drew, the mocking grin on his face was all the encouragement that she needed. As she continued to run her eyes along the rows of supporters, one face in particular caught her attention. When she turned back to look again he was gone. Lola thought it was Alex but she couldn't be sure.

Determined that she could turn this game around Lola took a deep breath as she stood in the centre circle along with Christopher who was hovering over the football waiting for the referee to restart the game. As the whistle sounded Christopher slid the ball to Lola, creating a bit of space. She passed it to Brendan before turning to make a blistering run up the pitch towards the eighteen-yard-box.

As Lola ran, she knew instinctively that the ball would be played long, allowing her to run onto it. Letting the ball do most of the work she nimbly slipped it past two players and made her way to the last defender. Her tormentor stood with his back to goal as she advanced. Dropping her shoulder to one side, she pretended to go to the left. The defender bought the dummy going left also, so Lola slid the ball between his legs, leaving him rooted to the spot. Pacing towards the goal it was between her and the goalkeeper now.

Revitalised by the cheering crowd, Lola knew there was only going to be one winner in that contest. Lifting back her foot she blasted the ball into the top of the net. The game was level and she still had plenty to offer. Lola now had the measure of the bulky defender, yet he and his side continued to defend well, managing to fend off a great shot from Brendan, which reverberated off the post. The clock was running down and no one wanted extra time.

With just two minutes of normal time remaining Lola received the ball on the right wing, just inside her own half. She edged her way forward, with the support of Michael and Christopher in midfield. Seeing a gap open in the middle of the park, Lola offloaded the ball to Michael, who chipped it beautifully into the penalty box. Lola never once took her eyes off the ball – this was the match winner – but just as she was about to pull the trigger, the burly defender came crashing into her with his foot, crushing her shin.

Lola fell to the ground dazed. The deafening roar of the crowd was all she could hear. Suddenly there was a free for all. As Lola lay wincing in pain, her brothers ran towards the defender and Christopher pushed him to the ground.

'It was a fair challenge, ref!' protested her attacker. 'If she can't take a fair hit, she shouldn't be bloody playing.'

Lola's teammates surrounded the referee calling for a penalty, while she lay trying to get her breath back. Her father had now come onto the pitch, with her mum trying to restrain him.

'Why don't you pick on someone your own size, you prick,' shouted her dad, making his way towards the big defender.

'Get off the pitch, Granda, before you take a heart attack.'

This only incensed her brothers further, as the referee stood blowing his whistle in a futile attempt to regain order. Lola hobbled to her feet, and tried to walk off the injury, calling her teammates away from the referee. The referee sported a scarlet face from all the whistle blowing.

'Are you all right, Lo?' asked Michael as he came to her side, supporting her as she tried to walk normally. 'That dirty bastard,' he fumed.

'Mike, I'm grand. Really, I'll be okay,' reassured Lola, but it felt as though her leg was broken. A roar from the crowd alerted them that the referee had made his decision. Lola smiled as he pointed to the penalty spot and pulled a red a card from his back pocket, which sent the stocky defender off the pitch. Brendan came striding towards her.

'Are you fit to take this, Lo?' he asked hopefully.

'I don't think so, Brendan. Chris will have to take it.'

'Okay, are you alright? I'll get that rat for that,' he said through gritted teeth.

'I'm grand. Forget about him, we've got the winner, that's all we need.'

Marching into the eighteen-yard box, Brendan set the ball onto the penalty spot, as Christopher stood waiting for the referee to blow the whistle. The crowd fell silent, and at the whistle Christopher struck the ball, aiming for the bottom left-hand corner, but unfortunately the keeper read it right, diving to his left he got a fingertip to the ball making a great save.

Lola could only watch as the scene played out in slow motion in front of her. The ball bounced out towards the oncoming defenders, but she hadn't seen Stephen standing on the edge of the penalty box. Sliding in, he managed to get a touch on the ball before the central defender could, beating him and the goal keeper.

After the goal was scored, the referee blew the final whistle, much to the elation of the crowd and the Paige entourage. Running towards her, Lola's brothers hoisted her up on their shoulders, as her mum and dad ran onto the pitch, followed by all her brothers' friends.

Shouts of 'well done' and congratulatory slaps on the back greeted Lola as she limped carefully towards the car, a large lump rising on her shin.

'Where are you going, Lo? Are you not coming out to celebrate with us?' asked Brendan as he walked into the changing room.

'Of course I am, Brendan. I'll meet you all in there, okay? I need to go home and get changed first.'

'Right-oh, don't be long.'

Getting into the car Lola was instinctively heading towards her parents' house, before remembering that most of their stuff had been move to Arthur's. The rest of her family had not fully moved in yet, but she and Aibgrene had been there for a few weeks. Her mum had felt it best for her to be there by herself for a while to get used to the idea, and was delighted when she heard that Aibgrene would be staying with her.

When she arrived at Arthur's house, Lola could tell that Aibgrene had been out in the herb garden again. The smell from one of her concoctions filled the house as Lola came through the front door.

'In here, Lola,' shouted Aibgrene from the kitchen. 'Did you win?'

Lola followed the smell into the large kitchen, where she found her friend standing at the gas range. Aibgrene didn't turn to greet Lola, concentrating hard on the herbs and other unidentified ingredients that she was adding into her black cauldron, now frothing and bubbling on the stove. Lola rolled her eyes in amusement thinking she'd seen it all.

'Double double toil and trouble, fire burn and cauldron bubble,' she mocked, putting on a witch's voice.

If Aibgrene heard her, she refused to acknowledged the jibe and remained busily picking through her tools – as she referred to them – which lay scattered across the oak benches. Finally finding what she was looking for, she lifted the boline, which she used for gathering herbs and plants, and cut the head off a primrose, before adding it to the smoky brew. Since she had discovered Arthur's herb garden, the young hedge witch was like a child in sweet shop. It had gotten to the stage where Lola didn't even ask questions, she was happy to leave her to her work.

'Yes,' shouted Lola, so she would get her attention. 'We did win and we're heading out to the local club to celebrate if you wanna come?'

Aibgrene cut some more primrose and added it to the pot, bending over to inhale the fruity aroma. After washing her hands, she finally turned to Lola.

'Lola! What on earth happened to you! Are you okay?'

Lola nonchalantly remembered her leg injury.

'Oh that? Yeah I'm fine. I told you, we won!'

'If this is what you look like when you win I wouldn't like to see the other team. Sit down, I've got something that can sort that leg out for you,' insisted Aibgrene.

Despite protesting that she was perfectly fine, Lola was forced down onto a chair, while Aibgrene disappeared into the pantry in pursuit of a herbal remedy. Minutes later she emerged with a clear bottle of a yellowish liquid, which resembled urine, and a green candle.

'Really, Aibgrene, I'm fine, the swelling will go down, it's not that bad,' protested Lola.

'Just sit there, it won't take a minute,' demanded Aibgrene. 'The swelling will go down, but I'm afraid I won't be able to stop the bruising.'

Aibgrene lit the candle and began to dab the oily yellow liquid onto to the large lump on Lola's shin.

'What is that stuff?' winced Lola. 'You didn't say it would hurt!'

'It's better that you don't know, now stop being such a baby and sit still.'

'That's encouraging,' moaned Lola, her leg throbbing more than ever. She had almost forgotten about the pain until Aibgrene mentioned it.

'Shush, I need to concentrate,' said Aibgrene, rubbing her hands together for a few moments. She closed her eyes, holding her hands just above the tennis-ball sized lump, murmuring as she moved her hands in a circular motion.

'*Flesh be healthy, spirit strong, dancing feet and joyful song, health restored and revitalised, this leg be recovered before thine eyes.*'

As Aibgrene recited the words over and over, Lola could feel the intensity of the heat from her hands, as the lump began to slowly shrink, until it was hardly visible at all.

'There you are,' said Aibgrene with a bright smile, as she examined her work. 'You're as good as new.'

Lola sat stunned, looking at the place on her leg which just moments ago had been swollen and bruised. 'How did you do that?'

'The power of magick,' laughed Aibgrene. 'Now, are you not supposed to be going dancing?'

Now that she was sitting down, Lola realised how tired she actually felt. She could easily have put on her pyjamas and gone straight to bed, but she didn't want to let her teammates down.

'I suppose I'll go and get ready. Do you fancy coming along?' asked Lola hopefully.

She thought it would do Aibgrene some good to get out of the house for a while and let her hair down. In truth she felt a bit guilty about going out and leaving her on her own.

'Not really my scene, Lo, plus I have been looking at Arthur's log books, and I think I could be on to something, but I would rather be sure first. I'll fill you in when you get home.'

'Are you sure you'll be okay here on your own?'

'Lola, I have never felt safer in my life than I do here,' said Aibgrene reassuringly. 'And besides, I have the mighty Cuchulain here to look after me. Isn't that right, boy?'

'Well if you're sure. I won't be that late anyway, I'm absolutely knackered.'

It didn't take Lola long to get ready. She pulled out the very first dress she saw from her wardrobe. Slipping on the vintage pink summer dress with a peter-pan collar, pussy cat bow and short skirt flaring out from the waist, she matched it up with a pair of pink peep-toe heels that had a little red bow on them. Running the straightening irons down her long hair, she finished off her make-up, applying eye liner and mascara.

After saying goodbye, Lola left Aibgrene – under the protection of Cuchulain – immersed in Arthur's log books in the study, and walked to the end of the snaking driveway to meet her taxi. Her timing was perfect as the cab was coming down the avenue as she closed the gates behind her.

CHAPTER 28

Friday night in Ballyvalley was always a busy night, but the football
final had brought people in from all over the district and surrounding
towns. This meant the local nightclub, Chariots, would be very busy.
On Fridays at Chariots there was a Golden Oldies night, with the DJ
playing sixties and eighties music. Wednesdays and Fridays were the
main nights at the club and during the summer months, it was the
place to be. Lola, Ruby, Clara and Orla were there without fail every
week, but this year it would be different since the girls were in Cape
Cod all summer.

After paying in at the door, Lola made her way up the long dark
corridor, which was lit by blue and white floor lights into the main
disco. There was a huge crowd in tonight and she had to negotiate her
way through the throng. She headed towards the cocktail bar, where
she knew her teammates would be. Sure enough, as she entered the
circular room, with its cushioned booths around the perimeter and
a bar at the centre, she could see the cup which they had won being
passed along a sea of hands, the liquid contents sloshing out of it as it

went. Lola made her way over to her brothers. As she passed through the crowd she felt random pats on the back from well-wishers she had never seen before, congratulating her on her performance. Thanking them as she went, she finally caught up with her brothers who were in high spirits.

'Sis, there you are,' slurred Christopher as he threw his arm around her shoulders. 'Come, on and try some of this stuff – it's rocket fuel,' he laughed.

Taking her by the hand he grabbed the cup from one of the entourage and handed it to Lola, urging her to take a drink. Not wanting to offend, Lola took a mouthful of the cocktail and forced it down her throat.

'What is in that?' spat Lola, trying her best to hold down the volatile mix. 'That's so strong. I think I need to go and get something to wash it down with.'

'Okay,' laughed Chris. 'We're going to head to the dance floor, meet you there. I'll be the one busting the moves.'

'Then I'd better call an ambulance, Chris,' jibed Lola, 'because that could get quite messy.'

Laughing, Lola headed for the bar which was ten deep.

Patiently waiting in line, she finally spotted an opening, as a girl made her way out of the crowd, drinks in hand. Lola was about to slip into the empty spot, until she was obstructed by the same girl who was now gazing doe-eyed at someone behind her.

'Oh hi, do you want this spot?' she asked smiling as if her life had depended on it.

Lola was about to protest, when she heard a familiar voice decline the invitation.

'Thanks very much, but I think that girl was ahead of me.'

The girl turned to look at Lola, as if she had not even noticed she was there, shrugged her shoulders, and made her way out of the crowd. There was a loud drumming noise inside Lola's head, the same sound that she always heard when Alex Stein was around. She was sure he could sense this. Pretending that she hadn't noticed Alex, Lola waited patiently for the barman to take her order. All the while she could feel Alex close behind her. Finally the barman got to her. Lola ordered a cranberry juice and then waited for what seemed an eternity before it was set in front of her.

'That'll be two-thirty please,' said the barman.

Lola was about to hand over the money, when she felt a hand on hers.

'It's alright, Lola, I'll get this,' said Alex. 'Just try not to throw this one all over yourself – that's a lovely dress, you wouldn't want to ruin it.'

Lola could hear the humour in his voice, but she didn't offer any reply. She was momentarily stunned by the touch of Alex Stein's perfectly smooth hands on hers, and by the electricity that erupted throughout her entire body. Still with her back to him, she pulled her hand away and paid the barman, who was now looking impatient.

'It's okay, I'll pay for it,' she smiled, handing the barman a ten-pound note. She waited for her change.

'You still playing hard to get, Lola?' laughed Alex, with his usual confident delivery. Lola paused to collect her thoughts before turning to him.

As always, he looked extremely handsome, dressed in loose jeans and a designer navy cardigan, with a crisp white t-shirt underneath. Lola took a drink to settle the butterflies dancing about her stomach.

'Playing, Alex? I don't play,' she said beaming up at him. 'I am hard to get, and, unlike the women you're used to socialising with, I prefer to pay my own way. But thanks for the offer.'

Smiling serenely, she left Alex Stein at the bar and headed for the dark of the dance floor as quickly as possible, her heart still in her mouth. The crowd in the club had doubled since Lola came in and it was a struggle to find her brothers. After a few laps of the dance floor, they were nowhere to be seen. Tired, she decided to call it a night and left.

The cool night air offered a stark contrast to the over-crowded and sticky heat of the club, so Lola decided to make the most of it and walk the short journey home. She crossed over the river, making her way towards the most popular take-away restaurant in town. There were already a lot of people outside the shop eating their chips and hamburgers; some looked as though their night had ended early, having had too much to drink.

Lola was walking past the restaurant when she heard someone calling her name. Turning around, she smiled when Sebastian emerged from the chip shop with a large box full of chips and chicken. It smelt delicious, reminding Lola that she hadn't actually eaten all day.

'Want a chip?' he grinned, sticking the box under her nose.

'Are you heading home early tonight, Seb?' asked Lola as she plucked a few chips out of the box.

'Yeah. You could hardly get moving in there tonight. Are you walking home on your own?'

Lola was oblivious to the subtle implication in Sebastian's voice. When it came to boys and her, she usually was a bit slow. She could never see the signs, or tell if they liked her, unless they made it really obvious. Lola's mouth was full, so she just nodded until she finished her chips, they were delicious.

'I'm just heading home now, I'm so tired. It's been a long day.'

'Well done by the way, you were amazing,' enthused Sebastian, his dark almond eyes glistening.

Lola, as always, fobbed off the compliment by changing the subject to work and the paper. Suddenly their conversation was interrupted by the loud roar of an engine as a flash black sports car accelerated towards the chip shop. Lola took a quick glance, rolling her eyes in distain as she turned back to Sebastian. She was never impressed by the boy-racer type, doing laps around the town at night in their fancy cars, trying to impress members of the opposite sex.

The car pulled up at the kerb just behind them, and the crowd outside fell silent admiring it. Lola tried to see what the fuss was about, but the people around the car, most of whom were male, obscured it and the driver from view. It must have been quite a car judging from the 'hmmms' and 'aaahs' that were being uttered.

A tall ginger-haired boy came out of the shop with a mouth full of chips, the contents of which dropped to the floor when he saw the small black streamlined car crawl to a stop at the kerb.

'Oh my God,' he spat excitedly, 'a top of the range Audi R8. No way! Move over there, lads, let me get a look at that thing.' Pushing his way through the crowd he began to touch and stroke the car like it was some ancient priceless treasure.

'Idiots!' laughed Lola, bemused at the notion that a piece of metal with four wheels could evoke such emotions. 'Listen, Seb, I'd better get a move on, I'm starting to wish I had worn a coat.'

'You can't walk back on your own, it's dangerous, let me walk you home.'

'Don't be silly,' laughed Lola. 'I'll be fine, it's two minutes up the road. Anyway, you live on the opposite side of town. Who would be walking you home?' joked Lola, unaware that she had given Sebastian the brush off.

Clearly disappointed by her gentle snub, Sebastian accepted defeat and returned to his friends, who had all been watching the car intently. As Lola made her way up through the centre of town, the car that had everyone transfixed was on the move again, its loud purr echoing off the shop windows on both sides of the street.

The car was slowly moving alongside the kerbside giving Lola a chance to look at it. The windows like the paint were black, save for a red flash at the side of the car running from the roof to the back wheels. She couldn't see the driver as the windows were tinted. Feeling a little self-conscious that whoever was in the car could see her, she put her head down and continued to walk, trying to ignore it.

Suddenly there was a toot of the horn, making her jump slightly. Refusing to acknowledge it she lifted her head and tried to cross the road, but the car accelerated, forcing her back onto the pavement. Setting her foot tentatively onto the road again, the car jutted forward, causing Lola to jump back.

'Wise up will you, if you're going, then go!' shouted Lola at no one in particular.

Reluctant to walk out in front of it again, she tried walking around the back of the car, but the driver put the car in reverse. Then it dawned on Lola that there was only one person that she knew who would be so annoying and rich enough to own a car like this one. Just as she realised this, the electric window glided down, revealing an amused Alex Stein.

'Can I give you lift, Lola?' beamed Alex, clearly impressed with himself.

Lola struggled to keep a smile from spreading across her face; he was beginning to wear her down, and if she was honest she was quite enjoying the attention. Even though every part of her being was propelling her towards the car, and the gorgeous Alex, something else was holding her back. It was like she was fighting a bitter-sweet force field every time she was around him, and like the forbidden fruit, it was tantalising.

'Thank you, but I'm fine. It's a lovely night and I don't mind the walk.'

Just as she spoke those words the treacherous sky betrayed her and the heavens opened up with rain. In a matter of seconds Lola was totally saturated, her pink dress almost transparent as the relentless rain continued to fall.

'Lola, stop being such an idiot, and get in,' pleaded Alex. 'You're going to catch your death out there!'

Reaching over, he flicked the handle and the passenger door swung open. The seats were very low and Lola struggled to get into the soft white leather seat with any elegance. She had hardly the door closed when Alex hit the accelerator and headed towards the Scarvagh Road. The seat was heated and while she welcomed the warmth of the car, the window began to steam up as the damp rose from her wet body.

'How do you know where I live?' asked Lola, as Alex headed in the right direction.

'I don't,' he smiled. 'Just a lucky guess I suppose.'

Alex continued to look at Lola from the corner of his eye, examining her shapely legs. Her skin was pale, but it suited her and he liked it. The rain had soaked her dress through and her underwear was clearly visible through the thin pink cotton, another reason why he couldn't take his eyes off her.

'So where to now?' asked Alex as he hit the volume button on his sound system, the Arctic Monkeys booming out. They were one of Lola's favourite bands and it was their first album he was playing.

'You like the Arctic Monkeys?' asked Lola clearly impressed. 'I didn't think that would be your thing at all.'

'So what did you think would be my thing?' retorted Alex rolling his eyes, clearly anticipating Lola's insult.

'I don't know,' she laughed. 'I suppose one of those manufactured boy bands – something you could relate to.'

'Do you ever quit, Lola? Are you always going to be this impossible?' said Alex, his cold blue eyes seeming to soften as he held her gaze.

Lola wiped the window and realised that they were now halfway up the Scarvagh Road, just as her favourite song came on.

'Now that's what I call timing,' laughed Alex. 'That song suits you perfectly.'

'I'm not a Mardy Bum,' said Lola, a bit defensively.

'Whatever you think, Lola,' smiled Alex. 'Where to?'

'Oh just on up the road a bit. You see those two small gatehouses on the right-hand side of the road, just turn in there.'

Alex could feel the tension in the car. He could not quite place the feeling he was experiencing, the same feeling he had every time he was near Lola. It was like she was drawing him in, he could feel her energy, and he could feel how pure and strong it was. Checking out her legs again he could see the tiny white particles that still clung to a certain spot – it looked like magick to him, but he couldn't be sure.

'Did you hurt your leg?' asked Alex.

The question was already out before he'd even thought about it. There was no visible evidence to suggest that she'd had an injury. He cursed himself as Lola's reaction gave him all the confirmation that he needed.

'No, no, it's fine! Why, what made you ask that?'

'I just thought there was a bit of bruising on it, that's all.'

'Are you looking at my legs, Alex?' mused Lola mischievously, trying to embarrass him, but her question did not have the desired effect.

'Yes I am,' replied Alex serious now as he stopped the car at the large gateposts.

The rain seemed to intensify with his stare, and Lola couldn't break away from it. What was she doing? How did she get herself into this situation? They sat in silence. Lola kept telling herself to get out of the car, but her legs and body refused to move. Leaning in closer Alex could smell her hair, which smelled of apples. Stroking the side of her face he tucked a loose strand of hair behind her ear. Lola couldn't move; it was like he held her in some sort of trance. She sat hardly breathing now, as Alex gently cupped her face in his hands, he moved closer, his tongue tracing a line across her lips, unsure if she was going to reciprocate. But despite what her head was yelling at her, Lola didn't recoil. She couldn't restrain herself, lifting her hands she ran them along his muscular shoulders and neck, pulling him closer. She could taste his hot minty breath as she returned the kiss.

Every part of her body began to explode, and her lips reciprocated with the same intensity. Alex ran his warm tongue along her mouth, sensing that bitter-sweet thrill of submission and resistance running through her body all at once. Lola could no longer hear the rain pelting on the roof of the car, all she could hear was the pounding of her own heart as it nosily filled her ears.

Finally breaking apart, it took them both a few seconds to reorientate. Lola felt embarrassed and vulnerable, the game was up, and Alex Stein had won. He had gotten to her, broken her down bit by bit, but there was no trace of his victory on his face. He lifted Lola's chin up to meet those intense blue eyes, which were now glowing.

'You're not blushing are you, Lola?' he smiled gently.

'Just a bit,' replied Lola honestly. 'I didn't put up much of a fight, did I?'

'You lasted longer than most, but they all come round in the end, so don't beat yourself up.'

'You are so full of yourself,' laughed Lola, hitting Alex a punch on the arm playfully, before jumping out of the car to open the gates. The rain had eased up, but Lola was still soaked through, and her body began to shiver as she fumbled with the key trying to use the car's headlights to her advantage.

It was only when the car door was open that Alex sensed the force field around the large estate. It hit him immediately. He began to panic, there was no way he would be able to cross the threshold. Sitting rigid in the driver seat, he watched as Lola unlocked the gates, trying to figure out how he was going to get out of this one. Starting up the engine again he noticed a large dog trotting up the path towards Lola.

'Cuchulain, you big wolf, what are you doing out on a night like this?'

Looking straight past Lola, at the car, the large Irish wolfhound's ears pricked up. Arching his back he bent into a predatory crouch snarling at Alex. Lola had never seen Cuchulain react so aggressively towards anyone before, and she stood momentarily shocked, as the normally placid hound lurched towards the car snapping his teeth and barking.

Alex closed the door of the car quickly, as Lola tried to restrain the dog.

'Cuchulain, stop! What's gotten into you? You silly mutt,' said Lola, as Aibgrene appeared suddenly at her side, helping her to pull the dog back. It took all their strength to restrain him. Aibgrene strained to see the person inside the car; she knew that the dog sensed something was not right. As Lola approached the car apologetically, Alex wound down the window, the concern on her face breaking his concentration momentarily.

'I'm so sorry, Alex; I don't know what's got into him. He's never like this.'

'Don't be silly, Lola,' grinned Alex. 'He's just protective, that's all.'

Lola was embarrassed, she had never witnessed Cuchulain behave like that before. 'Are you sure you're okay?'

'I am, Lola,' reassured Alex. 'I'm fine. I better go, I'll see you soon.'

Alex exchanged a brief glance with the girl who was still straining to keep the dog at bay. He could tell that she was curious about who he was, and when he saw her face he understood why.

Alex turned the car, and sped off up the avenue. Closing the gate behind her, Lola caught up with Aibgrene and Cuchulain, now transformed back into the temperate creature Lola knew him to be.

'So who was that?' asked Aibgrene.

There was something in her tone that put Lola on the defensive straight away.

'Oh, just a fella I know, he gave me a lift home,' replied Lola flippantly.

'So, does this fella have a name?' continued Aibgrene.

'Alex, Alex Stein,' replied Lola.

Aibgrene had thought she recognised him and judging by the car it made sense.

'Do you know him?' enquired Lola, detecting from Aibgrene's reaction that she might. Ruby was right, thought Lola, everyone knew Alex.

'I know of him, and his father. Not a bit of wonder Cuchulain went berserk, he must be a good judge of character.'

Again that wave of embarrassment came over Lola. After all, this was the second person in as many days that she'd spoken to about Alex Stein, and they both seemed less than impressed. Just as she had been the first time they had met, she began to think that perhaps her gut feeling about Alex was right after all.

'Don't you like him?' asked Lola trying not to give her feelings away.

'They own Stein Corporations!' said Aibgrene, as if she had said something bad. Lola remained silent letting her explain. 'Well, Stein Corporations is a large development and regeneration company, and I use the term regeneration very loosely,' scoffed Aibgrene. 'All they really care about are their coffers and making money. We used to have our shop in North Street Arcade, but it was mysteriously burnt down, and then all of a sudden Stein Corporations bought the complex for redevelopment.'

'Do you think they were behind it?' asked Lola, a hint dismissively.

'Judging by the way Cuchulain reacted to your friend I wouldn't be surprised,' suggested Aibgrene, wondering again, as she had done many times before, what special qualities Arthur had seen in Lola. It was obvious that she had a beautiful soul, her light energy was clear for all to see, but she was naive about the world she was living in.

'He's not as bad as you think,' defended Lola lamely. 'He's okay when you get under all that arrogance and pretence.'

It sounded as though she was trying to convince herself more than anyone else.

'And you've clearly managed to do that then,' laughed Aibgrene, nudging Lola gently with her elbow.

'Behave, Miss Moone!'

'Well come on, dish the dirt. I couldn't really get a good look at him, but from what I did see, he's certainly handsome and rich,' commented Aibgrene. 'That's a top of the range R8 he's driving and those things retail at about one hundred k.'

Lola looked at Aibgrene, feeling a little bemused.

'Aren't you quite the little petrol-head? I thought a car like that would go against your green morals? You being a big tree hugger and all that!'

'Humph, you're one to talk. I thought a boy like that would be against your morals, you being a socialist and all that!' countered Aibgrene.

'Touché,' conceded Lola smiling.

'Well, we're all allowed our guilty pleasures, Lola. Supercars are mine, and arrogant rich boys seem to be yours. Come on, we may get you inside before you catch your death! No wonder he couldn't take his eyes off you, you can practically see through that dress! Here put this on,' said Aibgrene in a motherly tone, as she handed her coat to Lola. Slipping her arms into the padded jacket, Lola was grateful for the warmth. 'While you've been out courting, Ms Paige, I have been a very busy girl, and I may have a bit more information about Arthur's master plan.'

Over the last couple of weeks, with the football final and her work at the newspaper, Lola hadn't been able to spend as much time with her new friend as she would have liked, or maybe she was only fooling herself. Maybe it suited her that way. Aibgrene must have anticipated an oncoming apology, because before Lola could speak, she shook her head to dismiss it.

'There's no need to apologise, Lola, you will come good. I know it. I understand how very hard all this must be. You deserve to let your hair down and pretend your life is normal every now and then,' said Aibgrene soothingly.

She had completely understood how Lola was feeling, but Lola knew that she couldn't hide behind things forever.

'You are glowing tonight,' declared Aibgrene, as she looked around Lola. 'You must really like this Alex Stein.'

'I think I might,' giggled Lola, as she led Aibgrene and Cuchulain in through the door.

CHAPTER 29

It was almost four in morning when Alex pulled his car into the double garage of Chateau Bacchus. The wind was howling around the large stone edifice that was his home and he could hear the white frothy waves as they crashed off the side of the cliffs below. Taking the lift from the garage to the second floor of the house, he emerged at the top of the hallway just outside his father's library where his own large bedroom lay.

At first content that he had avoided his father, he froze when he heard voices coming from his library. The strong wind outside was barely audible inside the house, but it was still loud enough to make it difficult to hear what was being said. Knowing that his father would want a full account of the night's events, Alex stood in the hallway to compose himself.

He thought about going straight to the shower to wash away what was written all over him. He felt weak whenever he was with Lola because of the way she made him feel, or rather because she could make him feel. He could tell how unsure she was about him tonight. He could tell that she didn't trust him. He knew she'd been very cautious in letting her defences fall, but for the first time in his life he appreciated this.

Alex knew this girl was different, he genuinely cared what she thought about him, he wanted her to feel the same way he did, and this upset him – Lola Paige was getting to him. He thought about her constantly, and each time she left he couldn't wait until he saw her again. His father would sense it immediately, and this terrified him; everything would be compromised, he had to gain control of the situation and quickly. But he was not sure how to do that, as he had never had to in the past. Alex thought about cutting all contact with Lola, but realised that was out of the question. His father was aware of the link between Lola and the old man, and he expected Alex to make full use of that. Besides, he would only be fooling himself if he thought he could stay away from her. She was infectious, so different, so refreshing.

Standing in the dimly lit hallway, Alex could hear the faint voice of a woman. It was soft, tranquil, and even though there was an edge of pain to it, her voice was still very composed. There was something melodic in the way she spoke that sounded vaguely familiar to him, like he had heard it countless times before. But he knew this was impossible because he had never laid eyes on Celeste Moone, until he'd seen her on the floor of his father's room weeks ago. Alex stepped towards the door, but stopped dead when he heard the change of tone in his father's voice, he was readying some form of punishment.

'What does she know, Celeste?' asked Carl Stein aggressively.

He could tell that his father was growing more and more irate. Carl had been trying to break Celeste Moone's spirit for the last couple of weeks, but to Alex's surprise she was somehow holding out, despite the odds. His father's power was growing more intense, and he could tell that Carl was enjoying the little resistance that Celeste could muster. The fact she had withstood so much punishment already told Alex that she was a very powerful witch indeed. But there was no doubt in Alex's mind that his father was keeping her alive for some reason; otherwise he would have disposed of her long ago.

'What does who know, Carl?' wheezed Celeste.

'Don't play games with me, woman. You know we have no secrets.'

Celeste let out a laboured snort.

'Secrets and lies, Carl, you would know all about those, wouldn't you?'

Carl Stein was momentarily caught unaware. He admired Celeste, and always had, she was a very powerful and astute exponent, despite the fact that she was female and on the wrong side. It shouldn't have surprised him that she had finally put it all together, but it did.

'So have you told Alex all your secrets, Carl? Does he know who he is and what you did?'

Celeste's words were so loaded that the pain and hurt spilled through in each syllable. Carl knew the damage that she could cause with this information; he had worked tirelessly to protect Alex from it. Yet, knowing that she could still ruin everything, he decided that he needed Celeste for just a little bit longer.

'What does he know, Carl?' goaded Celeste. 'What does Alex know?'

For the first time Carl Stein's composure broke. Alex stood hardly breathing, listening behind the door. There was a loud slapping noise as if someone had been struck.

'Don't you ever dare speak his name, you filthy witch!' shouted Carl.

Alex could hear that his father's breathing was heavy now, as if he had put all his force into the blow. With all his powers Carl had no need to physically attack his subjects, this was most unlike him, clearly the woman had touched a nerve. Unsure what to do Alex went to move away, but a creak in the floor gave him away. Composing himself, he knocked the door and entered the large vaulted library to find his father sitting exhausted behind his desk with Celeste Moone lying unconscious on the floor. The blood oozed from the side of her mouth where his father's ring had caught her.

Startled, Carl Stein got up to greet his son.

'Alex! I wasn't expecting you tonight, when did you get back?'

Alex had never seen his father so dishevelled before, but there was something else, something that he would never have believed was possible. His father was afraid. He clearly feared the frail woman that lay in front of him. It was unmistakeable, his father feared what Celeste Moone knew, and he knew that his son could see this.

'I've just got in this minute, Father, and I have some news that may be of use,' said Alex, ignoring Celeste as she lay unconscious on the floor, while he filled his father in on the night's events. He, of course, omitted the part about falling for his nemesis.

'So this Lola Paige is now living in the Delphian Estate with the Moone girl? How do you know it was her?'

'I caught a quick glimpse of her as I was leaving. She's very like her mother, same long golden hair,' said Alex, nodding towards Celeste who was now beginning to stir.

'That is very interesting, if she wasn't aware of what she has in her possession, then she is now. Our contact confirmed that Arthur was very fond of the girl, and that she was at the cremation, which means she knows about the Order and the Club. And let's not forget she's also been to see Felix, although that could just have been about Arthur's Estate.'

Alex watched his father continue to pace up and down as he talked out loud.

'Were you with her tonight, Alex?' he asked Alex directly.

'I managed to convince her to take a lift. She's cautious, Father. Do you think she suspects something?'

Deep in thought, Carl Stein shook his head. 'I don't think so. Look what happened when that street urchin tried to snatch her bag, that was magick, but our source is certain she knows nothing of magick. Mmmm, I wonder…'

Carl Stein's mood had changed, buoyed by his own revelations. 'The only kind of magick that could offer that level of protection would be an amulet or talisman. It would have to be very strong indeed. We haven't had any luck in tracking Markus down, he has gone into hiding, and from what we know, he's made no attempt to get in touch with the Order or the girl.'

Alex stood in silence as his father continued. He had never seen him so frenetic before, he was always calm and collected.

'It must be Delphian's ring. She must have his ring.'

'I'm not sure, Father, I would have noticed it on one of her fingers, I'm sure of it. I would have been able to sense such powerful magick.'

'Not necessarily, Alex.'

His father's cold stare ran through him like a knife and he knew that his anxiety had finally registered with him. Like a blood hound his father could smell fear a mile off.

'You would not have sensed it if your head was elsewhere, but now is not the time to move, Alex, you need to gain her trust. I need you to get close to this girl, to find out what she knows, then we can make our move. In the meantime, we need to arrange for a little breaking and entering.'

'That might not be a very good idea,' replied Alex. 'The place is under some sort of protection spell. It starts from the main gatepost to the house, I could feel it. There is no way it would have let me pass through. It has multiple layers and seems to work on a level I have not seen before.'

His father considered this for a moment, the force field would cause problems, but nothing they couldn't overcome.

'That's only a minor setback, Alex,' he said assuredly, a dark smile spreading across his face as he let out a chuckle. 'This is just too easy – what an old fool. He has put all his faith in some working-class student, thinking that she could somehow outwit me.'

Celeste had come to in time to hear most of the exchange, but that was not what interested her. What interested her was the subtle shift in Alex's demeanour when his father spoke about Lola, which gave her hope and the promise of more time. But Carl had finally discovered Lola, and there was little Celeste could do to protect her. The only comfort now was that Aibgrene was with her at the manor. She knew they would be safe there, after all she had been with Arthur when the various enchantments were placed over the estate. She tried to get up again, but Carl Stein was soon standing over her, the same taunting smirk on his face.

'It looks like you were telling the truth, Celeste. You could still be of some use to me! I think it's time to restore you to full health. I'd like to save you for a special occasion. Then the pair will be complete!'

Nodding to his bulky bodyguard, Carl Stein motioned towards Celeste.

'Derek, kindly escort our esteemed guest back to her quarters,' he ordered.

The bodyguard grabbed Celeste by the arm, and hoisted her limp body off the floor, throwing her over his shoulder. She hardly had the energy to speak, but managed a faint whisper as she passed Alex on the way out the door.

'You love her.'

Alex didn't flinch, his face like stone as he pretended not to hear her, though his insides were churning.

'This Lola Paige needs to be taken care of, Alex. She has the Cosmic Cube, I'm sure of it, and the best part about that is that the stupid girl probably has no idea that she has it.'

Laughing, Carl Stein poured himself a glass of his favourite bourbon before sitting back down, his composure now fully restored.

'I'm actually quite intrigued as to what Arthur saw in this girl, why her? I think I would actually like to meet her.'

Alex's stomach tightened in a knot, his father was quick to notice it this time.

'What is it, Alex?' he asked.

'It's just been a long day, Father; I'm going to go to bed, good night.'

Turning to leave he froze in the doorway as his father spoke.

'So, when will you invite her to dinner?'

'As soon as I can, it shouldn't be too much trouble,' replied Alex, confidently returning his father's grin.

Leaving the room he felt sick. he wasn't a bit tired, there was no way that he would be able to sleep. He was relieved that his father had been so preoccupied when he entered the room that he had not sensed how nervous Alex was. Suddenly Celeste's words came back to him, 'You love her'.

There was such hope and relief in the way she had said it. How could she have known that, when even he didn't? A fresh wave of panic began to erupt inside him as he knew that his father had an inkling of something, but then Alex had seen a different side to him tonight. Clearly his father and Celeste knew each other, what secrets was she referring to?

Without thinking about what he was doing, Alex made his way to the kitchen and then to the east wing of the house, to a small room where Celeste Moone lay.

CHAPTER 30

Whatever Celeste was talking about, she had clearly rattled his father. Opening the door, the light from the hallway spilled into the darkened room, and Alex could see that Celeste lay curled up on the bed like a child. Her state was deteriorating; he recognised the effect of his father's poisonous brand of magick. It was invading her body, despite her best attempts to repel it.

All his life Alex had been sure of who he was and what his role was. He had been brought up to have no mercy for the weak – it was his birth right to keep the masses ignorant and subjugated. He would one day take over his father's mantle, in the meantime his wealth and good looks always ensured that he got what he wanted. Women were there for his enjoyment, pawns in the larger game, he used them and disposed of them as and when he pleased. Their lives were honoured in the best way as a sacrifice to their deity. That's what he had been raised to believe. Survival of the fittest was the natural order of the universe.

But lately, he had been growing weary of this way of thinking. There was a constant voice deep inside him that began to question it all. He was unsure whether he wanted to follow in his father's footsteps, he often felt ashamed, feeble and scared that his father would not accept or tolerate weakness.

Standing in the doorway staring at the pitiful figure before him, Alex couldn't help but feel bad. Celeste didn't turn to look at him; she seemed to know it was him. Her breath was laboured, and her mouth was dry and cracked, as she tried to speak. Alex didn't know what to say, though he knew that Celeste wanted him to hear something. He walked into the room and set the water, bread and fruit that he had taken from the kitchen onto the small French table that sat beside Celeste's stark bed. He knew it was wrong for him to go to her, even stupid and reckless. But as he was about to leave, he heard Celeste's hoarse voice and stopped.

'You are so like her, Alex, more than you know.'
Initially Alex thought that Celeste was talking about Lola. But the sadness in her voice made him think otherwise. Still he couldn't speak; he just stood there close to the doorway as Celeste began to sob.

'How did I not know? I loved her so much.'
Alex couldn't understand what she was saying, who she was talking about. Then Celeste dropped the bomb shell.

'Your mother, how did I not know? What sort of person abandons their sister?' continued Celeste, sobbing uncontrollably.

Alex's head began to spin and his knees felt weak. He quickly left the room, closing the door behind him without a word. He stood outside for a moment; Celeste was alone again in her cell, she was lying, trying to trick him. He reasoned with himself that it was all a lie; she could sense his weakness and was trying to turn him against his father. Climbing the large staircase to his room, he removed his clothes and fell into bed in a daze. Lying in the dark, he listened to the wind and rain as it lashed at his window, struggling to make sense of what he was feeling. What was happening to him?

He tried to tell himself that this feeling would pass, and for a moment it did. But then he realised that ever since the night he had met Lola something in him had changed. That first night, standing staring into Lola's vivid green eyes, a transformation in him had occurred. It was like she had reached into the dark depths of his soul each time she looked at him, igniting it with pure light. But his feelings for her would have to be suppressed at all costs. She was now standing in the way of his destiny and that could not be tolerated. He knew that she would have to be terminated.

Lola's humanity and light energy were infectious, and he knew that once his father met her he would see this immediately. His father would then realise that she was neither common nor stupid, and as a result would want her for himself. His father would greedily consume the powerful force within her, and there was nothing that Alex would be able to do to prevent it.

Alex lay in the dark with Lola, his father, the Club and his mother all racing through his mind. The storm beyond the stillness of his bedroom continued, perfectly mirroring the internal tempest that raged deep within his soul.

CHAPTER 31

Lola woke the next morning to the sound of her mother's voice echoing off the large entrance hall at Brook Mill Manor. Eileen Paige was stressed, Lola could tell from her high-pitched tone. It sounded as though she was directing the delivery men to the various rooms with the countless boxes from their old house. It had been emotional leaving 33 Cottage Park, she and her brothers had never known anywhere else. Her parents had debated whether to move into Brook Mill Manor at all, but Lola couldn't bear to see it go to someone else. Arthur had left it to them, and although it had initially been difficult for her to be there without him, it was much better than the thought of some stranger living in it. So eventually the Paige family officially moved into the Estate.

It took Lola and her siblings some time to get used to having so much space. They had to acclimatise themselves to running from one end of the house to the other in order to find each other. Her brothers all had their own rooms now, whereas previously they had to share, four of them in two sets of bunk beds. Being an only girl, Lola had been used to having her own room, and she decided to keep the large spacious room next to Arthur's library and observatory for her own use.

There was a large king-sized bed in it and the several rectangular windows brought in the morning light. She had a wonderful view of the sprawling green lawns, which were flanked by beds of lavender and roses. The room was painted a pale grey, which added to the airy feel of the place. Most of her stuff still lay in boxes, as she hadn't got around to unpacking it yet. Just off her room lay a large dressing room with built-in wardrobes and a long antique mirror, next to that was her en-suite. Apart from the fireplace, this was Lola's favourite part of her new bedroom. The bathroom had an antique bath which sat in the centre of the large room, perched on four golden paws. Directly above the bath the ceiling was painted a beautiful midnight blue spotted with tiny golden stars. At night, when lying in the bath, Lola would extinguish all the lights, and lie gazing at the starry firmament embedded into the ceiling, it was enchanting.

Lola's mum hadn't stopped since moving in, working day and night to make new curtains and quilt covers for the boys' rooms, and she finally was beginning to put her own touch into the house. Her father and Liam, her youngest brother, helped in the gardens. To Liam, Brook Mill Manor was wonderland, so many rooms and cellars to explore, and with Cuchulain at his side, he was never short of an adventure.

By now Aibgrene had settled into Brook Mill Manor like one of the family, and Lola noticed that Liam was not the only brother who seemed fascinated by her – Christopher also seemed to be hanging around a lot lately.

Arthur's library soon became headquarters, where the pair of them went to mull things over. Lola had managed to find a white board, and they had the library set out like an investigation room, with all the information they had to date on the board and on random pieces of paper. This would have taken a lot of explaining, had anyone walked in on them, but they were never disturbed. Her brothers and parents seemed to accept that this was Lola's private place, where she could be closest to Arthur, and they respected that. Liam would often try to get a sneak peak at what they were doing, and for weeks he had been trying to figure out how the door unlocked, but much to his exasperation he hadn't managed it yet and Lola was confident that he wouldn't.

Work was going to be busy for Lola; she would now be making up news and sports pages as well as having to find enough copy to fill them. She was beginning to feel a little stretched, working as hard on their investigations as she did in the office. Aibgrene had been working on her own during the day, but together, they seemed to be getting nowhere in their investigations, which was frustrating.

Stretching in bed, just awake, Lola thought briefly about her encounter with Alex the night before, but she was quickly reminded how every part of her body ached after the gruelling football match. She could easily have gone back to sleep, but checking her watch, she couldn't believe that she had slept until noon, half the day was gone already. Pulling her dressing gown on over her flannel pyjamas, she headed to the kitchen for a cup of tea.

She could hear her father scolding Liam, who'd been messing about with the service bells again. The bells had been installed when the house was built over two hundred years ago. Liam thought this was fantastic, no matter what room you were in you could call for service. Lola had been similarly impressed when she had first discovered them, and knew that the novelty would soon wear off.

Passing the library on her way downstairs, Lola heard Aibgrene talking to herself. Popping her head around the door, all she could see were Aibgrene's feet on the top step of the staircase, the rest of her body having disappeared through the ceiling level to the highest shelves.

'Talking to yourself? That's a sign of madness, you know?' shouted Lola, before taking a seat on Arthur's rocking chair.

'You didn't decide to get up did you, sleepy head?' said Aibgrene looking exhausted as she descended the spiral staircase. There were dark rings underneath her eyes and her hair was even more unruly than normal.

'By the look of you, you didn't get any sleep,' remarked Lola concerned.

'I didn't,' said Aibgrene. 'What time is it?' Her face was serious now, the tiredness showing.

'Just after 12, what kept you up all night, Aibgrene?'

'A few things. I had to make the most of the full moon, and then, like I told you, I had been looking at Arthur's log books, which led me to other things.'

'Why didn't you waken me? I could have helped you,' replied Lola.

Walking over towards Lola, Aibgrene closed the door, and then took a seat in front of her.

'I discovered a few things last night, Lola, but I wanted to be sure before I said anything. To be honest,' said Aibgrene, yawning and rubbing her eyes, 'it has given me more questions than answers.'

Lola was excited to hear what she had to say, but her friend looked like she needed some rest.

'Aibgrene, you look dead on your feet. Why don't you go and get some sleep and then we can talk about it. We've waited this long, I'm sure a few more hours won't make much difference.'

Aibgrene didn't protest, instead she handed Lola a dusty book in a red casing. It looked and smelt old.

'Have a look at that, it might make things a bit clearer for you later,' said Aibgrene, as she got up and left the room, heading for bed.

Tucking the book into the pocket of her dressing gown, Lola headed towards the noisy kitchen to get some breakfast. There were boxes everywhere, some with labels and some without. Lola still felt a little groggy as she took a seat at the large oak table in the kitchen. She was just in time as her mum was filling the kettle.

'Morning, love, or should I say afternoon,' shouted Eileen from across the spacious kitchen. 'Did you have a good night last night?'

'Yeah, I didn't stay long, Mum. I was home early. I was tired.'

'Unlike your brothers, they're still in their beds. They didn't come in until eight this morning. They'll have right sore heads today!' fussed Eileen as she filled the teapot, getting some cups ready.

Lola sat and chatted to her mum for a while before heading back up to the book room. She always felt closer to Arthur in there, and despite having spent most of her time in the study, she hadn't yet ventured up the spiral stairs to his observatory.

She stood at the bottom of the oak steps, and decided now was the time. Slowly she climbed up the spiral staircase, finally passing into the upper observatory. Nothing had changed since the last time she was up there – the circular room, with its large iron dome and the moderate telescope that sat in the middle. The few books that lay on the shelves beside Arthur's writing bureau had been disturbed, and

Aibgrene had left the light on. About ten dusty logbooks sat opened on the walnut desk along with a very old copy of Johannes Kepler's Mysterium Cosmographicum written in 1596. Very heavy reading indeed.

Over the years Lola had picked up the history of astronomy and its main exponents, but it was a very complicated area of study, and once maths and equations were thrown in, she was lost. Yet one thing had stuck with her and that was the majesty and the perfect order that existed in the universe and in every living thing. Despite her distaste for maths, she could see that it provided the script to the universe's divine order and majesty.

As Lola looked around the sparse room, she felt as if Arthur was still present, his memory lingered in every crevice and corner of her mind and this large house. She remembered being an eight-year-old child gazing into the large telescope for the first time, how Arthur had introduced her to the heavens and all its wonders. Constellations, galaxies, nebula. That feeling of awe and wonder had never left her. Lola always had an insatiable desire for knowledge, even if the topics, as she thought, were well beyond her intellect.

She took a seat at the bureau, running her eyes over the page that Aibgrene had been reading. It was Kepler's model of measuring space between the orbits of the planets. The language was very complex, but Lola remembered Arthur explaining how groundbreaking the model was at the time. Kepler had thought that he had discovered God's Blueprint, like Euclid, Pythagoras and Plato before him, he used what was known as the Polyhedra or the so-called 'perfect solids' to explain the order and shape of our universe.

According to the sixteenth-century German astronomer, the perfect solids consisted of five three-dimensional shapes, each different, but whose faces were all identical. Kepler even made a diagram to illustrate this, a replica of which sat in the corner of the observatory. Lola walked over to the large copper spherical object that sat on four legs; the instrument had always fascinated her.

It was like gazing into time itself with its layers upon layers. It seemed infinite to her. Inside the first circle was a six-sided cube, inside the glass cube lay another smaller circle, which housed a pyramid with four sides, then inside the pyramid was another circle and inside a dodecagon, with twelve sides, then as Lola gazed deeper, she could see another circle. This time the shape inside it was an icosahedron which had twenty sides and finally inside yet another circle lay a three-dimensional octagon. Lola's head was dizzy.

Her concentration was broken by a movement downstairs. Thinking it was Aibgrene, she made her way down, and was surprised to find DCI Campbell standing examining the painting on the roof.

'Excuse me, but how did you get in here, Detective?' she asked, thinly veiling her annoyance. Unperturbed, the young detective met Lola with a warm smile.

'Lola, just the person I'm after. You're brother Liam said I'd probably find you up here.'

Lola's temper began to flare, as the detective scanned his eyes across the room. 'I see you found the key then?' The remark caught Lola unaware. 'The key to the room, we couldn't get in here, when we first came to the manor. A pity really, this is really worth seeing.'

'I take it you didn't come here to admire the view, Detective. How can I help you?'

Lola had never felt so uncomfortable, she felt like she was under scrutiny. Walking towards the door, Lola expected DCI Campbell to follow, but when she turned he had seated himself in Arthur's chair.

'You don't mind if we have a chat in here? It's such a lovely room.'

But Lola did mind, and she knew that the detective sensed this.

'No not at all, sir,' she lied, as she took a seat opposite him on the sofa. 'So what was it you wanted to see me about?' asked Lola impatiently.

'Was it not you who wanted to see me? I'm sorry I never got back to you sooner, but you know how it is.'

'That was a work matter, Detective,' said Lola coldly.

'We'll that's not why I'm here, Lola. I really just wanted to know if you had thought of anything else that may have come to mind about Arthur, maybe some new developments?' Lola's palms began to sweat as she shifted in her seat. She was the worst liar, and she feared that DCI Campbell knew this.

CHAPTER 32

'Like what, Detective? I mean, I told you all I know. I was away the weekend that Arthur died, you mentioned the note and as I said to you before, it was a quote from Socrates.' Lola swallowed hard, hoping that she sounded convincing.

'I know it has been a very troubling time for you, Lola, Arthur was a great man and he'll be sadly missed.'

'You say that like you knew him, Detective. Did you know him?' asked Lola clearly confused.

'Yes I did. He knew my father well.' Just as Lola was about to probe further, she was cut off. 'But that's not why I'm here today,' he smiled. 'Our investigation has come to a dead end, and something you said about the note has stuck with me,' he said still smiling as he rocked back and forth in the old wooden chair. 'You said that the original quote by Socrates was, "The end of life is to be like God, and the soul following God will be like Him", but that Arthur had changed the Him to a Her. Why do you think he did that?'

Of course Lola knew why he'd done it, but she wasn't sure that it would benefit her any if she explained this to the detective. She had thought about what the note had really meant and what Arthur had been trying to say to her. She could tell the detective suspected her. Not of the murder, but of knowing more than she was clearly divulging. In truth he was right. After some consideration she decided that honesty was the best policy.

'Well, I think it was a private joke,' said Lola seeing that DCI Campbell wasn't following her logic.

'A joke? From a dying man?'

'Not really in that sense,' stuttered Lola. 'You see I always used to joke with Arthur about how everyone always referring to God as a man annoyed me. History has been written by men, Detective, and the role of women has been rewritten to that of the temptress and villain. In my opinion, that voice deep inside is the word of God, some people like to call it intuition. In my experience, women are as close to God as anyone, yet it's mostly men that create religion, which I believe, for what it's worth, has very little to do with God at all. I mean, who says God's a man? My God isn't.'

A condescending smile spread across the detective's face.

'So your God is a woman, Lola?' he laughed.

'Not necessarily, if we are all created in the likeness of the divine, my conclusion is that God is a bit of both.'

'What?' snorted the detective, 'some sort of He/She? Well, I've heard it all now.' Lola rolled her eyes. 'So that note was like a little private joke between you and Arthur?' continued DCI Campbell, all humour gone now. But Lola was unphased by the implication.

'Perhaps it was. The truth is I don't know.'

'You have no idea what it might mean?'

'I'm not sure what you want me to say, Detective. You clearly think that I am withholding information from you. I loved Arthur, more than you can ever understand. You know nothing of what I've lost, or how my life has changed since his death. There's nothing more I can tell you.'

'I didn't come here to upset you, Lola. I'm just trying to get to the bottom of this.'

The detective got up out of the chair to leave.

'I read your article in the paper this week, you've been covering the Vikki Jones story.'

'Yes.'

'She went missing in Portstewart the weekend Arthur died. You were up there that weekend, weren't you, Lola?' It was more of a statement than a question, but Lola didn't like where it was going. 'I got the impression that you don't think that she took her own life.

What made you think that?'

Lola just wanted to get him out. She didn't trust him. He seemed to be taking a very close interest in her and her whereabouts.

'I'm not sure what you mean, Detective,' replied Lola, as she ushered him out of the book room. 'I was just quoting her friends and family. They don't believe that she took her own life. You're working that case too? As you know, I tried to contact you about it.'

The detective nodded.

'Well you deemed it as suicide. Despite the evidence.' Lola couldn't resist the jibe, but immediately scolded herself for revealing too much.

The detective pounced on it straight away.

'Evidence? What evidence? If you've uncovered something, Lola, I would strongly suggest you bring it forward,' he warned.

Lola didn't know if she could trust this man now. It seemed strange to her that he would be covering Arthur's death and Vikki Jones's. He made her feel uneasy so she went with her gut. There was no way that she was going to discuss the voicemail. Besides, he'd probably already heard it and obviously dismissed it.

'You are clearly a very busy man, detective, and I wouldn't like to take up any more of your time.'

Lola ushered DCI Campbell to the top of the stairs and watched as he left the house.

She was annoyed with her brother Liam for letting DCI Campbell into the house without her notice, and she would soon let him know when she got her hands on the little imp. Lifting the small book that Aibgrene had given her out of her pocket, she headed back to the book room. Sitting in Arthur's chair, she opened the battered book, which was yellowed and bore the smell of an old book shop. Lola began to read The New Epoch by Dr Roberta Emmett.

It took Lola a while to get into the book, as the language and astrological diagrams were difficult for her to interpret. Eventually she got the gist of the subject, which was discussing the new Age of Aquarius.

From the little she could grasp, each of the twelve astrological signs of the Zodiac had an age associated with it, and each one of those ages lasted approximately two thousand years or more. The example the book cited was that of the current age or epoch – Pisces/

Virgo – which the book stated was ushered in by the birth of Jesus.

Lola tried to recall what Markus had said at the fort on the evening of Arthur's cremation about the new age, to see if it had any relevance to what she was reading. The writer·claimed that these epochs could be charted through astronomy and were determined by the equinox procession. This phrase caught Lola's attention because Arthur had been observing the spring equinoxes. Frustrated, Lola threw the book to one side, deciding to wait until Aibgrene was there to explain it to her.

That's when she saw DCI Campbell standing in the side garden with his head cocked to one side, as if he was trying to figure out some sort of puzzle. Lola suddenly felt sick – from her high vantage point she could see the entire picture. Aibgrene must have forgotten to clear her things away last night. There in the garden lay the remnants of her moon ritual. The large circle of petals and salt, along with four white candles, lay scattered in the dewy grass. It was most unlike her to leave her things, as she was usually very discreet.

Lola had become accustomed to her ways, and had even partic-ipated a few times in the rituals and really enjoyed it. This particular ritual was performed every month, as Aibgrene followed the cycle of the moon. But Lola was only too aware how this would look to an outsider, especially an already curious one.

Lola watched from behind the curtain as the detective stepped around the circle. He bent down, and picked up some salt, rubbing it between his fingers. It was as though he was investigating a crime scene. From his body language and the way he was moving, it was clear that he understood what he was looking at. He must have sensed that someone was watching as he looked up towards the window, but Lola quickly ducked away, undetected.

Two hours later a bleary-eyed Aibgrene staggered into the book room, still half asleep.

'What time is it, Lo?'

Lola glanced at the large walnut grandfather clock that sat beside the doorway. 'It's 10 to 5.'

'I can't believe I slept for so long, why didn't you wake me up?'

'You needed the sleep, Aibgrene, there's no rush. By the way we had a visitor.'

'Who?' asked Aibgrene, half yawning.

'DCI Campbell,' said Lola, rolling her eyes in distain. 'He suspects that I know more than I'm telling him. Well, I suppose he's right. He just wandered into the book room and said that Liam had told him that's where he'd find me. I'm sure he could tell that I was very annoyed by his sudden presence.'

'What did he want?'

'That's a good question, Aibgrene. He said he wanted to ask me about the note that Arthur had left and the wording of it. I told him the truth, that I didn't know, but I could tell he didn't believe me. But here's the interesting thing. He's not only working on Arthur's murder, he's also leading the investigation into Vikki Jones's death as well.'

Aibgrene had guessed as much, despite the fact that she hadn't mentioned anything to Lola about it. Lola noticed the subtle shift in Aibgrene's body, like she was hiding something.

'Do you think he's one of them?'

'I don't know, Lola, he could be, but then how would he get through the sphere?'

Lola was never that convinced about the invisible shield that encapsulated the entire estate. This was mainly due to the fact that someone had penetrated it before – the night Arthur was murdered. She was about to explain this point when Aibgrene cut in.

'I know what you going to say, Lola, but there could be a number of reasons why whoever is responsible for Arthur's death got in. Perhaps the spell was only cast afterwards, or maybe he knew the person. We really don't know yet.'

'He knew his killer? I'd never thought of that,' said Lola shocked at the implications this would have.

The thought had never crossed Lola's mind. To her, Arthur's killer could never have known him, because if they had, they could not have done what they did. Suddenly she realised how naive she sounded. It made perfect sense that Arthur would know his killer. How else would they have gotten in past the spell, and past Cuchulain? Lola sat in silence for a few moments.

'He knew Arthur. He said he knew Arthur,' murmured Lola.

'Who did?' quizzed Aibgrene.

'DCI Campbell, earlier today when he was here, he said that he had known Arthur through his father. Oh my God, Aibgrene, he was in here, looking about. How could I have been so stupid? When he left I came back in here and he was out in the side garden, where you were last night. You'd left your things there and he was examining them, like he knew what he was looking at. He's one of them, and he knows all about Arthur and us!'

Lola felt a sudden panic, as she realised that such a scenario made perfect sense, and that explained why he was pushing her on the note.

'We don't know anything for sure, Lola. He's a policeman, and he's just doing his job and everyone knew Arthur, that's no surprise.'

'You're wrong, Aibgrene, I know it! He's working for the Hell Fire Club. The only thing that doesn't make sense is why would he be working on the Vikki Jones case, what has that got to do with Arthur?'

Aibgrene shifted nervously, looking down at the floor. Lola had seen that look before, and knew she was hiding something.

'You know something don't you?' asked Lola directly.

She would be hurt if Aibgrene was keeping information from her, after all they were meant to be in this together. If Lola couldn't trust her, who could she trust?

'Well?' Lola persisted.

'Calm down, Lola. I don't know anything for sure, and I wanted to be sure before I discussed it with you. You could be right about the detective, but we don't know that for certain. I do have a theory about Vikki Jones and Arthur in that I think their murders could be related.'

'How? I mean they were miles apart and they didn't know each other, did they?'

If Aibgrene had been withholding this information, what else was she not telling her? Could she be trusted? Now that she thought about it, what did Lola know about Aibgrene? The truth was that she really knew nothing about her, she could be anyone, and could be working for the Hell Fire Club too. Lola's head was spinning now. She wasn't sure about anyone, or anything. She felt confused and suddenly alone. She had been warned about new people that would come into her life, but she never for one second suspected Aibgrene, not until now.

'So how are these murders related, Aibgrene?' asked Lola calmly.

If Aibgrene sensed the slight chill in her voice, she didn't acknowledge it.

'It came to me a while back, when you first started working on the Vikki Jones story. The fact that she went missing on the same night that Arthur was murdered. So I started to look into it a bit, and it turns out that another girl, around the same age, disappeared about two weeks before that.'

'That doesn't explain how the murders related to Arthur's death,' said Lola drily.

'You see the Hell Fire Club have been known to make sacrifices to their deity. Mostly these sacrifices are animals, like goats and lambs – it really depends on the occasion. The more important the occasion, the bigger the sacrifice, and they have offered women to their God before. There is no doubt that Arthur's death would have been celebrated and would have been merited by the biggest sacrifice.'

Lola couldn't bear to think about the implication of what this would mean, so she changed the subject. Aibgrene had promised her answers, and she was determined to get them.

'What about the other stuff you talked about? What did you find in Arthur's log book?' asked Lola.

'Did you have a look at that book I gave you?' Aibgrene asked Lola in return, motioning towards the discarded book lying on the sofa.

'I read a bit, but I thought it would be best if you explained it. I got as far as the twelve epochs, which last over two thousand years, and that they are associated to certain astrological signs, like Pisces/Virgo.'

'Good,' smiled Aibgrene. 'You've got the basics then. I'll not bore you with all the details, but each age changes, as you said, after every 2,150 years or so, and this is determined by what sign appears on the morning of the spring equinox. That is why Arthur had been monitoring it for the past fifty years or so. I found tons of data dating back over two thousand years. It looks as though members of the Order have been tracking these ages for millennia!

'According to Arthur's calculations, the dawning of the Age of Aquarius could occur in the next few years. There are a lot of geometrical symbols beside this particular calculation and I'm not sure what they mean. By the spring equinox of this year, which falls on 20th March, the epoch will have shifted to Aquarius/Leo. I'm sure the symbolism isn't lost on even someone like you, Lola?'

'Of course,' said Lola. 'It makes perfect sense, Aquarius, the water bearer, pouring spiritual understanding upon humanity, illuminated by the sun sign of Leo; the sun, which represents the divine light of creation, the source of all life, cleansing our perceptions of our world!'

Lola looked up to the domed ceiling, scanning the gold-leaf letters that where inscribed around it. Finding the words she was looking for, she read them aloud. '"If the doors of perception were cleansed, everything would appear to man as it is, infinite. For man has so closed himself up, till he sees all things thro' narrow chinks of his cavern". Is this what this is all about? Change?'

'Yes, Lola, and you have a huge part to play in that.'

'So the Tuatha Dé Danann and the Cosmic Cube must fit into all this somewhere?'

'You took the words out of my mouth,' Aibgrene laughed. 'That's where I was drawing a blank.'

Getting up she motioned for Lola to follow her, as she disappeared up the spiral staircase. 'Look at this, Lola, and tell me what you think.'

Lola examined the strange geometrical shape etched in pen on the yellowing paper of Arthur's log book. It reminded her of Kepler's model that sat in the corner of the observatory.

'I can make out about five different shapes,' said Lola searching for the right word. 'The polyhedra, that's it.'

'Well done, Lola,' enthused Aibgrene, as though she was genuinely surprised that Lola had managed to figure it out. 'What you're looking at is the Cosmic Cube or better known as Metatron's Cube, or the five platonic solids.' Aibgrene looked thoroughly pleased with herself and Lola was duly impressed. She would never have figured it out on her own.

'So do you think that the Cosmic Cube is related to the new epoch then?' asked Lola. 'Maybe it's some sort of portal or vehicle to bring in the energy needed for the new epoch to begin?'

'That's amazing, Lola,' gushed Aibgrene. 'It took me all night to try and figure that out and you got it in about twenty seconds. I suppose you are the chosen one,' she laughed.

'Don't sound so surprised,' chided Lola. 'I'm not as stupid as you think. And what do you mean by the chosen one?'

Aibgrene smiled waving her hand to dismiss Lola's comments.

'Lighten up, Lola. I don't think you're stupid. You're anything but! I'm only messing with you.'

Lola returned Aibgrene's soft smile, immediately feeling guilty for having doubted her.

'You've done a great job, Aibgrene. Really you have. I would never have figured this all out. It makes so much sense now. The Hell Fire Club doesn't want to see this new age, as it will challenge everything they have, it will destroy them. And whoever controls the Cosmic Cube controls the fate of humanity. No pressure there then!' smiled Lola sarcastically. 'All we need to do now is figure out what Arthur has done with it.'

'Although we don't have it, the good news is, neither does the Hell Fire Club,' declared Aibgrene confidently.

Lola looked up, rubbing her weary head, waiting for an explanation.

'I know because they have my mother and she's still alive. With each full moon my connection is growing, but time is running out, Lo.'

CHAPTER 33

The weeks raced by for Lola, and the Vikki Jones story had almost become an obsession for her now that she realised that there could be a link between her death and Arthur's. She'd been given a great lead from the Jones family explaining that their daughter was seen by one of Stein's cleaners leaving the house at around 4am on the morning she disappeared. Their source, who Lola was guessing was a private detective, also told them that she was seen getting into a black car, which confirmed Sarah's voicemail. There was so much about the case that was troubling.

This would be a great exclusive, if she could only find an opening, but there were no witnesses – save Sarah Byrne – who were willing to speak to her. It seemed that people were afraid to come forward, this wall of silence made Lola even more suspicious.

Then there was the added complication of Alex Stein. She'd been seeing quite a lot of him lately, and knew that she was in way over her head. Aibgrene never talked about him, and Lola could tell she didn't approve. Why? She wasn't exactly sure, but perhaps her friend felt that she should be giving all her time to finding Celeste. Lola knew Aibgrene was right, but it was too late now – she had fallen for Alex

Stein. He offered her an escape from the pressures of the Order and that part of her life that she was still trying to run away from. Besides, she was reconciled with the fact that she couldn't deprive herself of him, even if she wanted to.

Lola's phone buzzed twice before she picked it up. She had just finished her front page lead and was checking over it before it went to the sub-editors desk.

'Hello, Lola speaking.'

'Lola, Bryce here, could you come and see me for a minute, please.'

It was almost five o clock, and as always Lola was very nervous when she got a call from her editor. Climbing the aged stairs to her editors office, Lola's mind was working overtime trying to think what he might want, but nothing prepared her for what she was about to hear. Knocking the door, she waited for Bryce Neal to call her in before she entered the room. Lola's heart sank when she saw the stern look on his face, she could feel the tension in the room and she knew that this was serious. Bryce didn't lift his head to look at her when he spoke, which only heightened her panic.

'Take a seat, Lola.'

Doing as she was told Lola waited for him to speak.

'Listen, Lola,' he said, his tone firm but not too harsh. 'To date I have been very happy with your work, and very glad to have you here, but I just had a very interesting phone call from Carl Stein's solicitor, and they are very concerned about the inquiries you have been making with regard to the Victoria Jones story.'

Lola was struggling to comprehend what he meant, straining to find a connection between this Carl Stein and Vikki Jones. Then it finally dawned on her: Stein. He was Alex's father, and the last person who the dead girl was seen with was his son. Lola waited for her boss to continue.

'It has come to my attention that you've been harassing some of his staff and saying that you have reason to believe this girl did not take her own life. You need to be very careful, Lola – that is a very loaded statement, and could get this paper into a lot of trouble,' he warned.

'I was given information that one of the cleaners saw Vikki get into a black car the morning she disappeared,' stammered Lola, trying to hide her nerves. 'This information has since been backed up by one of Vikki's friends, and it also appears in the police statement. That's why I contacted the company, but the person that I needed to speak to no longer works there. So, I tried to get a contact number. That's all. Why would Mr Stein be interested in that, and why would his solicitors want to warn us off? Seems a bit strange to me,' added Lola defiantly.

'The truth is that this girl killed herself. The police and coroner's reports verify that. You are going on the word of a grief-stricken father and friend. That is not professional, Lola! When you're a journalist you must always deal in facts – nothing more, nothing less. So that's it! The story is closed.'

'But I'm trying to find the FACTS, sir! I'm a reporter, is that not what reporters do?' argued Lola. But this didn't wash with her editor, who stared at her, stony faced.

'I don't think I'm making myself clear, Lola,' hissed Bryce. 'No more investigating or trying to find the facts. The story is closed. End of!'

'But, sir....' protested Lola.

'Do I make myself clear? Do I?' pressed Bryce aggressively.

Lola's face had flushed scarlet and she feared that her emotions would betray her. She was tougher than that, but suddenly struck by a heady mixture of embarrassment and frustration she wanted to cry. Lola fought hard with herself to choke back the tears and the dry lump in her throat that housed all her anger. She couldn't allow herself to speak in case it all poured out. Instead, she just nodded her head meekly, hoping that would be enough. But it wasn't. Bryce Dixon had broken her and he knew it. Her editor wanted to make sure that he was understood and that he would not be challenged.

'Is that a yes?' pressed Bryce.

'Yes, sir,' croaked Lola.

'Okay, it's time you were leaving.'

Rising from the chair, Lola left the room with whatever dignity she had left. She was relieved that the office was empty when she returned to her desk. After shutting down her computer, she shuffled through the drawers, gathering all her material on Vikki Jones, and headed home feeling dejected.

Stomping up the driveway to the house, Lola's temper was in

full flight. She slammed the front door behind her, disturbing the large crystal chandelier in the hallway. Heading straight for the stairs she made her way to the book room, throwing herself onto Arthur's rocking chair before finally allowing the tears to flow. Deep down she knew that it was her pride more than anything that had been bruised and that she would get over it. But to think that Carl Stein had gone to such lengths to stop her making enquiries, and the fact that Alex had not even mentioned it to her, didn't seem right.

Then again Carl Stein's son was the last person to be seen with the victim. Lola expelled the thought as quickly as it came into her head. That was way too messed up. Alex was arrogant, rich and spoilt, but a killer? That was too much.

Lola looked up to find Aibgrene standing in the doorway in a lovely lavender dress which flowed to the floor. As usual, she wasn't wearing any shoes and her hair, although dishevelled, was tied up off her face. Aibgrene was enchanting. Her warmth and radiance affected all in her wake. Lola could often see a beautiful apple-green haze around her, especially when she came back in from working in the garden or from concocting one of her potions.

She had begun to notice this same strange egg-shaped force field around her parents and siblings too. Her mother's was a mixture of light and dark yellows, which often changed quite a bit over time. Sometimes light grey spots appeared here and there, but only when she was anxious about something. Her father's was a clear vibrant orange, like the sun, and it fascinated Lola to see how her parents' auras engaged with each other, how both seemed to complement each other perfectly.

Out of her brothers, Liam's haze was by far the most fascinating – it changed from indigo to light blue, with flecks of pink, swirling and altering all the time. But there were others that she could not detect, or that simply were not obvious to her. Alex was one such person, she couldn't see his. Perhaps that was because she didn't know him as well as her family, or maybe because deep down she didn't want to see it. Well, not if it was a true manifestation of the soul, like some people said it was.

'What's wrong with you?' asked Aibgrene.

'Oh nothing, I'm just being a girl. I got my wrists slapped in work today.'

'Why what happened? What did you do?'

Lola blew her nose before she began to answer, fearing that a fresh wave of tears would start. She noticed that Aibgrene didn't seem that concerned, as she flopped down on the sofa.

'I've been pulled off the Victoria Jones story,' began Lola, but she was distracted by the slight smile at the corner of Aibgrene's mouth.

'What are you so happy about?' muttered Lola sourly

'Nothing, I've just got a bit of good news that's all.'

'It's well for some. So, are you going to share this bit of good news, or are you keeping it to yourself?'

'It's nothing, I've been invited to a wedding and I've accepted, so we will be heading there tonight. I think you could do with a break, Lola.'

'That's great news, but I'm afraid you'll have to go solo, I've work tomorrow.'

'Call in sick, sure you only have a few more weeks to go,' encouraged Aibgrene.

'Oh right, call in sick after I get a telling off, that looks really professional, Aibgrene!'

'This trip is important, Lola. We can kill two birds and all that. I need you to bring the parchment and the letter Arthur gave you. There will be someone at the wedding who might be able to help us, plus it's Lughnasadh, which is a very important festival for me. It's vital I'm there and I can't go without you. So we're going. Okay?'

'Whatever,' replied Lola with a wry smile.

'So, grumpy girl, tell me why he pulled you off the story?'

'That's the frustrating part. One call from Carl Stein and that's it. You want to have heard him, he was livid.'

Aibgrene stiffened, all traces of humour now extinguished from her face.

'Hold up, hold up. Your editor received a call from Carl Stein's solicitor? About what?'

'Well, I'd been led to believe that Vikki was seen getting into a car by one of the Stein's cleaners when she left their house earlier that morning.'

'The dead girl was in the Stein house the night before she disappeared! How did you know that?' asked Aibgrene shocked at this revelation.

'Well… Well, I saw her!'

'Okay, Lola, back up there. What do you mean you saw her there?'

'Look, it's a long story. The girls and I went to a party there the Saturday before they left for America, which was the night Arthur died.'

Lola was momentarily distracted by her own words, but Aibgrene waited patiently for her to continue.

'Anyway, someone spilt their drink over me and I went upstairs to try and find a bathroom, that's when I had my first encounter with Alex. He was on the phone to someone and came out accusing me of listening. We had a very unpleasant exchange, and then I left, but before I left I saw him with her.'

Lola guessed where Aibgrene's train of thought was leading. Lola watched her as she sat trying to put the pieces of this puzzle together, but before she could give her prognosis, Lola interjected.

'Aibgrene, I know you dislike Alex because of his father. I know you think I shouldn't be spending my time with him, and it's clear you don't trust him, but a killer? That's ridiculous!' scoffed Lola. She could hear the panic and pleading in her voice.

'I didn't say that, Lola. You did,' replied Aibgrene, her words falling like a lead balloon between them.

'Yes, because I know what you're thinking!'

Aibgrene didn't offer any further explanation. Lola was right; she didn't trust Alex Stein. There were so many things that didn't sit right with her. For example, the way Cuchulain had reacted to him or the way he always collected Lola at the end of the driveway and never accepted her invitations to come up to the house and the look on his face the night he saw her.

Arthur's death, two girls missing, Alex Stein coming into Lola's life – it was all connected. Aibgrene was sure that this was no coincidence. But she would never utter a word of this to Lola until she was sure. She could see how happy Lola was with him, she was deeply in love and this was blinding her, maybe jeopardising everything, that's why she'd made the decision to leave Lola and the sanctuary of Brook Mill Manor.

'Calm down, Lola, I'm not suggesting that at all,' she lied. 'All

I'm saying is that there is a bigger picture here. Everything is connected. You must understand nothing happens by chance.'

Aibgrene got off the sofa, kneeling in front of Lola, a look of pleading on her face.

'This is your destiny as well as mine we're talking about. I've tried to understand where you're coming from, Lo, but we are going to get nowhere as long as you continue to bury your head in the sand and pretend your life is normal. You will have to face these truths sooner or later.'

Aibgrene's eyes dropped before she began to speak again.

'I can still feel her, you know, my mum. She's still alive and getting some of her strength back, which means she doesn't have long left. So I have a very small window of opportunity to find her!'

Lola didn't know how to react, or what to say. She had let Aibgrene down, let Celeste down and Arthur too, but she didn't know what it was she should be doing. They were all wrong, she had no special gifts, otherwise she would've put a stop to all of this.

'I'm going to pack my things, Lola. You don't have to come with me if you don't want to. It's your choice, but if you do come, you may see and hear things that will force you to make some very hard decisions.'

Aibgrene left the room, leaving Lola alone rocking in Arthur's chair, mulling over how stubborn and selfish she had been. Jumping out of the seat, Lola called after her.

'So what do you wear to a tree hugger's wedding then?' joked Lola.

This brought the warm familiar smile back to Aibgrene's face.

'Wear whatever you like, you won't be wearing it for very long anyway.'

And with a wink Aibgrene disappeared down the stairs to gather the rest of her things, leaving Lola wondering if she was serious or not.

Lola went back into the library and pulled out the illustrated collection of Blake's work. She opened it at the middle page to make sure that the parchment was still there. Closing the book again she went into her room to pack a bag. Once she had collected some bathroom essentials, she ran to the library to lock the door. Arthur's cardigan was still hanging over the chair, lifting it off she put it on and ran downstairs to meet Aibgrene, who had started packing her things into the car.

'Lo, you may need to take some wellington boots with you. The weather has been good, but we are in Ireland, so that could change at any time.'

'Okay, I'll go and get them, anything else while I'm there?'

'Do you have a sleeping bag and some blankets?' enquired Aibgrene.

'Why? Do I need one?'

'Well, we're going to be sleeping in a tent, and I know how much you hate the cold, so it might be a good idea.'

'Now come on, Aibgrene,' protested Lola. 'You didn't tell me we would be camping? Can't we get a B&B or something?'

This only amused Aibgrene even more.

'Come on, Lola, you can play football and get kicked about by boys ten times bigger than you are, but you don't like sleeping outdoors? Stop being such a girl, you'll be fine. It'll do you the world of good to reconnect with mother nature, and no better place to do it than the spiritual epicentre of Ireland.'

Unconvinced, Lola stomped into the house. It took her almost twenty minutes to fish out a sleeping bag and some blankets from the various boxes that lay around the house still waiting to be unpacked. Her mum walked them to the door to see them off.

'Okay, girls, you be careful now and have a great time.'

'Okay, Mum,' said Lola, as she hugged her goodbye. 'I'll see you when I see you.'

Lola was getting into the car, as Aibgrene embraced Eileen.

'Eileen, I just wanted to say thank you so much for everything. I will never forget your generosity. Could you tell the boys and Joseph the same?'

Eileen was touched by Aibgrene's show of emotion, although she was a very warm person Aibgrene was quite reserved when it came to demonstrating her affections.

'Ach, Aibgrene pet. You are more than welcome. Are you not coming back?' joked Eileen.

'I won't be back for a while, Eileen,' explained Aibgrene awkwardly. 'I'm going to be staying with family for a while. You and Joe have done more than enough for me here, and it's time I moved on.'

'Don't be silly, darling,' protested Eileen. 'You're always welcome here. You know that.'

'I know, I know, but I would like to spend a bit of time with my family and friends. I haven't seen them in a while.'

'Well you know there is always a place for you here, pet!'

Eileen had begun to cry, she couldn't describe how good it was having Aibgrene around. There was something about her that had such a soothing and calming effect on all those she came in contact with. Even the plants and trees around the estate seemed to respond to her. Eileen had noticed all these things, but said very little, and she would really miss her. She returned the embrace and finally released Aibgrene.

'Bye, pet, and we will all really miss you. Don't be a stranger!'

'Bye, Eileen,' replied Aibgrene struggling to fight back the tears.

It was not a decision she had made lightly, but she knew that she needed to be with her own people if she was to stand any chance of finding her mother.

'Oh before I forget, this is for Joseph, for his arthritis.' Aibgrene produced a small clear bottle with thick green oil inside, handing it to Eileen. 'It's very strong, so tell him to only use a little bit. He can put a few drops into the bath, it'll work wonders!'

Lola stood stunned, glaring accusingly at Aibgrene as she climbed into the passenger seat.

'Come on, Lo, we need to get a move on!'

Lola got in and turned on the engine. Without saying a word she headed down the driveway of Brook Mill Manor waiting for an explanation from her friend, but Aibgrene didn't speak, instead she acted as if everything was normal. This only enraged Lola more until she couldn't hold her tongue any longer.

'So when were you going to tell me that this trip was a one way ticket for you?'

'You wouldn't have agreed to come if I had told you that,' replied Aibgrene without looking at her. 'Time is running out for my mum, Lola. She's not going to be able to contact me again, so I need to find her. Travelling on the astral plane is a family gift, you might say, but I never got the chance to learn how to use this power properly. I need to be with people who can teach me how to use it. It's our only hope.'

Lola turned to met Aibgrene's gaze and was instantly disarmed by the agony in her eyes.

'It was a very difficult decision, Lo, but that's why I have to stay at Tara.'

'That's where we're going? Tara?'

'Yes. The spiritual epicentre of Ireland, and it's Lughnasadh tomorrow, so expect one heck of a party.'

'But you're leaving me, what am I going to do now? You'll be gone. Arthur's gone, Celeste is gone. What am I supposed to do now?' pleaded Lola, her voice beginning to crack as that familiar dry lump started to restrict her throat again.

'You need to accept your own path, Lola. No one can make you do something you don't want to. In all of this universal order, nothing can compete with the soul's free will; this is the ultimate gift from the divine creator. Deep in your soul, you know this more than most, Lola.' Lola didn't want to hear anymore. She wanted her old life back. Turning on the radio, Lola let the music fill the silence between them, as they headed towards the mystical Boyne Valley.

The stretch of brand new motorway sprawled out before her cutting through fields and countryside, which were still visible on the periphery. This new road from Belfast to Dublin was evidence of the 'New' Ireland, an improved Ireland, and although Tara had been untouched by time for centuries, it too could not escape this so-called progression. The modern Ireland had caught up with it, leaving its dark scar in the form of another controversial motorway running through its ancient lands. Aibgrene had been looking out at her wing mirror for some time now. Lola was just about to take over the car in front of her when Aibgrene put her hand on the steering wheel, her eyes still fixed on the wing mirror.

'Lo, stay in this lane, and slow down, will you please.'

'You want to get there tonight, don't you?'

'Please, I think we are being followed!'

Instinctively, Lola looked in her rear-view mirror; she had noticed the car behind but hadn't paid much attention. Taking a closer look she could see it was a black Mercedes, its windows tinted. A feeling of dread began to invade her already tense body once she realised that she had seen this car before.

'I know that car, Aibgrene, I've seen it before. That's the car your mum got into when I dropped her off after the cremation.'

Lola was panicking now, there was no way Ruby's Figaro could outdrive that car and they had still miles to go.

'Are you sure, Lola?' asked Aibgrene calmly.

'Are you sure it's following us?'

'It's been on our tail since we passed Newry. Whoever is driving that car has had plenty of opportunities to bypass us.'

'We're like sitting ducks!'

'Do you have the ring on?' asked Aibgrene.

Lola groped at her chest, searching for the ring, her hands trembling, until she finally located it under her t-shirt.

'Yes, I have it, but how is that going to help us, if they decide to ram us off the road?'

'Pull in at the next filling station just to make sure,' ordered Aibgrene.

Lola continued to drive at a steady pace, gradually slowing down, but their pursuer still trailed behind. After driving about five hundred yards they saw a petrol station up ahead. Indicating left, Lola checked her mirror again, praying that the black car would continue on and that it was all a mistake. For a fraction of a second she thought it was going to pass by, but as she pulled off the motorway to the station, the car followed.

'Okay, you need to calm down, Lola, and act normal, alright? Can you do that?'

Lola nodded her head in agreement, but every part of her body was on edge. Bringing the car to a halt, she sat rigid in her seat, her knuckles white from gripping the steering wheel so hard.

'We need a distraction. Just fill the car or something and leave the rest to me.'

Aibgrene leaned into the back seat searching for something in her travel bag. Finally locating it, she lifted her hand bag, left the car and walked towards the shop. Lola got out of the car in as carefree a manner as she could, removed the petrol cap, and put some fuel in, taking a sideway glance at the car behind, the driver hadn't emerged yet.

She could feel the ring beginning to pulse next to her skin as her anxiety grew. Replacing the fuel cap, she walked around to the bonnet of the car, lifted it and pretended to search for an imaginary fault. Suddenly feeling bold, she strode to the car behind and knocked on the dark window. She could tell that the driver had not been expecting it and was unsure how to react, but another car had pulled in behind him and he had nowhere to go without looking suspicious.

After a few seconds the electric window came down, revealing a hulk of a man dressed in a black suit with a white shirt that looked like it was restricting the blood flow to his thick neck. He had a scar along the side of his face and his head was completely shaven, adding to his menacing look. If he was surprised by Lola's approach he didn't show it.

'Alright there, love? How canna help ye?'

He had a very thick Belfast accent and for a moment Lola thought she'd heard it somewhere before, but couldn't quite remember where. Focusing on the task at hand, she put on her best damsel in distress act, and even resorted to twirling her hair aimlessly.

'I'm really sorry to bother you, sir, but I think I'm having a bit of trouble with my car. I think it needs water, but I don't know where it goes,' said Lola smiling helplessly, and praying it would work. 'I'm such a girl when it comes to these things, would you be able to give me a hand?'

'It's not every day you get approached by a beautiful woman at a petrol station, so I'm sure I can,' grinned the huge man, revealing a row of nicotine stained teeth.

Lola moved away from the car door as the man got out. She couldn't disguise the shock on her face when she actually saw him up-right. He was well over six feet tall and nearly as wide – he was pure muscle. He was clearly used to women looking at him, and mistakenly took Lola's reaction as a compliment.

Aibgrene emerged from the shop, and now she was looking nervous – the confusion written all over her face – wondering what on earth Lola was doing. As the man continued to look for the water opening, Lola watched as Aibgrene made her way around the back of the Mercedes, her hands full.

Suddenly Aibgrene dropped the contents of her bag and bending down to pick them up again, she withdrew her boline knife from its sheath and ran it across both back tyres. The blade was so sharp that all it required was a gentle slash. The air started to escape from the wheels with a slow hiss.

'What's up, Lola?' chirped Aibgrene, feigning surprise.

'Oh nothing, I thought I might need some water in the car, and this gentleman has been kind enough to help me, but everything looks fine.'

'Yeah, it seems okay to me,' said the huge man, looking a little bewildered, as his eyes darted furtively from Aibgrene to Lola. The girls knew that he may have realised he'd been discovered.

'Well everything seems okay; I'd better be getting on. I have an important meeting to get to.'

'Like I said, I have no idea about these things. I'm sorry to have wasted your time. Thanks a million for your help.'

Closing the bonnet Lola watched as the monster of a man made his way back to his car before she climbed back in behind the wheel. Turning the ignition, she made her way onto the motorway, with the Mercedes in pursuit.

'What was that all about?' demanded Aibgrene.

'You said create a diversion, so I did. Plus, now we know who's following us. Mind you, I think I'd rather not know. Did you see the size of him? He's built like a brick shit-house.'

'He was big, wasn't he!' laughed Aibgrene. 'Let's just hope our little ruse works.'

Just as she spoke, there was a loud screeching of brakes confirming that it had. As they both looked behind them the black car was forced onto the hard shoulder.

'And it looks like it did!' grinned Aibgrene.

'What did you do?' asked Lola.

Lifting the boline knife out of its leather cover, Aibgrene slashed at the air.

'Remind me to consecrate this again when we get to Tara.'

'You slashed his tyres? Genius! Give me a high five for that little piece of ingenuity.'

Lola was buzzing now, the adrenaline of the chase made her feel that she could handle anything.

'I think that we should come off the motorway,' said Lola.

'You're right, Lo,' agreed Aibgrene. 'Take the next turn off for Slane, and we'll take the back roads. It's safer.'

'Did you get the number plate?' asked Lola hopefully, she'd been so busy trying to distract the man that she had forgotten to.

'Yes,' said Aibgrene, lifting a pen out from the glove box, and then scribbling down the registration onto the back of an old receipt.

'W10 RNU1,' said Aibgrene proudly. 'We've got it now!'

'What are you going to go with it?'

'I have a friend, you'll meet him later, and he's very adept at finding stuff online. If you know what I mean,' said Aibgrene with a wink of her eye. 'He might be able to trace who the car is registered to. Another thing, Lola, there are only two people who know that Celeste is missing. I think that the Order has been compromised. We don't know who we can trust. Daithi and my mother's friend, Darragh, are the only people I've told.'

'So tell me a bit about this Daithi!' teased Lola. She wasn't fooled for a second. Every time Aibgrene had mentioned his name a thin smile crept across her face. Lola knew that he was more than just a friend.

'He's very special to me,' mumbled Aibgrene, a light pink flush blushing on her freckled cheeks. 'He's a very gifted druid. He could have easily been part of the Order, but Daithi is a free spirit. He prefers to travel his own path.'

'A very powerful druid?' grinned Lola impishly. 'Is he indeed! And does he have a very impressive magick wand as well?'

'Lola Paige! You saucy mare,' said Aibgrene laughing and giggling like a little school girl. 'Maybe he has,' she suggested slyly, 'but that's for me to know.'

'I'll ask you tomorrow night then?'

'Well you might get to see for yourself,' said Aibgrene now serious. 'You know how us tree huggers are? Everyone gets to join in.'

The smile immediately slid from Lola's face.

'That's the second time you've said that! What goes on at these gatherings? No, don't tell me, I can only imagine. Well, I can tell you I'll be keeping myself to myself, and that goes for my clothes as well.'

Aibgrene couldn't hold her laughter for long; she could hardly get the words out for laughing. The frivolity did Lola good. She hadn't had much to laugh about in the past few months.

'You want to see the look on you face! It's priceless. What do you take us for, Lo?'

Smiling in amusement, Lola watched the road ahead, taking the turn-off for the town of Slane. From there, Tara was only a few miles away and the sun, which was beginning to dip, guided them towards their final destination.

CHAPTER 34

Getting out of the car Lola stretched her aching bones, realising how tense she had been. Closing her eyes, she inhaled the earthy, sweet smell of the countryside. The sun was still strong as it made its decline in the evening sky, but Lola could feel a different form of heat running through her body. It was the energy of the trees and hills all around her as it seeped into every part of her body.

'Can you feel that?' asked Aibgrene closing her eyes, allowing her other senses take over. 'This is where my soul belongs, where it yearns to be, in mystical and ancient Teamhair. I feel as though I'm completely plugged into source here, it's amazing.'

Lola shared her peace, and tried to imagine the thousands of people that had descended on this site for millennia, each one of them trying to experience its wisdom and peace.

'Come on, let's get our stuff and get sorted for tomorrow.'

Lola started to unpack with a feeling of anticipation as the ancient hills of Teamhair beckoned her, whispering their secrets in the soft evening breeze. It took a couple of trips to the car before Lola and Aibgrene retrieved all of their things. Walking up the stony laneway, Lola could see the church of Saint Patrick stationed like a sentry. Legend had it that upon coming to Ireland, Patrick recognised what an important place Tara was, and in order to quash the old religion and magick, he knew he had to conquer it if Christianity was to flourish. The church was erected and rebuilt over the centuries, but now it was used as a visitors centre.

There were still a lot of tourists at the centre, enjoying the last of the evening sun and sights of the Boyne Valley. They were clearly intrigued by the large group of people that were erecting marquees and other tents on the site. Lola followed Aibgrene through a small vertical slit in the stone wall that surrounded the church and old grave yard. She had heard all about Tara and its legends from Arthur, but she had never been there before.

Tracking through the graveyard, they came to a small opening in the hedge, leading them out on to the hillside, where the wide expanse of the Boyne Valley was laid out in a vivid blanket of green as far as the eyes could see. Lola looked around her in all directions and drank in the breathtaking panoramic view. It was said that the fires of Tara could be seen from all over Ireland, and standing there Lola believed that it may well have been true.

To her left stood two large satellite mounds. The sign which sat atop a long metal pole read 'The Mound of the Nine Hostages', the other pointed towards one of the most import features of the site, the 'Lia Fail' or the 'Stone of Destiny'. To the unobservant tourist, it may have been difficult to imagine Tara in all its splendour as the Royal Fort of Ireland, but Lola could feel the energy of the place, the calm, the serenity. Although she had never been there before, it seemed so familiar to her.

'Come on you, get a move on!' said Aibgrene, bringing Lola out of her daydream.

Lola trudged after Aibgrene as she passed a group of men who were erecting a large circular white tent. It reminded Lola of a circus tent, without the red and white stripes. Each of the men was dressed in loose canvas trousers and t-shirts, the colours varying, but the look was essentially the same. They reminded Lola of the eco-warriors that lived in forests throughout Ireland and England. She had seen them on the news years ago and more recently protesting against the motorway that cut through the Boyne Valley.

It was difficult to guess the age of the men, but it was clear by their faces that they were used to working outdoors. They were all in deep concentration, each holding onto a taught rope, pulling out in different directions as the large structure began to take shape. They were almost there when one of the workers deserted his station, his eyes catching Aibgrene as she passed. The chorus of shouts and curses informed Lola who the deserter was, as dropping his rope the whole structure collapsed, imploding in on itself.

'Daithi! What are you doing, man? We nearly had it there!' The young man who was running towards Aibgrene was oblivious to their protests.

'Aibgrene, you made it.' said Daithi, embracing her and lifting her up, before twirling her around, and then setting her back onto the ground. The feeling was clearly reciprocated, as they held each other's eyes intently, before kissing, much to the delight of the group who were now watching, whooping and shouting in encouragement. Lola stood feeling a little awkward. She'd been right about them being more than friends. Aibgrene turned towards her introducing the young man.

'Daithi, I would like you to meet a very good friend of mine. This is Miss Lola Paige.'

Stepping towards her, with his hand extended and a wide smile radiating from his face, the tall dark-haired boy shook Lola's hand.

'Hello, Lola, I've heard a lot about you,' he smiled. 'It's lovely to finally meet you.' He looked a perfect match for Aibgrene, thought Lola as she examined him. He was a bit taller than her and had jet-black hair, which fell in curls around his elfin features. His dark green eyes sparkled with a gentle kindness. Lola instantly warmed to him.

'Lola, this is Daithi O'Neill, my friend and soon-to-be husband,' declared Aibgrene, barely containing her excitement.

'What?' Lola felt was sure that she'd picked her up wrong. 'It's your wedding? Why didn't you tell me? I haven't even brought a present! Oh my God! Congratulations, to the both of you.' Lola couldn't hide her delight, grabbing them both into a group hug.

'She didn't tell you, Lola?' laughed Daithi. 'Aibgrene!'

'Well I wasn't sure if I was going to go through with it,' she smirked, as he chased after her.

Lola watched as they kissed once again, before following them to the campsite nestled at the foot of the hill. The large tents and small caravans that lay scattered about the site were all deserted, as everyone was up on the hill preparing for the wedding.

CHAPTER 35

Walking through the warren of tents, Lola stopped when they came to a small circular stone cottage at the edge of the site. It was like the small satellite mounds that where dotted throughout the Boyne Valley, but Lola cold tell that this building was modern. The enchanting cottage had two small windows in the front and a wooden door with a grass roof. Pots of herbs lay along the window sills, and at the side of the house a vegetable plot housed potatoes, carrots, lettuce and other vegetables, which Lola couldn't identify. It looked so quaint.

There was an open fire built into a small forge, with black pots and a hot plate for cooking. From the outside the cottage looked tiny and Lola wasn't entirely sure that they would all fit in. As they approached the door, Daithi lifted Aibgrene, her shrieks of laughter echoing over the site. Pushing the door open with his foot, he carried her over the threshold. Lola hesitated outside, feeling a little like a third wheel. Aibgrene and Daithi hadn't seen each other in a while so she guessed that they could do with some time alone.

'What are you doing, Lo? Come in.'

'It's okay, guys. I'm going to go for a walk, you two need a bit of time on your own.'

Aibgrene was about to protest, but Lola remained adamant.

'Really, Aibgrene, I need to stretch my legs, it was intense coming down the road, and a bit of fresh air will do me the world of good.'

'Okay, but at least let us show you where you'll be sleeping,' said Aibgrene, seeming quite excited at the prospect, which made Lola instantly suspicious.

A night under the stars was preferable to sleeping in the cottage with the soon-to-be husband and wife, so she was delighted when Daithi and Aibgrene led her to the side of the house where an old horse-drawn caravan sat. It was one of the most beautiful things Lola had ever seen. The long cylinder caravan had been fully restored; it's turquoise roof and red inset looked as though it had been freshly painted. Five small steps curved up to the entrance of the wagon, which had a hand-painted stable door.

Stepping inside Lola was completely enchanted. At the bottom, the main feature was a sofabed, which had two posts. The green satin bedding reminded Lola of Aibgrene's wispy apple-green aura. The padded cushions and pillows that lay scattered on the sofa bed were a pallet of varying shades of green. There was a wooden frame around the bed, and muslin draping from the two white wooden posts. Much to Lola's surprise there was a tiny shower cupboard and toilet. At the entrance lay a minute kitchen space with a bench, some old cupboards and a small wood burner. It was so bohemian and Lola fell instantly in love with its charm. She could imagine herself quite happily living there, giving up the modern world travelling from place to place, packing up her troubles as she went.

'So what do you think, Lo? Do you like it?' asked Aibgrene and Daithi in unison.

'It's fabulous guys, I could live here. Did you do it up yourself, Daithi?'

'Yeah, it's a present for Aibgrene. It has been in my family for years. It still needs a bit of work, but I'm getting there.'

'A present?' said Lola turning to Aibgrene, getting ready to list the many reasons why she couldn't possibly stay in it first. But, for the second time her friend anticipated her reaction.

'Don't start, Lola, we are only too happy to have you stay in it.' Dropping her things Lola lifted Arthur's cardigan off the top of the pile.

'Thank you both so much, it's really great. I'm going to head back up to the hill. I'll see you in a while.'

When Lola emerged up the side of hill she was startled by how much the vast sea of green had been transformed. In the short space of time that she'd been down below, the huge marquee that Daithi had abandoned earlier was now fully erect, and a steady flow of foot traffic flowed in and out of it as tables and sheets of linen, glasses and cutlery were brought inside. Not really sure where to go, Lola headed for the mound of the Nine Hostages. This was where Niall, one of the great Irish High Kings of Tara, was said to have kept nine royal hostages in order to keep his enemies at bay. Sitting down on the grassy mound, Lola wrapped Arthur's worn cardigan around her body. Inhaling its scent resurrected so many happy, but painful memories.

It amazed her how something as simple as a smell could trigger such bitter-sweet emotions. Lola missed him desperately. Every day she thought about him and every day she missed him more and more. She thought sometimes that she could hear him, especially when she was in Brook Mill Manor. Just the other day when she was passing the book room, she could have sworn she heard him calling her name and she could have sworn that she heard his familiar footsteps padding along the carpeted floor, but when she turned to see, she was alone.

The truth was that his loss was still very raw and the constant ache that gnawed at her stomach could only, at best, be ignored. Now that she was in Tara, Lola understood that she needed him now more than ever. She wondered how he had ever let her become so embroiled in this madness. What was she meant to do?

As she sat tangled in her own questions, the small signet ring around her neck began to pulse. Without actually knowing why, or how, Lola climbed to her feet and descended the mound. She moved to the other side of the tent, where the second largest mound lay, which displayed a large phallic stone, carved from granite. Lola absently walked towards it, examining the bright white haze emanating from the stone as it beckoned her.

Like a magnet, the ring chain began to pull and tug at Lola's neck as if it too recognised the stone's energy field. Lola's vision began to blur and her head felt light as she stood inches away from the Lia Fail.

Closing her eyes, she felt as though she was spinning around and around, getting faster and faster. She could hear a female voice, at first it was a soft whisper but as the spinning intensified the voice grew louder and more audible.

'Cad a thagann faireim leirionn gan,' said the mysterious female voice.

'What lies within, reflects without,' repeated Lola rhythmically, as she forced her eyes open.

Suddenly the entire Boyne valley was rotating around her, but all her eyes could focus on was the large stone, as she repeated the words that were carried on the wind. She felt at one with the ancient rock. Its magnetism was overwhelming like nothing she had ever felt before. Her body was tingling all over and she felt cold and warm at the same time. She reached out to touch the stone and her hands could feel the warmth of the force field around it, but her fingers fell short of the stone itself. The voice began to intensify, until Lola fell, losing consciousness.

She was running through a dark forest, guided only by her instincts and the light of the full moon. Snow had begun to fall as it blanketed the soft needled floor below her feet. Cold panic rose in her stomach as she realised that her pursuers would be able to see her trail, but she didn't have time to worry about that, she had very little time left as it was almost dawn. She had to get to the temple.

Reaching for her hip she grasped for the comfort of her sword and wound her snow-white hand gratefully around its hilt. The item she carried stirred as its white light crept out through the bag's thick stitching. She could tell that it too sensed that it was almost home. A loud bark ripped through the still night air forcing her feet to move ever faster and although the snow muffled their frenzied shouts, Lola could tell whoever was chasing her was closing in. Drawing the silver sword from its sheath, Lola caught a reflection of her jade green eyes, which at first looked like they belonged to her. But they were harder than hers, more defiant. Then she saw it, flowing in the soft breeze, a flash of flaming red hair. In a moment of lucidness, Lola realised that the features reflected in the swords steely gaze were not her own.

'LOLA. LOLA!' Aibgrene's panicked voice drifted closer as Lola woke to find herself sprawled out on the bed of the wagon. Aibgrene was wiping the sweat from her clammy face with a cool flannel. She felt as though she'd been run though a spin cycle and spat out.

'What happened, Aibgrene?'

But Aibgrene only answered with another question. 'How are you feeling? Are you hurt?' she asked softly.

'Hurt? What happened? How did I get here?' demanded Lola.

'Sean said he saw you standing by the Lia Fail, he said that you were murmuring something in Irish and then you collapsed. He couldn't bring you around, so he carried you down here to us.'

'Carried me. How did he manage that?' quizzed Lola still disorientated and suddenly mortified all at once. This only made Aibgrene laugh.

'You're hardly the heaviest person, Lola, plus Sean is quite well put together, I'm sure it wasn't too hard for him.'

Stepping to the side Aibgrene motioned towards the caravan door. Lola's head still felt fuzzy, but she could see Daithi standing outside in deep conversation with a tall, fair-haired boy. He towered over Daithi, who was over six feet tall, and was quite well built. He wasn't too bulky, but Lola could see that he would have no trouble carrying her and a few others.

'I see what you mean,' she croaked apologetically.

'Lo?' asked Aibgrene, sternly. She sat down on the bed taking Lola's limp hand in hers. 'What happened up there?'

Lola could sense her anxiety which scared her a bit. Aibgrene was always composed and self-assured, but clearly whatever had happened up on the hill had frightened her.

'I don't know,' she answered honestly. 'One minute I was standing by that stone, the next I was gone, out cold. It was so strange, it was like a dream. I remember Arthur's ring began to pulse again and the next thing I was beside the Lia Fail. I can't describe it but it was as though it had some hold over me. The ring was going crazy. This might sound stupid, Aibgrene, but it was almost as if the two were communicating. It was as if they recognised each other.'

Lola paused, trying to sit up. She reached for the glass of water at her bedside. Gulping it down in one go, she hadn't realised how thirsty she was. Aibgrene didn't say anything, but Lola knew she was contemplating some facet of what she had been told.

'I could hear this voice, it was only a whisper at first, but as I got closer to the stone it became clearer. She was speaking in Irish, but I could understand what she said. "What lies within, reflects without."

She was repeating this over and over. Then everything started to spin and the next thing I was somewhere else … or someone else.'

'Somewhere else? What do you mean?'

There was something in Aibgrene's voice that gave Lola the impression that she knew more than she was divulging, but as she was about to continue, Daithi came into the cabin, along with Sean, who had to stoop a little to get in through the door. Feeling quite self-conscious Lola stopped talking.

'Lola! You're back with us I see,' said Daithi as he moved towards the bed, looking relieved. 'You had us worried there!'

'Sorry about that. I don't know what happened,' replied Lola. Sensing her uneasiness and embarrassment, Daithi didn't push the conversation.

'Well it's just as well Sean was there to save the day.' Looking behind Daithi Lola found Sean standing beaming, and lifting his hand he waved at her.

'Nice to meet you, Lola, or should I say nice to meet you again.'

This lightened the mood straight away, which was a relief for Lola, as Aibgrene sat scrutinizing her. She wasn't off the hook yet.

'Well, girls, we'll leave you to it,' said Daithi as he turned and gave Aibgrene a gentle kiss on the cheek, before making his way out of the caravan. 'See you in the morning, Lola.'

'Bye, lads, and thank you so much, Sean.'

'No worries, Lola, but don't be making a habit of it,' he quipped before ducking out the door.

'Daithi, will you take a look at that for me tonight?' shouted Aibgrene after him.

With a knowing nod, Daithi and Sean left, leaving Lola to face her inquisitor once again.

'So you said that you went somewhere else?'

Lola tried to get the vision or the dream clear in her head, before she began to speak.

'It's not so much that it was a different place, I was running through this wood and it was dark. It was snowing and I was trying to get to somewhere. I don't know where, but I felt like I was running out of time.'

'What were you like in this dream?' asked Aibgrene, catching Lola's attention.

'What makes you think I was any different?' asked Lola suspiciously.

'Nothing, I was only asking, that's all,' murmured Aibgrene.

Continuing, Lola tried her best to remember the details but it was all so fractured and hazy.

'I was wearing strange clothes; it felt like animal skin or something and a long cloak with a hood – not a good fashion choice to say the least. I even had a sword. It was made of silver or something and it was engraved, but I can't remember with what. I think I was being chased, I couldn't see any faces, but they had torches and dogs. Then my bag began to glow like there was something in it. I drew out this sword and that's when I caught my reflection.'

Closing her eyes Lola tried to recall the feeling when she saw someone else's face.

'It was quite surreal, I was the same person, it felt like me running through the wood, it was my body. My eyes were the same, but my hair was flame red. It was me but someone else. It sounded like a story Arthur told me many years ago. It was about Brigid. That sounds crazy, doesn't it?'

The caravan was in darkness now, but Lola welcomed the cool night air that was filtering in through the opened door. She lay in silence waiting for Aibgrene to say something, hoping she would offer an explanation as to what was happening to her, but it didn't come.

'Well, what do you think?' Lola asked, but Aibgrene was just shaking her head in bewilderment, before getting up off the bed.

'You need to get some rest, Lola, for the big day tomorrow. I'll be in the cottage if you need anything. Okay?'

Despite the fact that she wanted answers, Lola felt too drained to mount a protest and laying her head on the pillow she closed her eyes and tried to find sleep.

CHAPTER 36

She woke again a little later with the moon shining into the caravan, flooding it with a pale white light. Getting out of bed she shuffled to the small cupboard that housed the toilet. Stepping into the small cubicle she closed the door behind her still half asleep.

Far off in the distance she could hear the faint sound of music and singing as it drifted down towards the campsite. Washing her hands in the sink, Lola could hear someone talking close by. Listening closer she could make out Aibgrene and Daithi. It sounded as though they were arguing. Not wanting to eavesdrop, Lola was just about to go back to bed when she heard her name.

'Lola deserves to know, Aibgrene,' protested Daithi. 'You can't keep this from her forever.' There was urgency in his voice, but no aggression just gentle reasoning.

'Not now, Daithi, it's not the time, plus we're not sure. Don't you understand that I'm trying to protect her?'

The emotion and agony in Aibgrene's voice touched Lola, as she stood intently listening to the exchange.

'We have been brought up in this lifestyle, this culture,' pressed

Aibgrene. 'Can you understand how difficult all this is for her? She must be terrified. She's lost Arthur and hasn't even got the chance to truly grieve. Add to that the guilt she feels every time she has to look at me, or hears me talking about my mother. She feels as though it's all her fault that Celeste was captured. She's trying so hard to step up, and I don't want to ruin what little normality and happiness she has at the moment.'

Daithi's tone was soft and reassuring now. 'I know, love. I know how important she is to you and how much you care about her, but she could be in danger, you're playing with fire here.'

'As long as she wears the ring, she'll be safe; no one can harm her. Now is not the time. We need to be sure.'

'That parchment is pretty clear, Aibgrene. This is the start of the battle. I think you could be right about Arthur's intentions. Looking at his log books he knew this time was coming and he recognised Lola's importance in all of this. Your mother could see it too, but why didn't they tell her who and what she really is?'

'To protect her, I suppose. I don't know, maybe they weren't sure either. It's not exactly something that you throw into normal conversation,' said Aibgrene.

'Maybe you're right, maybe they weren't sure. But you are, and she's bound to be wondering what happened up there today.'

'I wasn't sure at first. I thought the ring had Arthur's magick in it, but then I realised that she is the one controlling it. On me or you it would just be a normal signet ring, yet on her it holds such powerful magick, and it's getting stronger and stronger and she doesn't even realise it. Then there's the random Irish she has been speaking. After what happened today there can be no doubt. What she thinks was a dream was actually a glimpse of a previous life, a life she lived over three thousand years ago,' explained Aibgrene. 'Arthur's story was really about her.'

'So much rests on her shoulders, and I can understand why you want to protect her, but if Celeste figured it out and you figured it out, I'm pretty sure the Hell Fire Club know about Lola Paige,' warned Daithi, his ominous tone making the hairs on Lola's neck prickle.

'They do know about her,' said Aibgrene wearily, as if she had just revealed a great secret that had been a great burden. 'That attack outside our shop and the car that followed us today is proof of that.

That's why I made the decision to leave Brook Mill Manor. If I'm right, they know I'm with her but I really don't think they are fully aware of who she is and what she is capable of.'

Lola sat rigid as the panic rose in waves over her body. All she could hear was her own heartbeat as it accelerated. Yet while she should have been running and screaming for the nearest exit she just sat there. Trying to pick out bits of the conversation, she turned it over and over again in her head. She knew there had to be an explanation for the things that were happening to her.

But Aibgrene was wrong. It wouldn't be too much for her to take. She was well aware of the way that she was changing and how powerful the ring was becoming. Any doubts she had were eradicated when she stood in front of that ancient stone today. Yet part of her couldn't really believe it. Lola had felt her soul awaken, yet her mind – especially her ego – struggled to understand. This sort of thing didn't happen in the REAL world.

Finally getting up off the cold floor Lola climbed into bed. Lying there in the dark, she thought about her questions before the incident at the Lia Fail. She had been asking Arthur for answers and it looked as though she had been given them, however abstract they appeared to be. Even from her bed, Lola could feel the energy of this ancient and sacred site, a place that was so familiar. Clearly part of her soul recognised Teamhair as home.

CHAPTER 37

Lola stood speechless as Aibgrene emerged into the open living room of the cottage. She was shrouded in the most exquisite pale cream wedding dress. Like a vision, the lace dress, which was embroidered with an intricate Celtic Knot, dripped off her porcelain shoulders into a V shape, as the intricate stitching travelled down onto the bodice. It was impossible to tell where the golden knot started and where it ended. It was eternal, perfect for a wedding, thought Lola. The dress hugged Aibgrene's waist and hips cascading like a waterfall at the bottom. Her mum had done a fantastic job. The long bell sleeves added that romantic touch, as did Aibgrene's honey-coloured hair, which fell down her back in thick ringlets. Aibgrene stood looking in the mirror. She was so like her mother in many ways and she was quite unsure how she had managed to get through these last few months without her. Today was going to be the most difficult, but she had Lola and Daithi.

'Well, what do you think, Lo?' Lola lifted the garland of pink foxgloves, blue forget-me-nots and wild roses that lay on the table and gently placed it on her head.

'Perfect. Absolutely perfect,' beamed Lola, taking a step back to admire the view.

Her aura didn't glow. It pulsed. Lola drank in the beautiful wisp of apple green that she'd come to associate with her friend. Today, it was smattered with bright yellow and pink. It reminded Lola of a tie-dyed t-shirt she'd tried to make once. It was magnificent. But there, just on the edge of her aura, she could see a tiny fleck of light grey. Lola understood today would be a bitter sweet one for Aibgrene. The most important person in her life would be missing. Celeste wouldn't be there to hold her hand, to cry when she was married, to do all the things mothers did on the day of their daughter's wedding. Lola was in awe of Aibgrene's strength. At times it made her feel so ashamed.

'You're amazing, Miss Moone. Celeste would be so proud of you today,' enthused Lola, feeling the tears well up in her eyes, she tried to compose herself. 'Cad ata taobh istigh, Leirionn ar an taobh amuigh. What lies within, reflects without.' The words were out before Lola had even time to think about where they had come from. That had been happening a lot lately. But she seemed to be the only one taken aback by her new found understanding of the gaeilge language. A wide grin spread across Aibgrene's face as she clapped her hands in approval.

'You really are growing, Lola. You still have so much to discover about yourself.' Not long ago Lola would have rejected the notion, but after her little waltz with the Lia Fail, perhaps Aibgrene was right.

'I really don't know where all this is coming from. I mean I never studied Irish at school or anything. Arthur taught me a bit, but the stuff I've been coming out with... It's like someone else is speaking through me.' Lola didn't like the way Aibgrene was looking at her so she tried to change the subject. 'Anyway, enough about my craziness, this is your big day and you look otherworldly like a modern-day Ophelia. You're radiance is undeniable. Daithi is going to be blown away.'

'I hope I do a bit better than poor Ophelia did, driven to death by love and madness, found in a river of rushes and flowers,' laughed Aibgrene.

'I meant more like the picture than the character, you know? Serene. Beautiful.'

'I know what you mean, Lo, I'm just messing,' said Aibgrene serious now. 'It means so much to me that you're here, Lola. It wouldn't be the same without you. Thank you for everything.'
Aibgrene pulled Lola over into a warm hug.

'I wish my mum was here today, but I know she will be in spirit.'

As always, Lola seemed to think it was her fault that Celeste Moone wasn't there, but it wasn't until that moment, standing there looking at Celeste's daughter on her wedding day, that she realised that Aibgrene had been right. She had carried that guilt, a burden from which she had been trying to escape.

'It's my fault, and I'll make it right,' said Lola unable to look at Aibgrene. 'I'm so sorry.'

'Lola. Lola. Look at me!' pleaded Aibgrene, as she reached out and lifted Lola's chin. 'Look at me. I don't ever want to hear you say that again, do you hear me?' Her tone was firm, almost angry. 'It's not your fault. My mother is a very experienced witch, she knew what she was doing and she did it for a reason. It was not your fault. Okay?'

'If I'd only been more insistent ...'

'It happened the way it was meant to happen. Now that's it, Lola,' insisted Aibgrene. 'No more. This is supposed to be the happiest day of my life, let's lift the mood. It's not every day that I get to bind myself to my "Anam Cara".' Lola had never heard this expression before, but of course she understood the words perfectly. There was no doubt in her mind that Daithi and Aibgrene were soul friends. They were truly made for each other. Stepping out into the glorious sunshine, she followed as Aibgrene joined the procession of brides, all dressed in flowing dresses, holding small bouquets of posies and singing as they made their way to the hill top. It was quite a spectacle. The large marquee sat in what was once the Royal Enclosure, of Cormac MacAirt. Behind it sat the Lia Fail.

As she passed the large granite stone, the small signet ring began to stir and a sense of panic rose in Lola's stomach. The sound of a bell peeling out around the site helped her focus, and she fell back in line with the rest of the guests, following the trail of rose petals towards the makeshift altar that had been erected under a large hawthorn tree.

The hawthorn was in full bloom, its white flowers acting as natural confetti, sprinkling the altar whenever the gentle breeze blew. The tree itself seemed to be awash with colour and it wasn't until Lola came a bit closer that she realised that every branch had something hanging from it. There were ribbons of every shape and size tied to it and tiny crystals and pieces of paper wedged into it. It was truly magical and one of the most beautiful sights she had ever seen. The altar was adorned with pink and white roses and other wildflowers. Two large white candles sat on either side of the makeshift altar and Lola could smell perfumed incense which gave off a sweet apple scent – it was delicious.

Lola came to halt beside Sean and the other guests, as all six couples were called forward by the Priestess. Lola had met the Priestess the day before, while helping with the preparations. She had raven black hair, which was cut into a neat short bob. Her robe was made of pink silk and she wore a head piece like the one Celeste had worn, with a full moon in the centre and two crescent moons at each side. Her male counterpart was dressed in blue, and Lola had noticed him the previous day also.

He had caught her attention because he reminded her of someone, but she couldn't figure out who. He was quite tall, with grey hair and a long peppered beard. This was so far removed from any wedding ceremony Lola had ever been to. What stood out for Lola was the perfect balance between male and female. This parity appealed to Lola and all her sensibilities. To her that was the way it was intended. After all, man and woman were created by the divine, thus they were equal in their divinity.

Having been brought up in the Catholic faith, there was much about its dogma that didn't sit well with her. The main factor had always been that women were never treated as equals. They were put on pedestals for other women to live up to, but that always struck Lola as unfair and unrealistic, because to her, life was for living and experiencing, learning and growing. Many women and men could not live up to the archaic expectations that constitutional Catholicism imposed and she believed that this inevitably damaged their relationship with their God.

To her it was much the same for all organised religions, and she believed God and religion were two completely different things. Thinking about it, Lola realised she'd always been drawn to the female aspects of the church – Mother Mary, Saint Brigid and Saint Therese. The celebration of the sacred feminine had been choked and killed by men over millennia, not just in the Christian faith, but also in Judaism and Islam. Lola truly believed that it was the denial of the female aspects of nature that created a major imbalance in the world, yet here was a belief system, as old as time itself, still flourishing in an Ireland that had been torn asunder by dogma.

Stepping forward the high priestess was first to address the gathering.

'As with our ancient Kings and Queens, we are gathered here today at Tara on this most joyous festival, Lughnasadh, where we celebrate the bounties of the Earth Goddess and we offer a blessing to the east, south, west and north before we begin this hand-fasting ritual.'

CHAPTER 38

Lola listened intently, as the priestess and priest began their blessing. On cue, three harpists perched on a small ridge behind the hawthorn tree began to pluck the chords, and the sound that came out almost brought Lola to her knees – Johann Pachelbel's Canon in D fluttered through the air. The last time she had heard it was at Arthur's funeral, it was one of his favourite pieces of music. Lola had always been used to the full instrumental version, but today it was stripped bare, and the ethereal sound of the harps brought a tear to her eye. After lighting the candles and incense, the priest and priestess turned to face the gathering. The priest spoke first, his strong husky voice reverberating over the hillside.

'We gather here in a ritual of love with those who would be wedded. Aibgrene and Daithi please come forward and stand here before us, and before the gods of nature.'

As instructed, the couple stepped forward, with Daithi in front of the priestess, and Aibgrene positioned in front of the priest, as the priestess continued.

'Be with us here, O beings of the Air, with your clever fingers, tie closely the bonds between these two.'

At this signal Daithi held out his hand, while Aibgrene reciprocated, placing hers onto his. The priest began to tie a white ribbon around their hands.

'Be with us here, O beings of Fire, give their love and passion your own all-consuming ardour.'

This time a scarlet ribbon was produced and tied. Lola sat in rapture as the priestess continued. 'Be with us here, O beings of Water, give them the deepest of love and the richness of the body, of the soul and of the spirit.'

A light blue ribbon was added to symbolise the element of water. Finally, the Priest produced a brown ribbon as his female counterpart evoked the spirit of the earth.

'Be with us here, O beings of Earth, let your strength and constancy be theirs for so long as they desire to remain together. Blessed Goddess and Laughing God give to these before you; we do ask your love and protection. Blessed Be.'

Turning towards the altar, the priestess and priest lifted what Lola guessed was a piece of branch from the hawthorn tree. Holding it aloft between them they placed it on the hands of the newlywed couple as they spoke in unison.

'For the Goddess and the God are with you, now and always.'

There was a slight pause before they continued.

'Is it your wish, Aibgrene Moone, to become one with this man?'

'It is my wish to become one with this man.'

'Is it your wish, Daithi O'Neill, to become one with this woman?'

There was slight pause before he answered, but looking into Aibgrene eyes, he spoke softly and slowly,

'Tugaim mo chroí duit go deo – I give my heart to you forever.'

A soft murmur of appreciation rippled around the crowd. Tears began to fall from Lola's eyes at the beauty of the words spoken.

'Then, as the Goddess, the God and the spirits of Tara bear witness to this rite, I now proclaim you husband and wife.'

A loud roar and cheers erupted from the gathering, as the couple kissed to consummate their ceremony. This was continued down the line until each couple was bound.

The evening passed away at speed and each guest danced and ate their fill. As dusk closed in Lola escaped from the tent to enjoy the evening air. Climbing one of the mounds, she sat and marvelled at the beautiful sunset. To her left lay the Lia Fail, dormant now. Some of the guests had been gathering fire wood for the last hour and began to build a large bonfire.

Aibgrene had told her that this was always her favourite part of the evening when they would all sit around the fire, and the bard would tell stories of legend. A soft vibrating noise alerted Lola that her phone was ringing. She had put it on silent throughout the service and had forgotten to change it back. When she lifted it out the display read Alex. Hitting the answer button Lola tried to think of what to tell him. There was no way she could tell him the truth.

'Hi there, how are you?' she answered.

'Lola. Hi! I was calling to see if you would like to go to see a movie tonight.'

Lola sensed something in his tone; he seemed a bit more subdued than usual.

'Sorry, Alex, I meant to text you earlier to say I would be out of town this weekend. I'm in Dublin with a friend.'

'A friend?' he enquired, his tone considerably colder, as Lola caught his train of thought. 'Yeah, her cousin got married today,' lied Lola, 'and her partner let her down at the last minute, so she asked me to come along.' Just at that, the music in the tent came on, as Faithless began to ring out over the Boyne Valley, Lola couldn't believe her ears. 'It must be some party. I can hear the music, sounds more like a club.'

'I know I'm as shocked as you are to hear dance music,' laughed Lola. 'Let's just say it was a very traditional wedding, and this is the last place I expect to hear Faithless.'

Lola felt awkward, she could sense his irritation as the conversation began to run dry.

'The other reason I called you, Lola, was to ask you to dinner. My father would like to meet the young lady that has been taking up all of my free time.' Lola hadn't been expecting that. Lost for words, she began to stutter. 'You don't have to if you don't want to, Lola; it's not a big deal.' Lola could hear the disappointment in his voice, but there was relief there as well. She really missed him. It would have been great if she could have shared this occasion with him. So why couldn't she bring herself to tell him the truth? Lola accepted that here was no denying the fact. She didn't trust Alex Stein. She was only lying to herself if she pretended otherwise.

'Don't be so silly,' answered Lola, finally. 'I'd love to meet your dad,' she lied. The thought made her feel physically sick. 'When would you like me to come up?' Alex let out a sigh of relief; even the sound of his breath was enough to send her stomach fluttering. 'How does next Saturday suit you? You can stay for the weekend.' Lola couldn't deny the effect that Alex Stein had on her or how happy she was when she was with him. If only it was that simple, she thought, but life rarely was.

'That would be lovely! I'll give you a call when I get back. Okay?'

'Okay, Lola. I miss you.' Lola's stomach fluttered to the lyrical thrum of Alex's smooth American accent. 'You too, Alex. I'll see you soon.' Lola hung up and placed the phone back into her bag, feeling even more conflicted than before.

'There you are, Miss Paige. I've been looking everywhere for you,' sang Aibgrene, as she shuffled up the small satellite mound, struggling to keep her wedding dress off the ground. She had a thick quilted blanket with her. 'Here you are. I thought you might get a little cold later.' Aibgrene threw the patchwork quilt at Lola, as she slid down and took a seat beside her. Lola draped the blanket around her shoulders, grateful for its warmth.

'Do you want some?' offered Lola but Aibgrene waved off the gesture as she tried to catch her breath.

'No, I'm roasting with all that dancing about.'

'Speaking of which,' laughed Lola, 'What's that all about? A bunch of tree huggers listening to dance music, raving the night away. Just when I thought things couldn't get any stranger.'

'What?' laughed Aibgrene. 'Dance music is great for the soul. It raises the energy levels, which can result in very powerful magick.'

'Oh please, Aibgrene,' protested Lola, clearly not convinced.

'What was your first reaction when you heard it? I bet you smiled and there is no way you can sit still to it. Even if you don't like it, you have to move. It lifts the mood, I'm telling ya. Add a bit of Faithless or Tiesto to an energy lay-line like the one we're sitting on now and it can create a lot of positive energy, Lola. You confound me, Lo, you really do. You're surrounded by these things. You can see it, you can feel it, you can sense it, yet, you still deny it. Why do you do that?'

'I don't deny it,' protested Lola, slightly stung by Aibgrene's candidness. 'I just like to have an open mind that's all.'

'It's about time you did open your mind. Who was that on the phone?'

Lola didn't answer her straight away.

'You know rightly who it was, Aibgrene.'

'Where did you tell him you were?'

'Don't worry I didn't tell him the truth, I lied and said I was at a wedding in Dublin.'

'I know you didn't, Lo. That's not what I'm getting at. What I'm getting at is the fact that you chose to lie. You did that for a reason.'

Aibgrene's words hung thick in the air between them. Lola contemplated her reply. She didn't want things to end badly between them. It had been a magical day and she didn't want anything to spoil that. 'Let's not do this right now, Aibgrene. Okay?' suggested Lola amicably.

'Enjoying the view girls?' Lola was delighted to see Daithi climbing up to join them.

'It's something else, isn't it?' continued Lola, admiring the vista and trying to dispel the tension between her and Aibgrene.

'It sure is, Lola, and even though I live here, it never looks the same. There is always something new about the night time at Team-hair,' replied Daithi, in his usual gentle tone. The first stars were beginning to emerge as the sky descended into darkness. Shouts came from below and the music came to a halt as the guests gathered around the large bonfire that had been ignited. Lola couldn't prise her eager eyes away from the bright gibbous moon as the three of them walked towards the large circle of flames to join the other revellers. A few bursts of white light caught the side of Lola's eyes as she turned towards the hawthorn tree. At first she thought she was imagining it, but then tiny little sparks flashed and moved around again.

'I didn't know we had fireflies in Ireland, they're beautiful. Look!' said Lola.

Aibgrene looked towards the Hawthorn and began to laugh as she turned back to Daithi. 'Daithi, Lola didn't know there were fireflies in Ireland!' she said, as if they were enjoying a private joke, at Lola's expense.

'Yeah, Lola, they're everywhere! Enchanting, isn't it?' said

Daithi in response.

'What are you two laughing about? What's so funny?' asked Lola, slightly agitated by the obvious jibe.

Putting his arm around her shoulder, like a parent would do to their child who has just said something innocent, but funny, Daithi whispered into her ear. 'They're not fireflies, Lo, that's the Sidhe. If you look hard enough you might even see Queen Aine herself.'

CHAPTER 39

'Fairies?' snorted Lola, as her emerald eyes tried to catch the tiny dots of light that flitted around the hawthorn tree. But Daithi and Aibgrene didn't share her humour, as they left her alone to go and join the rest of the group. The wedding guests were beginning to settle down around the large bonfire, the Lughnasadh celebrations were underway.

'You're not having another one of your episodes. Are you, Lola?' said Sean as he stood beside her looking towards the tree with a large grin on his face. 'What's so interesting over there?'

Lola looked at him as though it was obvious what she was looking at.

'Can't you see the light?' enquired Lola hopefully, until she realised how crazy she must be sounding, immediately changing the subject. 'Oh, it's nothing, must be the light from the fire catching the crystals on the tree. Are you heading over to the bonfire then?'

Walking towards the rest of the group, Sean fell into step beside her. Lola realised he was tall, but standing beside him she was able to get a true sense of his dimensions as he towered above her. He was very good looking and spoke with a soft southern Irish accent. Sean looked familiar, but Lola couldn't quite place his face, she was sure she had seen him somewhere before, but that had been happening quite a bit since she arrived at Tara.

'I never really got the chance to say thank you, Sean, for looking after me, so thanks.'

'Don't be silly, Lola; I love all that damsel in distress stuff. I'm glad you're okay. You really scared me up there. You look a lot better today mind you.'

'I feel a lot better an' all. It's been a great day, they make a perfect couple, don't they?'

Lola and Sean looked over to where Daithi sat with Aibgrene in his arms. Sitting down across from them on a large log, Aibgrene caught Lola's eye and, nodding towards Sean, gave her a knowing wink. Lola laughed off the implication. The small group that had gathered around the fire sat talking quietly until the priest stood to address them.

'Today some of you have been joined in marriage, and others have come to celebrate this joyous occasion. As always, Lughnasadh is a very important day in our calendar and we have gathered here around this eternal flame to continue a tradition that is as old as the hill we sit on. For generations our kind has kept our oral traditions alive through stories passed from family to family, from generation to generation, over millennia.

'Tonight our bard is no other than Sean O'Neill, an international rugby player by day, and esteemed orator by night. If you would all put your hands together for Sean.'

Standing to receive his raucous applause, Sean was quite embarrassed, and quickly sat back down again.

'Aren't you a dark horse,' teased Lola, who recognised him now.

She had seen him on television a few weeks ago playing rugby for Ireland, he had scored the winning try. According to the pundits he was the next big thing. Had it been football then she would have recognised him immediately, but rugby was never her thing. The hum of the crowd quietened down and the only sound now was the crackling of the fire, its flames lighting the faces that sat around it waiting eagerly for Sean to begin.

'Some say they came from the sea in the west, others believe they descended in the high air from the north. However they arrived here in the mystical Boyne Valley, one thing is for sure, the Tuatha Dé Danann, or the People of the Goddess Danu were the most advanced race ever to come to Ireland. With them they brought four extremely powerful and magickal items from their homeland. From the city of Falies in the north, they brought the Lia Fail or the Stone of Destiny, which still sits at Teamhair to this day. This ancient stone holds such powerful energy and magick that only a true descendant of the Dé Danann can activate and control it. For millennia the high kings and queens of Ireland stood upon it waiting for its mighty roar to confirm them as the next rightful ruler.'

Lola's mind was racing now, she could see that Aibgrene had been looking at her, perhaps for some sort of reaction or eureka moment. The stone had spoken to her, of that she was sure, but surely this didn't mean that she was a descendant of some mystical race from the annals of Irish mythology. She had heard all the stories about the Dé Danann from Arthur, but she had always believed that it was folklore and nothing more. Lola listened intently as Sean continued, his voice growing more animated as he spoke.

'From the city of Gorias in the south, they brought with them the Sword of Virtue, which legend has it was passed down from the Good God Dagda, to his daughter Brigid, the Goddess of fire and healing. It is said that when battling the forces of darkness Brigid used her magick to ignite the sword with a silver flame, protecting all those around her. From the east and the city of Fiats came the Spear of Victory, a spear so powerful that no one could defeat it.

'Wars have been fought over its possession and when the Dé Danann was finally forced to retreat to Tir Na nOg it was because they had lost the Spear of Victory to the shadow masters of fear and deceit. Masters that are still at large today. Now, more than ever. They have been in possession of this object for the last two millennia.

'Some believe that it was the very same sword that pierced the side of Christ himself and later fell into the hands of Napoleon and Hitler. The final object, and possibly the most important, is the Cauldron from Muitas in the west. The Cauldron of plenty was the Dagda's greatest gift to his people. A source of eternal sustenance and life, no party ever left feeling hungry again. As we all know the Cauldron represented true alchemy, the transformation of the spirit back to its natural state of pure light and divinity. The legend of the Tuatha Dé Danann tells us that they will once again return to Ireland and this realm and, like the true Aquarians they are, they will usher in a new dawn for mankind.'

Sean fell silent for a moment, gazing into the orange and yellow flames that were dancing and swaying in the cool night air. Lola followed his gaze towards the bright fire that crackled and shifted, completely immersed in his every word. She had been struggling to make a connection between the Dé Danann and Arthur, to connect the dots, and yet this ancient site had yielded more questions than answers. Sean moved to his feet and gestured towards the druid who sat perched on a log at the opposite side of the pyre from her. Lola hadn't noticed him until then as the old man had traded his ritual robe for an inconspicuous pair of brown corduroy trousers and a cream aran sweater. His moses sandals were quite worn and his grey wiry hair was windblown and dishevelled. He had the distinct look of someone who lived by the sea. Lola guessed he was in his late sixties and despite his weathered and unkempt appearance she could see the knowledge and wisdom housed in every laughter line and wrinkle. Using the light from the growing fire Lola traced her eyes along the man's violet aura. She had never seen one like that before, it was so strong. With surprising agility, he jumped to his feet, giving Sean a gentle nod before he began to introduce himself. His textured voice was a soft and raspy hum that seemed to flow in rhythm with the dancing flames.

'Thank you, Sean! For those that do not know me I am Darragh Blaney and I'm from the West Country. I come from the Isle of Innis Mor, but have been living here at Teamhair for many years. In that time I've seen the fear machine and its mechanisms at work, played out on an international and local level. I know that opinion is divided on the times we are living in but we need to wake up.

'Some believe that the return of the Tuatha Dé Danann is only a child's story, a myth. But there are those amongst us that know that this time is very near. The signs are everywhere – if you know where to look. In the past ten years there has been a significant shift and increase in the intensity of this battle that is being waged by this sinister group. Their aim is to keep each of us in spiritual bondage.

'Some believe that this concept of an elitist agenda behind our wars, violence and lack in this world is but a conspiracy theory, concocted by some crazy old man like myself. But the truth is, they do exist and they are not just interested in power, they want our souls. They know the universal laws, they know our true divinity and they know what we are capable of, and this is what terrifies them. Because if we too realised this, our world would be transformed in the blink of an eye, and their power and control would be extinguished, forever.

'They can't allow this to happen, so they create and fund war, which in turn creates death and hate, and while we are busy hating and killing each other we are blind to the divinity that resides in each and every living thing on this planet. The light-workers have returned to our plane, and some sit here amongst us tonight. You might not yet know your true purpose, but in the coming days, months and years you will.

'There are more and more light-workers awakening from their slumber. They are aware that the time has come to stand up and help humanity accept and acknowledge her true nature – which is that of light and love. But in this dark night, we have much to do before the dawn of the new epoch can begin.

'These forces will stop at nothing to get what they want. They hide behind politics and the highest offices in the land. They hide behind big business, the law and organised religion. We only have to look beyond this hill to see their dark scar. How they have forced a motorway through our sacred lands here. We can switch on the television any time, day or night. Palestine, Iraq, Afghanistan – even our own island has been ravaged by thirty years of neighbour against neighbour.

'Fear and greed breed hate, which in turn spawns violence and war. It's no co-incidence that it's raging at one of the most powerful energy lay-lines on the planet. By creating fear and hate, by slaughtering innocents, by waging war at such a powerful site, this resonates throughout the world, and we can see evidence of this everywhere. All of the world's conflict is controlled by a relatively small number of people – known to us as the Hell Fire Club.'

CHAPTER 40

There was a loud round of applause and shouts of support for Darragh's appeal but some of those gathered around the fire started to shift and murmur. They looked quite uneasy, as though they were not really convinced that this was true. Lola wasn't one of them; she had heard both Celeste and Markus say the same thing at Arthur's cremation.

As a journalism student, she was well aware of the conflict around the world, so much of it didn't sit well with her. She had always questioned the 'truth' as told by various media outlets. Everyone had an agenda, and in recent years the right-wing press seemed to be winning that battle. In the light of what she had heard and experienced over the past few months, Darragh's insight seemed to make perfect sense to her now – the jigsaw puzzle began to fit together. She listened intently as he continued.

'Already, we're beginning to see evidence of a mass awakening. There are signs that the revolution by dissolution has begun. All over the world people are trying to take that power back. They are taking to the streets as the old institutions begin to crumble. This is no more evident than here in Erin. But while this rages around us, we too have our part to play. It is a crucial one that will have far-reaching implications.

'At this very moment we are gathered together at one of the most important spiritual and sacred sites in all of Ireland. Not just here at Teamhair, but the entire Boyne Valley which lies on the same lay line as the Tor in Glastonbury and the Pyramids at Giza. Just over the Valley is the home of the Dé Danann, who left many esoteric texts, which few have seen. Legend has it that it prophesises the return of the Goddess Brigid and her tribe. The very old rhyme, that my very own grandmother used to recite to me, tells of her return. It says:

> *When the Goddess with the emerald eyes returns,*
> *So too will her fiery light;*
> *Her healing and radiant sun,*
> *Will extinguish even the blackest of knights.*
> *What lies within will reflect without,*
> *Leaving all in her wake with little doubt.*
> *Hanging her mantle upon the sun,*
> *She'll bring Danu's light to everyone.*

'The fire that burns inside her will ignite a spark in even the darkest of souls. Only Her spirit can usher in a new day. Only a true descendant of the Tuatha Dé Danann can ignite the truth, and only she can protect Metatron's Cube from those that covet it.'

At that moment Lola and Aibgrene caught each other's eyes. So much understanding flowed between them in those few seconds, it was almost as if they were talking to each other, yet no words were spoken. There was no need for language. Was Lola a descendant of the Tuatha Dé Danann? Had Arthur known this from the first time they met? Did she believe it?

As Darragh finished, the music started and the sound of bodhrans, drums and tin whistles rang out over the Boyne Valley once again. Lola wrapped the warm blanket around her body as she gazed into the flames. She wasn't afraid anymore, in fact, the burning embers seemed to make her passion, strength and pride swell. Was she once a great warrior goddess? It seemed ridiculous, but something in her had stirred. Aibgrene was right when she had told her to open her mind; all the things that she had been experiencing were signs.

Deep in her soul Lola now acknowledged this truth, but she was still only a girl, living in a world that was dictated by the senses. There was that seed of doubt that had always been at the back of her mind, that self-doubt. She wasn't important enough or good enough, how could she be? Lola Paige, a working-class girl from Ballyvalley. How could she be anything other than what she appeared to be? It was a beautiful thought, that she could be governed by her gut, by her instincts, but still there was something extremely far-fetched about the suggestion that she had lived as Brigid over three thousand years ago. Deep in thought Lola hadn't noticed that she was shivering.

'Are ye feeling the cold, Lola?' said Sean looking down at her with a playful smile on his face. 'Come on get up and give me a dance, that'll soon warm you up.'

Lola didn't even have time to reply, as Sean lifted her up off the seat and swung her about in his arms. Her feet eventually touched the ground and she followed his lead as he whirled her around and around to the sound of a fast Irish reel. As the reel played by the musicians accelerated, Sean continued to spin her until she almost lost her balance, but once again he was there to catch her when she fell.

'I think I need to sit down,' said Lola, not noticing that they had moved away from the rest of the revellers, dancing around the fire.

'Is this how you get your girls, Sean?' asked Lola. 'You disorientate them and then lure them to a secluded spot?' she laughed, as she sat down under the hawthorn tree she had been admiring earlier. It took a few moments for her to realise what she had said. Embarrassed she tried to back-track. 'I mean. I don't mean me. I'm not saying you are trying to, you know ...me!'

Sean sat beside her enjoying her discomfort, letting her ramble on until she fell quiet.

'Well has it worked, Lola? Has my bold plan to get you on your own worked?' said Sean softly, as he began to move closer to her. Lola could feel the heat from his body next to hers and she quite liked it.

'Well, I suppose it has. We're here and they are over there,' smiled Lola.

'Good.'

Without another word Sean gently kissed her lips, breaking off momentarily to make sure that she was okay with it. Without a word, Lola reciprocated, not really thinking about what she was doing. It felt right. Lifting her on to his knee as though she weighed nothing, Sean pulled her closer to him, as Lola continued to kiss him.

It felt normal. It felt good, and despite his stature he was so gentle, his lips caressing hers as his hands found her waist. But there was something missing. It was that light feeling in her stomach, that tantalising wave of electricity that she felt when she was with Alex. She was really attracted to Sean, but he wasn't Alex. 'I'm so sorry Sean. I... I can't do this,' Lola broke off abruptly. 'I'm sort of with someone at the moment. You're such a great lad... But I shouldn't be doing this.' Sitting back down on the grass, Lola felt terrible. What had she been thinking? It must have been all that twirling and dancing. Her head wasn't straight. She was the worst liar, and there was no way that Alex wouldn't know. Not that he would care. Or would he? What was it they had anyway? He was Alex Stein after all and for all she knew he could be with a different girl every night. So why did she feel like she'd betrayed him, for a second time that day? 'I think it's time I called it a night,' said Lola awkwardly.

'Come on, I'll walk you to your cabin,' said Sean gently. 'I'm sorry if I was a bit forward – you're very hard to resist, Lola.'

'I wasn't exactly beating you off with big stick, Sean. I'm sorry too. You're a great kisser though,' smiled Lola. 'Friends?' she offered, extending her hand.

'Well if that's all there is at the moment, I'll take that,' said Sean as he reluctantly shook her hand. He and Lola walked across Tara to their campsite in silence, guided by the bright harvest moon. Most of the revellers had returned to the site after what had been a very long day. They passed the small earthen cottage and headed to the back of the garden, where the Romany caravan sat. Feeling quite awkward Lola stood up on the first step.

'Well, that's me home safe and sound,' said Lola, and reaching over, she embraced Sean, planting a kiss on his cheek. 'Thank you, Sean. I really mean that, thank you for everything.' Standing so close to him, Lola felt the urge to kiss him again, but it would be wrong to give him mixed signals.

'You're very welcome, Lola, you're a very beautiful person and whoever this fella is – he's a very lucky man. I just hope he's worthy of you.'

Not sure what to say, Lola didn't offer a reply, afraid that she might change her mind. Sean seemed like the perfect man for her, Aibgrene would certainly approve. He was funny, gentle, and aware of what she was going through at the moment, not to mention gorgeous – what was she thinking? But he wasn't Alex; Lola couldn't explain what she felt when she was with him. It was like she had no control over her emotions. She was inexplicably drawn to him, as to why, she couldn't say.

'Night, night, Mr O'Neill,' said Lola.

'Night, Miss Paige.'

Closing the cabin door behind her, Lola undressed and climbed into bed, exhausted. Lying there in the dark she could feel the power and energy of the ring around her neck beginning to awaken again. It felt as though it was connected to her now. It felt as though it was a part of her soul, and now that she had awoken, so too had it. She could feel the comfort of its warm embryonic protection and for the first time believed that she could become the young woman that Arthur thought she was.

Lola now understood that this was why Aibgrene had insisted on her coming to Tara. This was a test to see how she would react – to prove that her suspicions were correct. A fire had been ignited inside Lola, and like the Triple Goddess of the Celtic pantheon, she too would use that to fulfil her destiny. But that was not all she had gained from this trip – she had discovered her Anum Carra, Aibgrene was her soul friend too.

Chapter 41

Lola woke to the rain which sounded like a freight train as it fell in slanted sheets onto the roof of her caravan. It was a dull morning and the overcast sky made it impossible for Lola to tell what time it was. Her aching body implied she'd been asleep for quite some time. Lola checked her watch, it was almost 12 noon. She'd have to make her way home soon. Labouring out of bed to get washed she was a bit worried about making the journey alone, but just as the thought had entered her head, the amulet around her neck began to stir, reassuring her. Lola got washed and dressed, slipping on a pair of track bottoms and a t-shirt. Rummaging around she finally found Arthur's cardigan, and slipping it on she peeked outside.

The heavy rain had transformed the entire camp site into what could only be described as a swamp. Deciding she would need her wellingtons after all, she pulled on the red boots and headed for the cottage, hoping that Aibgrene and Daithi were awake.

Climbing the steps to the cottage, Lola could hear voices. Knocking gently on the door, she was beckoned in by Aibgrene's familiar voice. When she walked into the front room of the rustic building they were nowhere to be seen. There were two doors in the small room, one led to a bedroom, but it was empty. Then she heard Aibgrene calling her again.

'We're in here, Lo,' called Aibgrene.

Following the voice through the small wooden door, Lola walked into a large half-circular room which was filled with flat-screen computers and books. It was like some high-tech surveillance room.

'I bet you weren't expecting this, Lola, here take a seat and have a look.'

Lola sat down on the wooden chair that Daithi had pulled out as he, Aibgrene and Darragh made room for her.

'Lola, this is Darragh, he's a linguistics scholar and a very good friend of ours.'

Smiling Lola greeted the man who had presided over Aibgrene's wedding the day before and gave the rousing speech at the fire.

'Lola, good to meet you, dear. I hope you don't mind, but we've gone ahead and had a look at the parchment that you brought with you,' greeted Darragh in his vintage voice. 'I've been able to translate the majority of the text. Aibgrene has been explaining that you could pick out a few of the words yourself. You've done very well.'

Daithi had scanned the item and now it was on the large computer screen in front of them. Lola stared at the screen and the lavishly decorated gaeilge script and the colourful illustrations at the start of each passage. The computer screen had enlarged the text and illustrations, and now Lola could make out figures, a sword and a sun.

'What is it?' asked Lola, pulling closer to the screen to get a better look.

'Well we're not entirely sure, but if we are correct you could have in your possession one of the most treasured and oldest written manuscripts in the history of this island. It is something that has only been whispered about in legend and myth. If this is indeed what I think it is,' enthused Darragh, 'then this fragile parchment could lead us to the Lost Oracle of Danu, or the Oracle of the Golden Dawn as it has also been known.'

'The what?' asked Lola, both confused and intrigued.

'The Oracle of Danu, Lola, is a book that was said to have been scribed by the Tuatha Dé Danann, themselves. It is said to be made up of four folios, each containing deep esoteric magick, spiritual wisdom and knowledge of how we were all created. Contained in its sacred texts is the prophecy which tells of the Dé Danann and their light workers who will reincarnate to earth, in order to help us evolve spiritually. By now I'm sure you have heard of the Ancient Order of the Golden Dawn, but I'm not sure how much you know about them, Lola.'

Deciding that Darragh's question was a rhetorical one, Lola didn't offer an answer; instead she nodded, for him to continue.

'As you heard last night, the Dé Danann brought many items with them to Ireland, but one of the most important things was the written word and great universal wisdom that is contained in this book. Of course, we don't really know what's in the book, or if it even exists. That is, until now. All we have to go on are myths and stories that have been obscured by millennia. But just because they are myths and stories doesn't mean they are not true, or that there is not an element of truth within them. Some believe that when the Tuatha Dé Danann was forced to leave this realm by the invading Milesans, they bestowed this Oracle to a group known as the guardians, from which emerged the Ancient Order of the Golden Dawn.'

Darragh was becoming more and more animated.

'This book contained such powerful magick and knowledge which would have far exceeded the time, or any time for that matter. It would have been madness to keep it all in one place. As a result – and this is only conjecture – those who have searched for this item throughout all antiquity, believe that it was separated.'

'Yes!' exclaimed Lola. 'I remember this story Arthur told me once. I was very young. I mean it's maybe not related at all but… Well he told me a story about Brigid. She was like a warrior goddess and healer and she had a very important book. There were people after her, she had to get it to safety. So, Brigid split the book into four parts and entrusted it to her guardians, Delphius, Rocha, Luna and Manus. They then spread out across Ireland and Europe, passing the information down to the next generation. Arthur said some even went as far as Egypt. Yeah,' smiled Lola, thinking of Arthur. 'That was my favourite story.' Suddenly Lola felt very self-conscious and silly. This had probably nothing to do with what they looking at. It was only an old story.

Darragh was laughing now, which only compounded Lola's unease. 'That is more than just a story my dear. What Arthur was telling you was the legend of the lost Oracle. The group's leader,' continued Darragh, 'the leader of the guardians was from the Greek City of Delphi, and thus the Ancient Order of the Golden Dawn was born. Up until today, not even a fragment has been found of this mythical book. There are those scholars who maintain that the Book of Kells was modelled on it. Some even have gone as far as to suggest that the Book of Kells is actually the Oracle of the Golden Dawn in disguise, and that it is under a complex veil of magick. They argue that in order to protect it from the early church in Ireland it was transformed into a Christian text, but the right magick performed by the right proponent would reveal its truth. Indeed, this very parchment, which was passed on to you by no other than the head of the Order, could be the only historical reference that the Oracle exists.'

'That's quite a lot to take in, Darragh,' said Lola, slouching back on her chair. 'I mean you're talking Neolithic period here, there was no written word then, society would not have been that sophisticated. Would it?'

'Look around you, Lola. The Brú Na Bóinne was constructed then, a perfect and precise model of the cosmos, tracking the sun and the moon and the stars. Look at Stonehenge, the Pyramids at Giza. Each a perfect example of sophisticated, intelligent and sacred engineering, not to mention places of powerful energy. Where did that knowledge come from and why did it take millennia to rediscover it?' contested Darragh.

'I suppose it makes sense then for Arthur to have this, considering who he was. So what does it say?'

'Well it's written on very high quality calf vellum, like the book of Kells and you can see the various pictures and spirals. Can you see the triple spiral there at the start of the first paragraph?' They all leaned in closer as Darragh pointed it out. It was hard to see at first, in amongst all the other swirling art, but then they all seemed to see it at once. Lola recognised it immediately, but couldn't quite place where she had seen it before.

'Well that's what makes me believe this is the real deal,' said Darragh, his voice very emotional, almost breaking as if he were about to cry. 'I can only give you a rough translation as there are certain words I don't recognise.'

Taking a deep breath Darragh began to read the text aloud.

When the Goddess with the emerald eyes returns;
So too will her fiery light,
Her radiant sun extinguishing
Even the darkest of Knights.
What lies within will reflect without,
Casting light through shadow's doubt.

She will hang her mantle upon the sun,
Bringing freedom to all and one.
As the mystical Dé Danann once again awake,
The forces of darkness shall lie in wait.
Their time will be short and their mission hard,
As told to us by our greatest bard.

A time will come as blackness falls,
On the inside of our sacred Palace walls.
But lying there, as before,
Will be our Goddess with her blazon core.
Only she and she alone,
Through Her sacred spiral will lead us home.

The Oracle will free us all,
As she awakens to the divine cosmic call.

'Have you already seen this, Darragh? I mean, before today?' quizzed Lola. 'Didn't you say something like this at the fire last night?'

'No, Lola. What I recited was very similar, but it was only an old poem handed down through the generations of my family. Well at least that's what I thought until I saw this. To be honest,' said Darragh taking a seat, 'I can't really believe that we may have the only copy of this poem, or prophesy in the written word. It's more than I could ever have imagined.' Lola could see tears well in the old man's eyes, she could tell that this was quite a find, yet she remained slightly nonplussed by it all.

'There are a few things that stand out,' said Darragh as he traced his finger along the screen and read out the words aloud. '"Her radiant sun extinguishing even the darkest of knights." This is interesting because it is spelt KNIGHT, not night.' Lola sat gazing at the screen, hardly even blinking, picking out all the words that she recognised again and again. She could feel Aibgrene taking her hand, giving it a reassuring squeeze, but she didn't turn to face her friend. Looking at the illustrations painted in gold, green and yellow she suddenly remembered where she had seen that triple spiral before. She hadn't actually seen it, but had felt it. Her fingers had traced its deep grooves in the cold stone.

CHAPTER 42

It had been her dream, that same recurring dream she had for months about the cold stone chamber. A shiver ran over Lola's body at the thought of it. She had recognised that the dream meant something, even before all of this mess. Before Arthur had died, when her life was normal, when it was simple. Back then she was just Lola Paige. But that time was over. Aibgrene had warned her that she would see and hear things at Tara that she might not like or want to accept. This had been her awakening, her road to Damascus, her moment of eureka, so why didn't it feel good?

'Are you okay, Lo? Lola!'

Turning, Lola realised Aibgrene had been speaking to her.

'Oh sorry, Aibgrene! Yeah, I'm fine. I suppose I'd better make tracks.'

'Daithi and I are going to follow you up the road. Just in case,' said Aibgrene uncomfortably'

'Don't be silly, Aibgrene, I'll be fine.'

Aibgrene began to protest, but Lola just lifted the ring from under her top and waved it at her.

'Really I'll be fine, I know I will. I could do with a hand to the car with the rest of my things though.'

Lola got up off the chair, her cardigan disturbing some photos on the small table next to her. As they fell to the floor in a pile, Lola knelt down to pick them up. Suddenly Daithi was beside her. 'Please, Lola, it's fine, I'll sort that out, go you on and get your things together.' There was uneasiness in his smile, just like Aibgrene and Darragh. It seemed as though everyone was privy to some secret that she wasn't which made Lola suspicious. She couldn't see what the pictures were of, as they lay face down. Turning one of them over, she saw a picture of the black car that had followed them, the lens had zoomed in on the registration number. Written beside it in bold black maker were the words 'Car registered to Stein Corp'.

Lola lifted picture after picture, some of Tara and the motorway, highlighting the same words 'Stein Corp.' There were pictures of developments, old buildings, road works, and then at the bottom of the pile there was one of Alex and, according to the notes on the picture, his father, Carl Stein. They were both dressed in tuxedos, smiling brightly for the camera. The sign behind them read 'Stein Corp charity benefit'. Alex was a bit taller than his father, who had silver grey hair, with a tiny smattering of black around the sides. He was a very handsome man, but his son looked nothing like him. They only shared one similar characteristic and that was their eyes. Alex had his father's cold blue eyes.

'What's this all about, Daithi?' she asked.

'It's nothing, Lola, just a bit of work I've been doing, that's all.'

Aibgrene came forward to offer her explanation.

'I told you that I had a friend who could find things, Lola. I asked Daithi to try and trace the numberplate after we'd been followed coming down, and this is what we found.'

'The car is registered to Alex's father's company? Why would he send someone to follow us? I don't understand,' said Lola sitting back down on the chair, as Aibgrene and Daithi gave each other that same knowing look.

'We don't know, Lo, that's what Daithi has been trying to find out. It seems a little bit strange, don't you think? Arthur dies and suddenly Alex Stein appears in your life, he is everywhere you go. Two young girls have gone missing as well as my mum!'

'I think we've established how much you dislike Alex, Aibgrene,' spat Lola defensively. 'What are you saying? Even if it is the case, it's his father you are looking into, not him; maybe he's nothing like his dad. I know he's a bit out of my league, but …'

Lola could hear the distress and panic in her own voice again. It was all too much to take in. Alex was the only semblance of normality that she had, away from all the pressure she was under. But who was she kidding? Normal! There was nothing normal about their relationship. Then something that Alex had said came back to her, his dad had wanted to meet her.

'He wants to meet me,' whispered Lola in a daze.

Aibgrene was on her feet now.

'What? You're not going. Are you Lola?'

'Are you asking or telling me?' replied Lola defiantly.

'Oh, why do I bloody bother!' said Aibgrene impatiently.

Daithi stepped in to try and defuse the situation, all the while Darragh sat in silence.

'Come on you two, please don't be fighting. Lola, Aibgrene is just worried that's all. But you're right, we don't know anything for sure. I know how hard this must be for you, Lola, but Aibgrene only has your best interests at heart.'

Lola knew this was true, but she was sick of everyone telling her how they understood, without them having any idea just how hard it was.

'Everyone keeps on saying that,' she was almost shouting now. 'But you have no idea what this is like for me. It's like my life isn't mine anymore. I feel so restricted that I can't even make up my own mind about what to think and what to do, who to see and how to feel about them.'

Neither Daithi nor Aibgrene spoke, they just sat in silence for a while.

'Maybe you're right, Lola,' said Darragh.

Lola turned towards him having almost forgotten that he was still in the room. Slightly embarrassed, she played with her fingernails, not wanting to look at him.

'We can all see how special you are, and now we know for sure that Arthur knew this from the day and hour he met you. In fact, I would go so far as to say that he knew it before he met you. You need to do what feels right for you, Lola,' advised Darragh calmly. 'If you want to meet this man, then go and do it. I know that you will instantly see his true nature, and if he is who we think he is, then unfortunately he will also see yours. Then, I'm afraid, there can be no more protecting you.'

Lola just nodded her head, thanking Darragh, before leaving the room. It only took a few minutes for her to get her things together, and Daithi and Aibgrene helped her to the car. Packing the rest of her things into the trunk she turned to Daithi first.

'Thank you, Daithi, for everything, you have been wonderful. I'm sorry about earlier, I really didn't mean to be so rude to you.'

'Please, Lola, don't apologise, you are more than welcome. Take care and let us know when you get home okay.'

Pulling her into a warm hug, Daithi wished her well and headed back towards the site, leaving her alone with Aibgrene.

'I'd better be going,' said Lola, her temper still hot, and although she didn't want to leave on bad terms, she was too stubborn to apologise.

'It's been a lot for you to take in, Lola, thanks for coming. I'll be in touch. Okay?'

Aibgrene was crying now, her tears visible even in the heavy rain. This broke Lola's resolve as she pulled her into a warm embrace.

'I'm so sorry. I'm such an idiot. I know you were only looking out for me. Please take care, okay? And if there are any developments let me know.'

'I will,' promised Aibgrene. 'Be careful, Lo, and text me as soon as you get home. Do you hear me? Straight away!'

Aibgrene handed Lola a piece of soggy paper.

'What's this?'

'It's a safe number. I won't be able to use it all the time, Lo. They'll be watching us, but Darragh is going to help me with my astral travel, that will be the safest way for me to contact you, so don't be freaking out if I'm sitting at the bottom of your bed some night,' she laughed.

Lola watched Aibgrene and the Hill of Tara disappear from view as she wove her way along the narrow country roads towards the motorway. It was shortly after five o'clock in the evening when she arrived back at Ballyvalley. It had clearly been raining there too, but the sun was trying to emerge from behind the clouds. Heading onto the Scarvagh Road, she turned off the main road towards Brook Mill

Manor. As she drove down the avenue, a familiar black and red sports car sat at the gates.

Sensing her arrival, Alex got out of the car with a wide grin on his face. He sat on the bonnet of the car until she came to a halt beside him. Lola's heart began to hammer. He was the last person she needed to see right now, but he was the only person she wanted to see. Conscious that she looked a mess, she tried to fix her hair before getting out of the car. Alex as always was dressed impeccably, even when he was being casual. He wore a pair of baggy Abercrombie jeans and a sky blue designer polo shirt. He had light stubble on his face and his hair, as always, had that dishevelled look that seemed so appealing to her.

'Well? What has you around these parts, Mr Stein?' grinned Lola, clearly delighted to see him. Reaching out Alex grabbed Lola by the waist, pulling her closer to him. 'I was in the neighbourhood and thought I would call to see if you were home from your trip yet.'

Lola looked at him quizzically, her emerald green eyes intoxicating him as always. He could tell from the black circles around her eyes that she hadn't slept much. But she was still beautiful, and he'd really missed her. He pressed his lips to hers. He could taste her lip balm, it tasted like watermelon. Alex was relieved when she didn't hesitate this time. She instinctively followed his lead. He slipped his hands inside her t-shirt, feeling the soft flesh of her arched back. Suddenly there was a rustling in the trees and the sound of a child sniggering. Breaking away from Alex, Lola's face turned a light pink, as she turned to find her little brother. She was not amused.

'Okay, Liam, out you come, you wee stalker!' she shouted. Sliding out from behind one of the large oak trees in the drive, Liam stood beaming. 'What's up, squirt? What are you doing hiding behind trees spying on people?'

'I wasn't spying! Me and Cuchulain are playin' hide and seek actually!'

'You're playing hide and seek with the dog? So whose finding who then?'

'It's his turn. I don't know where he's got to, the silly mutt. So who's that?'

Liam didn't even look at Alex, he just nodded towards him. Stepping out from behind Lola, Alex introduced himself.

'Hi, I'm Alex, nice to meet you, Liam.'

'Alright,' nodded Liam, as if he was giving him the once over. 'Are you our Lola's boyfriend then?' Lola was totally taken aback by her brother's candidness, shooing him off in embarrassment.

'Right you, I think it was time you headed back up to the house!'

'I was only asking,' protested Liam innocently.

'Well then the answer to that is yes. I am Lola's boyfriend.' This did nothing to distract or appease Liam; instead he used it as a precursor to more questions.

'So are you from America then, Alex?'

'I was actually born here, but I went to school in America, and my dad's from America, but he lives here too now.'

'So where's Aibgrene, Lola?' asked Liam.

Lola stiffened, she was sure that Alex could sense this. Ushering Liam up to the house again, she changed the subject, but it didn't go unnoticed.

'I need to get washed and changed. Do you want to come up?' asked Lola, feeling that she really needed some company tonight. 'It would give us a chance to catch up.'

Reaching up this time, she kissed Alex, running her fingers through his tussled hair. Caressing her throat he whispered in her ear.

'I'm sorry, Lo, it was just a flying visit, and I have to get back home.'

'Oh alright, that's no problem,' she replied feeling silly for being so forward. Lola went to get back into her car, but Alex was right behind her now, his arms around her waist. That same volt of electricity coursed through her body again.

'I'm sorry, I have stuff to do for my dad. So are we still on for next weekend?'

Lola had forgotten all about his invitation.

'Yes. That's grand.'

'Okay, I'll pick you up on Friday evening then. My dad doesn't get back from the States until Saturday, so we will have the place to ourselves on Friday night,' said Alex, placing emphasis on them being alone for a night, which was not lost on Lola. She had never really had any quality time with him for much longer than a few hours. Pushing the thought from her head, she kissed him goodbye and headed up the driveway to the house.

CHAPTER 43

Falling in through the door, overloaded with bags and blankets, Lola found the house full. Hearing the commotion, her mum and dad came to the rescue and helped carry her stuff into the nearby kitchen.

'Well the traveller has returned I see. Did you have a good weekend, pet?' asked her dad, instinctively filling the kettle. He must have been able to read her mind as she was dying for a cup of tea.

'Yeah, Dad, it was great, very different, but good nonetheless. I met some very good people and wait till you hear this, it was a wedding. And guess who's wedding it was. It was Aibgrene's!' said Lola before either of her parents had a chance to answer. Lola was anticipating the same reaction she had when she found out, but they were quite subdued considering the news.

'How did she look? Did the dress fit her okay?' asked Eileen.

'You knew about this, Mum?'

'Well not really, love, she just asked me to help her out with a dress, she didn't go in to detail and I didn't ask, but I had an idea that it might be for her.'

'Nobody bothers bloody telling me anything these days,' huffed Lola. Rolling her eyes in bemusement she took a seat at the table.

'Where's Liam? Did he come back up to the house yet?'

'He's out gallivanting with that dog. He has that poor mutt tortured!'

Lola saw a copy of the Ballyvalley News and began to flick through it. 'Did you contact work, Lo, to let them know that you wouldn't be in?' asked her mum.

Pre-occupied Lola just nodded to her mum. She was reading the match report on the back page. 'The Town were beaten again, Dad? Were you and Liam at the game?'

'Yeah,' sighed her dad. 'They were unlucky, lost to a last minute goal, which was offside by the way, and they had a goal disallowed as well.'

'Some start to the season that is!' she replied. Flicking on through the paper Lola finally came to the front page. She noticed her mum and dad stiffen at the table as she read and then re-read the bold headline.

𝕭𝖆𝖑𝖑𝖞𝖛𝖆𝖑𝖑𝖊𝖞 𝕹𝖊𝖜𝖘

BALLYVALLEY MAN ACCUSED OF ENGAGING IN OCCULT ACTIVITY

IN an exclusive interview with Ballyvalley News reporter Abbey Williams, a close friend of the deceased astronomer Arthur Delphian has sensationally claimed that he was not the 'gentleman' that his local community believed him to be.

Mr Delphian was found dead in his Brook Mill Manor estate back in June after digesting a rare poison. A murder investigation was then launched by local detectives after they believed that all evidence pointed towards foul play. In this exclusive interview, our source, claims Delphian, was involved in occult activity and says that he was a guest at the estate on many occasions and saw Mr Delphian performing satanic rituals.

'Arthur would often invite me to stay at the manor and I didn't really like to refuse. There was this one occasion where about thirty men and women arrived and I just thought that it was a normal party. But after a while I realised that I was gravely mistaken. Let's just say that the good Christian morals that Mr Delphian built his reputation in this town on were nowhere to be found. I left the place soon after and refused to return.' Our Source also claims that mock sacrifices were made, where Mr Delphian and his followers would pretend to drink the blood of their victim. Since the revelation, many people have come forward to the Ballyvalley News to say that they had often heard the sound of drums and chanting coming from the estate late at night.

One man who lives in a housing development beside the 40-acre estate said that he always feared for the safety of the young girl that frequented the manor regularly because of the things that he had heard about the place. The Ballyvalley called Mr Delphian's solicitor regarding these allegations but he has refused to comment.

Lola shook uncontrollably with anger. She couldn't move, her body was rigid, if she had Abbey and Bryce in front of her now, she would have slit their throats without even a moment's hesitation. This was the Hell Fire Club; it had their filthy name written all over it. Her editor had published this poison, and yet forced her off what was a legitimate story. They printed this when Arthur was dead, thinking that there would be no one to defend him, but they were grossly mistaken. He had family and friends and there was no way they would get away with this. Lola lifted the phone and made a call.

Felix Tennyson's chirpy secretary told her he would only be five minutes, but she was on hold for ten. She didn't want to hang up, as she needed to speak to him before she headed for the Ballyvalley News. Listening to the hold music, Lola was growing more and more irritated.

'Lola, my dear, thank you for holding. How can I help you?'

answered Mr Tennyson.

The old solicitor's raspy voice wheezed down the line making Lola feel guilty for getting mad. She didn't want to be rude to the old man, nor take her bad mood out on him, so she tried to compose herself before speaking.

'Good afternoon, Mr Tennyson. I'm really sorry to bother you, but it was important that I spoke to you as soon as I could.'

'What is it, dear? Are you alright?'

'Well no I'm not, sir,' explained Lola trying her best to keep her emotions in check. 'I have seen the most disgusting story in our local paper defaming a dead man. The Ballyvalley News has printed a front page story claiming that Arthur was some sort of satanic abuser.' Lola spat the words out down the phone before Felix could muster a response.

'And what makes matters worse,' she continued, 'is that they claim they contacted his solicitor and he refused to make a comment. So I was hoping you would give me some sort of explanation. And I also want to know where I stand in taking the paper to court.'

'Slow down, Lola. Slow down, dear. Firstly let's get the record straight, I received no such phone call, and I am not aware of any such article. What I will need is for you to send me a copy of it. I'm not good at this inter-web stuff, emails and all that nonsense, so I will put my grandson on, and he can give you all the information you need.

'If indeed, as you suggest, Arthur has been defamed in any way, we can certainly look into that, but first we need to get in touch with the editor of the paper. Who is in charge now?'

'The editor is called Bryce Neal and I can email the Ballyvalley News contact numbers for you along with the article. I won't let this go, Felix, and just to let you know, there are sinister forces at work here.'

The old man considered this for a moment before answering Lola.

'I would guess you are right, my dear, but we need to play a shrewd game here. So please do not do anything rash, okay?'

Lola couldn't and wouldn't promise any such thing.

'Okay, Mr Tennyson, I'll try my best.'

Lola waited on the line, as he called his grandson to the room. Lola listened as he explained the situation handing the phone over to his grandson.

'Hello, is that Ms Lola Paige?'

'Yes, I take it Mr Tennyson has explained the situation to you, sir?'

'Oh yes. He has. Please call me Andrew; you don't sound much younger than me, Lola.'

Lola took down his contact details including his email address. As soon as she hung up the phone, she scanned the article, before sending it through to him. Next was the Ballyvalley News, Lola needed to clear out her desk and the rest of her things. But she wasn't going to show any restraint when she confronted her editor.

CHAPTER 44

Lola parked outside the newspaper office. She stormed in through
the door, bypassing Jane without even acknowledging her, as if she
too were co-conspirator in this front page story. Abbey, Sebastian and
Drew were all perched at their desks. Sebastian was the first to see
Lola come through the door. He was about to speak but Lola's face
was like stone, looking straight through him she glared at Abbey on
her way through the office.

'I'll deal with you later!' she spat venomously in her direction.

If Abbey could have crawled into the nearest crack she would
have. Slamming the door behind her Lola headed towards her editor's
office, picking up a copy of the paper as she went. When she reached
the top of the landing she could hear that he was on the phone. He was
clearly in a bad mood.

'Are you aware who owns this paper, Mr Tennyson?' said Bryce.
Lola stopped short when she heard the solicitor's name.

'Don't you dare threaten me, you little whipper-snapper!' he shouted.

With that Lola strode into the room, throwing the paper on his desk. Bryce Neal was still on the phone, surveying her with disinterest. His obvious arrogance only served to buoy her boldness. Lola stood glaring at him, waiting for him to get off the phone.

'I'm afraid we will have to continue this conversation later, Mr Tennyson, I see the cavalry has arrived,' he said putting the phone down, while meeting Lola's glare.

'"Facts are facts, Lola. You're a journalist and journalists deal in FACTS, Lola!" I don't think it's verbatim, but I'm sure it's pretty close to the bullshit lecture you gave me. So, in light of that conversation, can you tell me how this piece of crap ended up on your front page, Mr Neal?'

Lola was seething, but she was always good under pressure, she always seemed to find the right words and the right tone. Raising his eyebrow dismissively, her editor motioned towards the chair in front of him.

'Nice to see you too, Lola, would you like to take a seat?'

Laughing at his attempt to defuse the situation Lola refused his offer.

'I won't be staying long, sir. So who is this great source of yours then? Who is this person that knew Arthur so well?'

'That is none of your business, Ms Paige,' smiled Bryce. This only enraged Lola further, the fury growing and growing until she finally exploded.

'None of my business. How dare you, you pompous prick? Arthur was family to me, it has everything to do with me, and I will not have his good name besmirched by you or anyone else. I will take you and this excuse for a paper to court. Then we'll be able to see who this mystery source is that you're hiding behind.'

Leaning back in his chair, Bryce began to examine his fingernails petulantly.

'Are you threatening me, Miss Paige? Because that sounds very much like a threat.' Leaning over the table his voice was even but there was no mistaking the venom in it. But Lola wouldn't be backing down this time.

'You better believe I am. You Creep!'

No way would he get the opportunity to treat her like his subordinate again. Lola stared down at him, her eyes blazing, matching the veracity in his. Suddenly Bryce lost his resolve. He stood up in a burst, throwing the chair out from behind him, his jugular vein looked as though it was about to pop. His face was getting redder by the minute, and for a second Lola thought that he might take a heart attack. Slamming his hand down on the table he roared at her. It was so loud that she was sure those below could hear him. But she didn't even flinch. 'How dare you storm into my office and speak to me like that, who do you think you are?'

As he pointed at her menacingly, she saw the detail of one of his cufflinks. She was momentarily silenced when she recognised the tiny silver owl with the ruby-red eyes. That's where she had seen it before. Was he part of the Hell Fire Club? It all made so much more sense to her now.

'Who do I think I am?' shouted Lola. 'After the weekend I've just had, we could be here all day answering that question. The fact remains this paper had better be able to substantiate those vile accusations in a court of law. Otherwise, I will be expecting a full apology printed on the front page of your rag!'

'Court?' snorted Bryce sarcastically. 'Who would be paying for that? Social Services?' Lola was untouched by his snide remark. She had always known how men like Bryce Neal had viewed working-class girls like her. His type thought they were good for one thing and one thing only and it wasn't intellectual stimulation.

'You are pathetic,' mocked Lola. 'Really, you are! Haven't you heard the news?' she said smiling. 'You're not the only one with a very wealthy benefactor.'

Lola saw the confusion on his face turn to comprehension. Leaving her comment hanging in the air between them, she left the room slamming the door behind her.

Now it was Abbey's turn. Descending the stairs two at time Lola burst into the office like a demon, her belly full of fire. Work had stopped completely, and she saw Abbey standing beside Drew. Heading towards her, Sebastian stood up to try and block her.

'Come on, Lo, please calm down.'

But Lola looked straight through him.

'Out of the way, Seb!' she demanded, as she trained her eyes on Abbey, who stood out in front of Drew flicking her hair, with a look of defiance on her face.

'So what do you want, Lola?' mocked Abbey, the sound of her voice grating on Lola's nerves, bringing back every snide remark, every smirk that she and Drew had shared at her expense.

Lola had lost control as pure rage burned inside her. She knew that she would regret it but in that moment standing there with just inches between them she didn't care.

'What do I want?' hissed Lola between gritted teeth. 'I want your head on a stick, you poisonous bitch.'

Lola stepped towards Abbey, who slowly backed into the corner like a trapped animal.

'Who gave you the story, Abbey?'

Suddenly Drew stood in front of her pushing Lola back.

'Get out of here, you tramp!' he goaded.

'Tramp?' shouted Lola, finally losing her temper completely.

The ring began to pulse as if it was working in tandem with Lola's emotional state. Drew was about three stone heavier than her, but she knew he wouldn't stand a chance. She had never struck anyone in her life, except for self-defence in countless quarrels with her brothers. She had wanted to knock that sneer of his face from the first day she had stepped inside the Ballyvalley News. Lola could feel the power of the ring grow in harmony with her emotions. And then it just happened. She clenched her fist and then there was a flash of white light, too quick for anyone else to see it, but she did. Landing a punch right on Drew's chin, he flew up onto the table landing with a crash.

Lola was momentarily stunned. For a second she thought she had killed him. But then he tried to get up and fell back down. Abbey was in hysterics now crouched down in a ball in the corner sobbing uncontrollably.

'I swear... Lo-Lola, I don't know who the source is. Bryce gave me the story and told me to call a number. I'm sorry.'

Lola felt a bit sorry for her now, as her temper began to subside. She should have known that Abbey was only a pawn.

'Where is the number he gave you, Abbey?'

'It's in my desk,' said Abbey pointing to her top drawer.

Moving across the room Lola located a number on a yellow post-it.

'Is this it?' asked Lola, Abbey quickly nodded.

Turning to her own desk, Lola began to clear it out, throwing the contents and her Dictaphone into a clear plastic bag. Just as she was turning to leave, Bryce walked into the room to see the carnage that was Drew splayed out across the table.

'Jane, Jane. Call the police!'

Composing herself Lola strode out the door of the Ballyvalley News for the last time. She was totally calm now, as if the person in there had been someone completely different. How could Bryce have betrayed Arthur like that considering he had been so good to him? It was Arthur who'd given him his start in journalism, through his numerous contacts. That was why he'd wanted Lola to go to the Ballyvalley News in the first place because he felt Bryce would give her a chance to learn and grow. Starting up the engine she headed for home.

Lola could hear her parents chatting in the kitchen as she closed the large front door behind her. She couldn't face them right now. No doubt the police would be at her door at some stage. Exhausted, she headed straight to the book room. Closing the door behind her she lay sobbing on the couch. She had never felt so alone. She couldn't even talk to her parents and now Aibgrene was gone. She had no one to confide in. Totally exhausted she pulled the fleece blanket that laid over the sofa around her cold and tired body and fell asleep.

CHAPTER 45

As she drifted into sleep she became aware of a presence. A man with familiar grey hair and a beard sat in Arthur's chair, illuminated by the light, which added to his silvery glow. He was dressed in a familiar knitted jumper and trousers. Lola wanted to hug him, but was scared that it was only a dream. He was just staring at her and smiling that same kind, heart-warming smile.

'Arthur, is that really you?' she asked hopefully.

He didn't answer straight away. He just rocked back and forward, chuckling to himself.

'Of course it is, Lo,' Arthur finally answered.

Lola was confused, he seemed so at peace, and she had a million and one things to ask him, but she couldn't seem to formulate a coherent sentence.

'You are so close to the finish line, Lola. Please don't give up. You may feel alone, but we are always with you.'

'We?' asked Lola feeling confused; this was only one of the thousands of questions that were swimming around her head.

'There are many forces at work both behind you and against you. But you are never alone. Divine beings of light surround you. All you need to do is ask them for help and guidance.'

'Like angels?' asked Lola.

'Yes, Lo, like angels, sent to you by the Divine Source. Your path is a long and hard one, my dearest, but you are walking in the right direction. Trust your soul and your inner voice and you will find your way. Many trials still lie ahead, but you are getting stronger by the day. You will never walk alone.' Lola smiled at that. That was her anthem, her team's anthem. She liked the idea that though she walked through the wind and the rain, like the song said, she would never walk alone. Lola's eyes began to feel heavy again, she didn't want to fall asleep, or was she already asleep? She couldn't tell anymore. She tried to focus on Arthur.

'Please, Arthur, stay with me. Don't leave me. I can't do this without you.'

'Use the talents that come so naturally to you. Do not look past your training and how that can help you learn and prepare you for what is to come.' Lola could feel his hand in hers. 'I have never left your side, my dear. I have trust in you, Lola, and I love you,' he said as the light began to fade.

Lola woke to the early morning chorus of the song birds busy at their work. It was totally disorientating, she looked around the book room but there was no trace of Arthur. His chair sat empty and motionless. It must have been a dream, yet it had all seemed so real.

Glancing at the rows and rows of books, she waited for her lap-top to start up. She wasn't exactly sure what she was looking for, as her eyes scanned the spines of the books, most of which she had never even touched. Then something caught her eye, then another and another. Lifting the books out from the shelf Lola laid them on the ground just as her computer whirred to life.

Flicking through the first book, Lola located the page she needed, opening it out she examined the illustration of the bold red head that looked back at her. The caption at the side of the illustration read, 'Breo Sagit – Brigid of the Fiery Arrow'. But instead of holding a bow and arrow, the Celtic warrior goddess was holding an ornate silver sword in front of her, a single yellowy silver flame emanating from the blade. Her hair was flame red and her eyes emerald green, just like Lola's. She was dressed in what looked like animal skin trousers and a bodice, with a beautiful purple cloak that was secured with a triple-spiral broach. She looked as though she was ready for battle. Behind her were three crosses made from reeds. Flicking through the second book, again she found another picture of Brigid, this time she was depicted as the triple Goddess. Standing with her hair falling around her, she was dressed in green robes, holding a flame in her hands. At each side stood two maidens, one with a hammer in her hands and other with some herbs. Lola felt strange. It was as though she was looking into her own eyes as they looked back at her from the page. The ring around her neck began to pulse again, as if it too recognised its old master.

Looking at the first picture a little closer, Lola almost stopped breathing when she spotted the small ring. A golden band with an in-laid stone hung loose around Brigid's neck on a piece of worn leather. It was identical to the one Arthur had left her. Surely it wasn't the same ring? This book was Arthur's, reasoned Lola. Perhaps he had a replica made. Lola scanned the passage below the picture.

Known as the Goddess of healers, poets, fire, inspiration, and wisdom, Brigid is the Goddess of light and energy. She is the Goddess of fertility, and is said to lean over every cradle. She is associated with sovereignty and protection of her isles and the sea. Brigid is the classic Celtic Triple Goddess. She was the daughter of the Good God and Sun God, Dagda and thus one of the mystical Tuatha Dé Danann. The legends of old claim that Brigid was born at sunrise, and that a tower of flame could be seen reaching from the top of her head to the heavens. She is one of the most important Goddesses in the history of this island, but like most deities, much of her history has been lost since the rise of Christianity. While some scholars believe that she, along with her people, left a book detailing their magick and wisdom, it is widely believed that this is the stuff of myth and fantasy. Any written documentation that has survived appears to have been written after the church absorbed her, in order to convert the general population to Christianity.

In order to achieve this, the church transformed her into the Christian Saint Brigid. Through a blending of pagan Christian beliefs the veneration of Brigid the Goddess was absorbed into the Christian faith and the role of priestess became the role of a nun. But many who still follow our old religions believe that there will come a time when Brigid will return to Erin's green isle

Exhausted Lola leaned back on the couch so lost in the mire of her own thoughts she didn't hear her mum come into the room.

'What an amazing room! It's funny how I've never been in here before.' Lola turned to find her mum standing at the doorway. Eileen came into the room and sat on Arthur's rocking chair in front of her daughter. Lola knew that familiar look on her face, the same one she always seemed to bear these days when she was trying to guage if Lola was on the brink of another breakdown. 'I can see why you like spending so much time in here, pet. You can feel Arthur everywhere.' Lola tried to close the book discreetly but this only drew her mother's attention to it. 'So what's with Brigid?' asked her mother, nodding towards the open book.

'Nothing, was just having a look through some of the books. It's amazing that I've been coming here all these years and never really looked at them, never really saw them.'

'I don't think you look like a Brigid,' smiled Eileen. She could read her daughter's face like a book, each worry line and furrow giving her away.

'What do you mean? Was I almost called Brigid?' asked Lola, trying to keep her voice steady and even. It was all too much.

'Well, you know your dad and I are big Kinks fans, so it had always been Lola, but then whenever I had you...' Her mum paused as if she was regretting starting the story, but this only intrigued Lola more.

'Go on, Mum, what is it?' she encouraged. A light flush of pink appeared on her mum's neck, which only ever happened when she felt uneasy about something.

'Well, I've never actually told anyone about this before,' laughed Eileen nervously. 'It's silly really. You were born literally at sunrise on the 1st February, on Saint Brigid's Day. I had a good labour with you, Lo. In fact, you couldn't wait to get out, but I did take quite a lot of gas and air,' she laughed. 'As you know, your gran died a few months before. I must have been high as a kite because I could have sworn I heard mum talking to me through the whole labour. It was as clear as I'm sitting here with you now. As clear as a bell she was, telling me everything would be okay and to call you Brigid. Of course your da thought my head was away with the fairies.

'Then when you were born I could see this light all around you, it was beautiful. I just kept crying and saying to your dad, "Look, Joseph. Look. Look at the fire around her!". They all just ignored me because they thought I was doolally. I probably was, but it seemed so real at the time. Silly, isn't it? So, that's how you were nearly called Brigid. From the day you were born, I prayed to her every day. Your granny was a big believer in her too.' Lola didn't know what to say, or where to begin. How had she not realised that she shared the same birthday? It was all too coincidental. Turning back to the book, Lola scanned the text to see if it mentioned anything about Saint Brigid's day. Then she saw it.

'Imbolc - when Pagan's celebrated the coming of spring and the awakening of mother earth, day of celebration for Goddess Brigid, 1st February, which later became St. Brigid's day.' How had she not noticed this before?

'I'll leave you to it love, said her mum as she rose from the chair. She was just about to leave the room when she turned with a huge grin on her face. 'Oh aye, I forgot to say to you - our Liam tells us you've got yourself a man! Said he's some big yank with a fancy sports car. So when are we going to meet him?'

'Liam, wait till I get that wee git!' fumed Lola, as her mum laughed her way down the hall.

Cuchulain shuffled into the room, his long coat was damp and smelt earthy.

'Hello, my big wolf,' said Lola, ruffling his coat. Cuchulain was clearly as pleased to see Lola as she was to see him, but as always Liam wasn't too far behind.

'Come here, boy. Come here, Cuchulain,' called Liam. Obediently, the large animal got up to greet Liam, who was idling in the doorway, not sure if Lola would shout at him or not. 'What are you doing, Lo?' he asked. Lola could see he was as intrigued by the room as she had been the very first time she'd stepped inside it. She hadn't been very patient with her baby brother lately and she was feeling a bit guilty. When he was younger he was like her shadow, following her everywhere. Lola adored him. She still did. He was beyond his years in many ways and his interests fascinated her.

'Well are you going to stand there all day, or are you going to come in and sit down?' Not needing to be asked twice, Liam bolted into the room, slamming the door shut behind him. Jumping onto the sofa the first place he looked was at the ceiling.

'That is class! Did Arthur paint that himself?' That brought a much-needed smile to Lola's face, her baby brother's innocence and wonderment provided her with some light relief. Lola checked her emails. She had a full update, including pictures from Ruby and the girls. She couldn't believe that the summer had gone by so quickly. They would be coming home at the weekend and she couldn't wait to see them. It would be no time before they would all be heading back to university. Liam sat on the couch behind her reading the emails over her shoulder. There was nothing much in them so she didn't mind. Going through her inbox, Lola noticed an email from Daithi's cousin Sean. Opening it there was just a brief hello and a link to a popular online video page. Clicking the link Lola was re-directed to a video. The picture was grainy and the footage had clearly been taken undercover on a night vision camera. The shaky image zoomed in on a large fire that, as far a Lola could tell, had been constructed on a small island in the middle of a river or lake. In the middle of the island stood an altar, and towering above the altar was a massive statue of a stone owl, it must have been about thirty feet tall. There were about a hundred people dressed in cloaks chanting and dancing. Suddenly the person with the camera began to zoom out and started running through the dense forest. Then there was close up of the wooden entrance sign. It read Bohemian Grove.

Lola immediately understood what she was looking at. She remembered what Aibgrene had told her. This place was connected to the Hell Fire Club. Exiting out of the video Lola typed 'Bohemian Grove' into her favourite search engine, which responded immediately spitting out hundreds of links. Lola was quite taken aback by the amount of information available. It was hardly a top secret. Hitting the first link, she got a brief history of the place. The article detailed where in California it was located and that it was an all-male Club founded in 1876. There were even pictures of some of its members. Lola couldn't believe the amount of former heads of state that went there. It fitted the limited knowledge that she had about the Hell Fire Club. Then something caught her attention, the club's motto. 'Weaving Spiders come not here.' It was Shakespeare, from Midsummer Night's Dream. Before, if Lola had seen this she would have thought nothing of it, but she was different now. On the surface this Club was well publicised. They even had their own website, detailing how to join. Flicking on through some other sites the signs were everywhere.

'I nearly forgot to tell you,' said Liam, handing Lola her cell phone. 'That yank must really like you. He called you about ten times last night. You left your phone in your bedroom and the door here was locked so I couldn't get in to you. I told him you were at the cinema with your other boyfriend,' said Liam with cheeky grin as he jumped off the seat with Cuchulain at his side.

'Did you now?' laughed Lola.

Checking her phone, she realised he wasn't joking.

CHAPTER 46

There were actually ten missed calls and two text messages from Alex. Hitting the redial button she waited anxiously for him to pick up. 'Lola, where have you been? I've been trying to get in touch with you all last night,' answered Alex. Lola's voice was still a little groggy from the sleep.

'Sorry, Alex, I wasn't feeling too good and went to bed early. I left my phone downstairs.'

'You still don't sound good. Is everything okay?'

Of course he knew that it wasn't. He knew that she had been in Tara with the Moone girl and he had also heard about what had happened at the paper. Most of all, he knew that Lola wasn't going to divulge any of this information to him. She didn't trust him, yet she cared for him. He could see this conflict playing out in her eyes every time she was with him. He felt ludicrous for testing her in the ways that he did. Somewhere in his head he believed that she should trust him, but how could she when he had only ever deceived her. He could no longer deny that he cared about her too, that how he felt when he was with her was the only truth between them.

'I'm fine, Alex, really, just a bit run down.'

'Is that why you're not at work today?'

'I'm not at work today because the Ballyvalley News printed something they shouldn't have about Arthur. I was livid and went in yesterday in a blaze of glory, and let rip. I even punched Drew. So I would imagine that I won't be allowed to set foot in the place anytime soon. But, I'm sure you already know all this. So let's not play games, Alex.'

Lola's candidness caught Alex off guard, a million thoughts ran through his head – had she figured it all out, did she know who he really was?

'Come on now, I know Abbey would have been bursting to tell you about how mental I am,' jibed Lola.

Relieved, Alex decided to change the subject.

'So does that mean you can come up to Portstewart any time then?'

'I suppose it does.'

'How does tonight sound then? I can pick you up say around seven or so?' he asked.

'Okay. Why not!'

'Great, I'll meet you at the gates.'

Before Lola could change her mind, he had hung up. She cursed herself for not telling him to call to the house. Instinctively, Lola typed 'Stein Corp' into the search engine and picked through the official website, which gave an overview of the company, its holdings and stakes in other areas. It also gave a short bio on the company's founder, Carl Stein.

Born in New Orleans, Carl Stein was educated at Yale, reading architecture and antiquities. After leaving Yale top of his class, he set up his own architectural consultancy company. This company rapidly expanded, allowing him to diversify into engineering, construction and finance. Over the years Stein Corp has become a multi-million pound business, with offices in America, Europe, the Middle East and Far East. After visiting Ireland in the late 1980s, Carl fell in love with

the Emerald Isle, and decided to move there, feeling that he could create opportunity in what was a divided and fractured country. He re-located to Northern Ireland, a country ravaged by tribal violence at the time.

Currently Stein Corp and their affiliated companies provide over a thousand jobs throughout the whole island of Ireland, not to mention Mr Stein's extensive charity work. Stein Corp continues to grow and prosper in its vision of creating a New World Order.

The last three words made the hairs on the back of Lola's neck stand to attention. A 'New World Order'. There was something inherently menacing about the idea in this context. A new dawn, or a new world for mankind, yes she could accept that, but a New World Order, she didn't quite like the implications of this. Scrolling down the page she stopped at the picture of Carl Stein smiling back at her. His flawless well-shaven face and that all-American smile, painted perfectly white. He had a presence about him, she could even tell that from the picture. It was clear where Alex got his arrogance from, but again looking at him, apart from the eyes, it was hard to believe that Alex was his son. Lola wondered what his mother might look like. Perhaps Alex favoured her. Then it occurred to Lola, he never spoke about his mum, only his dad, and even when he spoke about him he always addressed him as 'father' not dad or daddy or even da.

It was obvious that he respected his father, but Lola respected hers too, only she didn't call him father. To her it sounded more like fear. It was subtle, but she could sense that Alex feared his dad. Looking at the picture she could see why, he had all the swagger of someone who was used to being in control. He looked like a man who always got what he wanted. How he would react to her would be interesting. She had thought a lot about that and now she was prepared to face Carl Stein.

CHAPTER 47

The past few days had been pure bliss for Lola as she and Alex lazed around on the beach, cooked, read and watched movies. It had been a perfect escape after an intense few weeks, but deep down she knew that she would have to face her new reality sooner or later. She had seen such an entirely different side to Alex in the days and nights they had spent alone. In a stroke of fortune, Ruby's father had called her and asked her to check out the cottage. It was between summer tenants and he wanted to make sure that everything was as it should be. When Lola had explained that she would be heading to the coast for a few days he had kindly offered her the use of the place. She loved Pebble Cottage, it had a great energy. It was so relaxing.

The weather had finally broken and Lola was soaked through as she and Alex ran towards house in the rain. She watched him ahead of her, carrying her bag and blanket. He was even breathtaking in the rain. His white t-shirt was drenched and Lola noticed how it clung to his well-toned torso. Finally they reached the refuge of the cottage, out of the rain and out of breath. Alex expelled his luggage on the floor and pulled Lola towards him. Still breathless from the exertion of running back to the cottage, Lola traced the contours of his face with her fingertips. He had been tense all day and she knew it was because they were having dinner with his father that night. But his mood seemed to have lightened as he pulled her closer, his words like a symphony in her ear.

'We'd better get out of these wet clothes.'

That familiar wave of electricity began to ebb and flow through her body in response. Taking her by the hand, Alex led her towards the bedroom. Lola knew what was about to happen. Over the past few days they had been steadily building up to this point. She had decided that she was ready. She was an adult now and the choice was her own. She'd never been this close to any boy before, or this intimate. For once she was going to do exactly as her heart dictated, no over think-ing it, no rationalising. Standing there looking into Alex Stein's eyes, in that moment she knew it was right. Lifting his t-shirt, she peeled it off his wet tanned skin, running her fingers down his sculpted chest. Alex reciprocated, much more adept than her – he unzipped the back of her wet dress, letting it fall to the floor.

'Are you sure you want to do this, Lo?' whispered Alex gently in her ear, but the sound of his deep voice only made her more deter-mined. Nodding she continued to let him undress her. 'Do you trust me?' he asked. Lola wasn't quite sure how to answer this question, because she really didn't know. All she knew was how she felt about him at that moment, standing there semi-naked and face to face.

'I trust how I feel and I trust that you feel the same way about me as I do about you,' she replied softly. It was the only honest answer she could muster. It was the only truth she could give him.

Alex understood that he really couldn't ask for anything more of her because that was also all he could give of himself. Her honesty and light touched him so deeply, and he could tell that she meant ev-ery kiss, every caress, felt every touch with the same intensity that he did. He'd had plenty of lovers, but – just like Lola – this was the first time he had ever made love. It wouldn't always be like this between them and he knew that Lola was aware of that too. So in the here and now they both decided to give themselves completely and unreservedly as they became immersed in one another, the intensity intoxicating.

After what seemed like an eternity, they finally broke apart gasping for breath and their bodies moist with sweat. Lola didn't hold any of the guilt or regret that she thought she would. She was completely vulnerable and for the first time in her life it didn't scare her. Glancing over at Alex, she couldn't believe her eyes when she saw a bright pink phosphorous glow around his entire body. This was the first time that she had ever seen or even sensed his aura. It was amazing. She just continued to stare at him in wonderment.

'What? What is it?' he asked, sensing her intense stare as he pulled her into his arms, kissing her softly on the forehead.

'It's nothing. I've just never seen you like this before.'

'Like what?' he laughed. 'Naked? I do look pretty good I suppose. You don't look too bad yourself, Lola.'

Lola couldn't very well tell him the truth, so she manipulated it again. 'I've just seen you in a different light that's all. So what are the plans for tonight?' she asked.

Alex was dreading the dinner. His dad would sense his feelings for Lola. The only thing worse than his father realising that he had fallen in love with her, was his father seeing how powerful she was. Since she had returned from Tara, there was a subtle change in her. It was as if something had changed inside and he could see it in her eyes. Alex often wondered if she was really as naive as she appeared. He didn't think so. Lola's energy was growing more powerful, and if he could see this, then so would his father. That would only mean that he would want her more.

Lola shifted uncomfortably moving the necklace and ring around to hang again at her front. Alex took a double take when he saw the signet ring as it lay dormant between her breasts. He hadn't noticed it before, but there, around Lola's slim pale neck, was the ring that his father had killed for.

Controlling his voice he ran his finger over Lola's toned stomach, following the grooves up to where the ring sat. 'That's an interesting ring. Where did you get that?' Alex couldn't tell if Lola was suspicious or not. Her tone gave nothing away as she lifted the ring, holding it between her fingers.

'Oh this? It was Arthur's,' she replied nonchalantly. 'He left it to me. I never take it off. It means he is with me all the time.'

'What, even now?' joked Alex, as he swerved to avoid Lola's slap.

'You know what I mean. He meant a lot to me, Alex. He was like a grandfather to me. Speaking of which, I remember seeing you at the funeral. I never asked you how you actually knew him.'

Alex was desperate to change the subject, but he couldn't take his eyes off the ring. All he had to do was just snatch it. It would be so easy. But that would require force, it would require him to hurt her and he didn't have the strength to do that. 'I was actually there on behalf of my father. I had heard of Arthur but I never had the privilege of meeting him,' he replied, praying that this would be the end of the questions, but he should have known better.

'So how did your dad know him, and another thing, why do you always refer to him as your father?'

'Well, he is my father.'

'Yeah, but it sounds so formal. Why do you fear him so much?' she asked expectantly. The words had escaped Lola's mouth before she had realised what she had said. She could see that her comment had wounded Alex. 'Sorry, Alex. That came out wrong,' she immediately apologised. 'I just meant that you have a different sort of relationship with your parents than I do, that's all.'

'Parent,' he corrected her. 'You said parents. There's only my dad and I. My mum died during childbirth.' Alex thought about what Celeste Moone had told him, but she was a liar. He never spoke to anyone about his mother; it wasn't encouraged by his father. But Lola was different. She brought light where there had only ever been darkness. He could tell that she felt she'd offended him, but she hadn't. He did fear his dad, but most of all he feared what he himself was. He feared that blackness deep within his soul. He feared that he would ultimately betray the only thing that he had ever loved.

Lola turned on her side to look him in the eye. 'I'm so sorry. I had no idea, Alex.'

'My dad and I are close in ways. I was always away at school in America and really only saw him during the summer, or when he was over on business. We've a good relationship, but we never talk about my mother. I haven't even seen a picture of her.'

Lying there in silence Alex pulled Lola close. He wanted to savour every minute of this. Once his father met her, it would be the beginning of the end for Lola Paige.

Lola noticed Alex grow more and more anxious as the day progressed. He was becoming very restless and couldn't sit in one place for long. Lola chose not to say anything to him. She really didn't know what to expect from this meeting. In many ways she was going in blind and that worried her. But she had to meet him; she had to see him with her own eyes.

CHAPTER 48

It was almost time to go and Lola headed upstairs to get dressed.
She had decided on the short red dress that she had worn to Arthur's
funeral and matched it up with a pair of flat pointed court shoes with
a tiny bow on them. Lifting her hair off her face she tied it back into a
ponytail with a slight bouffant on top. Finishing her makeup, she came
back downstairs to find Alex staring out at the water.

'Are you ready to go, Alex?' Turning around to greet her, Alex
caught his breath, she looked radiant. The red dress really brought out
the green in her eyes, she looked like something from a fifties Vogue
magazine.

'You look stunning, Lola. You really do!' Shaking her head dismissively, Lola took his hand. Locking the door they walked the short
distance to Chateau Bacchus.

The ground was still wet from the rain earlier that evening, but
Lola loved the sweet, damp smell of summer rain. Inhaling, she could
smell the sea air, with a mixture of earth and grass. Rounding onto
the Strand Road, her eyes found the turn-off to Alex's house; it was

exactly the same as the last night she had been there. The sandstone wall curved down towards the cliff-side mansion, while on either side of the wide entrance stood two stone owls. This caught Lola's attention. Perhaps it was just coincidence, she thought to herself, but her ring began to awaken as if gearing up for something. She could feel a shift in the energy immediately. Alex suddenly let go of her hand, it was subtle, but Lola picked up on it, she was beginning to feel quite uneasy now. Although the place looked exactly the same as it had when she was last there, if felt different.

The door opened as they approached and Carl Stein emerged with a wide grin on his face, his languid New Orleans accent breaking through the still night air, welcoming them in to the house.

'Come in. Come in.'

'Father, this is Lola Paige. Lola, this is my father, Carl Stein.' Lola noticed how Carl Stein examined her like she was some chattel. She followed his cold eyes, bemused as he looked at her and then around her.

'Nice to meet you, Mr Stein,' said Lola shaking his hand. 'Thank you very much for having me.' His hands were unusually soft for a man but his grip was firm.

'What a vivacious red dress. Why you look like Little Red Riding Hood.'

'So does that make you the Big Bad Wolf then?' retorted Lola, mimicking his fake smile.

'Perhaps, Lola. Perhaps,' said Carl, a slight knowing glint in his eye, as he thought to himself that perhaps he had underestimated this young girl.

'Dinner is almost served; shall we make our way to the dining room?'

Following behind both men, Lola ran her eyes over the house. She could see a bit more of the interior than the last time she had been there, but Lola could sense that something was different about the place. Walking through the living room, with its glistening white marble floor, Lola realised how vast the space actually was. A curved white couch sat in front of a gas fire and other smaller, circular white chairs were scattered around the room. It was very minimalist, too stark and clinical for her taste. Lola liked a home to feel like a home, and so far this place didn't. As they approached the glass staircase,

Lola laughed to herself thinking about her previous ill-tempered encounter with the structure. But her reverie was short-lived. As she ascended the steps Lola began to feel very disorientated. Her head began to throb and she thought for an instant that she might vomit. Shaking off the feeling, Lola put it down to not having eaten much that day. She continued to follow, walking down the red-carpeted hallway. All the doors were closed, and as she passed the first door on the left, she remembered her first encounter with Alex. He must have had the same thought, because at that moment he turned to look at her with an apologetic smile.

As she passed the closed door, she could have sworn she heard a faint whisper. The voice was familiar and it called her name. Slowing down a fraction she heard it again only it was even fainter this time. For a second her nostrils were filled with a briny smell that reminded her of corroded metal, then as quickly as the sensation had arrived, it was gone.

The dimly lit hallway seemed to go on forever, until the party came to a halt outside two huge black doors. Throwing open the doors, Carl Stein stood aside to let Lola and then Alex into the room. The large dining room had a massive vaulted ceiling and the main space was taken up by a huge antique banquet table. Scanning the seats Lola guessed it would have accommodated at least twenty or thirty people.

Around the brightly lit room were large mirrors and portraits, and underfoot lay thick golden carpet with a black band embroidered around the edges. Six crystal chandeliers dangled from the roof over the table. The entire room would not have looked out of place in some royal palace. It was all a bit intimidating for Lola, but she guessed that this was the point.

'You've an amazing home, Mr Stein, this room looks like something from the Palace of Versailles.'

Carl Stein seemed to be impressed by this observation.

'That is exactly what it was modelled on, my dear.'

Pulling out a chair, he gestured for Lola to be seated. They all sat at the bottom of this enormous table, which seemed a bit ludicrous to Lola. Alex had hardly spoken a word. He sat opposite Lola, with his father at the head of the table. Lola's head was still feeling a bit fuzzy and this feeling seemed to intensify each time Carl Stein trained his eyes on her. But the ring was soon at her aid, as she could feel its warm energy encapsulating her. Its presence was subtle, but she knew that she was safe.

'Shall we eat?' chirped Carl congenially.

Ringing a small silver bell at his side, he watched the door to the dining room open as service began. Lola had no idea what she was eating, but it was delicious, as course after course was brought in by two waiters. There wasn't a great deal of conversation during dinner, which was alien to her. In her house there were at least three rows before the dinner was even served. The dinner table was where the Paige family caught up on their news.

Finally dinner was over, and Lola could feel the obvious tension between Alex and his father, or perhaps it was just this place, she thought. 'That was delicious, Mr Stein, thank you.'

'You are more than welcome, young lady, and please call me Carl. Shall we retire to the smoking room?' suggested Carl, as he stood up from his chair, and headed towards a door at the back of the dining room. 'It sounds awfully pretentious, but I like to call it my smoking room, as I indulge in a few glasses of my favourite bourbon and a cigar or two.'

The atmosphere in the house was oppressive, and her head continued to throb. The smoking room was cosier and a bit more homely than the dining room. The fire had been lit and a few lamps illuminated the room, which consisted of a small bar and some plush chairs. Carl Stein sat in a large wing-backed chair, while Lola and Alex sat beside each other in front of him. Lola could anticipate that this was where the inquisition would start. She could see it in Carl Stein's gaze, and although he was very charming, his smile never reached those cold, calculating eyes.

Pouring himself a glass of bourbon, Carl Stein offered Lola a drink, but she politely declined.

'No thank you, Mr Stein. I don't drink.'

'Aren't you a sensible girl? Well I can see Alex has got himself a good one, you're absolutely radiant, Ms Paige. A slight departure from my son's usual partners, but don't you just glow, Ms Lola!' There was a hint of menace in his tone that didn't go unnoticed by Lola.

Alex was so on edge that he'd hardly looked at her throughout the dinner service. He had felt his father's eyes on them at the top of the drive, and he had seen that familiar covetous look on his face when he met Lola. He didn't have to say a word, Alex could tell that his father realised how much he had underestimated her. He could feel how powerful she was and he could tell that she didn't trust him. He knew this was all the more enticing for his father.

'I can certainly see why my son is so taken with you,' continued Carl. Lola laughed off the compliment, knowing that Alex's father didn't mean a word of it.

'I wouldn't say that, Mr Stein. You know Alex, it could be me today and someone else tomorrow.' Lola could see that Alex was quite stung by her comments, but his father thought this hilarious.

'So tell me, how'd you two kids meet?'

Lola thought about whether or not to tell the truth, but decided against it.

'We met through a mutual friend, and then I saw Alex at Arthur's funeral, and we sort of took it from there,' replied Lola. 'I believe you knew Arthur, Mr Stein?' Carl Stein was momentarily taken aback by her candidness, as he shifted in his chair feeling a little uncomfortable with Lola's tone.

'Yes I knew Arthur very well. We met many years ago through business. He was a shrewd old fox, but a great man. His death was a great tragedy of course. Were you close, Lola?'

'Yes. Arthur was one of my best friends. He was like family to me and I miss him a lot, sir.'

'He was a very worthy adversary,' commented Carl, as he became aware of Lola's intense stare and her somewhat familiar blazing emerald eyes. 'We often played chess for hours at a time,' he smiled. 'We discussed all sorts of things. Of course we had very different ideologies and I did get the better of him a few times, but yes a great adversary nonetheless.'

'I'm afraid that I never once got the better of him, he was way too good for me.' This was the second time tonight that Carl Stein had been surprised.

'You play chess?' Lola wasn't insulted by his shock; in fact she was used to it.

'Don't sound so surprised, Mr Stein. There are women that can play chess and even working-class women that can play,' laughed Lola. This brought a smile to Alex's face for the first time that night.

His father laughed along taking it all in good humour.

'Well, Lola, that sounds like a challenge and you know I love a challenge. Alex, would you go and get the chess board from the study. I think I'm going to have to test this young lady's resolve and see how well old Arthur has taught her.'

CHAPTER 49

You really are a diamond in the rough,' chuckled Carl as he took another sip from the crystal goblet. The insinuation wasn't lost on Lola
as she watched him rub his hands together and sit up excitedly in his
chair. Alex wheeled the chess board in between his father and Lola.
The chess set, like everything else in the house, was ostentatious. The
board itself was made of marble as were the pieces. The black half
was facing Lola. Sitting up she turned the heavy board around so that
she would be playing with the white pieces.

'The guest always plays with white,' offered Lola apologetically.
This seemed to amuse Carl. Lola could see the glint of excitement in
his eyes and she was sure that he would underestimate her again, as
he had done all evening. Lifting a small chair from the corner of the
room, Alex sat it in the middle, as his father and Lola scrutinised the
chequered board in front of them. His father was a great chess man, so
he assumed that this game would be over pretty quickly.

'So tell me, Lola, what should every good chess player know?'

Lola knew the four main principles of the game off by heart. Arthur had drilled these into her since the first time she played the game. 'Let's see,' she mused. 'Number one. Be patient. As Arthur used to tell me, if you haven't got patience you may as well forget it. That's the one I struggled with – a lot,' smiled Lola.

Carl Stein nodded in agreement. 'Patience is certainly a virtue and one of the few that I was born with.' Lola fixed her pawns in a row and then began to organise her back row as she continued.

'Number two. It's vital that you have a sense of timing.' All Lola could see was Arthur, his face furrowed as he examined the board, relaying this to her time and time again. And just when she thought she had him cornered, he would make his move. 'Checkmate,' he'd say, before adding, 'you need to know when to make your move, thus timing is essential.'

Carl Stein stared at Lola wondering if she was as oblivious to the subtext as she seemed. Alex clearly wasn't, as he continued to shift in his seat. Carl could taste his son's unease and he could see that he had fallen for Lola. In truth he couldn't blame him, her aura and presence were extremely intoxicating, even more so than the boy's mother's had been to him.

'Number three, Mr Stein – and being a successful business man yourself you would know all about this – know your opponent.'

'Most impressive, Lola, but you have left out the fourth and most important rule of chess. You must be willing to make any or all sacrifice to protect your interests.'

Lola stared directly into Carl Stein's eyes; there was no doubt in her mind that he made that decision every day of his life without so much as a sideways glance. Men like Carl Stein did not have a conscience, such was their conviction that they were always right. Lola could remember when Arthur had first introduced her to chess. It used to make him laugh how she couldn't accept that the pawns were there to be sacrificed. To her they should all be equal. She used to ask Arthur, why should the poor pawn be sacrificed for the knight or the rook for a king? 'You are ever the libertarian, Lola. But unfortunately in this world, my dear, there are those that believe that some are more equal than others,' he would say.

'Your move or mine, Mr Stein?' asked Lola.

Raising his eyebrow, Carl motioned for her to begin the game.
'Ladies first.'

Composing herself, Lola carefully examined the board. She
usually started every game in the same way, trying to get control of
the centre board. She made this move in her head, trying to anticipate
Carl's response and how she would counteract that. It took her many
years to learn how to do this effortlessly.

Lifting one of her pawns, she moved it to D4. This move, as
expected, was mirrored by Carl Stein who shifted his to D5. Again
Lola shifted another pawn to E4, as Carl followed to E5. He could
see where she was going with this and admired her tenacity. Lola had
learned the hard way that the closer developed pieces were to the centre, the more mobile they could be. Shifting her knight in to support
the pawns she could see eight possible moves.

Carl, after some thought, decided to bring his bishops into play,
but Arthur had always taught Lola to develop her knights before
bishops, as it was easier to find a good strategic place for the knight.
Of course in chess this wasn't a given, but she only brought in what
she needed in order to accomplish something. Inevitably, as the game
progressed most of the pawns were taken out of play, with Lola claiming one piece more than Carl. Gradually, they came to the endgame.
Lola could see that the end was in sight; with one more move she
would have Carl Stein in check. The game had slowed to a crawl and
all traces of humour had evaporated. The atmosphere was thick with
tension. But just as Carl Stein was about to make his move, there was
a knock on the door bringing them both out of their trance-like state of
concentration.

'Do you mind, Lola?' said Carl Stein. Getting up out of the chair
he opened the door. Lola's view was obstructed, so she couldn't see
who he was speaking to.

'Mr Stein, sir, there's an important call. I've put it through to
your study.' Lola thought that she had heard the deep voice that came
from behind the door before, but he was gone before she could be
sure.

'Okay, Derek, thanks. I'll be there in a minute.' Returning to
the room Carl Stein apologised, saying that he would have to call it
a night. 'It looks like we will have to have a rematch, Lola. We will
have to continue where we left off.'

'I think you were saved by the bell, Mr Stein,' retorted Lola with a cheeky grin.

Carl Stein returned her smile, knowing full well she had almost outwitted him.

'We will never know,' he replied cunningly.

Leaning down he kissed her on each cheek.

'It was certainly a pleasure to have you here, and I look forward to seeing you again. Soon.'

'Thank you for having me, sir, and enjoy the rest of your evening.'

Walking back up towards the hall Carl Stein went into his study, closing the door behind them. Lola walked ahead of Alex. He had hardly spoken all night. Aibgrene's concerns were not unwarranted. It had been a risky move, perhaps even a stupid move coming to Chateau Bacchus, but she had to know who and what she was up against. Chess rule number one, know your opponent, thought Lola. But while she had gained an insight into her enemy, her newly acquired knowledge was not without its casualties. She had rehearsed everything she was about to say, countless times. His withdrawal during the evening made what she was about to do easier. Waiting until they were outside, she rounded on Alex and although this was her exit strategy her stomach was churning and her heart was breaking. Tears began to stream down her face, the only semblance of honesty in tonight's exchange.

'What was that about?' she raged. 'I have never been made to feel so cheap in all my life. Who do you think you are, Alex Stein? Making me jump through hoops, like some circus act, to prove my worth.'

Alex stood momentarily stunned until he realised what was happening. She understood it all. He had completely underestimated her, yet again. But how much did she know about him? She could sense his father's thoughts and the covetous look in eyes. But Alex understood that Lola, however shrewd, was no match for his father. His dad had learned just as much as she had. He knew Lola had the ring; he'd worked hard to weave enough magick to make sure of it. There was no way she could have reached the top of the stairs without the ring. She had exposed herself and the only reason that she was allowed to walk out of the house tonight was because his father must have another purpose for her. With all that in mind, Alex decided to partake in her charade.

'Why did you invite me here if you are so embarrassed to be with me?' continued Lola, pushing him now. A lump had settled in Alex's throat.

'Lola, I don't know what you're talking about,' he shouted back. 'I mean it's not my fault you have some sort of chip on your shoulder. It's not my fault you're ashamed of where you come from.' Alex knew that last comment would really sting her, because he had never met anyone more proud of their family than Lola Paige. So he didn't move to avoid the palm of Lola's hand as it came crashing down on the side of his face. He deserved it.

'I want to go home. Now!' demanded Lola, trying to fight back the tears.

Carl Stein watched this interesting display from the shadows as Lola stormed off. He had truly underestimated her. Like her mentor, she was a very worthy adversary, but the time for playing games was over.

CHAPTER 50

It only took a few minutes for Lola to gather her things, and by the time Alex's car pulled into the yard she was locking the door to Pebble Cottage. She would never forget what they had shared there. It was exactly as she had intended: a perfect end to things. She got the distinct feeling that Alex had seen through her performance outside Chateau Bacchus and had decided to play along. It was ludicrous to Lola, all the subterfuge and deceit, one big mummer's farce. Yet, they both chose to overlook each of those dark colossal truths that were so cruelly anchored between them.

Usually Lola encouraged Alex to drive sensibly, but tonight she just wanted back to the safety of Brook Mill Manor. So she was happy when he pressed his foot on the accelerator as they sped down the motorway towards Ballyvalley. Her headache had cleared the moment she stepped off the boundary to Alex's house and the heaviness that she had struggled against lifted. The silence stretched out between them like a black abyss. What was there to say? Lola didn't want to hear the truth from his gorgeous mouth. She didn't want to hear what he truly was, but most of all she didn't want to accept who and what she really was. Aibgrene was right. Despite everything she had seen and heard, despite everything she had experienced for herself, she still couldn't free her mind. She still couldn't shed the skin of the Lola Paige she understood herself to be. Lola gazed out of the passenger window blindly, as town after town zipped by. Finally, after an hour, Alex's R8 had them in Ballyvalley. Up until that point she hadn't been paying attention to the music, but just as Alex made the turn off towards the manor, the lyrics of the song on the radio hit her like a wrecking ball, rendering her immobile and unsure if she would be able to get out of the car. As the song continued each word washed over them as she and Alex sat in perfect stillness. The chorus ringing around them: 'I was standing, you were there, two worlds collided and they will never tear us apart.' It was an old song, but the artist singing was a young woman. Her voice fell like velvet on Lola's ears, soft and mournful.

Lola turned to face Alex for the first time since they had left Portstewart. She could no longer fight back the tears she had fought so relentlessly to suppress, yet his face remained stoic. But there in a flicker of his eyes was the truth that she so desperately needed to see, that she so desperately needed to believe. Because while Alex's face was a void, his eyes churned in turmoil. The love he had felt, the loss he was about to experience, the complete hopelessness and inevitability of their situation, and it was all right there, in those deep pools of frigid blue. Lola had risked a lot tonight, she had shown her hand, but at that moment, looking at the most beautiful man she'd ever known, it had all been worth it.

Finally, Lola found the strength and will to climb out of the car. She could see the outline of the embryonic shield that surrounded Brook Mill Manor; it seemed to be stronger tonight. Collecting her bag from the boot, she crossed between the gateposts before turning to take one last look at Alex Stein, knowing that he could not follow her, even if he'd wanted to. They stood just inches apart, each knowing that they would never touch again.

CHAPTER 51

As the weeks passed by Lola didn't venture too far from the sanctuary that Brook Mill Manor offered. She spent most of her time outside in the gardens and in the greenhouse tending to Aibgrene's herbs and vegetables, readying them for the sparse winter that was almost upon them. Liam was eager to have someone to share all his discoveries with and Lola was happy to indulge her little brother. The girls had returned from America and had called every day to try to break her melancholy mood. The days and weeks went by in a haze, and Lola couldn't begin to explain what had happened.

Even if she did, she doubted they would believe her. A global occult had killed Arthur and the same group wanted her dead too. Lola could just see their faces when she told them that. They'd more than likely think she needed to be institutionalised. In truth, there were days when she believed that herself. It was all so surreal. So instead of coming clean Lola gave them a diluted version, a partial truth, but truth nonetheless. She was grief stricken by Arthur's death and she was heartbroken by the fact she could never have the man she loved. Not because her love was unrequited, but because he was, by default, her enemy. Lola understood that she had always known this. She had felt it in every fibre of her being from the instant they met, yet some invisible force had pulled them towards each other. Something much stronger than all the mistrust and doubt she had felt.

So, it was easier for her to play the game with the girls and her parents. It was easier and safer for them if they didn't know the truth, whatever that was. Yet, despite all this newly acquired gnosis, there still wasn't one day that went by when Lola Paige didn't think about Alex Stein. She hadn't expected any contact from Alex, yet in spite of herself she craved it. And then it came. It was a small envelope addressed to her. Without knowing why, she took it to the book room before opening it. When she did, all that Lola found was a CD and a short note in Alex's handwriting. The smell of his aftershave on the paper awoke the aching and longing, cutting open all those harsh emotions like an old wound. 'Our collision has left us both irrevocably transformed. I'm sorry'. That was all the note said. When she placed the CD in the player, the voice of the young girl she'd heard in his car came spilling out from the speakers. Her lament, Lola thought, was a perfect eulogy for what had passed between her and Alex. But that time was over. Now each of them stood on two opposing sides and the demarcation lines had been clearly drawn. At first, she listened to the song continuously. It was the only reminder that she would allow herself. The only reminder that she had loved and been loved in return. But, in the end, she could not and would not permit any man to define Lola Paige – whoever that was. So she determined to find the strength. To wake each day and be thankful for every lesson and every blessing she had in her life, no matter how small.

Soon autumn came to Brook Mill Manor, Lola's favourite time of year. She loved to be among the towering oaks that had now turned umber and red as Mother Nature prepared for her winter sleep. The changing leaves meant it was time to return to university for her second year of journalism. For a while she'd been toying with the notion of staying at home and travelling back and forth to Belfast each day, but Ruby, Clara and Orla wouldn't hear of it. They had talked her into staying at their shared house and she was glad they had. She had to get on with her life. She couldn't put it on hold for something that might never happen.

Throwing herself into her school work and the university newspaper, Lola kept very busy. She had brought the parchment and sun catcher with her, as she felt safe when it was there.

Aibgrene's power was becoming stronger and stronger as she visited Lola almost every night. Lola had thought she was dreaming the first time she saw Aibgrene sitting at the bottom of her bed. Her friend explained that travelling on the astral plane was becoming easier and easier for her, and Lola was becoming used to seeing her now. It gave her a great deal of comfort. Having someone that she could discuss her worries and concerns with openly was a real relief. Of course it was hard to lie to her friends when they reported hearing her talking to someone late at night. She tried to palm them off by telling them that she was talking in her sleep, but a very astute Clara, who slept in the room next to hers, said that she could hear two voices. For weeks the girls had been trying to talk her into going to the university's annual Halloween party. It was fancy dress and Lola wasn't sure she was in the mood for it. She had been talking to Aibgrene about this, and was advised to go and enjoy herself.

Halloween was a very important night for Aibgrene. At Samhain, as she called it, the people of the Old Religion celebrated their New Year. For them, it was a time to honour the past and to give thanks for the new. She explained that it was a time when the veils between both worlds were at their thinnest. This was far removed from the commercial view of Halloween that Lola had been used to, and the thought of dressing up made her feel a bit silly, but she needed to let loose and enjoy herself, so eventually she decided to go.

After much deliberation on what to dress up as, Lola decided to go as a Celtic warrior goddess – it would be her own private little joke. In truth she wasn't feeling much like a goddess lately and thought that maybe dressing up might ignite that side of her once again. Lola got her mum to make her costume. She really wasn't sure what a Celtic goddess looked like, but she went with faux leather trousers and corset. Her mum also made a mantel and a head band, which she engraved with a triple spiral.

Ruby had managed to get her a red wig, which fit perfectly, and she found a sword and pouch in a toy shop. After getting dressed, Lola stood looking in the mirror, shocked at how much she resembled the girl she had encountered at Tara. Running into the bathroom to get a wipe, she returned to the room to find Aibgrene standing like a spectre at the bottom of her bed, forcing Lola to shriek with fright. Aibgrene had never come this early before – usually it was late at night – so Lola instinctively knew something was wrong.

'Aibgrene, you nearly gave me a heart attack,' said Lola, but Aibgrene just stared blankly back at her.

'I've found my mum, Lo, I've found her. She's by the water. Where the owls are. I don't have much time. He's going to kill her tonight,' sobbed Aibgrene. Lola was almost floored when she got a flash of Aibgrene's vision. She found herself transported; she was hovering above the foamy sea now looking down onto a cliff-side mansion. Across the beach on the cliff top stood Mussenden Temple. Lola wasn't sure why her eyes had been guided towards it but she understood it was significant. Red light leaked from its latticed windows and she was momentarily hit by the same oppressive feeling she'd experienced in Chateau Bacchus. Lola knew instinctively where Celeste was.

'You can't go alone, Aibgrene. Where are you now?' asked Lola. But it was too late, Aibgrene's form started to fade, until it finally disappeared in a milky wisp. Struggling to orientate herself, Lola scrambled over her bed searching for the small notebook where she kept the mobile number that Daithi had given her to call in emergencies. Ripping the page out of the book, she descended the stairs two at a time.

'Ruby, Ruby! Where are your car keys? I need to borrow your car.'

'What is it, Lola? What's wrong?' asked Ruby.

Lola didn't know what to tell her, but she couldn't lie, not again. Grabbing Ruby, Lola hugged her best friend.

'Oh, Rubes, there's so much I can't tell you. All I can say is that someone really important to me is in trouble, and I need to help them.'

'What'd you mean? Lola, you're really freaking me out. Please, Lo, what's going on?' pleaded Ruby. But Lola didn't have time to explain.

'The keys, Ruby. Where are they?' Taking the keys from her pocket Ruby handed them to her hesitantly. Checking that the ring was still around her neck Lola snatched the keys and bolted towards the door. 'I love you, Rubes, and I'll be okay. I'll call as soon as I can,' assured Lola.

Lola didn't care that she was doing sixty in a thirty zone, or that she might get caught. When she finally got onto the motorway, she dialled the number on the crumpled piece of paper. The phone rang for what seemed like hours, before Aibgrene's familiar voice answered.

'Aibgrene, where are you now?' Aibgrene shared none of Lola's panic, her voice was perfectly calm and even, it sounded as though she was sedated.

'We've just come through Belfast and are on our way up the M2,' replied Aibgrene. They weren't that far away, which meant they would get to Portstewart around the same time, thought Lola.

'Listen to me, Aibgrene. I'm not far away so don't do anything rash. I have the ring, we'll be fine. Okay?' Aibgrene began to protest, begging Lola to turn back, but there was no way she could. This felt right. Lola could feel the power of the ring growing with her resolve, giving her courage and clarity. She had to do this; in fact, she knew that she was the only person that could save Celeste. 'Listen to me, Aibgrene, I need to do this. You won't have a chance of rescuing Celeste on your own. Wait by the entrance to the beach for me if you get there before I do. There's a house there with a white fence around it and it's called Pebble Cottage. I'll meet you both there. Okay?'

CHAPTER 52

Lola didn't lift her foot off the pedal once as she pushed Ruby's beloved car to its limit. With her mind racing, she tried to work out what their plan of attack would be. She knew exactly where Celeste was even before she had seen Aibgrene's vision. 'By the water where the owls were,' she had said. Lola had known all along, she had even heard Celeste's voice the night she was there, she was sure of it. The thought made her sick to the core. The idea that she had been just metres from Celeste the entire time she was in Chateau Bacchus was devastating. Lola commanded herself to re-focus. She was sure that Carl Stein would not be expecting her, so they could use the element of surprise to their advantage.

Lola felt so alone. 'Oh, Arthur, what will I do? I wish you were still here!' she called out in desperation to the only person who could help her now. No sooner had Lola cried those words when a feeling of total calmness enveloped her and a voice inside her head assured her that everything would be okay. She wasn't sure if it was her own voice or Arthur's but she felt that she would know exactly how to act when the time came.

After about ninety minutes, Lola arrived in the small sea-side town of Portstewart. The town was busy as students in fancy dress made their way in and out of the bars and clubs, all oblivious to what was unfolding a few miles up the coast in one of Northern Ireland's most iconic landmarks. Lola envied their ignorance. Turning onto the Strand Road Lola slowed the car, her heart pounded in her throat as she took in the number of cars on the roadside as she crawled the car past Chateau Bacchus on her way to the cottage. To her relief Daithi and Aibgrene had already arrived and they had taken her advice. They were both standing outside the car. Aibgrene shifted impatiently waiting for Lola to emerge. Aibgrene's face was ashen and her body was trembling.

'Everything's going to be alright, Aibgrene,' promised Lola, as she held her in her arms. She could tell that her friend wasn't entirely convinced. Lola could understand her apprehension, but she had never been surer about anything.

'Well at least you've come dressed for the occasion, Lola,' jibed Daithi nervously, trying to break the tension. Aibgrene looked her up and down. Lola realised for the first time that she was still in fancy dress. They all burst out laughing at how ridiculous the situation was.

'Carl Stein is going to get some shock tonight,' laughed Lola. 'It'll be like déjà vu.'

'You know it's him?' asked Aibgrene.

'I've known all along, I think,' replied Lola. She couldn't bear to look her friend in the eye. She felt so ashamed that despite Arthur's advice and Celeste's warnings, she hadn't trusted her inner wisdom. But now was not the time for an apology, reasoned Lola. It was time for action.

'So where do we start, Lo? She could be anywhere.'

'I know where she is!' declared Lola with authority. 'And I'm sure there's access through the house. But first things first, we need to be prepared. The element of surprise will only get us so far.' Lola was growing bolder by the minute. She had no idea where this was coming from. Was it actual intuition or perhaps just adrenaline? Either way she was happy to let it take over.

'We need blankets. Daithi, do you have any blankets or bags

in the car? Daithi nodded and moved to the boot of his car, where he pulled out a quilt and a sleeping bag and handed it to Lola. 'Perfect,' said Lola placing one along the back seat of her car, crumpling it up to make it look as though there was someone lying underneath it. She did the same with the sleeping bag, this time placing it on the back seat of Daithi's car.

'Now, Aibgrene, you take my car, and Daithi can take his, and park just up the road. When I get Celeste...' Lola didn't get a chance to finish her sentence.

'No, no, hold up there, Lola! What do you mean, when you get Celeste? I'm coming with you. You're not going in there alone. No way!' protested Aibgrene. Lola didn't want to argue, after all it was Aibgrene's mother, what right did she have to tell her not to come? She was just trying to protect her.

'Okay then, Daithi, you'll have wait out on the road,' suggested Lola.

'I'm not letting you go in there on your own, Aibgrene, not a chance!' protested Daithi.

'Listen, guys,' reasoned Lola. 'We can't all bloody go in! We need to get Celeste to safety as soon as possible. Are you forgetting who we are dealing with here? They have contacts everywhere. We need to split up. Create a decoy.' Lola's voice was raised now, but it wasn't the usual panic, it was authority that she exuded. Aibgrene soothed Daithi, and finally he agreed to let her go alone with Lola. Checking her watch, Lola guessed they would have to wait just a little bit longer. 'Follow me in the car,' she directed, jumping into Ruby's car. Lola drove back up the street at a crawl, with Aibgrene and Daithi following behind her. She couldn't risk parking too close to the house as her car, which was bright yellow, would certainly attract some attention, so she motioned to Daithi to overtake her.

Daithi pulled up onto the kerb a few yards from the rest of the cars, Lola slowly pulled in behind him, happy that her car would be obscured from view. Aibgrene got out and headed towards Lola. Just as she was about to climb into the passenger seat there was a screeching sound as a car rounded the suburban street at speed. Reacting quickly, Aibgrene crouched behind the bonnet, doing enough to stay out of view. Lola caught a glimpse of the side of the car as it disappeared into the driveway of Chateau Bacchus. The car and the driver were unmistakable – it was Alex. Lola's stomach leapt to her throat. He was coming to join the party too. Why did this surprise her? She scolded herself. Secretly she'd hoped that he wasn't like his father, that he had nothing to do with it, but that was delusional at best.

'I see your boyfriend has just arrived,' said Aibgrene, with obvious venom in her voice. Although she was right and had been right all along, the words stung Lola, but she knew that her friend's anger was not directed towards her. 'I knew from the first night I saw him, I could just see it in his eyes,' continued Aibgrene.

'Aibgrene, now isn't the time, okay!' said Lola. What they were about to attempt required all her focus. 'Let's go!' Lola slid out of the car seat and pulled up the hood of her mantle. They were the only people on the deserted street. Daithi rolled down the car window as both women approached. Lola could see the worry and torment in his eyes.

'I've left the keys in my car, Daithi. Wait here for us,' said Lola quietly.

Reaching out to take his hand, Lola tried to reassure him as best she could.

'I'll get them both back to you safe and sound. Okay?' Daithi just nodded.

'Celeste will need to travel with me, because I have the ring, so when we come out you go north through the town, and I'll go in the opposite direction. We will meet at Brook Mill Manor, that's the only place where we will all be safe. Try not to raise suspicion. We don't know who or what they know.' All this flowed from Lola's mouth with confidence. 'Are you ready?' Lola asked Aibgrene. She shook her head and kissed Daithi goodbye, before taking Lola's hand and heading towards Chateau Bacchus to rescue her mother.

CHAPTER 53

As soon as they turned the corner towards the driveway of Chateau Bacchus, Lola and Aibgrene were hit by an invisible wall of dark energy.

'We're definitely at the right place,' wheezed Aibgrene. Lola felt short of breath too, as if she'd been winded or struck in the solar plexus. She could see the murky force field around the house. It started where the two large stone owls sat perched on columns on either side of the pathway. 'We're going to have to find another way in, Lola. That magick is too strong, it could kill us,' spluttered Aibgrene. They didn't have time to drive up the coast, thought Lola, and besides that would mean they would lose the element of surprise. She had no doubt that Carl Stein would have the perimeter guarded.

'We have to go in this way, it's our only chance.' Turning back Lola found Aibgrene hunched up against the wall struggling to breath. Her nose had started to bleed and she was retching. 'Aibgrene! Are you alright? Maybe you should go back to the car.' But Lola knew that she would risk the chance of dying before she would go back, if it was her mother in there she would feel the same. Although she could feel the heaviness, and her head was starting to hurt, it didn't seem to affect Lola the same way. Then she realised that this may have been simply because she was wearing the ring. Fishing it out from under her clothes, she took it off the chain and slid it onto her index finger. It was a perfect fit and the effects were immediate.

Closing her eyes she tried to channel her energy, and the power of the ring. She could feel the warmth and see the light as it expanded around her entire body like a shield. Aibgrene sat with her mouth gaping, awestruck. Lola was relieved when Aibgrene's breathing began to regulate itself.

'I told you I knew what I was doing,' winked Lola smugly. 'Come on let's do this.'

Although she could only see a slight silver ripple in front of her, Lola could feel the powerful auric shield encapsulating the two of them. 'Here goes nothing,' said Lola. Stretching out her index finger once again she led Aibgrene over the threshold. There was quite a bit of resistance, it felt as though they were wading through deep water. Finally they reached the door.

'Quick follow me,' whispered Lola, as her intuition guided her towards the glass staircase and the upstairs level of the house. Aware of what she was looking for, and more familiar now with the house, Lola managed to avoid making the mistake she made that first summer night. She skirted nimbly around the outside of the transparent structure, and was just about to warn Aibgrene, but it was too late. She collided with the staircase letting out an involuntary yelp. Lola sprang towards her friend who was now sprawled out on the floor almost knocked unconscious. If their predicament hadn't been so serious it would have been funny. Lola froze as she heard movement on the corridor above – it was coming towards them. Their cover had been blown! Grabbing the still disorientated Aibgrene, she pulled her across the polished marble floor, taking refuge behind the long white sofa at the other end of the room. Someone was at the top of the staircase and about to come down when a phone rang. Lola recognised the ring tone immediately, and knew who it was before Alex answered the call.

'Hello. Yes, Father, I'm at the house now, I am on my way. I'll be there in a few minutes.' It was Lola's turn to hyperventilate now. Despite everything that had happened, the sound of Alex's deep soft voice made her heart ache.

Aibgrene was coming round and was sporting a massive lump on her head. Touching it she winced with the pain. 'I feel like I've just been hit with a baseball bat. Was that who I think it was talking on the phone? Or am I still out of it?' Lola just nodded, she was always grateful that Aibgrene never used his name; it made it easier for her.

'Are you sure that you're okay to continue?' asked Lola, but Aibgrene glared at her making her immediately regret asking such a stupid question.

'Are you?' retorted Aibgrene. There was no venom in her tone, only concern. Lola didn't reply.

'I think it is safe now. Let's try this again, and watch the staircase this time,' laughed Lola.

'Very funny, Lo, my little accident saved our hides. He was still up there,' replied Aibgrene.

'I know,' smiled Lola, rolling her eyes in relief.

'Stupid staircase, who makes a staircase that you can't see?' mumbled Aibgrene as she climbed the steps.

Lola laughed to herself. She had the same reaction when she first encountered it. When they reached the familiar long corridor, Lola tried to recall at which door she'd heard Celeste's voice.

'Where to now?' whispered Aibgrene, growing more and more anxious.

Passing the first door on the left Lola stopped and walked back towards it.

'I think it's in here. I heard Alex saying on the phone that he would be there in a few minutes. So there must be some sort of passageway to the temple from the house. It makes so much sense – no one would suspect anything!'

Putting her ear to the door, Lola listened, but there were no giveaway sounds. Opening it gently, she let it slide ajar before stepping into the room. Following behind, Aibgrene closed the door with a soft click. They were in a library with large vaulted ceilings. The wall space was completely covered in books and at the top of the room sat a black desk and large chair with the initials C.S. embedded in gold lettering onto the cracked leather. Aibgrene's face turned white, and for a moment Lola thought she was going to faint again.

'She was in here. I can feel her. He had her here all this time.' Aibgrene's words hit Lola like a kick to the stomach. Celeste was in this very room the night she had passed that door? Had Celeste sensed that Lola was near? 'The passageway could be anywhere,' said Aibgrene, as she frantically moved around the room pulling random books from the neat shelves. Looking around the vast room, with row upon endless row of books, Lola felt unsure for the first time that night.

Her eyes scanned the library, finally resting on the chessboard that sat by Carl Stein's desk. It lay untouched. Not one piece had been moved since the night they had played. One more move, thought Lola, and she would have won the game, and Carl Stein had known it. He had completely underestimated her and that was her trump card. Lifting the white rook to G8, Lola ended the game. 'Checkmate, Mr Stein,' she said aloud. She wondered if after all this was over he would notice he had lost the game. Looking out of the small arched window, she could see the temple silhouetted by the bright silver moon, perched high in the sky. Looking to the left of the window, Lola noticed a tower structure with small slit-like windows here and there, a perfect place for a stairwell. Moving slowly across the book shelves, she tried to position herself adjacent to the tower, hoping to find some sort of gap.

'Have you found it?' asked Aibgrene, the urgency clear in her voice.

Lola didn't answer and continued to feel the wooden frames and shelves, not really sure what she was looking for, until she felt a gentle stream of air brushing across her face. Stepping back, she examined the shelf. It was very subtle, but her eyes traced a rectangular doorway. But how was it opened? All the books in that shelf were old and bound in leather casings mostly with Latin names that Lola couldn't understand, but right at the centre of the stack there was one that was clearly out of place. Moving closer to take a better look, Lola began to laugh.

'Clever,' laughed Lola. 'Very clever!' This was one example where research had proven invaluable.

'What is it, Lola?' asked Aibgrene nervously.

'Shakespeare,' chirped Lola, pleased with herself. *'A Midsumner*

Night's Dream, to be exact!'

'I'm lost, Lo,' said Aibgrene, with mild irritation.

'I was doing a bit of research on the Hell Fire Club a while back. Do you know they have an official website? Well on that website they have a motto, and if I'm right this book will lead us to their temple!' Stepping forward Lola pulled the book out. After all, this is what they did in all the movies and it worked every time, thought Lola. But this wasn't the movies, this was reality and lives were at stake. Nothing happened.

'I was sure I was right,' said Lola deflated. She stood back examining the rows of books again.

'Maybe it's another book, Lola. Let's try them all!' Aibgrene began to pull at books here and there, but again nothing happened.

'No. It has to be this book, it makes perfect sense,' protested Lola. 'Their motto is "Weaving spiders come not here".'

'I'm drawing a blank here, Lola, and time is running out. We don't have time for a Shakespeare lesson. It's almost midnight and we need to get a move on!'

'Look, Aibgrene. Look at all the other books around it, it's totally out of place and it's also positioned right at the centre. The Hell Fire Club's motto is from A Midsummer Night's Dream. It's the First Fairy's lines to be exact. Magick, other realms, do I need to continue?'

Instinctively, Lola slid her finger down the worn spine of the book, and suddenly there was a soft click. The bookcase slid across, revealing a dark staircase that plummeted into the bowels of the cliff.

Holding onto the wall as they descended, each step brought them deeper and deeper into the darkness below. Lola could tell that they were nearing the water. The sound of the waves as they crashed against the cliffs was getting louder and louder. Finally, they were at the bottom, but it was impossible to see.

Taking Aibgrene's hand, Lola inched forward with her other hand stretched out in front of her, trying to find a tunnel or passageway. Moving forward a few steps, she came to a painful halt, almost tripping over a large metal construction.

'Stop, I think there are tracks here,' said Lola. 'But it's nearly impossible to see anything. We need a light, this is useless.'

'Move over,' said Aibgrene pushing Lola to one side, suddenly offering a soft yellow glow to light their way. 'It's clearly a transport line to get them to the temple quickly without being detected above ground.'

'I can't believe you had a lighter the whole time!' said Lola slightly irritated, rolling her eyes in disbelief. They followed the lines, eventually coming closer to a small carriage which sat on the track.

'I just remembered I had it, sorry. Come on, get into the carriage.' Aibgrene climbed into the small craft first as Lola followed. Lola was still getting seated when it took off, almost throwing her out. Reaching for Aibgrene's hands she was finally seated as they accelerated through an endless sea of black. Lola's head began to throb and ache again as that same familiar feeling of heaviness began to bear down on them. Sensing her anxiety, the ring stirred and emitted a bright blue beam encapsulating both of them in its warm womb again.

The carriage began to slow and they could see a pale light up ahead. The loud baritone chants from the temple above them could be heard, as the small craft came to a halt at the bottom of another set of stone steps. Lola had never heard anything so chilling; a cold shiver ran right through her.

'She's up there; I need to get to her,' said Aibgrene striding towards the lift cage, but Lola pulled her back.

CHAPTER 54

'Surprise is the key, Aibgrene!' urged Lola, struggling to keep her nerves in check. 'Remember we don't know where that lift will lead us!'

Without a word, Aibgrene turned and bolted up the stairs taking two at a time, with Lola struggling to catch her up.

'Wait, Aibgrene! I can't protect you if you're that far away.'

But Aibgrene didn't care, all she wanted was to get to her mother, and Lola could understand that. Finally Lola caught her at the top of the stairs. The chanting had stopped and the only sound now was the languid and silky voice of Carl Stein.

'My brethren, you're all most welcome here tonight on Samhain Eve to celebrate in the offering to our great deity, Mollach. As we usher in our New Year, we have much to give him thanks for. The Ancient Order of the Golden Dawn has been destroyed, and its servant Arthur Delphian disposed of.' Cheers and laughter rang through the air in approval. 'But that's not all. We are close to acquiring the ring and the Cube and we all know what this means, my brothers,' laughed

Carl Stein. 'This means any opposition to our new world order will be destroyed.' Again a roar of appreciation rang through the air. Lola stood rooted to the spot; an indescribable rage surged inside her. She wasn't sure when to make her move, or even if she could, it felt as though she was paralysed.

'But now let's get back to the matter at hand,' continued Carl Stein. 'Tonight we offer the most prestigious sacrifice to our Lord. I have had the pleasure of sampling one of the legendary Moone family in my day and I must say I am most looking forward to this.' Unable to stand it anymore, Aibgrene burst into the room before Lola had even realised what had happened.

'Get your filthy hands off her, you bastard!' shouted Aibgrene at a bemused Carl Stein. Celeste lifted her weary head searching for her daughter, who was now hurtling towards her. But Aibgrene never even got within a yard of her mother as she was lifted up and thrown against the wall by a flick of Carl Stein's hand. Dazed, she fought to get to her feet, but she was no match for Carl Stein who stood over her, pinning her down onto the stone tiles by some invisible force.

'Well, well. What a treat. Now I have completed the set,' he sneered. Thick globes of blood oozed from Aibgrene's head. Kneeling down beside her, Carl Stein ran his fingers across her head. He examined the blood before smearing it over his thin lips.

'Mmmm, such life. Such energy!' he cried, as he gave a nod to two of his cloaked followers to pick the dazed Aibgrene up. Lola was still rooted to the spot not sure what to do as Carl strutted around the large stone table where Celeste lay with the blood weeping out of her arms into the thirteen small recesses carved in the stone table. Her hair had turned white and her once vibrant violet auric shell was a dim glow. Lola could see that she fought to hold onto life as the last drops of her life blood spilled onto the sacrificial table.

'I'm afraid you're too late, my dear,' declared Carl with mock apology. 'In a few moments your mother will be gone, but fear not, you won't be far behind,' he laughed.

Struggling to break free, Aibgrene threw herself at the table, and sobbing, she kissed her mother's pallid forehead. 'No please! No! Mum, it's me. It's me, mum! Please stay with me, it's okay we're going to get you out of here!'

'How touching,' scoffed Carl, much to the amusement of his

flock. 'We?' he said, turning around to the gathering.

'But you are completely on your own, my dear.' Carl looked dramatically around the circular room. It was now or never, thought Lola as she stepped out of the shadows.

'Well, that's not entirely true, Mr Stein, or do you still prefer I call you Carl?' She knew she had succeeded in the element of surprise; the mocking smile on Carl Stein's face was gone, replaced with a look of rage.

'This is going to be a most interesting night indeed,' he said, opening his arms towards his followers, calling for their assistance. Lola tried to blank out the faces around her so she wouldn't have to look at Alex, but another familiar face suddenly emerged from the group and tried to grab her. She wasn't at all surprised to see him there. It all made perfect sense – the cuff links, the Victoria Jones story and it must have been him that had told that young boy that she would be with Felix Tennyson the night she had gone to see the old solicitor. He must have been listening to her calls.

'I wouldn't try that if I were you, Bryce,' said Lola, her voice calm and unwavering. It felt as though someone else was speaking. Her old editor ignored her words of caution. Stretching out her index finger, Lola could feel the power and rage rise through her body, and she knew that what was coming would be much stronger than what she had conjured outside Mystic Moone all those months ago. Again it all happened in a blink of an eye. As he tried to grab her arm for the second time, a white bolt of pure light rippled across the circular room shaking it to its core and sending Bryce hurtling across the room. He collided with Carl Stein before sliding to the floor. Unlike the last time, Lola was totally focused now, her doubts and fears replaced with courage and absolute trust.

'Aibgrene,' she commanded, 'get Celeste, it's time we were going!' Grabbing her mother, Aibgrene pulled her off the stone table and into her arms.

'Do you think you can outwit me?' snarled a still visibly disorientated Carl Stein. 'Do you think that ring is any match for me? Even if you do get out, where are you going to go from here?' Lola moved to position herself between him, Celeste and the door.

'Aibgrene, get her out of here now!' ordered Lola. 'I'll meet you at the bottom.' Aibgrene hesitated for a second. 'Go now!' shouted

Lola, never once taking her eyes of Carl. She could feel his power trying to break through her defences, as he regained his composure.

'I've outwitted you once before, sir, and it looks to me like its checkmate, again,' threw back Lola smugly. Gradually the rest of the men started to get to their feet, except Bryce who was still out cold. Inching forward they began to form a wide circle around Lola. Stepping back she tried to reposition herself nearer the exit.

Lola remained calm, looking at the men around her, surprised at how many faces she recognised. There was a High Court Judge; she couldn't recall his name, but remembered seeing him on television recently. Another face stood out, he was a politician with a prominent role in local office who often referred to himself as being a committed Christian.

'Well I must say, Mr Stein,' shot back Lola, 'you have some very esteemed guests tonight.'

'This is nothing, Ms Paige,' he snarled. 'I'm sure there are some you know and others you don't. But you are familiar with my son Alex, aren't you?' Lola hadn't seen him behind the others, but as he emerged from the group with a cold, emotionless expression on his face, she began to lose her resolve. She had to get out of there and quickly. 'I believe you two know each other quite intimately. Alex and I usually like to share our playthings, it's a pity you didn't stick around a little bit longer, Lola.'

'I'm afraid you're not my type, Mr Stein, but I imagine that hasn't stopped you in the past. I'm sure you weren't Karen Watson's type or Victoria Jones's type either. Raping and murdering is hardly a consensual thing after all.'

'You really are very astute, Lola, but I can't take all the credit,' chuckled Carl. 'Alex, perhaps you could persuade your friend to stay.' Suddenly Alex began to edge closer to her.

'Get back, Alex, or you'll end up like poor Bryce over there,' cautioned Lola trying hard to keep her voice from breaking. But he continued to move forward. Lola had no idea if the ring's magick would work to repel him. After all, he had broken her defences before. His face wore a stony expression. He looked at her as though she meant nothing to him. The words of the song that he had sent her came into her head making her stomach churn. How could she have believed that what had happened between them was real for him? He was almost within reach when the ring ignited again, sending him hurtling across the room. It was much stronger than before as all the windows exploded sending shards of glass raining down around the room. The blast threw Lola backwards towards the door.

Darting out to the stairwell, she slammed the oak door shut and headed for the lift. Once inside, it seemed to take forever to descend towards the small craft, where Celeste lay half-dead in Aibgrene's arms. Jumping into the carriage they headed back towards Chateau Bacchus. They wouldn't have much time. There was no way Carl Stein was going to let them get away.

'She's lost too much blood, Lola,' sobbed Aibgrene. 'I tried a spell, but the wounds are too deep.' Aibgrene continued to whisper her spell rapidly, but there was no change in Celeste. Without knowing why, Lola ran her ring down the deep vertical slits in Celeste's arms, then watched in amazement as its light began to heal the wounds.

Finally the craft came to a halt. 'You take her legs and I'll take her arms,' ordered Aibgrene. Doing as she was told, Lola grabbed Celeste's legs as they climbed the staircase. Celeste weighed very little – she was a shadow of the woman that Lola had left after Arthur's cremation. Making it into the library, they quickly moved out into the hallway on their way towards the glass staircase. Lola turned to check if Celeste was still conscious, but the shocked expression on Aibgrene's face wasn't warning enough and suddenly she felt herself being knocked to the floor, after being hit across the face with what felt like a slab of stone.

Disorientated, she writhed around on the floor, with blood pouring from her mouth. Aibgrene's screams sounded suddenly distant, as Lola's vision slowly returned. She quickly realised that the weapon that had struck her was a fist and it belonged to the man-mountain, who was now standing over her, readying to pummel her again.

'Didn't your mother tell you that it's very rude to walk out on your host? Mr Stein would like you to stay,' he said in a thick Belfast accent. Lola recognised him immediately. It was the man who had tried following them to Tara. As if he had read her thoughts, he drew his arm back again. 'That was for Mr Stein, and this is for my tyres you bitch!' Grabbing Lola by the hair, he drew back his fist, but Lola got in first. Lifting her foot, she drove it as hard as she could between the legs, managing to roll out of his way before he fell. She clambered to her knees, while he writhed about on the floor. Lola stood to catch her breath while trying to help Celeste up onto her feet. It looked as though her assailant might get up again, and reaching out he tried to grab Lola's leg. But this time Aibgrene came to her rescue. Lifting the only thing that was to hand, Aibgrene pulled one of the paintings off the wall and struck their assailant over the head with it.

'I hate to waste a Jackson Pollock on someone like you, but didn't your mother tell you never hit a lady, you piece of shit!' spat Aibgrene. 'Now can we please get the hell out of here?'

'Please,' smiled Lola through her bloodied mouth. Aibgrene hoisted Celeste up, throwing her over her shoulder, as the three of them broke out of the house sucking in the fresh air. They were half-way up the driveway when Lola noticed Alex's car with the keys still in the ignition. 'Aibgrene give me your mum,' said Lola, stopping.

Aibgrene tried to urge her on. 'What are doing, Lola? Are you mad? Come on now.'

'No,' continued Lola. She'd had another brainwave and her instincts hadn't let her down. 'Put her in this car, Aibgrene.' Lola pointed to Alex's sports car.

'What are you on about, Lola? Come on we need to get out of here. Now!'

'I'm going to take Alex's car,' said Lola, already in the driver's seat. Reaching over, she opened the door. 'Put her in, Aibgrene, this car will get us to safety in half the time. You take my car; they won't be looking for us in this car. It's her only chance!'

Aibgrene put her mother in the passenger seat, gently placing her seat belt on.

'Are you sure you can handle this car, Lola?'

'We'll be fine. I'll meet you at mine. Now go!' assured Lola.

Aibgrene kissed her mother then turned and ran towards Daithi who was still waiting in their car as Lola sped off up the street.

CHAPTER 55

It wasn't the first time that night that Lola had lied to Aibgrene; she had no idea how to handle a car like this. Taking the roundabout at the top of the street, her gut guided her towards the next town over. Although the motorway was the quickest option, Lola decided it would be safer if she took the back roads home to Ballyvalley. Celeste continued to drift in and out of consciousness. Beads of cold sweat clung to her frail body. Her chest bones protruded as did her cheekbones; she looked as though she was teetering on the edge of death.

Taking off her ring, Lola slid it on to Celeste's finger hoping it would aid her recovery. Celeste began to shiver. She needed heat. Pulling over on to the side of the road, Lola took off her mantle and wrapped it around Celeste's infirm frame. She was a shadow of the woman that Lola had met at Arthur's funeral. Celeste was babbling incoherently.

'Shush,' soothed Lola. 'We'll be home soon, Celeste.'

She needed more heat. Lola remembered that there were heated seats in the car so she began pressing random buttons, hoping to eventually find the right one. A small screen emerged from the sound system. The seats began to heat. Lola turned the heat up on the air-conditioning, then started the ignition and took off at speed. Concentrating on the road ahead, Lola paid no mind to the screen, assuming it was some sort of built-in satellite navigation.

As she passed through Coleraine and other small towns, Lola made sure to keep her speed down to avoid any unwanted attention. But Alex's car wasn't exactly low profile. In unfamiliar territory, she decided to check the navigation system. At first she thought it was broken. It showed the car travelling down the main M2 motorway. Then an automated voice announced, 'Lola approaching Belfast city. Lola is now approaching Belfast city.' She couldn't believe her ears, with one eye on the road ahead, and one eye on the navigation system, she stared in disbelief, as a miniature picture of Ruby's car drove towards Belfast.

They had been tracking her car this whole time. Alex had known exactly where she was. He had known she was at Tara. Of course he knew, that's how his bodyguard had been able to tail them, that's how he had been able to tell when she would be arriving home. Surely, thought Lola, that meant he had known she was in Portstewart tonight, parked yards from his house. So why hadn't he informed his father? Lola's head began to swim with all the 'what if' and 'buts'.

The heat in the car was suffocating so Lola slid down the car window, as if the cold air would help expel Alex Stein from her head. He wasn't her concern tonight, nor should he ever be. They would know that his car was missing by now. Then it occurred to Lola that Carl Stein probably had a tracker on Alex's car too. She hadn't thought of that. Taking the next turn off for the motorway, Lola decided to break cover.

The R8 roared to life, as she slid it into sixth gear, pinning Lola and Celeste back into their seats. The dial was hitting one hundred and thirty, which meant Lola was on the other side of Belfast in less than thirty minutes. Keeping an eye on the tracker, she was relieved to see that Aibgrene wasn't too far from home. Leaving the M1 Lola took the dual carriageway to Ballyvalley. Her speed had dropped to ninety. The gods had been with her tonight.

There was very little traffic on the roads, and that included the police. Finally, she began to relax when she saw the sign for Ballyvalley. 'Only five miles to go,' she told Celeste. It was after 2am when she drove into town. The local nightclub had just spilled out, forcing the car to a crawl on the main road. There was a heavy police presence, which made Lola feel very uneasy, and the car was attracting a lot of attention. Lola noticed a uniformed police officer taking a look at the plates. The Halloween revellers continued to flood across the road and even though the lights were green, she couldn't move. A tapping on the window startled her. For an instant she considered hitting the accelerator, but thought the better of it. Taking a deep breath Lola pressed the button on the door, allowing the window to slide down.

'Hi, Officer,' said Lola.

'Hi, sorry to bother you, madam,' said the police patrolman. 'I just wanted to let you know that we are trying to clear the road, and we will get you on your way as soon as possible. Nice car by the way!'

'Do you like it?' asked Lola, trying to sound as flippant as possible.

'I've never seen one up close before, it must be amazing to drive.'

'Yeah, it really is a great car.'

Lola had no idea about car speak, so she was relieved when the young officer changed the subject.

'I take it you were out yourself tonight. What happened to your face?' asked the officer.

Lola had completely forgotten about her costume and her busted face. She didn't even feel the pain she was so preoccupied. She could see the policeman's eyes darting suspiciously between Celeste and her.

'Make-up, Officer, and my friend, she had a bit of a rough night as well. Too much to drink, you know?' laughed Lola nervously, as the lights suddenly turned green again, and there was a parting in the foot traffic. 'The lights are green. I'd better get her home.'

Lola took off again, her heart pounding and her palms sweaty as they gripped the steering wheel. Relieved that she was now on the Scarvagh Road, she checked the navigation system, and breathed a sigh of relief that Aibgrene had almost made it to Ballyvalley.

Pressing down on the accelerator, she sped up the driveway, coming to a halt outside the house. Every light in the house was on, and Lola wasn't out of the car before the front door swung open. Her mother and father were quickly at her side.

'Lola. Oh my God, are you okay?' cried her mother before launching into a tirade 'Where the hell have you been, young lady? You had me and your dad worried to death,' fumed her mum. 'We were about to call the police.'

Now it was her dad's turn. 'What the hell happened to your face, Lola? And where on earth did you get this car from?'

'Oh my God, her face. Jesus, would you look at her face, Joseph?' said Eileen, pacing back and forth. It had been a long time since she had seen her parents this angry and worried all at the same time. Ruby must have told them.

'Ma. Da!' shouted Lola. 'I don't have time for this right now. Okay?' Eileen Paige was about to launch into another scolding, but Lola never gave her the chance. 'Help me get Celeste into the house.'

Pushing past her mum and dad, Lola opened the passenger door to get to Celeste. There was a unified gasp from her parents, as they ran their eyes over the crumpled pile of skin and bones that lay motionless on the car's passenger seat.

'Jesus, Joseph, is she dead?' said her mum, covering her mouth. Eileen moved out of the way as her husband lifted Celeste's limp body out of the car.

'Quick, Dad, bring her inside, put her on the couch. Mum, get me some hot water and blankets, lots of blankets, she's lost a lot of blood.' Eileen Paige stood rooted to the spot, horrified by the thin vertical slits that were carved in Celeste Moone's transparent arms. 'Now, Ma!' barked Lola. 'There's no time to spectate.'

'I think we need to call an ambulance, Lo.' Her dad laid a gentle hand on her shoulder. 'I don't think she is going to do, love.'

'We can't, Dad. Aibgrene will be here soon, she will know what to do.' Her mum soon returned to the room with a large quilt and some hot water and a cloth. Lola wrapped Celeste in the quilt, cleaning the dry blood around her arms where they had been cut open. Lola ran to the window when she heard the sound of tyres screeching to a halt on the stones outside. It was Aibgrene and Daithi – they were safe. Relief washed over her as they came bursting in through the door. Aibgrene ran straight to her mother's side sobbing uncontrollably.

'She's lost a lot of blood, Aibgrene, she may need to go to a hospital,' said Lola hopefully. But she understood that Aibgrene wouldn't permit it.

'We can't, Lo. We don't know who to trust – it's too risky.' Aibgrene ran her fingertip along the groove in her mother's arms. 'The ring has healed these wounds well; it has given us a fighting chance, Lola. I don't know how to thank you, Lo, you saved our lives in there tonight. We owe you everything.'

Lola began to choke up, as she permitted herself to cry for the first time that night. The tears came, first in a trickle and then in torrents as she and Aibgrene just stood sobbing in each other's arms. No one had noticed that Liam and Cuchulain had joined them, until the dog let out a playful bark running towards Lola.

'Cuchulain, you big wolf, come here boy,' shouted Lola, as she knelt, embracing the dog, as he licked her face in delight. All the while Daithi had just sat in the corner calmly. Lola felt bad when she saw him.

'Daithi, I didn't get a chance to say thank you for tonight. I can't imagine how hard it was for you sitting out there not knowing what was going on.' As always, Daithi's kind smile spread across his face.

'I think I have you to thank, Lola. What you did in there tonight, words can't describe how indebted I am to you for bringing her back to me. We owe you everything.'

'You really don't, Daithi. It was my fault that Celeste was there in the first place.' Eileen was now by Aibgrene's side, as they tried to make Celeste more comfortable. 'I think we should try and move her upstairs to a bed, pet, she would be much more comfortable there.' Nodding in agreement, Aibgrene asked Daithi to carry her mother to Lola's bedroom. Eileen disappeared upstairs with Daithi and Aibgrene, leaving Lola alone with her dad and Liam. Lola could see the worry in her dad's face, but she knew that he didn't want to push it right now.

'You look terrible, pet; you should go and get yourself cleaned up,' said Joseph. Lola tried to reassure him that she was fine, but he wasn't convinced.

'Really, Dad, I'm fine, just a sore jaw. But apart from that, I'm okay.' The adrenaline that had coursed through her body just hours ago had prevented her from feeling any discomfort, but now Lola could feel every ache and pain. Her jaw throbbed where the mountain's fist had made impact. She could even taste the metallic dry blood that caked to her swollen lips. Liam couldn't take his eyes off her, but he didn't ask what happened, which was unlike him.

Lola's heart jumped when she heard the gentle ting of the door-bell. Even her father froze for second. Getting up he looked through the window.

'It's the police,' he said with a nod, as if he had been expecting the late call.

'The police?' said Lola as she jumped up from the chair, not sure what to do or where to go.

'What's wrong, love?'

'You can't let them in, Dad!' panicked Lola.

'What are you on about, Lola? I have to let him in now that you're okay. We were worried sick and with everything that has happened we didn't know what to think when Ruby called us.'

Ruby! Lola had completely forgotten about the girls, they would be sick with worry. 'I need to call the girls!' she said. Walking to the hallway, her dad answered the door, while she made for the phone in the kitchen.

'Hello, Mr Paige. Sorry it took me so long to get out to you. May I come in?' Lola listened, with her heart in her mouth as her father nervously guided DCI Campbell into the living room. Closing the kitchen door she called Ruby's mobile. Ruby's hysterical voice answered after just two rings.

'Rubes, it's me…,' were the only words that Lola got to utter. It was Ruby's turn to admonish her. Lola felt totally expired, so she listened as her best friend let loose in between sobs.

'We tried calling and calling and there was no answer! You just left, and then I had to call your mum and dad, what else could I do? What is going on, Lo? How could you put us through that?' Lola let Ruby continue until she was all shouted out.

'I'm sorry, I didn't mean to worry you,' said Lola, struggling to find a better explanation. She knew that it didn't cover it, but what else could she say? 'I'm safe now, Rubes. I'll give you a call first thing tomorrow. Okay?'

'Okay,' agreed Ruby. Lola could tell that she was still mad at her and in truth she couldn't blame her.

'Love you,' said Lola warmly.

'You too, Lo. And don't ever do anything like that to us again. Do you hear me?'

'Yes. Promise.'

Hanging up the phone Lola decided to avoid DCI Campbell and headed for the shower, but just as she was about to go upstairs, the living room door opened, and her father came out with young detective.

'There she is! Lola, you had your parents very worried tonight,' he smiled as his attentive eyes flitted from her costume to her bruised face. 'It looks like you had an eventful night.' Even though his tone was congenial Lola didn't trust it, his eyes missed nothing.

'You know what Halloween can be like, Detective!' offered Lola, moving up a step trying to indicate that she was finished with the conversation.

'That's some motor parked outside! Is it yours?' continued the detective. Trying to stay calm Lola returned his smile before answering.

'No it's my boyfriend's. He was good enough to lend it to me to get home tonight.'

'Yes. I heard some of the guys at the station talking about it. They said they spoke to a young girl tonight in a state-of-the-art sports car. Small world, isn't it?' Lola knew he could sense her discomfort, he knew a lot more than he was giving away, but she was determined to play the same game. 'How is your friend by the way? Did you get her home safely? The officer I was speaking to said that she was quite drunk.' Lola's heart was in her throat but she didn't show the slightest bit of hesitation.

'She's safe and sound, Detective. Thanks for asking. I'm very grateful that you've taken the time to come out. I'm sure you don't normally personally deal with every call from a worried parent,' replied Lola sarcastically.

'Well I better be off! Let you all get to your beds. Good night, Mr Paige, and once again I'm sorry for imposing on you so late.'

Just as the young detective was about to leave there was a shrill scream from upstairs. Lola's mother stood at the top of the sweeping staircase, calling for her daughter. Lola took the stairs two at a time. She burst into her bedroom to find Aibgrene on her knees sobbing and shaking uncontrollably.

'It won't work, Lola! My spell won't work, she's going!' sobbed

Aibgrene. Lola ran to Celeste, she could see that her aura, a dim di-luted shade of violet, was fading. The ring could only do so much and Carl Stein's magick had proved too strong. Lola had no idea what to do, she just stood there motionless. Time seemed to stop still. She had failed them again. She felt numb.

Lola and the others didn't notice DCI Campbell come into the room. They just stood there shocked as he checked Celeste for a pulse and then lifted her out of the bed and ran through the house towards the herb garden. Lola joined Aibgrene and Daithi, as they rushed out behind him. When they got to the garden DCI Campbell began shout-ing out orders to them, asking Aibgrene to bring salt, candles, white sage and juniper. Aibgrene wasted no time darting for the large green-house, and returned seconds later with the items in hand. The young detective gently laid Celeste out on the damp grass and Aibgrene sprinkled salt in a wide circle around her mother's deteriorating body. Lifting the candles, DCI Campbell placed them at the cardinal points of north, south, east and west. A small knotted bundle of dry herbs was handed to each of them as they formed a loose circle around the dying Celeste.

Lola noticed that the plump moon that punctuated the crisp night sky seemed to swell in tandem with their movement. It seemed to grow brighter and brighter as Aibgrene and DCI Campbell made incantations, moving around the circle and dousing Celeste's ghostly frame with the smoke from the burning juniper and sage as they went. Aibgrene's voice was shaky as she repeated the spell in perfect unison with the detective. 'Moon be strong, Moon be bright, clear this poison out of sight, Moon be whole, moon of the soul, free this woman from death's hold.'

Feeling useless, Lola began to chant the words praying that it might make some difference. Taking her lead her mother and father joined in, each repeating the rhythmic words of the spell.

Lola's parents looked on in awe as Celeste's breathing began to become steady and even again. DCI Campbell looked totally exhaust-ed when he finally stopped.

'That should do it,' he sighed. 'She's still very weak but most of his poison is out of her system. That was close,' he said to Aibgrene. 'Lola, I think you and I need to talk.'

Lola remained outside while the others moved Celeste indoors.

'I think we need to start again,' smiled DCI Campbell. 'Maybe we have both been a bit sparing with the truth. My name is Wayne,' he smiled as he offered Lola a hand of friendship. Lola felt ashamed, he had just saved Celeste's life and she owed him a great deal.

Moving to the summer seat, Lola and Wayne sat side by side. 'I think I owe you an apology, Lola,' he started. Exhausted, Lola only offered a smile in way of response. 'I am a real detective, as was my father before me. I followed in his footsteps. My father was one of the best detectives on the force but he was also a friend of the Order's and a friend of Arthur's. Like him, I only deal with occult cases, Lola, that's why I was investigating Arthur's death and the Vikki Jones case as well. When I was assigned to both cases, the powers that be were trying to say it was a suicide. Carl Stein's reach goes far and wide, but we are closing the net on some of his minions, Lola.'

Feeling her jaw tentatively, Lola spoke slowly as it hurt to talk. 'I can attest to that. There was a high court judge and a minister in there tonight, as well as the editor and chief of the Ballyvalley News.'

'I know,' said the detective solemnly. 'I've been tracking their activities for some time, but I can't do anything without evidence, Lola. It's so infuriating. I knew you didn't trust me and I wasn't sure what you knew about the Order or what Arthur had entrusted to you, if anything. Then there was your relationship with the Stein boy. You weren't keeping very good company, Lola. It wasn't until I was in the book room that day that I realised that you knew more than I thought. I could see that you had been busy.' Lola's heart sank. Had everyone seen so clearly what she could not, or would not? Alex had only been using her.

'You made sure that Arthur's death was treated as a murder, Wayne. So what happened to the Vikki Jones case?' enquired Lola. 'I mean, Sarah Byrne gave you the evidence that Vikki had got into a car on the night she disappeared, why did you dismiss it?'

'You need to understand, Lola, that I'm in the lion's den. The Hell Fire Club has people at every level in every organisation. I realised the true extent of this when the press release was issued to the media and a statement made to her family before I even had a chance to hand in my report. I'm fighting against my own department, Lola. They made sure that the mistakes made in Arthur's case would not be made twice.'

'So what happened to Arthur?' Lola wasn't sure that she wanted to know.

'Well, I'm still trying to piece the puzzle together. I mean the biggest puzzle for me is how did they get in? How did they get past that gate post?'

'They must have known him. Arthur must have known his killer,' said Lola through gritted teeth.

'Or,' offered the detective. 'Or, he allowed them in. I agree with you about Arthur knowing his killer, Lola, but I will go a step further and say that he knew that an attempt would be made on his life that night. When his visitor slipped that hemlock into Arthur's wine glass, I believe the old man knew exactly what was happening.'

Lola sat rigid. Of all the things that she had heard, this was the most ridiculous. Why would Arthur allow himself to be killed? He would never knowingly leave her to deal with all this shit on her own. 'You're wrong, Detective,' spat Lola with more venom than she'd intended. 'Arthur loved me. He would never have left me on my own to deal with all this crap.' Lola realised that she was crying. 'There is no way he would abandon me.' DCI Campbell touched her hand.

'I'm sorry, Lola, I didn't mean to upset you. It's just a theory, that's all.'

'Detective,' croaked Lola as she ushered her tears away with the back of her hand. 'Are we ever going to be able to get to these men? Carl Stein is too powerful.'

'That's not true, Lola. You won tonight by saving Celeste. He has underestimated you and now you three are the first witnesses ever to survive, surely that's a start.'

Lola shook her head, rejecting the idea. 'I have managed to help Celeste, that's true, but I have not won the battle, instead I've shown my hand. Carl Stein knows I cannot, or will not, go to the law. You've said it yourself, Detective, his tentacles are far-reaching. Besides,' added Lola, 'this battle transcends the realm of law and order. They make their own rules.' Lola's words hung between them as they both sat in silence. Lola was shivering from the cold.

'It's late, Lola, I'd better be going and you better get inside. I'll be in touch. But one more thing, Lola, you know this is only the beginning?' Lola understood it was more a statement than a question. She nodded her head wearily. One thing she understood and accepted

was the fact that this was only the start of things to come. Both players had shown their hand tonight, both had stepped out of the shadows
and into the unforgiving light of the arena. Lola may have defeated
Carl Stein on the chequered board, but this game of chess was a perilous one.

CHAPTER 56

Lola managed to get a few weeks of leave from university to try to get to grips with things. Her parents had been great; they seemed to take it all in their stride. They were relieved that she was safe. Joseph and Eileen didn't ask too many questions, but Lola felt that she owed them some sort of explanation to all this craziness. She skirted around the more intricate details, but explained that Arthur and Celeste belonged to the same fraternity. She told them how the same people that had murdered Arthur had tried to hurt Celeste too. That was as much as she could divulge, mostly because she felt that the less they knew, the safer they would be.

Aibgrene and Daithi had taken over the kitchen, making various concoctions to help nurse Celeste back to health and although it was almost winter the weather had been very mild so Lola spent a lot of time outdoors. The tranquillity of the gardens around Brook Mill Manor helped to quiet her chaotic mind. Weeks had passed and no one had made an attempt to retrieve Alex's car. It sat for days outside the front door, where she'd abandoned it the night they rescued Celeste. Lola was grateful when her dad moved it to the side of the house, she couldn't bear to look at it, to the extent that she even avoided leaving the house through the front entrance.

Lola was watching the last of the oak leaves as they sky-waltzed to the ground below when she decided that it was time the car was returned to its owner. Weeks before, Daithi had checked the Audi and disabled the tracking device. It took him longer to find the tracer on Ruby's car but once he did, he disabled it with ease. Lola declined to mention any of this to her best friend when she returned the car. Besides it was high time that she'd her own means of transport, especially now that she had the means to buy it.

Lola had always loved Volkswagen Beetles and after days of scouring the web, she couldn't believe her luck when she found one being sold locally. It had only one female owner and the lady selling it had just given birth to twins so she now needed something a bit bigger. The car was metallic black with a white hood and matching white leather seats. Lola fell in love immediately. Daithi checked the mechanics, but it wouldn't have mattered what he'd said, this was the car for her. She bought it there and then.

After a few more days of putting off the inevitable, Lola finally built up the courage and sent a text message to Alex, informing him when and where to pick up the car. Her palms were clammy with sweat and her heart pumped ferociously in her mouth as she hit the send button. She didn't know if he would respond but something familiar and unwarranted stirred in her when her text alert sounded seconds later. It was Alex. Lola's stomach jolted as she opened the message and read the curt reply. Okay, was all it said and although it was only four letters on the screen, she must have stared at it for hours. It was best that she did this on her own, so she didn't mention her plans to anyone, especially not to Aibgrene. Lola knew how her friend would react and that was a confrontation she could do without, so she organised the pickup for a time that Aibgrene and Daithi would be away from the house.

Each Tuesday, the two of them went to the city for more supplies. Lola watched from the book room as they disappeared down the driveway in Daithi's beat-up van. She'd stashed the car keys in a small green wooden box that sat on the windowsill overlooking the herb garden.

The car sat covered in a silver tarpaulin in an outhouse that lay to the back of the manor. Lola pulled off the cover and gently eased herself into the driver's seat. As she secured her seatbelt her nostrils caught the unmistakable scent of Alex's aftershave. Unbidden, a tsunami of memories hit Lola, ripping open that hole in her heart that she had tried so hard to close in the days and weeks that had passed. Smell could be such a cruel and emotive sensory device. Thought after punishing thought swam through her mind like a spectre. Had she not been already sitting down, Lola was sure that each one would have brought her to her knees and even though Lola had forbidden herself to shed another tear for Alex Stein, still they came. At first the tears leaked out of her eyes in a trickle and then in torrents as she let them fall freely onto the cracked leather seat. Pulling her knitted jumper over her hand, Lola forced the tears away. Alex was always on time and she needed to be ready when he arrived – she could not appear weak and broken. Turing the ignition, the car's V10 engine roared to life shattering the stillness, bringing Lola back to the present. She awkwardly put the car into reverse and eased out of the garage. She had told him that the car would be left outside the gateposts of Brook Mill Manor and that's exactly where she left it.

Lola was walking back behind the gateposts when a familiar Black Mercedes pulled off the road, stopping at the top of the avenue. Lola checked her watch, it was two o'clock in the afternoon and, as always, Alex Stein was right on time. She waited nervously as he strode down the avenue with the winter sun bouncing off his blonde hair. He looked amazing, dressed in loose indigo jeans, light tan desert boots and a cream padded jacket. Stay strong, stay strong, show no weakness, show no weakness, commanded Lola to herself. Alex showed no signs of discomfort and she would have to act accordingly. Alex locked his cold blue eyes on her. His face was emotionless as he came to a standstill just inches from Lola. All that separated them was a thin sphere but this gave Lola the protection and courage that she needed as she mirrored Alex's granite stare.

Lola wondered how she could have been so blind. She wasn't even convinced that she had been blind. She had known what Alex was like from the very first time they had met yet she had allowed herself to fall in love with him. Love, with all its passion and brutal intensity, had given her an excuse to deny what she'd always known. Yet, standing there looking at him now, Lola's brain still found it hard to accept that it had all been a lie. She recalled seeing that beautiful phosphorous pink glow around him after they had made love. But as hard as it was to stomach, Alex Stein was a fraud, it was all a fallacy. There was no need for words, there weren't enough words in her vocabulary to describe all that had passed between them.

'You're more like your mother than you know, Alex,' a voice said. For a moment Lola thought that the words had come out of her own mouth, but the voice was soft, like music. Lola turned as Celeste, aided by Arthur's walking stick, walked through the gateposts towards her nephew. 'You have her light,' said Celeste, as Alex glared at her.

'And what do you know about my mother, witch,' he spat back at her. Lola could see that Celeste had touched a nerve but she didn't know whether it was hate or fear that she saw in Alex's contorted face.

'As a matter of fact, I knew her very well, Alex. After all, she was my twin sister. I assume from your reaction that your father didn't tell you this. Did he even tell you her name?' she asked gently, without waiting for a reply. 'It was Aurora,' continued Celeste. 'She was named after the Goddess of the Dawn. She was so gentle and so loving but love can sometimes make us blind. She thought that she could change your father and for a time she did. For years your father fought against the darkness that raged inside him and gradually your mother became a constant reminder of what he was. Her light cast him in constant shadow. I have no doubt that he would have killed her sooner, but then she became pregnant with you, Alex, and Carl knew he would soon have his heir. I suspect that he killed my sister moments after she gave birth to his son.'

Lola could not believe what she was hearing. Alex was Celeste's nephew. His mother was Aurora and Carl Stein had murdered her. Lola was floored. She looked at Alex, but that momentary burst of emotion had vanished from his face and was replaced once again with the customary void.

'Don't be like him, Alex,' urged Celeste. 'Be like your mother.' Without a word Alex got into his car and disappeared up the avenue.

CHAPTER 57

Celeste never mentioned their encounter with Alex to her daughter; she didn't even discuss it with Lola after that day. How she knew that he would be there was still a mystery to Lola, but for once in her life she let the question remain unasked. She was sure that Aibgrene would not take the news that Alex Stein was blood in the best taste.

Celeste had been growing stronger by the day and although she wasn't back to her full strength, her progress while at Brook Mill Manor had been impressive. So when both Celeste and Aibgrene sat her down to say it was time for them to leave, Lola was devastated. She really needed them with her but that was just being selfish. Aibgrene explained that it was best for her mother to be among her circle of friends and the many healers that they knew. She had said that it would aid her recovery. Lola couldn't really argue with that, both women had already been through so much.

Despite herself, Lola often thought about Alex and what Celeste had told him. She found herself wondering if he had listened to Celeste, and if it had crossed his mind that there was indeed a different way.

Lola returned to university the week Celeste and Aibgrene left Brook Mill Manor. She hadn't realised how much she missed school. It was great distraction from her worries. She had over three weeks of work to catch up on, so most of her time was spent going between classes and the library. The staff at the university newspaper were delighted to have her back working with them, as things had been hectic for them without the extra help. For the first time in a while Lola totally immersed herself in her work. She had always been sceptical of how people could concentrate on studying when they were troubled, but it did actually help to clear her mind.

Gradually her life seemed to be getting back to normal, but she knew that Carl Stein wouldn't give up that easily. Normal service resumed for Carl and Alex Stein. Lola had caught glimpses of them in the papers and magazines. One picture was taken at a dinner at Stormont, the Local Assembly in Northern Ireland. The caption said that it was held in honour of local businessman Carl Stein for efforts in creating employment. Lola couldn't help but laugh when she saw the Minister for Trade and Commerce standing beside Carl in the picture with a sling on his arm. The last time Lola had seen him, he was lying sprawled out on the floor of Mussenden Temple.

The first semester passed by quickly and the Christmas break was approaching. Having the car was great; it meant that if Lola felt like going home, or needed to get home in an emergency, she could. It also meant that she could share the driving with Ruby. The girls had been fantastic. They never quizzed her about where she had disappeared to on Halloween night, but Lola knew they must have had their suspicions. They were very protective of her and made sure she was rarely on her own. Lola suspected her parents' hand in that. In truth she knew she was safe because she had the ring. Celeste had returned it to her before she left, and as long a she wore it, Lola always felt safe.

Preoccupied with assignments and preparing for exams, Lola was enjoying a rare weekend at home, helping her mum to put up the Christmas decorations. Her mum and dad had worked tirelessly and the house looked fantastic. Arthur had always placed a large tree in the entrance hall and her mum didn't depart from tradition. A garland snaked around the staircase, fixed with a large golden bow at the end of the railing and the smell of pine permeated the house. Arthur had been on Lola's mind all day, as he often was. It was late afternoon and it wouldn't be long until it was dark. Dropping the small box of red and gold baubles, Lola headed for the wet room. Lifting her winter coat and scarf she walked to the car, not really sure where she was heading. Taking a right turn at the end the avenue, Lola drove towards the fort. She hadn't been there since Arthur's cremation. Lola stopped at the roadside, shut off the engine and pulled on her coat before she got out of the car. The iron gate at the entrance was locked, so she had to climb over it. The ground beneath her feet was solid and even though it had been a bright day the sun hadn't been able to penetrate the frozen earth. Making her way along the two outer rings, Lola noticed how different the place was in winter. Clumps of variegated holly with scarlet berries bobbed in the faint breeze. This was the only colour and life that the fort offered now.

Lola's familiar feet made their way to the centre of the fort, as she took a seat at the foot of one of the large oak trees. Lola pulled her coat and scarf tightly around her ears, as the frigid wind lifted. Without really knowing why, she closed her eyes, recalling the countless times she had been there with Arthur and Cuchulain. She remembered every story he had told her, and he had been right, the place was full of magick.

Lola felt much more attuned to it now. She could feel it ebb and flow above her, below her and all around her. She wondered if Arthur's spirit still lingered there amongst the ancient oaks. She realised that was really what had brought her to the fort today. She longed to be closer to him. Brook Mill Manor was increasingly becoming her family's home now and it felt less and less like Arthur's. It was even becoming harder and harder to feel his presence in the book room and she was the only person who was ever in there.

'I never doubted you, Lola. You've come such a long way.' The voice was in her head, but Lola understood that it was not her own. Lola squeezed her eyes shut as if this would make it more real.

'You can open your eyes if you want, I'll still be here,' chuckled Arthur, but Lola didn't want to just in case it was all a dream. She wanted to keep him with her for as long as possible. 'Although you feel alone, I am always by your side. Never once will you walk alone. Think of what you have learned,' urged the voice in her mind. 'Think of what you have achieved. This is only the beginning. There is still much greatness to come.' This was Lola's opportunity to ask him anything, she had so many questions. Where should she begin? 'Always such a busy mind, Lola Paige! Yet you have all the answers you need,' chided Arthur. He was wrong. She didn't have the answers. She was lost without him. Lola was about to tell him so but she was interrupted by her cell phone ringing. Then the moment was lost and the voice was gone. Peeling her eyes open, Lola found herself alone. Reaching for her phone she answered the call.

'Ruby. What do you want?' said Lola, unintentionally allowing her frustration to spill out.

'And hello to you too, Miss Congeniality!' chirped Ruby.

'Sorry, Rubes,' apologised Lola. 'You caught me at a bad time.'

'Well I'll not keep you then. I just wanted to tell you that we are heading back to Belfast early and that we're gonna pick up our tickets for the Vintage Ball. You're still going, aren't you, Lo?' Lola understood that there was only one answer that her best friend wanted to hear. Reluctantly, and under duress, she'd promised the girls ages ago that she'd go to the dance, plus her mum had already started to make her a dress for the occasion. Lola couldn't see how she could back out now.

'I'll take that as a yes,' said Ruby. 'I'll see you when you get down.'

'Okay. See you later, Rubes.' Putting the phone back in her pocket, Lola decided it was time to head for home. The sky had turned a deep crimson as the sun began to fade. Heading out of the clearing, the wind picked up again, and for a second Lola heard Arthur's gravelly voice carried in the wind.

'You hold the answers, Lola. Remember, what lies within, reflects without!' Climbing over the gate, Lola prayed he was right.

CHAPTER 58

'It's amazing, Mum,' beamed Lola, as she turned from side to side surveying herself in the long antique mirror. 'You could be designing haute couture at one of the top fashion houses, Eileen Paige.' Lola ran her hands over the light golden fabric of the long debonair skill gown, smoothing it out as she traced over her hips and curves. 'It feels great on, Mum, it fits like a glove.' She had always told her mum that her talents were wasted and this piece of artwork was evidence of that.

'Are you sure, pet? Does it fit okay?' asked Eileen, her face furrowed with uncertainty.

'Look at it, Mum,' chided Lola. 'It's perfect!'

Usually Lola didn't like to spend too much time in front of the mirror, but she couldn't take her eyes off the dress. It was the most beautiful hue of liquid gold, which almost looked molten when she moved, accentuating her slim figure and curvaceous hips. The high, square neckline was lightly embellished with intricate gold and green beading, which had been hand stitched. From the front her dress looked modest as it hugged Lola's slim waistline, falling seductively over her hips and thighs and fanning out at the knees. The subtle embellishment along the top of the dress guided the eye towards the thick shoulder straps to the back of the dress for the pièce de résistance – the rear view. The dress took a dramatic turn as it plunged to the bottom of her back, the green and golden stones framing the contours of her pale form.

'The green brings out your eyes,' said her mother, who, standing up, laid her hand tenderly on her daughter's face. 'You look so beautiful, Lo. I know this has been a really tough year for you, honey, losing Arthur and then having your heart broken by some boy who will never be worthy of you, but things will get better. I promise. I can see that sparkle back in your eyes tonight. It hasn't been there for such a long time.'

The emotion in her mother's voice almost brought Lola to tears. There was so much that she didn't know, that she could never know. Lola wasn't the same person that she had been a year ago – her world and life were so comparatively simple back then. Her only worries had been exams, clothes and having enough money to go out. She had changed so much since Arthur's death, her mother was right about that.

But the old Lola would never return again, she was gone forever. Yet, tonight, for the first time in months, Lola actually felt light and happy, determined to enjoy her night out with her friends, banishing the uneasiness that had settled deep inside her for so long now.

After all nothing had been resolved. The Hell Fire Club had not gone away, and while Aibgrene and Celeste were now safe, she knew that this would not deter Carl Stein from getting what he wanted, and now that was her.

'Do you know how much I love you, Mum? I know I've been a bit distant, but I need to figure things out for myself.'

'That you do, Lo! You were always the same, pet,' said Eileen. Kneeling down she fought back the tears as she fussed around the hem of the gown.

The door to the dressing room creaked open as Cuchulain came padding in, dropping himself at Lola's feet, and bringing a smile to her face that broke the uneasy silence that hung in the air between her mum and her.

'Well, boy, what d'ya think?' laughed Lola. 'How do I look?'

Looking up through his brow of wiry grey hair, the dog barked his approval, reaching up to lick Lola's hand. The light was beginning to fade outside and Lola could see a light crust of frost begin to settle on the lawn of Brook Mill Manor.

'Come on, Lo, let's get you out of that, it's nearly five o'clock, you need to get a move on.'

Lola raised her arms to let her mum unzip the dress. Stepping out of the gown, she quickly dressed, slipping on a pair of baggy grey track bottoms, a matching hooded top and her favourite pair of winter boots. Feeling uncharacteristically organised, Lola lifted her bag packed with her shoes, make-up and her change of clothes, and scanned the room one last time to make sure she had everything. She descended the stairs and went out through the front door to her parked car, with her mother and father following.

'Here, honey, you daren't go without this!' Lola took the long dress, now wrapped in a dress cover, from her father, draping it along the back seat of the car. 'Now, are you sure you've everything? You know what you're like. You've a head like a sieve.'

'Yes, Mum, the hair's done, the make-up is almost sorted, I've got the dress, and the overnight bag. That's everything!' confirmed Lola with a nod of her head.

Cuchulain, trotted out to join the sending off party sniffing the cold night air, as he stood like a sentry by Lola's side.

'How's my big wooliff?' said Lola, as she ruffled his hair, scratching behind the large dog's ears, much to his delight. 'Now, will you look after them all while I'm gone?' she whispered.

A light chill fluttered over Lola's body, which made her reach for the talisman around her neck. Cuchulain seemed to share her unease, as his ears pricked up, looking towards the large circle of trees that surrounded the walled garden. He let out a deep growl.

Lola raised her head towards the sky, her eyes searching for the invisible force field that had protected her family and Brook Mill Manor since Arthur's death.

'What is it, boy? Are you after more rabbits?' said her dad lightly, looking down towards the bottom of the garden in search of whatever had stirred Cuchulain's interest. But it was impossible to see anything in the fading light.

'Lo. Don't forget these, love.' Lola didn't answer her mother as she was concentrating hard to find what she was looking for. Then in the falling dusk, she caught a faint shimmer as her eyes gratefully traced the almost invisible line from one side of the estate to the other. Satisfied that her family were safe, Lola finally turned to her mother.

'Sorry, Mum, just looking at the stars. It's a beautiful night.'

'Okay,' said her mother, not entirely satisfied with her daughter's answer. 'Your shoes for tonight.'

'I thought they were in the bag already,' grinned Lola sheepishly. 'Sorry, Mum.'

'Where's Liam?' asked Lola. It wasn't like him not to be in the middle of everything.

'He must be in the house somewhere,' said her dad. 'Be careful going down that road tonight, love. You hear me now? They said there's a chance of snow.'

'Okay, Da, I will,' replied Lola, reaching over to give her parents a kiss and hug. 'Big loves, and I'll see you tomorrow!' Lola's stomach was alight as she pressed against the accelerator, watching in her rearview mirror as her mum and dad disappeared back into the house.

The clock on the dashboard read five forty-five as Lola made her way onto the main carriageway towards Belfast. She was delighted to find that the traffic was very light heading city-bound as most of the daily commuters headed out of the city after their day's work. The sky had turned a deep dusky pink with splashes of blue and crimson as the last vestiges of light began to fade away.

Glancing ahead, Lola could see Venus as it shone like a beacon guiding her towards Belfast and the Vintage Ball. It was taking the car ages to heat up and Lola was fumbling with the heating switch when her mobile phone began to whir. Hitting the answer button on her hands free set, she was greeted by an unusually jittery Ruby.

'Lola, where are you, it's nearly 6 o'clock!' demanded Ruby anxiously.

'I'm on my way up the road now, Rubes, I'll be there in about twenty minutes or so. What's the panic?'

'The limo's coming around seven o'clock,' continued Ruby, clearly annoyed by Lola's flippancy. 'And we're all heading around to Luke's place first, remember?'

The truth was that Lola didn't remember. She had quite a lot on her mind at the moment, between exams, saving the world and having her heart broken, she was sure that she had a justifiable excuse.

'Of course I remember,' she lied. 'I'll be there soon, and if I'm not then you guys just go on, I can meet you all in there.'

This was actually a preferable option for Lola, as she was the only one out of the group that would be going without a partner. Up until a few weeks ago, she, Ruby and Clara had planned to go as a threesome, but then Dave asked Clara, and Ruby met Luke. Lola had toyed with the idea of not going at all, but she knew that this would only upset the girls, and more to the point, her mum had spent ages on her dress, so she decided to do the right thing and tag along with the rest of them.

'I don't want you in the house on your own, Lo, so hurry up, okay?' said Ruby.

'Okay, boss. I'll see you soon.'

Just as Lola hung up the phone, the stream of traffic ahead began to slow, their red brake lights blinking in synchronisation. Slowing to a crawl, Lola began to curse her luck. As she rounded the corner, she caught sight of the flashing blue lights of an ambulance crew and the police up ahead. There had been a car crash and the emergency services were working to move the wreckage off the motorway and on to the hard shoulder. Turning on the radio, Lola listened to end of the 6 o'clock news bulletin for any information. By now the traffic had come to a halt, only edging forward every now and then. Lola's mobile lit up again indicating another incoming call.

'I'm stuck in traffic, Ruby, there's been an accident, and I'll be there ASAP,' answered Lola urgently.

'Lola,' said the voice one the other end of the line, startling her momentarily as she had not heard it in weeks.

'Hello, Lo, it's Aibgrene, are you okay?'

'Yeah, yeah, I'm fine I thought you were Ruby. Are you okay, where are you? I've been worried sick, Aibgrene, you could have at least called me, or something.'

Lola hadn't heard from Aibgrene since she had left Brook Mill Manor with her new husband and Celeste a number of weeks ago.

'I mean, you all just disappeared and left me to deal with all that shit on my own,' continued Lola, a lump growing in her throat, as she tried to fight back what she had been clearly suppressing for the last few weeks.

'I'm really sorry, Lo, but I knew you would be safe as long as you had Arthur's ring and were still at Brook Mill Manor. Besides, my first priority was my mum,' replied Aibgrene defensively.

Embarrassed by her own outburst, Lola's thoughts immediately turned to Celeste. She had never been as scared as she was when she saw her that night on the large stone table in Mussenden Temple. She recalled seeing the faint glow of her violet aura disappear as Carl Stein's dense cloak of dark magick began to choke and kill it. She had watched in horror as the last remnants of Celeste's life spark began to fade from her golden hazel eyes.

'Celeste, how is she?' whispered Lola.

'She's getting there! It's going to take some time before she is back to normal. Stein's magick has become very dark and extremely potent, but we are both safe and with friends. I can't talk for long, they could be listening in on our call. I just want to warn you to be careful tonight and be vigilant.'

Lola began to reassure her that she would be fine, but Aibgrene cut in before she could answer.

'I know you're fine and capable of looking after yourself, Lo, but you know that tomorrow is the 21st December, the Winter Solstice. Mum and a few others of the Order think that the Hell Fire Club could have something planned. So make sure you have Arthur's ring on you at all times, and return to the Manor as soon as possible. Okay?'

Lola sat in silence for a moment, absorbing Aibgrene's words. She wanted so desperately to reassure her friend, but something deep in her heart told Lola that she could be right. She had felt it, she was sure of it, so she must be prepared.

'Okay, I will. Thanks.'

'I mean it, Lola,' urged Aibgrene, her voice thick with concern.

Lola suddenly realised how much she had missed her, and how much she needed her support right now.

'Have you heard from him? I mean has he tried to contact you?' continued Aibgrene.

Lola knew exactly who 'he' was, and the name Alex Stein cut like a dagger through her heart every time she heard or thought it.

'No. Nothing,' murmured Lola. She had to continually remind herself that Alex Stein was the enemy.

'Good. If he tries to contact you, Lola, don't believe him!' warned Aibgrene. 'I know you loved him, Lo,' Aibgrene's tone was softer now, 'but he's no different than his father. No matter what my mum says, he's nothing to me.' There was a light whisper in the background; someone was urging Aibgrene to get off the line.

'Listen, Lo, I have to go. We love you and please take care. I promise I'll be in touch soon.'

A car horn sounded, alerting Lola that the traffic had begun to move again. Both lanes reopened as they passed the spot where the accident occurred. Lola hit the accelerator, hoping the girls would still be home. She was disappointed to pull up outside an empty house. Struggling to carry all her bags inside, Lola kicked the door shut behind her before climbing the stairs towards her room, which lay at the end of the dark hall. A crashing sound from the direction of her bedroom startled Lola, rooting her to the spot in panic.

Lola held her breath as her eyes adjusted to the enveloping darkness. Her mind raced while her hands groped blindly around the hallway for something of substance to lift but all she could find was an umbrella. Slowly dropping her bags to the floor, Lola slid her keys between her fingers, each acting like a knife. They would at least allow her to put up a fight.

Lola crept forward in silence; the only noise now was the sound of her racing heart, clanging in her ear. Approaching the bedroom door gingerly, she listened hard to see if anyone was there. With her tooled fist in front and her other hand resting on the ring and chain around her neck, she edged into the room tentatively. If there was any danger the ring had not sensed it yet.

Lola scanned the dark room. Suddenly there was a flapping noise, which made her jump. Her porcelain jewellery box, which normally sat on her windowsill, lay smashed in a hundred pieces on the floor. Looking up she realised that her bedroom window was wide open and the curtains and blinds were fluttering in the chilly breeze. Relieved, Lola flicked on the light and closed the window tight before drawing the curtains.

Ruby's bathrobe lay on her bed so she deduced that her friend had got ready in her room and left the window open. Taking a quick inventory, Lola was satisfied that all was as it should be and began to get dressed. It didn't take long, and while touching up her make-up and hair, she called a taxi. Slipping on her coat and shoes, she crammed the essentials into her small golden clutch bag, which resembled an oyster shell.

Switching off the light, Lola headed for the door, relieved when she heard the sound of the taxi pulling up outside the house.

CHAPTER 59

The five minute ride to the university's Great Hall gave Lola time to try and compose herself. She had been tempted to get into her the car and drive home again, but how could she have explained her actions to her friends. Besides, she would rather die than let her mother's dress go to waste, so she decided to pull herself together and try and make the most of the night.

'Is it alright if I drop you off here? It's harder to get stopped out on the main road,' asked the taxi driver.

'No, this is perfect,' smiled Lola. 'Thanks a million. How much do I owe you?'

'That'll be £4.30, love.'

Shuffling through the contents of her purse, Lola pulled out a five pound note and handed it to the driver.

'Have a great night, young lady, and you look stunning by the way. There'll be some lucky boys in there tonight!'

'I don't know about that,' laughed Lola, lifting her dress as she climbed out of the black cab.

The taxi had dropped her off on a street situated at the side of the university. She walked past the main library towards the front of the large Tudor-styled hall. Streams of revellers were heading towards the Lanyon building where the Vintage Ball was being held. Red carpet had been rolled out leading into the entrance hall, or the black and white hall, as it had become known, because of its large chequered floor. It always reminded her of the entrance hall at Arthur's.

Lola retrieved her ticket from her purse, shivering as she entered the warm foyer where a statue of Galileo in deep contemplation sat as the centrepiece. A line had developed at the small door on the right-hand side of the room that lead to the Great Hall. Lola felt quite self-conscious as she stood alone in the queue, as everyone else seemed to have a partner. Lola handed over her ticket to the young girl on the door and made her way with the others up the narrow sandstone stairway to one of the most imposing rooms in the entire university. She had only ever been in the Great Hall once before and found it very pretentious and stuffy, like most of the people who frequented it. It was a magnificent room with vaulted ceilings, a raised dais and oriel windows, which allowed a great deal of natural light to penetrate the room, highlighting its ornate trusses and other features. However, once she stepped through the archway into the room, Lola was stunned to see how much it had been transformed. Any traces of the period room had completely disappeared. A white dance floor had been placed over the oak boards. The room was draped in a white canopy, which hung from the high ceilings and along the walls. There were large bunches of mistletoe with red and gold bows tied around them, suspended from the ceiling. The entire room was lit in hues of soft icy blues and whites, with frosted branches and icicle lights suspended from the ceiling.

It was enchanting. Small round tables, lacquered in black and gold, surrounded the dance floor. Each table was lit by candlelight which added to the ambiance of the room. Along the back wall was the refreshment stand where waiters and waitresses in white overcoats and aprons handed out mulled wine, champagne and other beverages. The centrepiece of the room was the large stage, which had been erected at the top of the long room. In true 1930s style, the art deco stage was lit in a soft yellow light, with a fan shaped backdrop. On stage there was a swing band with a the female singer belting out a jazzed up version of 'Big Spender'. The university committee had managed to book one of the latest swing sensations. She was from Dublin with a voice like Billie Holiday and Aretha Franklin all rolled into one, Clara had told her. Lola scanned the corners of the room hoping to find the girls. Hanging up her coat, she headed towards the bar stand. After the fright she'd had back at the house she needed something strong. Lola didn't usually drink, so to her 'strong' was a glass of mulled wine. Thanking the barman for the drink, she downed the contents of the glass. The combination of mixed spices, cloves and lemon was delicious so she ordered another. Lola almost spilled her drink down her dress when a cold pair of hands grabbed her back.

'There you are!' beamed Orla. 'We were wondering where you'd got to. Ruby's doing her nut in!' Lola was relieved to see Orla, and gave her a tight hug; she could feel the cold night air that still clung to her garments.

'Let me get a look at that dress, Lo, give us a twirl,' said Orla, holding Lola at arm's length, motioning for her to turn around. 'That is just stunning. You're like a model, and that green beading really brings out your eyes.'

'Wise up, Orla,' said Lola, clearly embarrassed and trying to change the subject. 'You look beautiful, that colour is perfect on you. Where are the rest of them?' asked Lola as she searched around the packed room for the familiar faces of Ruby and Clara.

'They're leaving in their coats. So,' said Orla, rubbing her hands, 'what are we drinking?'

'I've just tried some of that mulled wine,' replied Lola, waving the glass in front of Orla. 'It's really good, in fact,' said Lola before draining the second glass,' I think I'll have another one.'

'Here,' said Orla handing Lola another glass of wine, 'I'll join you.'

'Cheers, bud.' Lola clicked her glass off Orla's as she filled her in on her journey up the road. 'And that Ruby one, leaving my bloody bedroom window lying wide open. She nearly gave me a heart attack. I thought there was someone in the friggin house,' rambled Lola, but her friend wasn't listening. 'Orla. Orla,' nudged Lola. 'Are you listenin to me?' Lola hadn't had anything to eat all day so the wine had gone straight to her head, or her knees – she wasn't sure. So it was a few seconds before she sensed that something or someone else, held Orla's attention. The venomous look on her friend's face told Lola all she needed to know.

She didn't have to ask her friend, she didn't even have to turn around because her body sensed his approach immediately. She could feel his eyes burning into her exposed back. All heat extinguished from her body and her blood ran cold. Orla was speaking over her shoulder but the deafening roar inside Lola's ears made it impossible for her to hear anything. Everything felt distant and strange as she leaned on the makeshift bar for support. He's the enemy. Keep it together, Lola.

Orla positioned herself between Lola and Alex Stein. Lola could feel him closing in, and although she willed her brain and her feet to move, they wouldn't abide.

'You have some cheek coming here tonight, Alex Stein. Don't you come anywhere near her,' barked Orla. 'Come on, Lola, let's get a table.' Orla, who had started to move through the crowd, turned around, annoyed to find Lola still embedded in the same spot. Catching Orla's eyes, Lola nodded for her to go on. She could handle this.

'I'll be with you in a minute,' she said, gulping down the rest of her mulled wine.

Lola didn't move an inch, he was right behind her now, and she could feel his warm breath on her back. Aibgrene had warned her about this – so why was she still there? The amulet around her neck lay dormant. There was no fear. She could never fear Alex despite the fact that he posed such a threat to all that she held dear. Slowly turning, there was hardly any space between them now. He looked as radiant as ever.

He had a drink in his hand. 'Would you like a drink, Lola?' She had longed to hear that voice. It had seemed like years since she had seen that smile. Nervously, she snatched the drink and downed the contents. She had to get away; she had to get out of there. Lola's head began to spin and for an instant she thought she might vomit right on the spot. As she tried to shove past Alex he caught her by the arm, pulling her back.

'Please, Lola,' he pleaded, 'just one dance.' And there it was. That look. He was back. The Alex Stein that she had fallen in love with. The Alex that she was still in love with. What is wrong with you? Screamed her head. But her heart answered. What harm could one dance do? What harm can come to us in a large room full of people? Go on, one dance won't hurt. So, intoxicated on mulled wine and Alex Stein, Lola took his warm hand in hers as he led them out to the middle of the dance floor. The familiar current of electricity that she felt every time she was with him surged unbidden through every part of her body. As he pulled her closer, Lola recognised the first few bars on the piano; the melody floated out onto the floor and the lady on the stage began to sing that song. The lyrics that she'd cried a river to for weeks suddenly fell on the hall.

All she could feel and see was Alex Stein and all she could hear was their obituary as it rolled from the singer's mouth in a beautiful lament. *'Don't ask me, what you know is true,'* she sang. *'I don't have to tell you. I love your precious heart. I, I was standing, you were there, two worlds collided and they could never tear us apart.'*

'Why are you doing this to me?' Lola asked but Alex didn't answer straight away. Instead, he pulled her closer to him as he ran his fingertip down the crease of her back.

Caressing her neck, Alex whispered into her ear. 'Because you have been the only spark in my eternity of darkness.' Lola felt more disorientated as the wine made the room swirl. Still the words of the song shrouded the two of them, not one word escaped.

'If we lived for a thousand years, if I hurt you, I'd make wine from your tears.' But Lola knew that Alex Stein would make more than wine from her tears, he'd make it from her blood. Lola thought that she was about to lose consciousness. She needed air and she need to get out of this room. She needed to get away from Alex.

Breaking free from his arms, she stumbled through the crowd and descended the stairs in a haze. Running out into the quad, Lola greedily sucked in the cold night air but it only made her worse. Her vision became blurred. Panicked, Lola staggered forward in a futile attempt to steady herself. Dad was right, she thought to herself, it's snowing. Lola's brain didn't register the neat set of foot prints that lay in the newly fallen snow. The quad began to spin and swirl around her.

'Have we had too much to drink, Lola?' were the last words that she heard, before the black abyss of unconsciousness took over.

CHAPTER 60

Lola was beginning to come round, her head was still thumping, and she feared that if she opened her eyes she would throw up. She could hear the soft hum of a car engine and could feel the motion as her clammy face clung to the leather seat. She must have been drugged, there was no way four glasses of mulled wine would have knocked her out. Her arms were like rubber as she tried to sit up. Giving up she slumped back down onto the seat again.

'Well, it looks like our guest has decided to join us, Alex!' laughed Carl Stein. Lola forced her eyes open, praying that it had all been a bad dream. But it wasn't a dream. There, facing her, were Carl Stein and Alex. Commanding her arms into action, Lola finally managed to sit in an upright position.

'Where are you taking me?' she asked, her speech still slightly slurred. 'What have you given me?' she demanded as she realised she had little control over her body.

Laughing, Carl Stein handed her a bottle of water. 'Why, Rohypnol, of course. It's most unfortunate, I usually don't like to use drugs, but after our last encounter, I guessed it would be good to even the playing field a little. It taints the blood,' he sighed, 'but where you're concerned, my little treasure, that's a sacrifice I'm more than prepared to make.'

Alex sat silently, looking straight through her as if she weren't there. She had been so stupid. He had clearly spiked her drink. Lola felt the wave of nausea forcing its way up to her throat. Yet again Aibgrene had warned her and once again she had ignored her. Lola wondered if she had seen something in her dream visions. She must have.

'I must say, Lola, you do look ravishing tonight, and you really do know how to dress for the occasion.' Lola watched as Carl Stein's eyes drank in every inch of her body. Normally she would have had some witty retort for Carl, but her brain wasn't working that fast at the moment. Instead she was using whatever grey matter was working to find a way out. Her eyes darted around the limousine for an escape route. 'There's no way out, all the doors are locked, my dear,' said Carl as he followed her eyes.

'You won't get away with this!' she said, feeling for the chain around her neck. Her heart sank when Carl dangled it in front of her.

'Is this what you are looking for?' Lola lurched forward in an attempt to snatch it, but her lethargic movements were no match for him.

'That ring is no good to you, Carl; it only obeys its master. So I'm of no use to you.' This seemed to amuse him even more, as he let out a deep chuckle.

'I must concede, Lola, I did underestimate you in the past, and you have surprised me, but my goodness you are naive, darling. You've had the Cube the whole time and to think,' continued Carl in fits of laughter, 'to think you used it as an ornament to hang from your window. Either you are very clever, or very stupid, my dear. My son here had a great time watching you dress tonight. I don't know how he managed to contain himself. You do make a man wild.'

Lola felt as though she had been winded, slumping back on the seat, her body started to sweat. Arthur had given her the Cube! The sun catcher was actually the Cosmic Cube! Then she remembered what had been missing from her room tonight. Alex had been there the entire time. He had watched her from the shadows. Lola started to hyperventilate. How could she have been so careless? Arthur was right; she had all the answers she needed. She cast her mind back to the note he had left her, 'Gaze upon it with infinite wonder and discover all the power it possesses, contemplate its mystic crystal revelations in your voyage to the mind's true liberation. Remember, What Lies Within,

Reflects Without!'

Now she understood. She had the Cube the entire time, and she even knew how to activate it. The smug sneer on Carl Stein's face never wavered.

'Alex, hand me the bag please,' he commanded.

Reaching under the seat, Alex gave his father a black velvet bag, from which Carl Stein pulled out the five crystals. Lola decided it would be best to play dumb, pretend she was as stupid as he obviously thought she was.

'I thought you had the Cube, Mr Stein,' laughed Lola, now seeing a bit of doubt creeping into his face. 'That's my sun catcher, you moron!'

She was beginning to feel a bit more like herself, her senses returning.

'Nice try, Ms Paige, but perhaps it's time for a little lesson,' he said, and holding up the shapes he continued. 'These, my dear, are what's known as the Platonic Solids. Do you know what that means?'

Carl Stein was becoming more and more patronising by the second. Lola glared at him.

'I'll take that as a yes,' he smiled sweetly. 'Well, as you may know, they are the building blocks of nature. Every living thing on this planet, from a sunflower to a snowdrop, will consist of at least one of these structures.'

'That may be the case, sir, but it's still not a cube, even I can see that,' commented Lola petulantly. Undeterred Carl Stein continued.

'And right you are, Lola. However all these shapes, these building blocks of nature and the universe, fit into a Cube perfectly.'

'So why are they still apart, why aren't they together?' said Lola, knowing the answer to her own question. Only a true descendent of the House of Danu could activate and control the Cube, which was why she was still alive.

'I think you already know the answer to that, Lola. Why else would you be here?'

'Ha,' snorted Lola. 'Do you really think I am going to help you? That ring is no good to you, and I'll die before I'll give you what you want. Arthur died to protect me and to protect the Cube. Do you think I would sell his sacrifice so cheaply?'

'How valiant of you! All you people are the same, so willing to give up your lives for others,' he taunted. 'This may persuade you to change your mind!'

Lola had almost forgotten that Alex was still sitting there. She had been trying so hard to block him out. He handed her a small flat screen.

'I think you might want to have a look at that before you make any rash decisions,' said Alex coldly. His voice was so harsh that Lola barley recognised it. Touching the screen she watched in horror as she saw Liam tied to a chair in a dimly lit room crying for help.

'I don't believe you, there is no way you could have got to Liam or any of my family,' said Lola, hoping that she was right.

'Liam and I are old buddies,' smirked Alex. 'All I had to do was offer him a ride in my car. It was that easy.'

Tears began to rise in Lola's eyes at the thought of her baby brother alone and scared. Propelled by the pure rage inside her now, she lurched forward and punched Alex flush on the nose with her fist.

'You utter piece of shit! If you dare, if you dare harm a hair on his head, I will kill you! I will. I'll kill you with my own hands, you monster.' Alex tried to push her off, but she was like a wild cat, punching and pulling at his hair. The car came to a sudden and abrupt stop and Lola was flung back onto her seat. She was about to get up again, but Carl Stein hit her a blow across her cheek, leaving a cut where his ring had broken the skin.

'Such energy!' he said somewhat excitedly. 'Hate is such a powerful emotion, isn't it, Lola?'

'You touch him and I will destroy you! Do you hear me, you devil?' she shouted back through the tears.

'If you're a good girl, and behave, and do as you're told, then he will be fine. I'm a man of my word.'

Alex wiped his bloody nose with a white handkerchief, as Lola rounded on him again.

'A busted nose will be the least of your worries, Alex, if Liam is hurt. You repulse me!'

'I didn't always,' sneered Alex.

'Oh you had me fooled, it's true. I thought, deep down, that there was some semblance of good in you. Something worth saving, but that vulture you call a father, stole that from you, and now your soul is as black and dead as his.

'I loved you, Alex, and because of that I could never hate you. I could never hate anything. I feel sorry for you, Alex, because you will never know what it is to love.' Lola's temper seemed to subside as quickly as it had erupted. 'I really do pity you.' There was no mistaking the honestly and tenderness in her voice now.

'I will never be ashamed that I loved. There is nothing wrong with love. It's what makes us human; it's what makes us different. You may have everything money can buy, but you have nothing, because you have never tasted love. You have allowed your nurturing to overcome your true nature. That man there,' Lola pointed an accusing finger at Carl. 'That man there extinguished that light when he murdered your mother.' Lola noticed Alex stiffen.

'Don't play the innocent little girl with me, Lola,' spat back Alex. 'You have always known what I am. You have never trusted me, yet you always went against your better judgement. You are only kidding yourself when you say I deceived you. You deceived yourself.'

He was right. She had known all along. Time and time again she had told herself he wasn't the bad guy, but the night they had first met told her all she needed to know about Alex Stein. Yet, in some twisted way she was drawn to him because of it. She was drawn to his darkness as much as he was drawn to her light.

'Even your father, the great Carl Stein is not impervious to the clutches of love, whatever his motives.' All traces of humour were now removed from Carl Stein's face and Lola could see that he was growing more and more uncomfortable.

'Have you been keeping secrets, Carl?' scoffed Lola. 'I thought you Stein boys liked to share everything? Well, since we are having a heart-to-heart, perhaps we should lay all our dirty little secrets on the table. I've started; I fell in love with a soulless swine. Now are you going to share, Carl, or would you like me to start for you?' goaded Lola. 'Okay then. You murdered his mother, minutes after she gave birth to your son. Isn't that right, Carl?'

Carl didn't offer a reply, but his face spoke a thousand words as the rage trembled inside him. Suddenly Lola felt her airway constrict as though a pair of hands were physically wrapped around her throat, choking her. Her head began to throb, she felt dizzy and slowly she lost consciousness for the second time that night.

CHAPTER 61

Lola woke with a start, brought round by the crisp night air. The car had come to a halt on the side of a narrow country laneway. Lola recoiled as a large pair of steely hands gripped her by the arm, wrenching her off the warm seat.

'Glad to have you back with us, Lola,' said the large burly man she had last violently encountered at Chateau Bacchus.

Carl and Alex walked towards the lane, as Lola was dragged behind them by Derek, Carl Stein's man-mountain bodyguard. A sharp pain shot through her ankle as the heel of her shoe snapped, forcing Lola to collapse in a heap on the ground.

'Get up now!' demanded Derek, pulling Lola to her feet, and dragging her along the pathway until they came to a wall with a narrow slit in it.

Tara looked completely different at night, but equally as beautiful, with its wide landscape now immersed in a pristine quilt of snow. Limping through the graveyard, Lola thought about making a run for it. The campsite was just over the hillside. But could she make it?

In reply to her musings, another sharp pain shot up her leg. She had twisted it badly and there was no way she would be able to run on it, besides there was no way that she would abandon the Cube and the ring. Arthur had died to protect it and Celeste almost died because of it. She wouldn't give it up without a fight.

It was hard to distinguish any landmarks in the white landscape, but Lola realised that she was standing at the foot of the mound that housed the Lia Fail. Lola had no idea what was happening.

'Give her the ring, Alex,' ordered Carl.

'Are you sure it's safe to, Father?'

'She is the only one that can unite the pieces, and it has to be whole before we can destroy it.'

Alex approached Lola cautiously, as you would a wild and unpredictable animal. But he need not have worried because the hulk of a man standing behind her had her arms pinned tightly behind her back. Slipping the ring over her neck, Alex stood back out of the way.

'Now, do what you were brought here to do, Lola!' said Carl, pushing her forward, as he handed her the five crystals.

Lola held them tightly in her shivering arms. She had been so stupid, so careless. All this time she'd had the Cosmic Cube. Fighting with the pain in her ankle, Lola struggled up the mound to where the Lia Fail stood, bathed in pale moonlight. It wasn't like it had been before, she was drawn to it but this time she felt more in control and she knew exactly what to do.

Stepping onto the circular stones which lay around the vertical piece of granite, Lola closed her eyes, letting the ancient stone's energy mingle with her own.

'What lies within, reflects without,' she whispered to it. Immediately, the ring began to awaken and the stone began to tremor, as though it was shaking off millennia of sleep. The tremors became stronger and stronger, almost knocking Lola off her unsteady feet, as the entire mound shook and roared to life. Grabbing onto the granite stone, Lola let the crystals fall from her arm, knowing that they wouldn't hit the ground. Each hung in the air. As the tremors intensified, the entire structure began to crack open, expelling a piercing blue light that shot straight out of the stone towards the sky like a beacon. Lola's ring reciprocated, as a shaft of light poured from it merging with the light stream emitted by the Lia Fail. And so too did the crystals. They began to rotate towards the light absorbing it and morphing into each other, until they formed a single translucent Cube made up of pure light and energy.

Lola stood mesmerised as the Cube absorbed the life force of the stone and the ring. Then as quickly as it had been ignited, the Hill of Tara was once again plunged into darkness. Exhausted, Lola collapsed onto the stone holding the Cube the entire time. It lay dormant in her arms and its appearance had changed. It was still as light as a feather but it looked like a block of granite. Lola was weak and failed to fight off Carl when he prised it from her arms.

'Thank you very much, Lola. What an impressive display! Let's get a move on. It's time for you to go home.' Too drained to protest, Lola allowed herself to be hoisted up onto her feet and dragged back to the car. 'You said that you would let Liam go! You've got what you wanted,' was all she could say.

'Remember our little chess game? Any or all sacrifice, my dear Lola. You have to be willing to make any or all sacrifice to win. Now come on, the best bit is still to come!'

Lola fell into the back of the car, there was no use trying to escape, not now. She had lost, and the Hell Fire Club had won, this was the real endgame being played out, and she was all out of options.

'Where are you taking me, Carl?' demanded Lola, trying to sound as though she had some authority over herself.

'Home, of course, to where it all began,' he teased. 'Chess 101, Lola, know your opponent,' mused Carl. 'Of course it took me a while to figure it all out. I could sense how strong the magick and light around you was the first night we met. But, I must admit, I did underestimate you, Lola. I can see why my son was so taken with you, but we all have our weaknesses, I suppose.'

There was harshness in Carl Stein's tone, it was subtle, and Lola could tell that it wasn't meant for her, but his son. A warning that his recent lapse was a one-off and that such weakness would not be tolerated again.

'Like I said, I had my suspicions, but I really knew for sure the night you staged your little coup. I knew that I had stared into those wild green eyes before, even though it was many years ago. I waited a long time for that.'

Lola agonised over how much she had let Arthur down.

'That sentimental old fool left you totally exposed! He must have thought you would be the warrior that she was once, but it didn't occur to him that you had forgotten everything.'

'Don't you dare talk about Arthur like that, you poisonous snake! You will burn in Hell for what you did to him,' said Lola, the pain pouring from her. Though her threat only served to amuse her host.

'Hell?' laughed Carl. 'Didn't your mamma tell you there ain't no such place? And may I add that I'm afraid I cannot take the credit for Arthur's murder, that's down to my son!' Lola felt as though she had been slapped in the face again. Looking at Alex, her eyes urged him to say something.

'How could it have been you? You were at the party, I saw you there!'

Alex didn't have to answer, because she suddenly realised how he did it. She had overheard him on the phone that night.

'You killed him, and you killed her too,' whispered Lola. This time she couldn't control her nausea. 'Stop the car! Stop the car!' she screamed between retching. 'I'm going to be sick!' The car window slid down, leaning out Lola heaved and vomited, the mulled wine spewing out. Wiping her mouth, she sucked in the fresh air trying to get her head together. He had deceived her time and time again. How could one human being be so deceitful, so devoid of humanity?

Lola had no idea how long they had been travelling, or what time it was. Carl pulled the glass screen between him and driver across.

'How long until we're there, Derek?'

'A few minutes, Mr Stein.' Lola closed her eyes, trying to think of where they might be heading, and hoped there was a way out for her that didn't include death.

Sitting back down Lola was dazed, as Carl continued his sermon. 'Well, of course Alex didn't have the pleasure of being there when we got the old man, that had to be someone he knew,' said Carl matter-of-factly.

Lola recalled the conversation she'd had with DCI Campbell. She would never allow Carl Stein the pleasure of claiming Arthur's death, so she took the wind out of his sail. This was the only act of defiance left to her.

'Yes I know, Carl,' she interrupted. 'It was Bryce, your stooge at the paper.' Lola smiled now. 'Arthur knowingly allowed Bryce into the house and knowingly drank the wine with the hemlock. Does a man of your intelligence really think that Arthur was killed?' Lola was enjoying herself now. 'Tut tut tut, Mr Stein. You have said it before, time and time again. Know your opponent.' Carl's Stein's face grew darker by the moment and Lola half braced herself for another attack. Yet, she continued. 'Arthur sacrificed himself. You, Carl, only took what he gave you.' Lola watched intently as he began to put the jig-saw puzzle together. The car began to slow down now, finally coming to a halt.

'Excellent,' exclaimed Carl as though Lola had not spoken a word to him, 'we're here in the nick of time, just twenty minutes until the Solstice dawn.'

CHAPTER 62

Lola didn't have to be yanked from the car. She was determined to take control of her situation and to meet death as bravely as Arthur had. To face it as bravely as she had the last time she was at the Brú Na Bóinne. Only she was Brigid then, not Lola Paige. Leading the way with a pair of metal cutters was Derek, followed by a triumphant Carl. Alex walked behind Lola in case she decided to make a run for it, even though there was nowhere to run to. She wouldn't last an hour out in the open in that dress, with her ankle now considerably swollen, barely able to lean her weight on it. With the padlock on the gate now broken, Lola followed them up the path. The snow had started to fall again obscuring the large circular structure at the top of the hill. It was the ring that registered it first and then Lola felt it.

That sense of familiarity. It was like nothing she had ever felt before. A connection that was so deeply ingrained in every fibre of her being. A different picture flashed before her eyes, but the grass was green and the grassy mound of the sacred Brú stood out like a beacon on the landscape. The Brú Na Bóinne, whispered Lola to herself. This was where she had lived and worshipped. Her people had built this, millennia ago, in honour of the great universal creator, in honour of where her people had come from.

It took Lola some time to make her way up the gravel pathway. The capstone, which was ornately decorated, was now surrounded by a wooden fence, and at either side there were steps that led to the opening of the passageway. Cutting open the gate, Carl Stein entered first, with Lola behind.

There was only darkness ahead, but Lola knew every stone of the narrow passageway. Closing her eyes she let her hands run along the walls on either side of her. She could feel their energy and suddenly she felt calm. Inhaling, she allowed herself to savour the smell of the ancient stone and dust that had once been so familiar to her. All her senses had been ignited, triggering memories of a past life that she hadn't believed existed. Not until that very moment.

The space began to feel open, and although all she could see was blackness, Lola knew that she was in the inner chamber, the very place that her journey had ended, almost 3500 years ago.

Intuitively, she positioned herself in front of the north recess. Stretching out her fingers she touched more cold stone. She was searching for something, but she wasn't exactly sure what until her fingertips found it. There, carved deep into the stone were three intertwined spirals, exactly where she had carved them with 'Soluis'. Her guardians had been there too.

The memories of a previous life came flooding back to Lola. She remembered it all now. The chase through the forest, the Cube, the book, Luna, Rocha, Manus and Delphius. Tears began to fall from Lola's tired eyes. It was true, she had lived before. As she stood there facing the darkness, she no longer feared death for she understood now that her soul had lived many lives. She could hear Carl's breathing, and she could tell he was growing more irate.

'And now we wait,' said Carl. 'But just in case you get any ideas, Ms Paige, …' Lola winced as the cold blade of his dagger pierced her back. The amulet began to pulse again, transmitting a faint light around the chamber. Lola could see Carl Stein's face now, it looked contorted and ravenous.

'It's time, Alex. Hold out her arms.' Lola backed further into the small recess as Alex moved towards her. 'Come on, Alex,' shouted Carl impatiently. 'Her arms, hold them out.' Lola watched as Alex moved slowly towards her and turned around to position himself between her and his father.

'No, father,' said Alex.

Carl Stein was stung by his son's defiance. He wasn't used to being disobeyed. The rebuttal sounded alien coming from Alex's mouth. Lola didn't dare breath, as she listened to the charged exchange.

'This ends here,' continued Alex. 'I won't let you take any more innocent lives.'

For a second, Lola thought it was another of his sordid tricks, that he was playing his mind games again.

'Enough, Alex,' screamed Carl. 'We can deal with this another time. Move out of my way, boy!' Lunging forward Carl Stein directed the knife right at Lola's heart. Closing her eyes she waited for the silver blade to pierce her flesh, but the impact never came. Opening her eyes again, she saw Alex standing in front of her.

'What have you done, you stupid boy?' Carl Stein dropped the Cube, falling backward against the stone with the blood soaked dagger still clasped in his hands.

Wheezing, Alex fell back against Lola who struggled under his weight. Falling to the floor she cradled him in her arms trying to process what had just happened. The air exploded with the smell of iron, her hands were covered in blood, as it oozed out of the small puncture wound in Alex's chest and onto her dress.

Lola sobbed as she clung onto Alex's limp body. His breath was becoming more shallow as he tried to speak. Shaking uncontrollably from shock, or perhaps it was the cold, Lola kissed his lips.

'Please stay with me, Alex, stay with me,' she begged.

He was trying to speak, but Lola urged him to save his breath, yet he wouldn't listen. 'I... I'm so sorry.... for the things I've done, Lola. You were wrong when you said that I had never tasted love. Your light saved me. I love you!'

She was losing him and she felt helpless as she lay on the frigid stone floor. The deep coldness was beginning to seep into her bones. There was no way out of that darkness, and she could hear Carl getting to his feet, could hear him walking around her like a predator stalking its prey.

'How touching,' he mocked, as he continued to pace. 'He loved you after all,' hissed Carl, sounding deranged now.

'He is your son, you monster!' sobbed Lola.

'Any or all sacrifice, remember?' he sneered.

What was the use, thought Lola. What hope did she have? Then the memory exploded into her head. Her nightmare had come true. After months of the same dream of that cold chamber, here she was about to die. Lola's resolve was finally broken. It would always come to this, this was her destiny, and she had known it all along. Lola closed her puffy eyes rocking Alex's dying body back and forth, waiting for Carl's deathly strike. If he didn't kill her the hypothermia would.

CHAPTER 63

At first she thought she was dead, all around her was a veil of blackness, but the dull pain emanating from her ankle told Lola she was still alive. She thought she was delirious. Then, there it was. A thin sliver of warm yellow light crept up the narrow passageway towards the womb of the chamber. Lola's eyes followed an orb of pink and green pulsing light as it danced off the walls, growing brighter and bigger. The light hit her bare and swollen foot. Its warmth was a welcome change to the cold and dark of her tomb.

Lola forced her weary eyes open, tracing the single thread as it slowly filled the chamber with a soft golden glow.

The orb separated from the sun's ray and moved towards Alex, who was barely alive. The wispy light danced over his punctured chest, pulsing up and down. Alex began to stir. Carl Stein's steely blue eyes watched as the luminous orb grew more dazzling, as it floated towards the north recess of the cavernous room, reactivating the dormant Cube as it floated past.

The sun's movement through the chamber finally caught up. Lola watched as the beam saturated the rear of the chamber, illuminating the ancient symbol of creation, the triple spiral. All the while Carl

Stein stood slumped up against the opposite wall. All darkness had been extinguished and there was no longer any place for him to hide. The colour had drained from his face as he gazed down at his son, who seemed to be miraculously recovering.

Lola couldn't take her eyes off the light now dancing around her head. She felt detached; everything seemed so surreal, like it was happening to someone else. She watched the light as it softly materialised into the most beautiful spectre that her aching eyes had ever seen.

A lady appeared before her, dressed in a flowing gown that morphed between vivid colours, first green, then pink, red, and yellow. Her face was kind and serene and her long flaxen hair fell around her in thick waves. The vibrant violet aura that shrouded her mantle made her seem fluid, or translucent. It was the same colour as Celeste's, thought Lola. She was pure love. Lola closed her weary eyes, bathing in the radiance, sure that this was the end for her. Was this what it was like to die? If so she liked it. Somewhere in the distance was Carl Stein's panicked voice. No matter how hard she tried to block him out, she couldn't.

'It can't be you. This is impossible,' protested Carl to himself. Lola could hear the sheer terror in his strained voice. But the lady of light didn't answer him; instead she just smiled gently as he tried to pull his son from Lola's limp arms.

Alex had finally come to; tears began to leak from his eyes as he gazed at the vision in awe. She was so beautiful.

'Mother,' he croaked as his father grabbed him under the arms and began dragging him down the narrow corridor.

Lola didn't have the energy to fight against Carl Stein as he left with his son and the Cube. She closed her eyes savouring the warmth.

'You have come far, my cosmic sister. You alone have made Delphius and the House of Dé Danann proud,' said the vision. 'Your path has not been an easy one, but your light has penetrated even the darkest souls,' said Aurora, smiling. Her voice was like a symphony, it was nothing like Lola had ever heard before. Suddenly she began to feel overwhelmed with emotion. Had she survived? Was she still alive? Lola began to sob uncontrollably as she lay in the cold, dusty floor of the Brú. She wished Arthur was there. It was agony, as though every piece of grief she had ever felt exploded through her body.

Aurora's energy and light continued to morph and intensify,

bringing a sudden calmness over Lola. With each vibrant colour that washed over her body, she felt more and more at ease.

'My son's body will heal and while his soul has been bathed in the divine light of our sacred Brú, it will take longer to repair, Lola,' she smiled.

'You were once called Brigid, a wonderful warrior of her people and now in this life, you are returned as Lola Paige. But you are still the great goddess of light and of the House of Danu. Now you understand the importance of our secrets and ancient wisdom. My dear, you have learned that there are those who do not want to see the new dawn approach. No more so than the poor wretch who has fled this divine womb. There is still much for you to do before the people of Danu can return to this realm, Lola. Your journey does not end here. It only begins. The Cube can only work with the Oracle. You must find the Oracle, Lola.'

Lola sat in rapture as Aurora and the sun's light began to retreat back along the ancient passageway. She wanted them to stay but couldn't quite muster the energy to protest at their departure. Lola sobbed uncontrollably as the chamber was once again plunged into darkness.

And there it was. The realisation of just how far she'd come. As Lola stared through the sea of blackness, she finally understood that the dark was nothing to fear – it was as much part of her as the light was. It wasn't about light versus darkness. Each of them possessed both, Arthur, Carl, her and Alex. That was the order of the universe, light and dark, a wonderful balance of opposites. Do you choose love? Or, do you choose fear? There was only one emotion that compelled Lola. It had driven every decision that she'd made, right or wrong. It was what had set her on her current course and it was the reason why she lay broken on the cold ground now. Love was what had coloured her decisions. Love for Arthur, for Alex, for Aibgrene and Celeste, for her family.

She knew this because tonight, and since Arthur's death, she had faced the darkness. Not only that which was embodied in Carl Stein, but the darkness within herself. She had climbed into the dark womb of the Brú and was reborn. She felt stronger now, in a way she had never experienced before. Instinctively she reached up to her neck, relieved when her fingers found the small signet ring that dangled on a chain. Carl and Alex had gone, and with them the Cosmic Cube, but this didn't matter, thought Lola boldly. She would get it back.

As her senses returned, Lola could hear panicked voices echo up the narrow passageway. She willed herself to her feet, grasping the cold stone walls of the chamber. She wasn't sure whose arms she collapsed into, all she could recall was the warmth of the blanket that was wrapped around her body.

Lola shielded her eyes from the bright winter sun. Looking up she smiled as she saw the worried faces of Aibgrene, Celeste and Daithi gazing back at her.

'Oh, Lola, I thought you were gone,' cried Aibgrene, as she softly kissed Lola's cheek.

Lola raised herself up into a sitting position, as she tried to orientate herself. She lay up against the large kerbstone outside the entrance to the chamber. She could feel the ancient stone's warm energy seeping through her back, filtering into her aching bones. The site looked equally as stunning in the daylight as it had under moonlight. The ground was still carpeted with snow as the sun danced and glistened off each tiny flake of ice. Her grasp of language now seemed so vulgar and limited as she tried to relay what she had witnessed inside.

It was as though the sun's light had altered her very being, cleansing and purging her consciousness, reinvigorating it with love. Celeste fought back the tears as Lola told her about her sister, and all that she had told her.

'I need to find this Oracle, I don't know how I'm going to do that, but Carl has escaped with the Cube. There is no doubt in my mind that he knows about the Oracle too. He'll be looking for it,' croaked Lola.

'All will be explained in good time, my dear,' soothed Celeste. 'I think we had better get you back to the manor. Your parents have been worried sick and there is a certain young boy there who is very eager to see you.'

'Liam. Oh my God,' cried Lola. How could she have forgotten about her little brother? 'Liam.'

Aibgrene squeezed her hand reassuringly. 'Our good friend, DCI Campbell had your editor under surveillance. He was holding Liam in the Ballyvalley News offices. The police raided the place, got

Liam and have arrested Bryce Neal. It's alright, Lo. Liam is safe, a little shaken, but safe.

'How did you know where to find me?' This time Celeste answered. 'We were all at the campsite, celebrating the impending Solstice. There was sudden shift in the energy field around the site. That alerted me first. My talents are not fully restored, Lola, so I thought I was imagining it. I was sure I felt the ground tremor. I immediately thought of the Lia Fail. When we went outside we could see the light blast but by the time we reached the top, you were gone. I knew then there was only one place he would take you. Now come on,' beamed Celeste, 'let's get you home.'

Lola struggled to get to her feet, 'No, no, Lola, you lay there,' cautioned Daithi. Letting out a loud whistle, he waved his arms, summoning someone up to the entrance of the chamber. Lola blushed when she realised who it was.

'We'll have to stop meeting like this, Lola,' jibed Sean impishly. 'I'm beginning to think you're doing it on purpose.'

Running her fingertips around the triple spiral carved deep into the granite kerbstone for one last time, Lola closed her eyes, smiling to herself as she felt the last of the sun's alchemical rays on her face. Reaching down, Sean scooped her up into his arms.

'My awakening is complete, Arthur,' she whispered to herself. This was her awakening and like the vibrant solstice sun that hung low in the winter sky, Lola knew she too would rise again to help usher in the light. The choice was a simple one. Would she choose fear? Or, would she choose love? But Lola understood she had already made her decision.

THE END

TO BE CONTINUED...

EQINOX

THE GODDESS RISES

THE

SOLSTICE
TRILOGY

BY
J.S. COMISKEY

WWW.FACEBOOK.COM/SOLSTICETRILOGY
WWW.TWITTER.COM/SOLSTICETRILOGY

DESIGN & PRINT
Artwork & production by Barry Rooney
brooney999@hotmail.co.uk
00 (44) 07716288821